OLIVIA

STEVE WEST

Westenheimer Publishing

ISBN-13: 978-0-9976571-8-0
ISBN-10: 0-9976571-8-9

Book design by: The Scarlett Rugers Book Design Agency *www.scarlettrugers.com*

For Joan

CHAPTER 1

Watching the sun rise over Pittsburgh is perhaps the closest I have ever felt to having a spiritual experience. In the early hours of the morning, long before the commuters are awake enough to yell at each other, there is stillness, like the eye of a metropolitan storm. The rivers surrounding the city seem to flow more gradually, as though conforming to the tranquility of the silence. The high-rise windows reflect the rays of the sun, a thousand prisms shining their light upon us like the grace of the almighty. The mountain peaks tower majestically in the distance, rivaling the regality of heaven itself. The crisp morning air rejuvenates the soul, filling your lungs with joy, love, and hope.

And yet, none of this is true when you have a hangover. Even the quiet morning sounds of distant horns and construction painfully drill through your head like the ringing of a cathedral bell; sunlight gently prying your eyes awake like some impudent brat with a laser pointer trying to burn out your retinas. The beams of light behind the buildings cast everything into shadow and give off the eerie effect as though the entire city is burning. The mountains are ominous beacons lingering in the distance. The cold air smells little of anything pleasant, but mostly reeks of waste, disease, and bad decisions. The reflections of the water only further expose the unfulfilled desires of dreams long since destroyed, and lay bare all the blights, betrayals, and broken promises that never needed to exist.

Mitchell Flynn opened his eyes to the new dawn, somewhat dismayed at being given the opportunity. So many times in the past months he had all but prayed to be shuffled off this mortal coil and still he remained. Lamenting the punishment of his continued existence, he sought to find the one thing that would alleviate his discomfort.

Mitchell tried to raise his head, but didn't get very far. It was like lifting an anvil, and pain immediately overwhelmed his system. He clasped onto both sides of his head, tightly clutching his temples in a vain attempt to alleviate the pressure building inside his skull. The sudden movement caused his ribs to burn, the sharp sensation forcing him to take shallow breaths to keep from reliving the moment.

Regaining some composure, his second attempt went much slower than the first. He latched onto both knees, carefully pulling himself into a seated position. His stomach turned violently, though he managed to keep from surrendering its contents. Heat pulsed through his torso, the veins in his forearms felt like they might explode at any moment.

Each morning since Evelyn had left, he experienced this same rude awakening. In the beginning, it had merely been a convenience to have that early drink, but it quickly escalated into necessity. Functioning without it was like trying to breathe underwater. Mitchell blindly reached out his right arm, hoping to connect with anything resembling a bottle, but his hand touched concrete.

Mitchell shook his head in despair. Knowing that something was dreadfully amiss, he reluctantly turned his gaze in that direction. He could see several rows of what appeared to be central heating units, each one set upon a pedestal. He groaned with displeasure as one of the machines came to life, emitting a loud humming noise. Despite the cool wind blowing and the open sky above him, it was not until his eyes fell upon the iconic Steel Building in the background that he finally began to make sense of his surroundings.

A roof? How the hell did I end up on the roof?!

Several other questions raced through his head as well, though none were as pressing as the sudden force he felt against his midsection. Scurrying to his feet, he moved behind the nearest unit and let loose the release valve. The thin mist forming by his feet reminded him of the morning's chill. Mitchell scanned the area for his usual trench coat as a shiver passed through his body. He let out a sigh of relief when he found it lying in a brown heap near where he had awoken. It would have been such a shame to have misplaced his favorite coat due to a drunken escapade.

Looking around, he spotted what appeared to be a bottle of liquid repast standing upright beside a heating unit on the far side of the rooftop. At first, Mitchell was certain that he had officially lost his mind. He rubbed his eyes to make sure that he wasn't just imagining it. When the container did not disappear, he hurried his task along, zipping up when he was through.

Temporarily forgetting about the cold, Mitchell eagerly advanced to the container of clear alcohol, which still retained about a quarter of its original contents. Unscrewing the top, Mitchell downed half the remainder in one gulp. As it burned through his esophagus, so too did it alleviate the aching in his head. Another slug of vodka and he felt ready to conquer the world.

With renewed vitality, Mitchell set out to discover his whereabouts. Most of what he could see of the city from his vantage point was too generic to be of much use though. There was a pharmacy, a corner grocery store, a women's apparel shop, a jeweler, a bank, and three coffeehouses. Just when the task seemed pointless, he spotted the most recognizable place in all of Pittsburgh.

On the corner three blocks from his perch was Ameline's. For most people, it is a place known for its incredible fine dining and seafood cuisine. But for Mitchell, it was the place where his marriage officially came to an end. It had been a memorable evening filled with surf and turf, followed by so long and good luck. Even though he could forget whole weeks at a time now, Mitchell still recalled every detail of that fateful night. He remembered what they ordered, and what she was wearing, and even that she had chosen the place because it was only three blocks away from her condo.

All at once, Mitchell realized where he was.

Having answered his first question, the floodgates let loose on a whole barrage of new ones. *What am I doing on Evelyn's roof? Had I talked to her? What had I said? How bad had the conversation gone that I'd ended up passed out on the roof? How long have I been on the roof?*

Mitchell reached into his pocket and pulled out his cellphone. The date said August 30th. Ignoring his surprise that August had already come and gone, he tried desperately to focus on the last thing he could remember. No matter how hard he tried, he couldn't remember a single event from the previous night. He took a swig from the bottle, hoping that it might jar his memory. It didn't.

Mitchell began to pace nervously back and forth. The phone had told him that it was now Monday, but the last thing he could remember was going out for booze on a Tuesday. Another swallow from the bottle did nothing to remind him of where he had gone after leaving his apartment that day. Blackouts were prevalent, but they usually resulted in him waking up back in his own bed, safe and sound.

Think...Think...Think... he urged himself.

As he went to take another drink, his foot caught on something, causing him to land hard on the concrete. As he fell, he managed to safeguard the bottle, preventing the loss of even a single drop. Mitchell was not as successful in protecting himself, however. The fall had rent his pants, as well as a sizable portion of his leg, blood trickling out of a newly formed wound. In a rage, Mitchell turned to face whatever had nearly caused him to lose his precious vodka. His fury turned to confusion, then to fear, and finally to panic.

Sticking out beyond the edge of the heating unit, where he'd been pacing the whole time, was a shoe. Attached to the shoe was a foot, and to the foot a leg, and to the leg was a middle-aged man who lay unconscious and not breathing.

CHAPTER 2

There's nothing quite like the sheer terror of awakening from a drunken stupor and not being able to recognize the person near you, or where you might have met them, or why they're dead. For Mitchell, this horrifying nightmare had become his reality, and without any better options at his disposal, he upturned the remainder of his bottle.

Hurling the empty container over the ledge in frustration, he was able to return his attention to the matter at hand. Mitchell cautiously approached the unconscious gentleman, wishing him to stir, to see any signs of life. Even from several feet away, the body reeked of putrefaction, the pungent odor only intensifying the closer he got. The skin was unnaturally gray, his face drained of any vivacity. Unblinking, the man stared up at him from the cold pavement.

With the head tilted to the side, Mitchell spotted a matted pool of blood that had soaked into the man's hair. Originating from a deep gash just below the occiput, Mitchell followed a trail of red until it terminated at the corner of the pedestal for the nearest heating unit. Mitchell analyzed the shape of the pedestal corner and the head wound, fitting the pieces together in his mind.

Unwilling to accept the man's demise, Mitchell attempted to jar him awake with a kick to the leg. The body wobbled for a moment, then went still, those dead eyes continuing to watch him. Mitchell tried once more, this time further up the leg. Again, no response.

Mitchell took his head in his hands, anxiously gripping the strands of hair between his fingers. Regardless of how much he pulled or tugged, he wasn't able to generate a single memory, explanation, or solution. All he acquired was panic as tormenting visions of what he could have done while blacked out plagued his mind.

Shaking off terrifying thoughts, he gazed down on the man, hoping to discover a clue as to what to do next. If there was some hint to be had, Mitchell couldn't see it. The body remained idle, the contorted facial expression taunting with a disparaging sneer. It was almost as if the old man were mocking him, even in deep repose.

Mitchell resented the ridiculing treatment he was getting from this lifeless fellow. He examined the man, seeking to utilize some defect to his advantage in bringing low the ego of this chastising wretch. Scanning the attire of his newfound enemy, he realized that the old man was the most expensive corpse he'd ever seen. Where most men are ushered toward their maker in classy garb, this individual was probably overdressed for the occasion.

The old man wore a black wool dinner suit, double-breasted, complete with the standard bow tie. Silk suspenders matched the cummerbund about his waist; both looked like they were fresh from the tailor. Gold studs ran the length of his shirt which, although tightly snug at the abdomen from gaseous bloating, fit as though it were custom-made. A diamond encrusted wristwatch shone brilliantly above an aged wedding band. The man's outfit raised more questions than it answered, including many that Mitchell thought he'd already solved.

He knelt down beside the body. Despite changing angles, the old man continued to look at him with that vacant, accusatory stare. Mitchell raised his hand to the man's forehead, bringing it slowly down toward him. With those eyes no longer watching him, he felt safe to go about his business.

Searching through the many pockets, Mitchell sought to find anything that might hold a key to this man's identity. Moving beyond his embarrassment at attempting to investigate the two false pockets on the jacket's anterior, he was able to find a set of house keys, a silver cigarette case, a lighter, a pair of reading glasses, and a fancy, ballpoint pen.

Reaching into the left front pants pocket, Mitchell felt something solid and metallic. Pulling it out, Mitchell recognized it as a business card holder, the initials JPF monogrammed across the silver lid. He removed the top card to reveal the name James P. Friedman. The name didn't trigger any memories for him, but he took note of the title of president. He slipped the card into his pocket and returned the case to Friedman's pants.

Mitchell reached into the right pocket and removed a single bulky item. His eyes lit up when he realized that he held a wad of bills in his hand. It was definitely too thick to be held by a money clip, thus a rubber band kept the greenbacks together. With eager excitement, Mitchell put his hand back in the pocket with hope of finding more. He immediately regretted the choice when his hand touched something that was neither solid nor metallic.

Returning to the cash, he removed the rubber band and began to count. At first there were the usual fives and tens, but then the quantities escalated rapidly until Mitchell was only counting hundred dollar bills. When he touched the final note, Mitchell was so elated by the find that he forgot how much he'd counted. Wrapping the wad back up, he took one last look at Friedman to make sure the eyelids were still closed before slipping the money into his own pocket.

Who was this guy? thought Mitchell with admiration. Still unclear, Mitchell redoubled his efforts. Reaching into the back pocket, he extracted a wallet. It was a brown, bi-fold made of pure leather and filled to the breaking point. The inner fabric had begun to tear due to the overzealous packing of business cards, credit cards, stacks of checks, bank receipts, worn pictures of relatives, a variety of identification cards, some hotel and casino memberships, and a slew of random papers. Finding nothing of interest, Mitchell gracefully slipped the wallet back in place.

With the quest complete, Mitchell glanced up at the rising sun. Pretty soon the city would be awake. It had been quite a profitable morning, but now it was time to get going. Eventually the fetid odor would be enough to attract attention, and Mitchell wanted to be long gone before the neighbors came probing. He looked back at the body of James Friedman.

"Thanks, Jim," he said, giving a friendly pat to the dead man's chest. "You're quite the philanthropist, you know that?"

Mitchell chuckled to himself. Standing caused him to lose his equilibrium, and he latched onto the nearby heating unit to regain his balance. Finding his feet once more, he moved toward the roof's exit. It wasn't until his hand was firmly gripping the door's handle that he suddenly recalled the coat still lying against the distant wall. Mitchell sighed with displeasure.

Briskly crossing the distance, he moved to retrieve his coat, and as he bent down, his hand struck something solid beneath the heavy leather exterior. He raised an eyebrow in confusion. He didn't remember leaving anything beneath the jacket.

Lifting it from the ground, Mitchell froze in place, staring in perplexed silence at the extraordinary revelation before him. Beneath where the coat had been, in the very spot next to where he had been curled in slumber, lay the completely naked body of a prepubescent girl.

CHAPTER 3

A sharp breeze blows across my bare skin, causing goose bumps to form along the naked flesh. I have never much cared for cold weather and this sudden invasive chill gives me a foreboding feeling about my surroundings.

The first thing I notice when I open my eyes is that the large overcoat I was using as a blanket is no longer covering me. Although I would have preferred the protective warmth of the coat, my current immodesty does not bother me. Having spent half of my near twenty-four years of life living in either this orphanage or that one, sharing a bedroom with who knows how many other girls, being seen in this state has ceased to be a cause for alarm.

Still, I would rather have enjoyed the comfort of my own bed to the merciless exposure of the open air. The concrete structure had been less cushy than sleeping on a degraded box spring; my body ached from the rock-hard surface. Battling the stiffness in my joints, I pushed myself away from the unforgiving floor.

Coming to rest in a seated position, I noticed someone standing in front of me. Long before my eyes found his, I already knew who it was. He was the reason I had endured the unpleasantness of rooftop camping. In spite of the harsh environmental conditions, having him nearby makes me feel safer than being alone inside my own apartment.

The prior evening's activities flood my mind, sending a different type of shiver through my body. If not for the muscular giant beside me, I know I would never have survived the night. And yet, he had been nonchalant about the whole endeavor, treating my rescue as though it were just another minuscule act of a passing Samaritan. The casual way he wrapped his coat about my body, vowing to protect me no matter what, made it seem less like an empty promise and more like an absolute certainty. With ease I had drifted off to sleep in his shielding embrace, though I would have gladly repaid his bravery with other affections had he only asked.

My body trembles. Focusing my eyes on his, I motioned toward the blanket with a tilt of the head, but he only returned a look of puzzlement. I raised a hand outstretched toward the coat, accidentally displaying myself to him. Always the gentleman, he was quick to avert his gaze. As my salvation, I didn't mind if he saw, but he blushed all the same. I smile up at him, hoping to put his mind at ease.

Though he towered above me, he looked like a frightened deer in headlights. All the confidence he'd displayed in the eventide perils seemed to have shriveled back into the cocoon from which it came. I couldn't care less. I was just happy to have him here with me.

When the girl shivered again, a pitiful whimper escaped her lips. I moved behind her, snugly fitting the coat about her bare shoulders. She pulled it around her torso, thanking me softly for the gesture. I tenderly applied friction to her arms, doing my best to generate any warmth I could.

As the heat formed beneath my hands, she let out a sigh of contentment. Whatever relief she may have experienced in that moment was nothing compared to what I felt just seeing her move. Although the body of the old man had shaken me, the idea of a young girl dying next to me while I slept off a drunken stupor was too much to bear.

Our lives are littered with decisions that dictate the people we shall become. They are the choices that define us. It's in the friends we meet, and the ones who abandon us. It's the judgment to work hard for a promotion, or the choice to tell the boss to piss off instead. It's the desire to be there for your father's funeral, but being too drunk to roll out of bed. Each showdown with Evelyn, all the regrets I attempted to forget through drinking, and every act of foolishness along the way has shaped me into who I am today.

And here I stand about to make another life-altering decision. Great philosophers like William James and Brian Greene postulated on the existence of other universes. In my quiet times, I have often wondered if there is another form of me out there somewhere who took the other option when given the opportunity. How much different would my life have been if I had dropped out of college when my high school sweetheart was put on academic probation? Where would my life have led if I'd taken that job teaching at the community college instead of the private school? Am I better or worse off for going left when I could have just as easily gone right?

Even as I pondered what to do about the small girl by my feet, unsettling thoughts about the future and its consequences came to mind. Hindsight is the great lament of the perfectionist, forever chastising himself for that which might have been. And yet, even not knowing then what I know now, I was certain that leaving her alone would ensure that her fate matched that of the old man. It was all the motivation I needed, damn the repercussions.

Bending low, I cradled her legs in one arm and her torso with the other. Bracing myself, I lift her with ease from the hard concrete, her tiny body weighing little more than the coat she is wearing. She takes hold of my shirt, pulling herself closer to my chest. I feel her lips connect with the underside of my chin.

My body stiffens. Her tender kiss is the most affection I've received in the last year, and I feel euphoria set in. Gazing down at the petite girl cradled in my arms, I recognize the look of trust in her eyes. She looks young enough to be my daughter, and I suddenly feel guilty about the elated emotions I'd experienced.

"Let's get out of here," I said confidently, trying to push the shameful thoughts to the back of my mind. My small charge closes her eyes and leans her head against my chest. Doing my best to shield her from the morning chill, we make our way off the roof.

Down on the sidewalk, the two encounter the first wave of commuters, strategically maneuvering the volatile seas. Most of those who pass by don't pay them much mind, but a few who noticed the unusual package in his arms turn to stare. Though seeing a thirty-two-year-old man carrying an unconscious adolescent girl is far from the norm, no one was concerned enough to interfere. Mitchell muttered a silent prayer that he did not encounter any of Pittsburgh's finest.

Up ahead, an inviting yellow glow rested above the familiar color pattern of the local taxi company. Mitchell marveled at his fortuitous luck, moving to intercept the vehicle. Slipping into the back seat, Mitchell relayed his address to the driver who input it into a GPS. The entire ten-minute cab ride, Mitchell apprehensively monitored the condition of his new companion and the reaction of the driver. She was mostly asleep, and he remained apathetic.

Arriving at the apartment complex, Mitchell paid the meter, slipping the driver an additional ten dollars to show his appreciation. The driver thanked him with a thick, African accent. Retrieving the bundle from the back, Mitchell began the trek to the front door, relieved to finally be home.

Gratitude was short-lived however, as he remembered that the elevator was out of order, and he would now have to walk up to the fifth floor. Though the climb seemed arduous, it passed uneventfully; the only other person in the stairwell was a young woman texting on her cell phone who didn't even bother to glance in his direction.

Apartment 502 rested on the other end of the hallway, as far removed from the stairwell as one could get. Even with the extra effort required to make the walk this morning, Mitchell had always enjoyed having the end unit. Fewer neighbors meant fewer problems.

Struggling with the keys, he gave the door an extra hard shove, pushing through the resistance of accumulated garbage. After getting the door to close, Mitchell waded through empty bottles and takeout boxes as he ventured toward the bedroom. The stench of stale beer and moldy food clogged his nostrils, forcing him to breathe through his mouth, which turned out to be an even worse prospect.

Arriving in the bedroom, the aroma of unwashed clothing was added to the list of things assailing his olfactory. Laying the bundle on a pile of dirty clothes, Mitchell worked quickly to strip the bed. He might have been willing to sleep in such filth, but he wasn't going to force that on anyone else. When his task was complete, he reflected on his handiwork, and how dissimilar it was to the way his mother had taught him.

Hoisting his tiny companion from her place on the floor, he carried her to the freshly made bed. After tucking her legs beneath the soft sheets, he delicately untangled the coat from around her body, letting it fall carelessly to the floor. As Mitchell guided her head to the pillow, he observed the changes that had occurred in his young friend in only a short amount of time. The warm air of the apartment had rejuvenated her young form, transforming a once fragile condition into the healthy vitality of youth. Instead of the old pallor, her skin shone with a vibrant pink tint. Her blond hair almost seemed to glow as the morning light cast upon it through the bedroom window. For a few brief moments, her tranquil beauty captivated him the same way Canterbury Cathedral enraptured pilgrims.

Catching himself staring too long, Mitchell felt blood rush to his face. He quickly pulled the covers up to her chin, tucking them protectively beneath her side. Without thinking, he leaned forward, lightly kissing her on the forehead. Feeling a sudden pang of remorse, Mitchell absconded from the bedroom, quietly pulling the door closed as he went.

Back in the kitchen, he rummaged through the cabinets, all the while trying to force the event from his mind. Finding nothing of interest, Mitchell moved his search to the living room bookshelf. Grabbing one of the false books, he removed a flask from its interior, and flopped down on the couch with his newly acquired treasure. A few swigs later, he drifted off to sleep.

I don't know how long I was out, but I was awakened by a sudden jolt of a heavy object being forcibly dropped on my midsection. "Time to wake up," said a voice cold as ice.

Reeling from the pain in my ribcage, my fingers touched a plastic shopping bag with a 10-pound bag of sugar. I marveled at the compassionate nature of my human alarm clock. Pushing the bag aside, I managed to sit upright, though feeling a bit light-headed.

"Jesus, Abigail. Couldn't you have tried shaking me first?" In response, she said nothing, choosing to flip on the bright, overhead light instead. Harsh illumination stung my eyes, and the headache that had been absent returned in full blast. I let out a moan of protest.

"It's almost noon," she stated curtly. "I've only got a few minutes before I have to get back to the office." She walked back to the kitchen and began to unpack groceries. I begrudgingly followed her, placing the bag of sugar on the island next to the other items before taking a seat at one of the stools. As she emptied the bags, I spotted the usual items: milk, eggs, pasta, bread, and toiletries. She held up a bottle of cleanser and waved it in my direction.

"I picked up some cleaning supplies for you. This place smells like a dump." She continued to unload the groceries, taking special effort to ensure that she made as much noise as humanly possible. It was all part of what Abigail likes to call "tough love", though most times I think she just enjoys being unnecessarily cruel. Unfortunately, it is very effective. I decided to go along with her efforts and proceeded to make coffee. Her mood softened ever so slightly.

"What are your plans for the day?" she asked.

"I don't know, Abigail. I just woke up."

Responding to the testiness in my voice, she probed onwards.

"Have you found a job yet?"

I rolled my eyes, making sure that she didn't see me do it.

"No," I stated without enthusiasm. It was the same question she had asked me every time I'd seen her for the last year. The truth was that I hadn't even been looking, but I knew that if I told her that, she'd just drag me down to the unemployment office herself.

"I hear they're hiring substitutes down at…"

"Come on, Abigail," I interrupted. "No school would take me now. Not after what happened."

She forcefully exhaled; clearly not ready to give up this conversation.

"You know you could always come work for us at the church," she offered.

I rolled my eyes again, letting her see this time.

"Don't you have enough people there to stroke Eric's ego?"

Abigail folded her arms in front of her, glaring at me like a cobra about to strike.

"He's your family, too, you know."

"Just because you chose him doesn't mean I have to accept him."

She narrowed her eyes at me. "And what's wrong with Eric?"

"I think you already know the answer to that. You're the one married to him after all."

She flared her nostrils.

"I'll have you know that he provides very well for his family, unlike some people."

I groaned with agitation.

"Thank you for the offer, but I think I'd rather hang myself."

"Well you can't just stay here moping about the apartment. You need to get out and do something; see the world. It's not good for you to stay locked up by yourself all the time."

The smell of brewing coffee dragged me closer to the still dripping machine where I lingered like a well-trained terrier. Abigail continued to drone on as I drifted in and out of the conversation. I already knew all the words, like watching a syndicated rerun. Maybe if Abigail had the occasional nuance with chocolates on a conveyor, I would be more inclined to listen, but it's always the same boring lecture time and time again. I was just about to reach for the coffee pot when an unexpected namedrop drew me back into the conversation.

"What was that?" I asked.

"I said 'Evelyn called me last night'."

I tried not to let my panic show.

"Did she now?" I asked, doing my best to sound disinterested.

Abigail nodded.

"She said you stopped by her apartment last night."

"I'm sure Evelyn says lots of things," I stated dismissively.

"Like that you were drunk?" she asked, her eyes bright with sentimentality.

I exhaled a deep sigh, turning away from her peering eyes. I've always found it difficult to compete with the truth.

"Yeah…something like that."

Abigail shuffled nervously beside me.

"Anything else?" I inquired, still not meeting her gaze.

She hesitated, as though searching for the right words.

"Yes…," she said finally. "She doesn't want you going over there anymore."

I gave a solemn nod.

"Ok."

"I think she really means it this time."

"Ok."

"I mean, she might call the police if you show up again."

"I got it. Thank you," I responded gruffly.

"And I don't want you trying to visit her either."

"Uh-huh."

"I just don't see why you insist on torturing yourself like this."

"Christ Abigail! Let it go. I got it the first fifty times."

I reached into the cabinet and retrieved a mug for the coffee. Swallowing my annoyance, I pulled a second mug from within and set it on the counter, closing the door afterwards.

"Would you like some?" I asked, gesturing toward the pot.

The tension left her shoulders, as though she were willing to accept the truce. Abigail shook her head.

"I really should be getting back."

I nodded in agreement as I poured a cup for myself. Returning the pot to the machine, I felt a warm hand upon my shoulder. When I turned, Abigail wrapped her arms about me in a tight-gripped hug.

"I'm sorry, Mitchell," she said. "It's just…you know that I love you, right?"

I reluctantly returned the embrace.

"It's ok," I responded, trying to sound as soothing as possible. "I know you only want what's best for me."

Abigail pulled away so that she could look at me with those cat-like green eyes of hers. There was something eerie in those malachite oculi that made it seem like she was searching far deeper than just my irises.

"It's my job to make sure nothing bad happens to you," she stated affectionately.

I chuckled to myself. The idea of Abigail watching over me seemed laughable considering the size differential. Before I could say anything in response, a noise came from the direction of the bedroom.

We both instinctively looked that way. Abigail only had to analyze the strange scenario for a moment before locking that soul-penetrating gaze on me again. I watched her eyes go from being full of kindness, to being filled with confusion, to overflowing with rage in the span of only a couple seconds. Indeed, the sight before us was one of such unusual caliber that it took me a few blinks to register the malicious way Abigail was leering at me.

Whereas I had already begun to acclimate to the presence of my newfound companion, for Abigail it was probably quite alarming to see the young girl standing in the doorway to the bedroom, clad only in one of my t-shirts, still rubbing the sleep from her eyes.

CHAPTER 4

The small girl in the doorway smiled at me, and the entire world fell away. Her warm expression penetrated past the barricades defending my heart, through the layers of bitterness, resentment, and hate, leaving weightlessness to reside in my chest. Even the pangs of hangover seemed to slip away. I don't know how she was able to generate feelings in me that I'd forgotten even existed, especially with such a minuscule gesture, but I allowed myself to be absorbed in the sweet overpowering bliss. I politely smiled back at her.

Something forcefully struck the side of my face.

Quickly returning from my respite, I focused my attention back to Abigail, who panted loudly with fuming volatility. Her arms hung tensely by her sides, both hands curled tightly into fists.

"What's the matter with you?" I reproached, still addled by the blow.

She slapped me again, this time with greater fury.

"What's the matter with ME?!" she screamed. "What's the matter with YOU?!"

"Will you keep your voice down?" I pleaded.

"WHY?! You afraid somebody might hear me and come see what you've been up to in here?!"

Abigail took another swing, hitting me near the eye.

"Do you have any idea what you've done?! Do you know the trouble you could be in if anyone finds out about this?! Do you have any idea how much trouble I could be in for not reporting it?!"

I glanced over at the girl and then back to Abigail. I had to admit that it probably looked pretty incriminating, but I knew that I hadn't done anything inappropriate.

"Don't you think you might be overreacting?"

I was ready to defend myself against another attack, but Abigail struck with the opposing hand. I reeled a step backwards as my ear began to throb. I held up my hands in surrender.

"Calm down. It's not…"

"Don't tell me to 'calm down'! Don't you realize how serious this is?!"

"You don't understand…"

Abigail tried to slap me again, but I was prepared. I deflected her attack, gingerly clutching her wrist in my grip.

"Would you stop hitting me?! I'm trying to explain to you…"

She swung with the other hand, and I took hold of that arm as well.

"If you would only listen for just one second…"

I wasn't ready for the kick that came next. Immediately relinquishing my hold on her wrists, I collapsed on the floor in front of her, tenderly cupping my nether region. The pain in my groin was so intense that my vision blurred, preventing me from being able to resist her attack.

Overhead Abigail continued to lash out, screaming obscenities and pummeling me with both fists. Several shots slammed into my skull as I struggled to protect vital areas from her assault. Desperately sucking oxygen and unable to push aside the throes of crippling affliction, I curled into a defensive ball. Both forearms ached from the incessant whaling, as though the bones might break from the onslaught. Without warning, she fell silent, and the beating ceased. At first, I was afraid that she had gone for the scalding coffee pot, wincing at the thought of searing flesh. When nothing happened, I snuck a glance from my crouched position.

Standing between me and Abigail was the young girl whose presence had started this whole confrontation. Unamused by this interference, Abigail glared angrily at her, the venom still flowing through her reptilian eyes. I was frightened for the girl, terrified of what Abigail might do to her in a fit of rage. I tried to open my mouth to speak, but no words came out.

To my amazement, the girl reached her hand toward an upraised fist, tenderly prying it apart and interlocking her tiny fingers with Abigail's coarse, phalangeal joints. Unsure what to make of this strange behavior, Abigail attempted to pull away, but my small companion held fast, flashing a loving smile up at her. Utilizing her free hand, she cradled Abigail's wrist, resting her cheek against the soft skin. With eyes closed, she rubbed the side of her face affectionately across the back of the hand, like a kitten unto its littermates.

Abigail stared at her in utter bewilderment. She shot me a questioning look, but all I could do was shrug in response. I took advantage of the confusion to get back to my feet.

The girl cooed softly, still delicately cradling Abigail's hand. Pulling her face away, the girl opened her eyes, giving Abigail a jovial smile.

"You have such soft hands," the girl commented.

Abigail glanced at me, then back to the girl.

"Um…thank you," she replied awkwardly.

The girl lowered the hand away from her face, giving it a tender squeeze with both hands.

"I'm Olivia," the girl stated warmly.

Abigail stood dumbfounded for a long moment.

"I'm Abigail," she said finally, moving her hand up and down.

I wasn't entirely sure what had just occurred, but somewhere between empathy and discord, they found understanding. With nothing more to say, my frail defender released Abigail's hand, and there was peace once again within my kitchen.

The young girl turned toward the coffee pot. As soon as her back was to me, Abigail pushed passed her, pulling me close enough to whisper.

"Who is she?" she asked disconcertedly. I could almost taste the acid in her voice.

I shook my head side-to-side.

"Apparently her name is Olivia," I whispered back.

Abigail glared crossly at me over this retort.

"I figured that out on my own," she growled quietly. "I mean, where did she come from?"

I watched the girl over Abigail's shoulder. She picked up the empty mug on the counter and poured herself a cup from the pot. Tilting her head backwards, she stretched her arms high overhead, releasing a reticent yawn. The oversized t-shirt was not as long as I would have expected and her upraised limbs pulled the fabric skywards, exposing her bare bottom to me. I quickly looked back to Abigail, hoping that she had not seen.

"I, um, I'm not sure," I stuttered. "I kind of found her."

"What do you mean 'found her'? Found her where?"

Thoughts of the rooftop, the blackout period, and the deceased old man play over and over in my mind like a broken record. Perhaps honesty isn't always the best policy.

"I found her down by the tracks early this morning. She was sleeping behind one of the trash cans."

I looked up to the small girl, wondering if she would contest my lies in front of Abigail. I watched her take the sugar bowl from beside the pot and add three spoonfuls to the mug before casually returning it to its normal spot. Either she hadn't heard me, or she wasn't going to argue about it right now.

"And you brought her back here?"

"I couldn't just leave her there, could I?"

"Why not take her to the police station? Surely, somebody is looking for her."

Honestly, I hadn't thought about that.

"Don't you think I thought about that, Abigail? It was too early in the morning to be dragging her down there; you never know what sort of riffraff will show up at a time like that."

Abigail considered this for a moment before eyeing me suspiciously.

"Wait…What were YOU doing down that way this morning?"

I hung my head in shame, glancing awkwardly at the floor before looking back at her. Abigail shook her head with disappointment.

"That's right, you were drunk. Big shocker there!" she said, exaggeratedly waving her arms in the air.

"I thought I told you to keep your voice down."

Abigail folded her arms across her chest, clearly not amused. She tilted her head in the direction of the small girl.

"So what are you going to do with her?"

"Well, we've been interviewing at all the elite boarding schools, and I think we're just about ready to make a decision…"

"I'm serious, Mitchell."

I sighed heavily.

"I'm going to find out where she lives and take her home. Lighten up, Abby. It's not that big a deal."

Abigail pursed her lips tightly, furrowing her brow at me. She has always despised the shortening of her name, and I thought she might start swinging again.

"Ok," she stated finally. "Just promise that you'll take care of it today."

I nodded in agreement.

"Of course. Not a problem."

Abigail nodded solemnly. Sneaking a glance over her shoulder, she peered at the girl and then back up at me. She inhaled deeply before moving to speak.

"Tell me the truth, Mitchell. You and her. Did you…"

"Nothing happened, Abigail," I interrupted. "She was in the bedroom while I slept on the couch. You saw it yourself."

Abigail nodded, noticeably relieved.

"But thanks for the vote of confidence," I added.

"I'm sorry," she said with a sad smile. "I should have trusted you more."

I attempted to give her a reassuring hug, but she held up both palms, pushing me away.

"I have to go," she said forcibly. "Just make sure you get it all sorted out."

She looked over at the girl standing by the counter.

"It was a pleasure to meet you," she said, though I doubted her sincerity.

When the door closed behind her, I sighed with relief. Abigail has always been there for me, and I love her, but sometimes she can be an unpalatable termagant.

When I turned back to the girl in the kitchen, she was checking the expiration date on the milk from the fridge. She opened the top, scrutinizing its contents. Sloshing the milk around a few times, she made a disgusted face at whatever was floating inside the jug. She upturned the container in the sink, the strange noise it made while draining piquing my curiosity about the liquid to solid ratio inside.

"There should be some fresh milk in there," I offered.

She nodded in understanding as she rinsed the empty jug. The small girl stood on her tiptoes to collapse the container, setting it beside the sink. As she retrieved the new milk, she gestured to the second mug beside the pot.

"Would you like me to fix yours?" she asked.

Seeing no harm in this, I gave her the go ahead, and took a seat at the island. As she poured the milk, I instructed her to add only a little milk and a little sugar. When she brought it to me, the color was much lighter than I was used to, the sweet taste a bit overpowering. I didn't complain, though I did sip it slower than usual.

The girl set her mug down on the countertop beside me, taking the stool adjacent to mine. Climbing up, the shirt pulled tight against her body, reminding me of the missing adornments beneath. I took another sip from my mug, trying to divert my attention.

"So…it's Olivia, right?" I clarified.

She looked at me with disappointment, as though my having to ask diminished her importance.

"Yes," she responded. "Though I suppose you can call me whatever you like."

I gave her a sideways glance.

"Olivia works for me," I stated nonchalantly. "It's a beautiful name after all. Did you know that there's a Shakespeare character named Olivia?"

She smiled awkwardly.

"Thank you," she replied. "Your name is quite interesting as well, though I don't know anyone else to have it."

"Wait…You know MY name?"

She gave me a puzzled look.

"It's Mitchell, isn't it?" she asked with confusion.

I nodded, sheepishly looking away.

"Yeah…it's Mitchell. I just hadn't realized you knew."

"You told me last night."

"Did I?"

She nodded affirmatively.

"Huh…I'd completely forgotten," I said, hoping that she didn't know what a blackout was. I raised the mug to my lips.

"Yep," she continued. "You told me your name just before you asked me to take my clothes off."

The words caught me off-guard, and the coffee spewed from my mouth, the hot beverage pouring down my shirt and across the top of my pants. I stood up quickly in a vain attempt to keep it from soaking through my trousers. When the coffee was once again under control, I glanced over to see Olivia shaking with restrained laughter, smiling at me over the top her mug.

"I'm sorry," she giggled. "I couldn't resist."

I gave her a chastising glare, though it only caused her to chuckle harder.

"Here, let me get you a towel," she said, setting her mug down on the island.

"They're in that drawer over there," I said, pointing the way.

She retrieved a red and white checkered towel and moved in my direction. When she came close, I reached out my hand to take it from her, but she ignored the gesture. Unfolding the cloth, she pressed it against my chest, holding it up with both palms. As she blotted the coffee spill, her soft fingertips slipped off the edge, delicately pressing into my torso. The familiar touch suddenly made me uncomfortable, but I resisted the urge to pull away.

"You should have seen your face," she said with a grin.

I let out a sarcastic chuckle, though her comment was still making me feel uneasy.

"I didn't really tell you to do that, did I?"

She looked up at me, analyzing my scared expression. With a comforting smile, she shook her head.

"No," she said, moving the towel south a few inches. "You asked politely."

My body stiffened against her touch. Olivia, feeling my reaction, held eye contact with me.

"I'm kidding," she said softly. "I was like that when you found me, don't you remember?"

My mind was a complete blank for the evening. I shook my head. She raised an eyebrow at me, her eyes reflecting both confusion and sadness.

"Well, you were very respectful," she assured. "Otherwise I wouldn't feel safe being alone with you."

I nodded contentedly, her words putting my mind at ease.

She moved the towel a few inches further down, her little finger grazing the top of my belt buckle. I instinctively placed my hand on top of hers, clutching the towel firmly between my thumb and forefinger. Olivia gazed up at me with apprehension.

"Thank you," I said. "I'll take it from here."

Olivia smiled bashfully up at me, slowly relinquishing her hold on the towel. Her face flushed pink as she stepped away, allowing me to quickly blot the remaining moisture from my pants. Thinking about what had just happened, I decided to chalk it up to the simple misunderstandings of naiveté. I tossed the wet towel next to the sink.

My stomach rumbled.

"Are you hungry?" I asked.

"Yes," she stated eagerly.

Olivia took a long sip from her coffee.

"Do you want me to cook something?" she asked.

The question caught me by surprise. It wasn't until college that I had garnered even the slightest notion of how to cook for myself. This girl didn't look like she'd even reached high school. I shook my head in response.

"You're my guest," I said. "I can't ask you to cook."

She shrugged.

I thought about all the groceries I'd seen Abigail put away.

"Do you like French toast?"

Her eyes lit up with excitement.

"I love French toast," she exclaimed.

Energized by her enthusiasm, I retrieved the griddle from the lower cabinet and a mixing bowl from the lazy Susan. Moving about the kitchen, I gathered eggs, cinnamon, and vanilla extract, all the while meticulously checking expiration dates. I was almost through cracking eggs when Olivia appeared beside me, looking to refill her coffee mug.

"So…what do you do, Mitchell?" she asked while reaching for the pot.

"What do I do with what?"

"You know…as a job?"

It was an innocent question, but too complicated of an answer.

"I used to be a teacher," I said. "But now I'm…retired."

She raised an eyebrow at me.

"Aren't you a bit young to be retired?" she asked.

I glanced over at the girl who appeared less than half my age.

"I'm glad that someone thinks I look young," I said jokingly.

"Too young to be retired anyway," she stated in earnest.

I nodded, placing the first pieces of bread on the heated metal.

"That's true," I admitted, looking to change the subject. "What about you? Do you work?"

"No," she said. "Mr. James didn't approve of the idea of me working; said it made him look like a poor provider."

I glanced at her inquisitively. It had been quite a wordy answer to a yes or no question. "Who's Mr. James?"

Olivia took a sip from her prepared cup.

"He was my adopted father."

"Was?" I asked, catching the operative word.

She nodded solemnly.

"He's gone," Olivia said sadly. "Though I think he died a long time ago."

"I'm sorry to hear that," I said, flipping the bread. An awkward silence developed between the two of us.

"So…if you had an adopted father, does that mean you have an adopted mother?"

"I did. She passed away a few years ago."

I felt guilty for bringing it up. I wanted to ask about her real parents but figured I could assume how things had gone for them.

"So who do you live with now?"

"What do you mean?" she asked, eyeing me with confusion.

I began another batch of French toast.

"I mean, with whom are you staying?"

She tilted her head to the side, shooting me an esoteric grin.

"I'm staying with you."

I groaned at her cheeky response.

"Yes, you're currently here with me, but where do you live?"

She shot me another sly smile.

"I live here."

"You mean your home is somewhere in this building?"

"I mean my home is here, in this apartment."

Abigail's stern gaze flashed through my mind.

"Absolutely not."

"It'll be a perfect combination. You cook, and I'll clean."

"You can't stay here."

"It's ok. I'll sleep on the couch if you want me to. It makes sense giving the bigger bed to the larger person."

"Now look…sleeping arrangements have nothing to do with it."

"And I don't eat much."

I sighed heavily, flipping the second batch.

"You don't hear the word 'no' very often do you?"

She suddenly stared pitifully at me over the rim of her mug.

"What are you doing?"

"Do you hate me?" she asked sadly.

"What? No, of course not."

"But you don't want me around?"

"I didn't say that."

"But you would prefer if I was living naked on the streets than in your warm living room?"

"I didn't say that either," I said, suddenly on the defensive.

"But you don't care if I'm hungry and alone?"

I let out an exacerbated sigh.

"Of course I care. I don't want anything bad to happen to you. That's why I brought you here in the first place, so you would be safe."

"So I can stay?"

"Wait…what?"

I felt dizzy, like I'd just gone for a long session on the merry-go-round.

"Good. It's settled then," she said cheerfully.

I removed the second batch from the griddle. Flipping off the stove, I carried the plate of French toast to the island. I set a place out for each us, refilling my coffee for the long debate that still awaited us.

"Why do you want to stay here anyway? It can't be the most pleasant place to live."

Olivia glanced around the apartment.

"We can work on that," she said, forking some food into her mouth.

Could nothing discourage this girl?

"Sometimes I like to blast loud music at all hours of the night."

"I'm a sound sleeper," she stated quickly.

"Plus I snore."

"I'll get over it."

"And when it's warm out, I like to walk around in my underwear."

She flashed me a wicked grin, glancing down at her current garb.

"Funny, I also like to walk around in your underwear."

I let out another sigh; it seemed to be just as effective as any of my other arguments.

"What about Abigail?"

Olivia paused for a moment, pursing her lips together.

"It's okay. She likes me. I can tell."

"Hmmm…" I muttered between mouthfuls. "I don't think that word means what you think it means."

Just like every other argument I'd ever had with a woman, I knew I was losing the war. Every issue I could create, she had a rebuttal ready to go. If not for Abigail's menacing voice in my head, I would have already given up in exhaustion.

"She was hell bent on throwing you out earlier, and I don't imagine a day full of clients has improved her mood."

Olivia pondered this information.

"You only promised to find out where I lived and take me home. It seems like you've already accomplished that task."

I raised an eyebrow at her.

"Wait…you were listening?"

"Of course I was listening. You were talking about me."

It was hard to argue with that logic.

"Fair enough," I admitted. "But do you honestly think she'll see it that way?"

Olivia tapped her fork on the plate, emitting a dull clanking noise as she seemed to mull it over.

"Well…would she have to know?" she asked innocently.

My eyes met those deep blue sapphires, and I was like a wayward sailor being led along by the siren song. I don't know what terrible karma I had accrued to deserve finding myself between a child's gloom and a woman's ire, but I wanted no part of it.

"I don't like where this is going."

"It is YOUR apartment though, right?"

"Yes, it's my place."

"You pay the rent?"

"Yes."

"So it's your rules?"

"I suppose…"

"And if you say it's alright if…"

"Now wait a minute. Even if I okay you staying here, which I haven't, it's not like I can hide it from Abigail forever. She's going to find out eventually. Then what?"

"We'll deal with that when we get there."

I took a deep breath.

"You're too optimistic for your own good, you know that?"

"Eh, I've been called worse," she said, shrugging her shoulders.

"I'm sure you will be if Abigail comes back and finds you still here."

I watched as she bit her lip, clearly wrestling with an idea in her head. After another moment of playing with the food on her plate, she locked eyes with me.

"I don't like the way she treats you," she said.

To say I was taken aback would be an understatement.

"Excuse me?"

"It's not right, the way she screams at you and hits you. You're a good person, Mitchell. You don't deserve that."

Where was this coming from?

"I know what it must look like, but she really does care about me, even if she has a hard time showing it."

"I just...how can you stand to live with someone that violent? You could do so much better for yourself."

I couldn't believe this near stranger was defending me so wholeheartedly. My ego was enjoying the niceties, but she had clearly gotten the wrong impression somewhere along the line.

"It's not like that at all," I explained. "Abigail might be a passionate woman, but she can be caring and charitable when she wants to be. I'm sure you would like her if you got to know her."

Olivia shook her head, as though unsure if she should continue.

"I know it's none of my business, but there are plenty of other fish in the sea, and most of them won't try to bite your head off when..."

"Enough," I interjected sharply, raising my hand to emphasize the point.

Olivia hung her head.

"I'm sorry," she said. "I shouldn't have brought it up."

Frowning, her eyes flickered back and forth over the food before her. After a considerable silence, she spoke, her voice much more sullen than before.

"You two seem very close," she stated solemnly.

I took a moment to reflect on her obvious change in mood. Perhaps I had been too harsh in defending Abigail. Maybe Olivia was more sensitive than I had expected.

"How long have you known each other?" she inquired, her melancholy inflection still present.

I took a sip from the coffee.

"Over thirty years."

"Thirty years?!" she asked with surprise. "How old are you?"

It was the question I wanted to ask her, but she had already beaten me to the punch.

"Thirty-two."

Olivia sighed with relief at the mention of my age, though it seemed an odd thing to be concerned about. Before I could inquire further, she cocked an eyebrow at me.

"Did you two meet when you were in daycare or something?" she asked with confusion.

I let out a soft chuckle, shaking my head genially to and fro.

"She was there when our parents brought me home from the hospital."

Olivia beamed brightly as she connected the dots in her head.

"You mean..."

I nodded.

"Abigail is my sister."

Olivia's despondent attitude evaporated as quickly as it had formed, leaving only her earlier convivial mood. Her face glowed with a renewed vitality, as if she'd discovered a brand new source for hope in the world. Noticing me watching her, she glanced down at the island in embarrassment, her cheeks flushing pink, but her smile never faltering.

"It's okay," I said understandingly. "You saw two people in the same household bickering back and forth and assumed we are a couple. It was an honest mistake; nothing to be embarrassed about."

"Mmmm… ," muttered Olivia in acquiescence. She gathered her plate and mine, carrying them to the sink, which still overflowed with dishes. Rinsing them off, she set them on the counter, promising to wash them later. Although I felt guilty letting her do chores about my place, I loathed doing dishes more, especially since I didn't have a dishwasher.

Standing from my spot by the island, I carried my mug to the coffee pot, setting the ceramic cup delicately atop the counter. For the second time that morning I felt two arms affectionately wrap around my midsection. I looked down to see Olivia, her cheek pressed firmly against my abdomen.

"Thank you for breakfast," she said, squeezing me tighter.

I don't know what came over me in that small act of sentimentality, but something in the moment made it feel right, and I hesitantly returned the embrace. Feeling the pressure of my hug, she pulled closer, nuzzling her face against my torso.

Olivia sighed with contentment. It was the happiest I had seen her since we met. I felt the warmth of the body pressed against me, and I thought how contrary it was to how I'd found her, shivering in the early morning air. Is that really what I wanted to send her back to?

I let out a heavy sigh, already regretting the decision I had made.

"Olivia…"

She pulled back from our embrace, staring up at me with those gorgeous sapphires of hers. It was like staring into the depths of the ocean, maybe even deeper. I raised my hands from her back, placing them firmly along the edges of her shoulders, making sure that she was paying attention to what I was about to say.

"Listen," I began, "I want you to understand that things are not all sunshine and rainbows around here, and it's not just Abigail that I'm talking about. There are days when all I do is sleep; I may not even get off the couch. I am the absolute worst roommate there is. I don't clean up after myself, I don't do the dishes, I haven't dusted in a year, I barely do the laundry, and I only take out the trash every other month. There are probably things in the fridge that should only be handled by the CDC."

As I continued to rant, her eyes never left mine. If not for the occasional head gesture or blink, it might have been no different than talking to a manikin.

"However, if you still want to stay here, in spite of all of those horrible things, in spite of me, then I suppose I can't say no."

Her eyes lit up with such intensity that it looked like they were shimmering.

"Do you mean it?" she asked excitedly.

I gave a solemn head nod, still unsure what I was getting myself into. Overcome by emotion, Olivia leaned forward. I barely had time to turn my head away, her soft lips touching my cheek instead of their intended destination. Despite the apprehension I felt over the gesture, an aura of tranquility washed over me. When Olivia finally broke away from our embrace, she was glowing vibrantly with joy.

"Thank you," she uttered softly.

I nodded a welcome, though Chopin's funeral march played in the back of my mind as I pictured Abigail's reaction.

Olivia stepped away from me and began opening the drawers of the kitchen. One by one she searched through the contents, apparently not finding what she was looking for. After her third failed attempt, I decided to offer my assistance; it was my home after all.

"Whatcha looking for?"

"Pen and paper," she answered, not bothering to look up from her rummaging.

"Why do you need a pen and paper?" I ask curiously.

Closing the current drawer, she spoke over her shoulder.

"Well, if I'm going to be staying here, I will need a few things. I'm going to make you a list so that you can pick them up for me."

The wad of cash felt heavy in my pocket, and I knew that financially it would not be a problem to purchase whatever she might need. However, the prospect of shopping for an extended period of time seemed a more daunting task than having another slugfest with Abigail.

"Wouldn't you rather go and pick up whatever you need yourself?" I offered. "That way it's guaranteed to be exactly what you want."

Olivia paused her searching and turned toward me, her face contorted in confusion. It was the same look of frustration that my high school teachers wore when focusing on my inability to solve calculus equations. Biting her lip, she seemed to ponder a way to make me understand what I was clearly not getting.

Suddenly, a mischievous grin crept across her young face. Lowering her hands to the bottom of the oversized shirt, she grabbed an edge in each hand. With one quick tug, she raised the garment until the lower seam rested even with her navel. My pulse quickened, and I felt heat flood my face. As she let the shirt fall back in place, Olivia flashed me a wicked smile, obviously pleased with herself.

"I…uh…might know where some paper is."

CHAPTER 5

By the time Olivia completed the list, it was already pushing three o'clock. With the day quickly getting away from them, she suggested that they delay the shopping until tomorrow, which suited Mitchell just fine.

The two spent the remainder of the afternoon conversing about a variety of topics, the most important being why Mitchell felt it necessary to lie to his sister. Apparently Olivia had been listening to the conversation and was not shy about expressing her displeasure at his dishonesty. *Lies create more problems than they solve*, she said. Still, it was too late to cry over spilled milk, and she'd agreed to go along with the current story, at least for the time being.

With their minor quarrel pushed to the back burner for now, Mitchell was able to focus on supper. He idly stirred the pot, reflecting stoically on the trials the last 12 hours had wrought. All in a morning's time, he had discovered a dead president, rescued a fair maiden from the top floor of a tower, and even battled a fire breathing dragon, none of which he ever wanted to repeat. Mitchell lifted a rotini noodle from the boiling water to his lips, thankful that all the day's troubles were behind him.

Almost...

"How's it coming along?" asked Olivia.

Mitchell lowered the empty spoon from his mouth.

"It's nearly ready," he said flipping off the stove. "Do you want to eat here or in the living room?"

"Whatever," she replied with an impassive shrug.

Using the wooden spoon, Mitchell pointed to the rack of DVDs in the corner near the television.

"There's some movies in there if you want to watch something while we eat," he offered.

Olivia's eyes lit up as she advanced toward the shelf, suddenly gaining an interest. She scanned the alphabetically assorted cases, almost squealing when her finger touched a familiar title.

"You have Bicentennial Man? I love that movie!" she exclaimed.

"What was that?" called Mitchell from the kitchen.

There was some shuffling in the living room and the next thing he knew, Olivia was thrusting a DVD box in his face.

"Let's watch this one," she said.

"Huh… ," Mitchell muttered looking at the box cover. It was one of the movies he picked up in a five-dollar bin somewhere. He knew he'd seen it once, but was confident that he hadn't bothered a second time. "I wouldn't have expected you to choose this."

"Why not? I'm a *huge* Asimov fan," she said emphatically. "Plus, I haven't seen this since it first came out."

Mitchell dumped the pasta from the colander back into the pot.

"It's fine by me if it works for you."

Olivia smiled, eagerly clutching the box with both hands, pulling it tightly to her chest as though he might change his mind if she gave him the opportunity. While she impulsively bounced on the balls of her feet beside him, Mitchell stirred in the sauce. Grabbing two bowls from the cabinet, he carried a dish for each of them to the living room, setting them down gently on the coffee table.

Olivia handed him the DVD to slip into the player. As he bent down toward the machine, curiosity got the better of him and he scanned the back cover for a release date. The movie had come out eleven years ago.

"Did you say you haven't seen this since it *first* came out?" he asked.

"Yeah. I went to see it with my sister," she said, her face suddenly going wistful. "It was the last movie we saw together in a theater."

Mitchell hung his head.

"I'm sorry. I didn't mean to bring up painful memories."

Olivia gave him a half-hearted smile, melancholy still emanating from her pale features.

"It's not your fault," she said, her sad eyes boring into him. "I just miss her, you know? It seems like a lifetime since last we spoke. I don't even know where she is, or what's she's doing, or even if she's okay."

"Did you two get separated after your parents…?"

Olivia shook her head.

"We weren't sisters by blood," she explained. "We lived together at the foster home until…"

Mitchell waited a moment, wondering if she would continue.

"Until what?" he asked eventually.

Olivia shot him that gloomy stare once more. She bit her lip, seemingly pondering how she would respond to his inquiry. Raising her hand, she patted the seat next to her on the couch.

"Come, sit down. I'm hungry."

Mitchell nodded, pressing the close button on the DVD player. He grabbed two remote controls and maneuvered to his designated spot on the couch. Quickly navigating the menu options, he started the movie before reaching for the bowls.

"Thank you," said Olivia weakly.

Mitchell nodded a welcome as he jabbed a fork into his bowl. Before he could take a bite, Olivia scooted nearer to him, her body resting against the side of his torso. She was so close that he could sense the heat radiating from her body. Feeling uncomfortable about this proximity, Mitchell moved further down the couch, only to have Olivia follow suit, this time pulling closer to him than before. He hesitated a moment, and then scooted over again, his hip pushed against the arm rest.

Not to be denied, Olivia moved again, trapping him against the edge of the couch. Resting the bowl in her lap, she took his arm and wrapped it about her like a blanket, placing his hand against her abdomen. When Mitchell attempted to pull away, she set her hand over his, holding him in place. She closed her tiny fingers about his larger hand, affectionately squeezing it tightly against her.

Mitchell's body tensed immediately. All the distress he'd had about her sitting too close magnified into full-blown mortification. He did not know if there was anything inherently immoral about their current interaction, but his uncertainty made him all the more apprehensive about the placid emotions he experienced in her tender grip. Neither he nor Abigail had any offspring, and he wondered if they might all behave like this. *Perhaps she had curled up like this with her father to watch television. Parents often held hands with their children when walking; surely this couldn't be that much different, could it?*

Besides, her tiny frame was barely noticeable pressed against his sizable physique. Fighting off the urge to forcefully free himself from her grasp, Mitchell relaxed, deciding that it really wasn't hurting anything, they were just watching a movie after all. He delicately returned her embrace, making sure not to move his hand up or down even an inch.

Utilizing his left hand, Mitchell clumsily raised the fork to his lips. He chewed thoroughly; the whole business with the DVD date had ignited his curiosity about her age, but experience taught him that women rarely enjoyed questions of that nature. Instead, he focused on solving the dilemma mathematically.

If she could remember going to the theater, she would have been at least four or five when it came out. But she hadn't mentioned going with her parents, only her sister. *At what age did children go to the movies by themselves? Twelve? Thirteen?* He and Abigail had been at least in double-digits. And yet, even if she'd been only ten years old, quite young to be out alone, that would still make her twenty-one today.

Mitchell gazed down at the girl by his side. She looked young enough to be in middle school. The idea of her being fifteen seemed farfetched, let alone twenty-one. *Perhaps she misremembered when she saw the movie.*

Olivia suddenly lifted her gaze.

"Is everything alright?" she asked innocently.

Mitchell felt embarrassed that he had been discovered watching her so intently. Not wishing to reveal his analysis of her age, he searched desperately for a response, blurting out the first thing that came to mind.

"I was just wondering...What's your favorite color?" he asked, feeling foolish as soon as he'd said it.

She eyed him suspiciously.

"My favorite color?" she asked, cocking an eyebrow at him.

"You know...for when I go shopping tomorrow," he added quickly.

Olivia studied him another moment, then gave a subtle nod.

"It's blue," she said cheerfully. "What's yours?"

Mitchell sighed with relief, feeling as though he'd dodged a bullet.

"I don't really have a favorite," he said. "But I've always really liked green."

Olivia nodded appreciatively.

"What about a favorite book?" she asked.

Mitchell pondered.

"Maybe *Dune*?" he said without conviction. "I don't know, it's hard to say. What about you?"

She shook her head.

"Too many to name," she said. "I'm not even sure I could pick a favorite author anymore."

Mitchell gestured toward the television.

"Not Asimov?" he asked.

She shook her head.

"Probably not. Don't get me wrong. I love his writing style, but I don't think I'd call him my favorite. I probably enjoyed his commentaries on social issues just as much as his books."

Mitchell pressed the pause button on the remote.

"Like what?" he asked.

Olivia smiled up at him, her eyes carrying an extra sparkle.

"Did you know that Asimov believed that students should have the freedom to learn whatever they wished rather than follow a set curriculum?"

Mitchell blinked in response.

"I did not."

She nodded as if to reaffirm the idea in him.

"It's true. He foresaw a world where students would be able to use personal computers to learn independently from their peers. Imagine if he had lived to see what computers were capable of today. I think he would have loved Wikipedia."

"I'm sure he would have," replied Mitchell. "What else?"

"He was a major advocate for gay rights, for one. Asimov felt that overpopulation was the number one issue facing our planet; that all the famine, disease, and even crime, were caused by there being too many people. He argued that homosexuality was the natural evolutionary response to the abundance in population."

Mitchell took a moment to respond. It was not the type of conversation he was expecting to come from a girl so small. Still, he could not help but chuckle at her comment.

"I see... ," he replied as his laughter subsided. "Though I don't think everyone would agree with your hypothesis that gays are the evolved form of men."

"Oh it's not *my* hypothesis," she clarified. "It was Asimov who said that. And how can you argue with someone who has a doctorate in biochemistry from Columbia?"

Olivia shot him a smug grin.

"Besides," she continued, "have you ever heard of the fraternal birth order effect?"

Mitchell shook his head.

"Apparently, the more older brothers a man has, the more likely he is to be gay, at least among biological siblings."

Mitchell blinked, twice.

"Is that true?"

Olivia shrugged.

"It's hard to say for certain, they're still doing research after all. But I think it would be interesting if it were true."

Mitchell nodded.

"Did you ever read the Symposium?" asked Olivia abruptly.

"The Symposium?! You mean by Plato?"

"Is there another one?"

"Well, technically yes, but I was just surprised is all. Most people that I've met have barely heard of it, let alone read it."

"So you know it?"

"I used to teach it."

Her eyes illuminated.

"You taught Greek literature?"

"Philosophy actually. But you can't really teach philosophy without the Greeks."

Olivia nodded in agreement.

"So why don't you teach anymore?"

Mitchell took a deep breath.

"It's complicated," he said. "Plus it's kind of a long story."

Olivia nudged his side playfully.

"The movie's on pause," she said, fluttering her eyes.

Mitchell sighed heavily. Despite her persuasions, he was quiet for a long time. Inside he felt the cold sting of that distant November morning when he'd found out his teaching career was at an end. With a shake of his head, he tossed the memory aside.

"All my life, I've enjoyed studying and discussing philosophy," he said finally. "I've read hundreds of books, earned a master's degree, and had several papers published in respectable journals. When I was hired for the position at the private school, it was the culmination of a lifetime effort. It was one of the happiest days of my life…"

Mitchell suddenly went silent, his face contorting with the heartache of lost dreams. Olivia interlaced her fingers with his, urging him onward with a reassuring squeeze. Mitchell swallowed hard before continuing.

"The first years went by smoothly. I enjoyed writing lesson plans, and the students responded well to my teaching style. I made lots of money, and I married my ex-wife Evelyn."

Olivia tensed at the mention of another woman, but Mitchell did not seem to notice.

"Everything seemed to be going perfectly, but then it began to change. It was slowly at first, a student here or there would show up late for class or someone wouldn't bother to turn in a homework assignment. I let it slide in the beginning, but it quickly developed into people playing video games on their laptops when they were supposed to be taking notes. I guess kids these days don't really appreciate the classics like they used to.

"It all came to a head when I had the *audacity* to fail one of the students who hadn't done any work the entire term. His mother was furious that her precious Enson had been persecuted. Rather than defend my decision, the principal sided with the irate parent. The kid was given a B plus, and I was suspended without pay for two weeks.

"Things just kind of went downhill from there. When I came back, everything was different. The students stopped paying attention to my lectures altogether, including the ones who used to care. No one turned in homework or read the excerpts I assigned or even bothered to show up for the tests. Why put forth the effort when you could get away with doing nothing at all?

"Eventually, I stopped going to class. I would show up to my morning office hours, and then skip out for a cocktail at the pub near campus. When the higher ups couldn't ignore my behavior anymore, they asked for my resignation. That was almost two years ago."

With his mournful reverie at an end, Olivia freed her hand from his, wrapping her arm across his chest in an affectionate hug. This time, Mitchell didn't even flinch at the sudden contact. He moved his arm about her, rubbing her back gently as she embraced him.

Mitchell didn't know what had come over him. He hadn't talked to anyone about the incident with the school, other than to say he'd been laid off due to the failing economy. Even when Evelyn was supporting them financially, he never felt it necessary to confide in her the truth about what had happened. *So why now? Why to this girl that he barely knew?*

"What was it you were saying about the Symposium?" he asked, trying to depart from the conversation.

Olivia pulled away so that she could look at his face.

"Watching this movie always reminds me of the Symposium."

"*This* movie?" Mitchell asked, pointing doubtfully at the television.

Olivia nodded.

"In what way?"

Olivia furrowed her brow as she pondered the simplest explanation.

"Do you remember the part where Aristophanes tells the origination myth about love?"

Mitchell knew the passage she referred to. It had been his favorite section in lectures about Plato.

"It's been a little while since I read it," he replied modestly. "Can you remind me how it goes?"

Olivia beamed at him, obviously delighted at the opportunity to recite the tale to him.

"You see, in ancient Greece, men of high standing would gather at events known as symposia to discuss or debate all manner of topics from poetry to athletics. In Plato's symposium, they are discussing the topic of love, taking turns to explain different aspects of it within the culture.

"When it was Aristophanes' turn, he told how human beings used to be in the early days. They were similar to how we look today, though they had four arms and four legs and two heads, like two people strung up back-to-back. There were three genders: one that had the body of two males, one that had the body of two females, and one that had a combination of male and female.

"Now these beings were far more powerful than humans today, and thus, they were very prideful. Their hubris made them forget the divinity of the gods and rebel against them, attempting to overthrow the heavens. The gods grew angry over their mutinous behavior, threatening to wipe out the entire human race.

"In the end, Zeus stepped forward, preventing our destruction. Instead of killing them all, he rained down thunderbolts, splitting them in half. Where there had been two heads, there now would be only one; where there were four arms, we have two. Then, to ensure we would not simply unite against them again, a giant wave was sent to scatter us throughout the world. Since that day, each of us has been trying to reconnect to our other half, the soul mate we lost so long ago."

When she'd finished, Olivia smiled warmly at him.

Mitchell was stunned. Whereas Nietzsche and Voltaire had been a piece of cake for him to learn, Plato had proven especially difficult to understand. And yet, here was Olivia, tiny in every aspect, easily describing every detail to him. Mitchell was fascinated in ways he did not understand.

"I love that story," said Mitchell. "And you tell it so well."

"Thanks," smiled Olivia cheerfully.

"So why does this movie remind you of that story?"

Olivia took a moment to gather her thoughts.

"Because Aristophanes' love myth details a connection far deeper than just our physical forms; those emotions might pervade throughout new generations. Like reincarnation if you will."

"Ok."

"And with reincarnation, there's the possibility that we may exist as different genders in different lifetimes."

"I suppose," responded Mitchell, waiting to see where this was going.

"Likewise, our soul mate might exist as a different gender. Over the course of several generations, we may even exist as all three of the combinations."

"I can see that."

"But unlike the ancient Greeks," she continued, "our modern society shuns homosexual unions. In some countries, it is still illegal to be gay."

"In some Middle-Eastern countries it carries the death penalty," noted Mitchell.

Olivia grimaced at the thought before going on.

"Of Aristophanes' three genders, two of them led to same sex partners, which means that you are more likely to be incarnated to have a same sex soul mate than to have one of the opposite sex."

"I suppose that's one way to look at it. Statistically though, there seem to be a lot more heterosexual relationships than gay relationships."

"There's a lot of unhappy people out there too," she countered. "The divorce rate is greater than half right now."

"That's true," agreed Mitchell. "And if they're getting divorced they must not have been soul mates."

"See?" she said.

Mitchell took a deep breath.

"I still don't understand what this has to do with the movie."

Olivia gazed at him with those deep blue sapphires.

"Well...what if we're in the wrong body?"

The gears began to grind rapidly in his mind.

"You mean what if the body that we're in keeps us from obtaining happiness because it doesn't match up with that of our soul mate?"

"Exactly!" she exclaimed.

"Huh...I hadn't really thought about it that way."

Mitchell scratched the back of his head.

"So, the robot...?" he began.

"Is changing his external appearance to match his internal self," she said, completing his thought.

"It's like he's transgendered?"

"Well, yes. But it doesn't have to be just that. There have always been barriers preventing love. It wasn't until 1967 that the United States banned laws prohibiting interracial relationships. In the 1800s, it was still a major issue for people of different religious backgrounds to marry each other. Under India's caste system, one was restricted to certain groups, and you could be ostracized for marrying outside your specific caste. Maybe that's why *Romeo and Juliet* is still considered a classic. It reminds us of our own struggles in love."

Mitchell smiled. It had been so long since he'd had someone around for intense intellectual conversation, and he was really enjoying their passionate dialogue. Olivia looked so full of life that it made him happy just to hear her speak.

They continued their discussion for another half hour before Mitchell pressed play on the remote. Feeling her head grow heavy, Olivia rested it upon his massive chest, draping her arm tenderly across his midsection. Mitchell instinctually wrapped his arm about her shoulders. Tilting her head upwards, she whispered into his ear.

"Do you think you could handle it?" she asked softly.

"Handle what?"

"Could you fall in love with someone, despite their physical appearance?"

Mitchell hesitated.

"You mean...like a guy?"

Olivia noticeably stiffened.

"Something like that," she responded.

Mitchell seemed to be pondering the question in his head. Finally he spoke.

"I've never been attracted to men, and I can't stress that point enough," he began jokingly. "However, if it was indeed my soul mate, I hope that I would be wise enough to look beyond a ship's unsightly mast to find its true essence."

Although she did not know much about boats, his elegant words put her mind at ease, and she nuzzled back down into her muscular pillow.

I hope so, too.

It was nearly ten o'clock by the time the movie finished. Somewhere during the more mundane parts, Olivia had fallen asleep, resting her head on Mitchell's lap. With the soft music playing in the credits, she suddenly stirred.

Pushing off Mitchell's thigh, she raised herself to a sitting position. Olivia stretched her hands overhead, once again exposing parts of her bare hip. After a quiet yawn, she turned to her former pillow.

"I think it's time for bed," she said sleepily.

Mitchell nodded in agreement.

"I know we agreed that you would take the couch, but I think you should have the privacy of the bedroom," he offered.

Olivia eyed him quizzically, though she was too tired to argue.

"Are you sure?" she asked.

"Yeah," he nodded. "I'm sure."

Olivia smiled sweetly at him, holding out her arms as though expecting a parting hug. As Mitchell leaned forward, she took his head in her hands, pulling his face close to hers. Electricity surged through Mitchell's body like a livewire, his mouth tingling with the sensation of her soft lips pressed against his own. He closed his eyes, allowing the waves of euphoria to pass over him. He felt a yearning, a desire for the moment to last forever. Sadly, after only a few seconds, she pulled away. When Mitchell opened his eyes again, he stared longingly into those sparkling blue sapphires.

"Sleep well," she said before moving toward the bedroom.

"Good night," he muttered, still dazed from their kiss.

After she was gone, Mitchell sat alone with his thoughts. The silence of the living room allowed his mind to run rampant, plaguing him with feelings of guilt and remorse. *What have I done?* Each image flashing through his memory panged him, their hands clasped together, her head on his lap, their touching lips, his desperate yearning to do it all again. He tried to convince himself that it had all come from a place of compassion and not of desire, but all he saw was a vulnerable girl of whom he had taken advantage. *She was just a child.*

Or was she? During their conversation, she had seemed so…adult; her thoughts reflecting a greater experience than her youthful appearance could allow. The interest she showed in other people and their struggles far exceeded the egocentricities of childhood. Olivia was filled with compassion and knowledge, and even hope that so greatly encompassed his own that he felt insignificant as an educator, and novice as a student.

But her body told a different story. All the maturity she showed mentally was vacant when he gazed at her delicate frame. He had seen every inch of her bare body and knew it not to be that of an adult, but that of a child. The carefree way she frolicked half-naked through his kitchen was like a youth through the water sprinkler, unafraid and unashamed.

He shook his head.

When did I become such a pervert?

Mitchell pushed himself off the couch, no longer wishing to wallow in his own thoughts. He moved to the bathroom, making sure to lock the door once inside. Shedding his clothing he noticed dark splotches across his chest, shoulder, and abdomen, spreading to fainter marks along his periphery. He pressed one of the marks on his chest, flinching at the pain. Mitchell tried to remember when he'd acquired the bruises, but no memory came to fill in the blank.

He moved the shower knob to hot, then thinking better of it, adjusted to lukewarm instead. Stepping into the tub, he grimaced at the pressure on his wounds. Noticing the accumulation of dirt by his feet, Mitchell suddenly wondered how long it had been since he bathed. It was taking him two lather cycles to get the grime off. Normally he wouldn't have bothered, but the house guest made him self-conscious of his aroma.

As he showered, he thought about the release date on the movie. *Had she really seen it when it first came to theaters? How old would that make her now? What if she had been really young when she'd seen the movie?* Each time he ran the math that magic number seemed to grow more distant. *Even if he got there, could he justify his actions on a girl half his age?* Panic settled over him like a dark cloud.

Why did I kiss her? Or had she kissed me? Did it even matter?

Reliving the moment in his head, he recalled the events with clarity. He could see the way her blue eyes glimmered in the dim light of the living room, the way her cheeks flushed pink just before she nervously leaned close, the overwhelming sense of jubilation that coursed through him like a torrent of ardor. And then it receded, just as quickly as it had come. He longed for it still.

Mitchell flipped the temperature to cold.

When he finished, he stepped from the shower, drying himself with the usual towel. It felt coarse to the touch and seemed to add as much dirt as it retracted water. Placing the towel aside, he grabbed his shirt from the floor. Holding it close to his face, he inhaled the atrocious odor, nearly gagging from the stench. He couldn't believe that Olivia had cuddled next to him when he smelled like that.

Wrapping the towel around his waist, he gathered his dirty clothes and snuck quietly into the bedroom. With the added light from the exterior, Mitchell could make out Olivia's sleeping form in the bed. She was curled up on her side with the covers pulled high over her body so that only her head stuck out above the blanket.

He cautiously navigated his way across the wooden floor, trying not to make any noise. At the chest of drawers, he retrieved a pair of lounge pants and a t-shirt. Soundlessly discarding the dirty clothes on the floor, he brought his hand to the towel, but decided to wait on getting dressed until he was in the living room. He left the bedroom, closing the door behind him, never noticing those prurient orbs watching in the darkness.

Safely hidden from view, freshly showered with clean clothes, Mitchell already felt a change in outlook. Perhaps the kiss he shared earlier was just a harmless gesture from a young girl to a man she trusted. Little girls kiss their fathers after all, so maybe it wasn't a big deal. He just breathed too much into it, that was all.

Mitchell exhaled a sigh of relief, almost smiling as the anxiety fell from him. It had been an awkward day to say the least, but it had been pleasant. He spent the evening in good company, eating some of his favorite food, watching a nice movie, and he participated in the type of lively discussion that he so enjoyed.

And yet, it mattered little when confronted by obsession. In spite of the pleasant evening, when that familiar craving set in, everything else slipped away...

CHAPTER 6

It was almost 10:30 a.m. when Detective Nick Hagan arrived on the scene of the investigation. The frigid morning air was doing well to match his mood. He had been awake since three o'clock when a phone call roused him from an already restless sleep. It was about the body of a Caucasian male whose remains had been found in a burned building. An accelerant was discovered at the crime scene, and arson was suspected. Then, around five, he questioned two college students about their involvement in a vehicular death. Apparently, there were drugs involved, and both individuals were arrested. It was always hard to watch when young people threw their lives away making foolish choices. While he was interviewing the students, a jealous wife shot her husband when he came home from supposedly having an affair with his secretary. Fortunately, the husband survived, so it was not his problem to deal with. He had taken a break to go home and nap, but was interrupted over this recent development. Hagan did not understand how the human race could survive when so many were hell bent on making sure that they did not.

Stepping through the roof doorway, he almost bumped into a member of the forensics team. She was noticeably shocked by his appearance, though she pretended not to notice. Although Hagan felt a temporary pang of self-consciousness, he understood the girl's discomfort. Dark shadows plagued the undersides of his eyes, clearly outlining the wrinkles that had begun to form earlier in the year. His facial hair had not been groomed since Sunday morning, and the stubble was an ugly, matted mess. His hair was disheveled and stuck straight up on one side of his head. He looked as though he had just fallen out of bed, which suited Hagan, because that's exactly what happened.

When his eyes adjusted to the sunlight, Nick saw his partner approach. Doug Werner was what everyone thinks about when they imagine a police detective, shirt always tucked in, shoes shined, even a tie clip to complete the set. In spite of his appearance, Doug was actually a very relaxed and easy-going person. Hagan had never seen him angry or upset, and the only time he ever heard him curse was when he was telling one of his infamous raunchy jokes. The two had been paired on a case four years ago, and something just clicked. Since then, they worked together on every assignment. Nick couldn't imagine working with anyone else, especially with the perks that came with having Doug for a partner.

As Doug drew closer, he extended his arm and handed him a cup of fresh coffee. Despite their grim surroundings and the horrible way Hagan felt from sleep deprivation, this small act of friendship made him smile. Hagan took a long swig of the coffee and exhaled a pleasant sigh.

"Thanks, Doug."

Hagan eyed his partner as he ingested more of that sweet nectar. Although Doug was older by nearly a decade, Nick's current state made him look as though he were the senior.

"No problem, buddy," said Doug thoughtfully. "You doin' alright?"

"Yeah…just haven't been sleeping well."

"You still using that CPAP machine?"

"Would that I could. Damn thing's busted."

"What happened?" inquired Doug.

"No idea. It was working fine, then the other night I couldn't get it going. I haven't had a good night's rest since then. Worst part is that the insurance company is dragging its feet on getting a replacement."

"How long do they think until you get a new one?"

"It's looking like another couple weeks."

"Oh, man. Sorry to hear that. What do you do 'til then?"

"Coffee," Nick replied, clinging to his cup as though he were guarding a precious treasure.

The two made their way to where the forensics team was analyzing the scene. As they approached, the smell of putrefaction flowed into their nostrils. The body that lay before them was a Caucasian male, maybe mid-to-late fifties. The decomposition process caused the body to bloat, and the smell intensified the scent of decay. Behind the body, a red color stained the concrete. A deep gash could be seen in the back of the man's head, and it appeared to match the corner of the concrete under the heating unit.

"Have you identified the body?" Nick asked the closest forensics specialist.

"His wallet identifies him as James Phillip Friedman," she responded without looking up.

Doug cocked an eye at this new information.

"Did you say James Friedman? Like, *the* James Friedman?" he asked.

The forensic technician said nothing, and Hagan motioned to his partner. The two stepped a few feet out of hearing distance before speaking again.

"Friend of yours?" asked Nick.

"Ha! I wish."

"You sounded like you knew him…"

"Of course I know him. Well, I mean, I know *of* him. He's a big investment guy on Wall Street. He's worth something like a hundred million dollars. I can't believe you've never heard of him."

"It must be this cave I've been living in. Terrible satellite reception in that place. Besides, when did you become Mr. Bloomberg all of a sudden?"

"Eh, Nancy's been trying to get me to better manage my 401K. I keep telling her that there's no way we'll be able to retire on my salary, but she insists."

"If things keep going like they have this morning, maybe you should think about a good life insurance policy."

"Probably not a good idea. Things have been going well between us lately, but there may come a day when she values the prospect of white sandy beaches above my company."

"Fair enough," Nick said before taking a large gulp from his cup. "So what do you think about this case?"

"I'm thinking we should see if forensics will let us back in there with a Ouija board so we can pick this guy's brain," replied Doug with a smile.

"Shouldn't be too hard, some of it's already spilled on the concrete."

Doug let out an audible groan. For some reason, Doug could handle any vulgarity about what went on in the bedroom or between a woman's legs, but comments on the tragic and violent ways in which people died seemed to send him running in the other direction. *It was good timing though*, thought Nick, *because it was time to get serious.*

Apparently their victim was famous, and a dead celebrity put a rush on the investigation. Pretty soon the media would get wind of the story, and they would need to contact the next of kin before the bombshell hit the six o'clock news.

Hagan motioned toward the roof entrance, and the two moved downstairs.

"Where are we headed?" asked Doug.

"To have a talk with management. Chances are if he was on the roof, he was living here."

"Good plan."

The two arrived at the elevator, and Hagan pressed the down button. As they waited for it, Doug pulled out his iPhone and quickly began searching websites. He started to relay information just as they were boarding the elevator.

"According to Wikipedia," he began, "Friedman's total net worth is $314 million. He graduated from Penn. He is listed as the President of Friedman Financial. And he was apparently Catholic."

"Any family?"

"Hang on… ," Doug replied while messing with his phone. "Yes. He was married to Elaine Prescott from 1976 until 2008, when she died from cancer. It also lists one child, but doesn't give a name or gender."

"Has he been married since?"

"Negative. But what can you expect after being married to the same woman for thirty years?"

"Wouldn't have a clue on that one. My longest relationship was with my houseplant Bernie, who died last winter. The investigation is still underway in that case."

"My money's on the butler," chimed in Doug.

"My bet is on the angry ex-wife. It was a long, frustrating custody hearing that did not turn out in her favor. I think she's the type to seek revenge."

Doug chuckled as they exited the elevator. They made their way to the front desk where a girl in her early twenties stood post, focusing more on texting and her ability to chew gum than her job. Hagan sighed audibly with contempt at the sight of the pierced nose.

"Excuse me, young lady," said Doug with a friendly tone and a smile. "Do you know what residence Mr. James Friedman is staying in?"

The girl did not hear his question or at least did not acknowledge that she heard him. Her fingers continued to nimbly finesse their way across the tiny keyboard. Her chewing seemed to grow louder to Hagan, and small popping noises were added to the aggravating sounds of mastication.

"Excuse me," tried Doug again. "Could you look up a resident for me?"

The girl rolled her eyes at the second invasion of her conversation. She shook her head angrily, and her finger depressions became more forced. Doug looked over at Hagan and shrugged his shoulders. Nick nodded at his partner. In one swift motion, Hagan ripped the phone out of her hand.

"Hey! What's your problem asshole?!"

Hagan quickly pulled out his badge and shoved it in her face.

"I'm Detective Nick Hagan from the homicide unit, and this is my partner Detective Werner. We're in the midst of a murder investigation, and the last thing we need right now is the attitude. Either you start cooperating, or I'm arresting you as a suspect."

The girl's eyes grew wide.

"Did you say 'murder investigation'?" the girl asked in a hushed tone.

"Glad to see we have your undivided attention," Hagan retorted.

Doug held up a hand to Hagan.

"We need you to look up a resident for us," Doug repeated.

The girl hesitated before responding.

"I'm afraid I can't do that. We're not supposed to give out the private information of our residents."

"Sounds like someone is looking to get arrested," chimed in Hagan.

"Ok. Ok," The girl said, putting up her hands. "Chill out Robo-Cop."

She turned to the computer on the desk, her fingers not quite as agile as they had been with the smaller keyboard. After a few moments, she turned to the detectives.

"What is the name?"

Doug repeated the name for her, and she typed it into the computer. When the information appeared on the screen, she recited it back to the detectives.

"Thank you," replied Doug. "And do you happen to know whether anyone was staying with him?"

The girl thought for a moment and then shook her head.

"Well, thanks anyway," said Doug cordially.

The two turned to walk away when the girl called out to them.

"Can I have my phone back?" she asked.

Hagan looked at Werner.

"Sorry, we're going to have to hold it as evidence," said Hagan.

Doug looked at Nick.

"Fine," said Nick unenthusiastically, handing the phone to his partner.

Hagan walked toward the elevator. With phone in hand, Doug returned to the girl behind the counter. He handed it to her with a smile. Taking the phone from Doug, she clutched it with both hands to ensure that it would not immediately be taken back.

"Just so you know, you and your partner have the whole good cop, bad cop thing down perfectly," she said.

Doug nodded.

"Actually, he's not a 'cop', he's a detective, and he's a damn fine one on top of that. And just so *you know*, if you want to avoid these types of confrontations in the future, you could try being a little less of a pain in the ass."

Doug turned away from her stunned expression and joined his partner by the elevator. After the elevator doors closed behind them, Hagan turned to his partner.

"You should have let me confiscate the phone."

"I was going to, but then I figured exposing you to that much technology all at once might make your brain explode."

"Yeah," chuckled Nick. "Plus, the neon pink cover wasn't doing anything for me."

"But it completely matches your eyes," laughed Doug.

The elevator carried the two detectives to the top floor where the penthouse apartments were located. They made their way to 1201 and pressed the buzzer. There was no response. After several more attempts, Doug turned to his partner.

"What do you want to do now?" he asked.

"Let's see if any of the neighbors are home. We'll split up. You take the doors that way, and I'll go the other way. Try to find out if anyone else was staying with him."

Doug nodded, and the two began their search. The first door yielded no response for Hagan, nor did the second. When Nick was about to knock on his third door, Doug came running over to him.

"The woman in room 1202 says that she knows James Friedman. Apparently he didn't really live here. He only uses this place when he's in town for business. She said that he's here about once a month for a few days at a time."

"Did she notice if anyone else was staying with him?" asked Hagan.

"Yeah. She said that he traveled with a young girl that she supposes is his daughter."

"How old is the daughter?"

"Um…" muttered Doug as he scrolled through his notes. "She said maybe ten or eleven. She wasn't quite sure."

Hagan paused, his eyes flicking rapidly back and forth. His face suddenly jolted to attention, and he turned to his partner.

"Did you say room 1202?" he asked anxiously.

"Uh…yes," responded Doug.

Hagan hurried past Werner and began knocking loudly on the frame until the woman came to the door. When the door opened, the smell of fresh baked goods wafted into his face. For a moment, Nick was not standing outside the threshold to this woman's home, but was in his mother's kitchen.

"Is everything alright?" she asked when the door was opened.

"Yes, ma'am," said Nick, regaining some of his composure. "My partner spoke with you a couple minutes ago, and I have a couple more questions if you don't mind."

"Sure, sure," she said. "But would you mind coming in? I've got cookies that are just about to come out."

With a gesture, she ushered them inside. As they entered, Hagan wiped his feet on a doormat reminding him to *wipe his paws*. As they followed the woman to her kitchen, they passed an array of pictures on both sides of the hallway. Familiar sayings about friends and family hung on signs above them. Nick began reminiscing about his mother again. He vowed to call her when he got home.

As they turned the corner into the kitchen, the woman quickly snatched an oven mitt and took a peek inside the oven for a few seconds before closing the door. She reached over and grabbed a timer off the counter and adjusted it for two minutes.

While she was handling the oven, a fat orange tabby made his way onto the linoleum floor. His oversized belly dragged as he lumbered toward the detectives. When he got close, Doug bent down and held out his hand. The tabby sniffed it hesitantly before rubbing his ear across Doug's fingertips. A deep purr emanated from the cat.

"That's Willard," the woman stated with a smile. "He's quite the cuddler."

Hagan nodded. He had never been a cat person, and the sight of this overweight tom wasn't enough to make him a believer. The tabby, seeming to sense his discomfort, migrated closer and began to rub up against his ankles. Nick turned to the woman.

"And what's your name?" he asked her.

"Muriel," she said with a smile.

"Nick Hagan," he said, extending his hand.

Muriel ignored his gesture and instead greeted him with a hug. She repeated this process with Doug, though he seemed to be more at ease with the added niceties. Before Nick could say anything else, the buzzer for the cookies went off, filling the kitchen with noise.

Muriel swiftly quieted the alarm and looked inside the oven again. Hagan marveled at how gracefully she maneuvered through the kitchen, despite her short, stout frame.

As she moved, her apron swished back and forth like the sails of a ship. Her curly gray hair shimmered in the glow of the kitchen light like fireflies hovering above a wheat field. Her inquisitive gaze switched to a smile. The cookies were ready.

Muriel pulled the tray out and placed it on top of the stove. Hagan did not have to see them to know that they were chocolate chip. The smell was strong enough to permeate the deep recesses of his holiday memories. As he watched them cool on the cookie sheet, he could almost taste the melted chocolate. Muriel flipped off the oven and unfastened her apron. Tossing the apron aside, she turned to her guests.

"Can I get you all anything? Coffee? Tea?"

"None for me. Thank you though," said Doug.

"No, thank you. I've still got some," Nick stated holding up his cup.

"Ok then," she said festively.

Muriel took a seat at the kitchen table and gestured for the other two to join her. She took in a few deep breaths before letting out a sigh.

"It's rough getting old," she stated plainly. "So what do you want to know?"

"I have a couple questions about the girl living with Mr. Friedman. Has she always been living with him?" asked Nick.

"I suppose so. I wasn't there when they moved in, but I ran into them the week after, and she was with him."

"And about how long ago was that?"

"Oh, golly," she thought. "Maybe a year and a half ago."

"About how old did she look then?"

"Then? Maybe about ten or so."

"And you said she looks about eleven or twelve now?"

"I suppose so. It's hard to tell with kids these days," said Muriel.

"Did she ever tell you her name?" asked Nick.

Muriel took a moment to think before responding.

"I believe it's Cecelia, though it might not be. I'm not great with names."

"Was there anyone else living there?"

"I don't think so. If there was, I never saw them."

"No wife?"

"Oh, no," she stated sympathetically. "Poor thing died some time before they moved here. She was so young. He didn't like to talk about it though. I think it was hard for him with the child and all."

"I see," said Nick with sympathy.

"Excuse me a moment, dear," said Muriel as she got up from the table.

She stepped over to the stove and lightly tapped the cookie sheet, testing its warmth. Satisfied, she reached into a cabinet and pulled out a large, colorful plate and set it gently on the counter. Next, she fished through a drawer until she found a spatula. After she had moved all of the cookies to the plate, she set the plate on the table and sat with the detectives. Nick stared longingly at the cookies.

"Help yourself," said Muriel, pushing the plate in his direction.

Nick thanked her and took one from the plate. For the next few moments, Nick checked himself out from work and into Thanksgiving at his mother's house. Doug took over the questions in his absence.

"Did the two of them seem to get along ok?" asked Werner.

"I would say yes. I mean, they sometimes seemed distant, but that age can be difficult for a young girl, especially without her mother. I told her if she ever needed someone to talk to that I was here."

"Did you two get along well, then?"

"Not especially, but like I said, it can be a rough age."

"You mentioned that they did not stay here year round. Do you know where else they lived?"

"No. I'm sorry, I don't."

"What about school? Do you know where she attended?"

Muriel shook her head.

"What about any other family?"

"He never mentioned anybody to me."

The questions abruptly stopped at an audible moan of pleasure from Nick. His eyes were closed as he was savoring the last bite of his third cookie. When he finished, he turned to Muriel.

"Those cookies are amazing," he said pleasantly.

"Thank you," she said with a smile.

"Thank *you*," said Nick enthusiastically. "You've been a wonderful help on this investigation, and we thank you for your time."

"No problem," said Muriel.

The three got up from the table and made their way to the door. As they got to the threshold, Muriel thanked them for stopping by and gave them each a departing hug. Just before stepping out, Nick paused and turned back.

"Just one more thing, Muriel."

"What's that, dear?"

"In your conversations with her, did Cecelia seem intelligent?"

Muriel pondered the question a bit before responding.

"She wasn't dumb, but she didn't seem particularly intellectual either. Maybe about average. It's a bit hard to gauge these days when young girls are only interested in boys and rock 'n roll."

"Ok. Well, thanks again. Have a great day, Muriel."

"You, too," she responded.

As the door closed behind them, Nick motioned to Doug, and the two made their way to the other end of the hallway. Once they were out of earshot of Muriel's residence, Nick turned to Doug.

"She's not his daughter," said Hagan.

"What?"

"Cecelia is not Friedman's daughter."

"How do you know that?" inquired Doug skeptically.

"Just go with me on this," began Nick. "Friedman's wife died two years ago, when Cecelia would have been around eight."

"Right."

"That means Cecelia would have been born around the turn of the millennium. If Elaine Prescott was only eighteen when she was married, then she would have been forty-two when Cecelia was born, but chances are that she would be even older than that. Women over the age of forty are highly susceptible to having children with Down syndrome. But Muriel stated that Cecelia had at least average intelligence."

"Maybe. But there's no guarantee that even with a late pregnancy her child would have been born with Down syndrome."

"True. By why would two people who had been married for twenty years wait so long before having a kid? It's not like they couldn't afford one."

"So...you thinking this girl is some kind of child bride he picked up overseas?" asked Doug.

"No, nothing that sinister. I think he would have kept her existence secret if it was something that illegal."

"Then what are you thinking?"

"Not sure yet. But I'd be willing to bet cash money that they are no more related than we are."

"So...where to?" asked Doug.

Nick checked his watch.

"It's the middle of the day on a Tuesday. I say we start checking the schools. We'll leave someone here to watch the door in case she comes back. For now, we will continue this investigation as though we're searching for Cecelia Friedman in an attempt to notify the next of kin."

Doug raised an eyebrow at his partner.

"Is that not what we're doing?"

Nick shook his head.

"James Friedman is dead. His only known family is this young girl, who now stands to inherit a fortune. It's all a bit suspect to me."

"That's some pretty impressive detective work there Mr. Hagan," joked Doug. "And all it took was a cup of coffee and some cookies. Do you think we should go back and get that recipe from Muriel?"

"Absolutely," replied Nick. "But right now all I care about is finding that girl."

CHAPTER 7

Olivia stood before the bedroom mirror being subjected to the merciless scrutiny of the girl on the other side of the looking glass. Every imperfection ruthlessly identified beneath the judgmental eye of her most adept critic. The harsh reflection made her pale skin seem translucent, like that of an elderly hospice patient. Her thin blond hair coarse and matted, feeling oily and disgusting when she ran her fingers through it. Her tiny frame bony and frail, making her appear less a woman to be desired, and more like a skeleton.

Olivia pulled the shirt she was wearing overhead, tossing it on the bed beside her. Focusing her attention back to the girl in the mirror, Olivia let loose a despondent sigh. While the rest of the country struggles with concerns over obesity, her tiny body possessed neither a hint of fat nor an ounce of muscle. She had never minded being thin, but narrow hips and a flat chest did little to express one's femininity.

Other than the long hair and the missing anatomy, I look just like a boy.

Olivia pressed her hands to her midsection, just beneath the sternum, attempting to push the extra skin tissue upward. When that did not yield a significant change, she tried again from the sides, cupping her pectorals and pushing inwards. She bent forward, hoping that gravity would help her along, but it didn't. Olivia grunted with frustration, wondering if other twenty-three-year olds dealt with these same emotions.

Turning away from her reflection, she caught one last glimpse of herself in the mirror. She paused a moment to simply admire what few assets she possessed. Swishing her hips side-to-side, Olivia grinned with smug satisfaction. *At least I have a cute butt.*

Outside the bedroom, and safely away from the mirror, she cast her analytical eyes on the rest of the apartment. From where she was standing, she saw piles of pizza boxes, empty bottles, old newspapers, dirty clothing, and random debris scattered throughout every inch of table and floor space. In the living room, on either side of the television, were bookshelves. Though the shelves were black, a thick film of dust had collected along the interior and exterior sections, giving off the effect of gray.

Her curiosity piqued, she made her way to the closest bookshelf. Brushing away the dust from one of the shelves, she began reading the labels. She recognized several authors by name including Immanuel Kant, Thomas More, Friedrich Nietzsche, William James, and Bertrand Russell, plus others that she had never heard of. On the next shelf she found books by Plato, Aristotle, and Marcus Aurelius. Below that she saw many books on world religions and religious philosophy. She scowled at this recent discovery and decided to search the shelves on the other side of the room.

The other shelf yielded more fruitful prospects. Among these were some of her favorite authors. There was Asimov and Terry Pratchett, Frank Herbert, Rowling, and many more authors that she had spent hours being immersed in their creations. She was just about to reach for something she had not heard of before when the sounds of the Imperial March filled the room.

The sudden noise in the quiet room startled Olivia, but her curiosity quickly overcame her shock. She followed the ominous music to a cellphone which had been left on the kitchen island. Olivia peeked at the incoming name. It was Abigail. *It's a fitting theme*, Olivia thought. She pondered answering the phone, but decided against it since, according to Abigail, she wasn't supposed to be here in the first place.

Eventually the music ended, and Olivia waited with nervous anticipation. *Would she leave a voice message? What would it be?* Olivia had to remind herself to breathe. Her nails digging into her palms, she began counting away the seconds. As her counting hit the double digits she sighed with relief. Olivia walked away from the phone back toward the bookshelf.

The phone made a beeping noise.

Olivia snatched the phone off the counter and examined the screen. A message indicated that there was a new voicemail. Olivia recalled the good old days when people had answering machines with a delete button. She hesitated for a moment, debating the decision in her head.

She pressed the send button.

The phone did not dial, instead, a female voice answered immediately. It prompted her for a password. Olivia hesitated again. She didn't like the idea of invading his privacy, no matter the reason. The voice prompted her a second time. Olivia took a deep breath and decided to go for it. She typed in four ones and then pressed the pound key.

At first, nothing happened. The seconds ticked by slower and Olivia was certain that the factory password had not worked. Then, the female voice told her that she had one new voice message. Olivia could hardly contain her excitement as she heard the sound of Abigail's voice.

"Hi Mitch, it's Abigail. Sorry for going off on you like that before. But, anyway, I called my friend Samuel Brandt over at the child welfare office."

Olivia's heart sank.

"Unfortunately, they seem to be swamped at his office. He says he won't be able to get a caseworker out until Thursday morning. Sam suggested that we contact the police and at least make a report so they can start tracking down the girl's parents. My last client is at seven, and I will be done around eight. I'll be by after that to pick the child up and take her to the police station. Make sure that she's ready to go when I get there. I have to go now, my next client just walked through the door. See you tonight. Bye."

The female voice returned, prompting her with another choice. Olivia chose to delete the message. Realizing what this phone call meant for her, she slammed the phone down on the island in frustration, thankful that its protective case saved it from her aggravations.

It wasn't fair. All her life she had remained reticent and docile, never acting up, never making demands, never anything but her best behavior. Now that she finally found someone who actually listened to what she had to say rather than dismiss her ideas as the nonsensical ramblings of a child, someone who had been willing to defend her against a terrifying adversary, someone who had seen her as more than just her adolescent façade, it was all being ripped out from under her.

For one fleeting moment, everything appeared to be going in her favor. She'd finally found a man worth having who seemed to enjoy her company almost as much as she desired his. But now it looked like that pipedream had ended. As if in a daze, Olivia went back to the living room, plopping herself down on the couch. Pulling the throw blanket over her head, she lay with her back to the room and the floodgates let loose until emotional exhaustion ferried her off to sleep.

Mitchell stood facing an entire wall of underwear in despair. Where men had managed to survive with boxers, briefs, and boxer briefs, women had clearly taken the torch and run away with it. There were classic briefs, high-cut briefs, low-cut briefs, bikini style panties, something called hipster, and even a variety of garments called boyshorts. And then there were the designs: striped, solid, polka-dot, some with butterflies, some with Disney characters, a pair with a superman "S" on them, various designs that featured fruit, and many with words across the back that Mitchell couldn't imagine using in everyday conversation. All appeared to be available in every color that Mitchell could name, and even some he couldn't.

He double-checked the list to see if it miraculously presented more information. It still just said "underwear" with a size written next to it. He didn't know how many he was supposed to be picking up. What seemed like a simple errand had morphed into a futile task.

"This is hopeless," he muttered under his breath.

Out of the corner of his eye he saw someone enter the aisle near him. She clearly did not work here, but at this point he was willing to take help in whatever form it came. He approached the woman.

"Excuse me, miss," he began. "Do you think you could help me pick out some women's underwear?"

The woman said nothing, but her eyes grew wide for a moment before she evacuated the aisle, clutching her purse as she went. Mitchell let out a despondent sigh as he reflected on how this would be his last shopping trip in this particular store. He grabbed his cart and made a beeline for the checkout, hoping that he could make it through the exit before security started searching for a weirdo in the women's underwear department.

Fortunately, he made it out of the store without a hitch. He pulled out his checklist and reexamined it. He had been successful in finding most of the items on the list, including clothing, an apron, various toiletries, a coat, and even some sleepwear that was not on the list. All that remained now was underwear and a pair of shoes.

For all of the items, Olivia had been vague in details. Mitchell assumed perhaps she was trying to be as accommodating as possible, but the effect was less helpful than if she had just requested specific items. Her ambiguity in the clothing department had led him to wrongfully ask for assistance from the customer relations people. They supplied him with every fashion tip from the last twenty-five years, and he had been unable to comprehend much beyond the first couple sentences. In the end, he used what he thought was his best judgment and decided to hope for the best. It was only in the shampoo selection that Olivia had put down any details. He could only assume that she did not favor his choice of shampoo because she double-underlined her selection and put a large circle around it.

Since he was at the mall, he decided that he would look for the shoes next. *It certainly has to be easier to find a pair of shoes than underwear*, thought Mitchell.

Olivia awoke shortly after noon. Her body was stiff from the unforgiving nature of the couch. She wondered how Mitchell managed to sleep on it last night.

Listening to the stillness of the apartment, she pushed herself up, peering out over the top of the cushioned backing. There was no sign of Mitchell. All of the lights were still off, the bedroom and bathroom doors were wide open, and she hadn't heard him come in.

He must still be shopping, she thought to herself.

Sliding from her sleeping spot, she made her way to the bathroom. While washing her hands, she splashed cool water on her eyes, hoping to alleviate some of the dry irritation. Glancing in the mirror she could still see redness, but at least it felt better.

Olivia emerged from the bathroom with a renewed sense of purpose. Abigail might be trying to get rid of her, but she wasn't about to give up just yet. Olivia was confident that with enough time and effort she could win over any nemesis, no matter how disagreeable they appeared. All she had to do was prove herself to be a valuable houseguest, and she'd be allowed to stay.

First things first, she thought, *this place is too quiet.*

Olivia moved to the living room searching for a CD player, stereo, or record player. In the lower left cabinet of the television stand she discovered an iPod docking station which still had the device in it. She was pleasantly surprised by the collection of familiar artists, a selection almost identical to what she would have created for herself. Setting the device on shuffle, the soothing sounds of the Blue Oyster Cult filled the room. As the music played, she began to dance, her body flowing gently back and forth in rhythm to the relaxing chords.

The swaying movements carried her into the scattered debris; her bare foot striking an empty bottle. She was broken from her trance when the glass clanked loudly against others as it rolled across the floor. Her eyes followed the trail of bottles to where they had colonized behind the apartment door. Between where she stood and the pile before her, Olivia estimated that there must be more than a hundred empty bottles.

Shaking her head with disgust, she walked to the kitchen, rooting in the cabinet underneath the sink. She found several cleaning products, some scrubbing sponges, even a bottle of vodka, but no trash bags. She checked the other drawers around the room. Still nothing. On the counter she found a shopping bag, presumably one that Abigail brought which had not been unloaded.

"Ah ha..." she exclaimed as she found what she'd been searching for.

Pulling one of the large black bags from the box, she headed to the pile of empty bottles behind the door. With the exception of a few random soda bottles, each discarded container had once been a carrier for alcohol. In her heart, she hoped that they had taken a long time to accumulate. The idea of Mitchell being a lousy housekeeper seemed a better option than the alternative.

When the bag was full, Olivia tied it, leaving it lying behind the door. Even if she had known where the trash chute was, there was no way she could leave the apartment looking as she did. With one bag completed, Olivia retrieved another from the box.

Mitchell exited the shoe store at 2:15. When he told the store manager that he was in search of a pair of shoes, the manager insisted that no single pair could cover all occasions. Mitchell, who had been wearing the same shoes for every occasion in the last six months, disagreed, but was wise enough not to get dragged into a debate over the issue. In the end, he compromised, opting to buy two pairs instead.

Mitchell checked the mall directory and found that the only reliable merchant in the underwear field was Victoria's Secret. Although it was not a place that he felt comfortable going into, especially for the sizes he had been given, Mitchell gathered his courage and made his way to the other end of the mall.

From the moment the store came into view, a sense of panic enveloped him. *What if his story didn't make sense to the manager? Would they call security? What would happen to Olivia if he never returned?* Pushing those thoughts aside, he took in a deep breath and entered the store.

Perhaps it was just his imagination, but Mitchell felt eyes peering at him from all corners of the store. He was the only male patron, and his presence changed the entire shopping atmosphere. Where there had been friendly and boisterous conversation when he approached, now there were only hushed whispers and sideways glances. When a store associate approached him, Mitchell felt a sense of relief and another of trepidation.

"Good afternoon. Is there anything I can help you find?" she asked with a hint of defensiveness in her voice.

"Hopefully," Mitchell said nervously. "I need to find some underwear."

"Well, we definitely have that here. Who is the underwear for?" she asked apprehensively.

"My niece," Mitchell responded, just a little too quickly.

The woman's whole body tensed.

"You see," he continued, "she's up here on a visit from Florida, and the airline lost her luggage." Mitchell raised the bags in his hand, displaying them to his inquisitor. "I've been going around getting some stuff for her to wear until it gets straightened out."

The woman relaxed her shoulders.

"I'm sorry to hear that," she stated sympathetically. "That happened to my boyfriend when we flew to Las Vegas last summer. They got it cleared up by the next day. I hope it all works out for your niece."

"Thank you."

"Do you know what styles she likes?"

Mitchell shook his head.

"I don't even know what type of styles there are."

"She didn't mention anything to you?"

Mitchell shook his head again.

"All she gave me was a size."

Mitchell showed her the line on the checklist. She looked at the size and then quickly examined other items on the list. Satisfied that the list matched his story, she looked back up at him.

"An extra-small…She's quite the petite one isn't she?"

Mitchell nodded.

"How old is she?"

Mitchell took a moment to ponder the question.

"I think she may be twelve or thirteen."

"Oh wow," she commented, eyeballing Mitchell's stature. "I guess she missed out on the good genes."

Mitchell chuckled cordially.

"So, I'll show you what we have and you can decide what you think is best."

She took a step away from him, but Mitchell did not move.

"Actually, I was thinking…"

The woman stopped and looked at him curiously.

"Would you maybe pick out a few things in her size for me."

The woman laughed.

"Men… ," she said rolling her eyes. "I can do that. Does she have a favorite color?"

Mitchell smiled.

"She likes blue," he said.

"What about a bra?"

Mitchell frantically searched the recesses of his brain but came up empty.

"I don't know," he said.

"Ok," she responded with sympathy. "I'll grab one just in case."

Mitchell sighed with relief. As the woman turned away, he suddenly recalled something.

"Oh, miss!" he called to her.

She stopped and he approached her, speaking in a hushed voice.

"Nothing too…childish," he said.

The woman smiled warmly at him.

"I know," she said. "I was once that age myself."

The woman disappeared behind the walls of the main showroom, briskly moving about the back end of the store. After a few minutes, she returned to the front, her arms loaded with colorful delicates. With a motion of the head, she gestured Mitchell to the register and he was quick to comply.

"I picked out six pairs of panties, which should get her through the week if nothing else."

She held up the bra that she had selected. It had a blue, green, and white striped design.

"This bra should match all of the panties. The smallest we had is a 30A, but she can return it if it doesn't fit. Just make sure you hold onto the receipt."

Mitchell nodded, but had one question.

"If she has a week worth of panties, won't she need more than one bra?"

The woman laughed and rolled her eyes at him again.

"It will be okay. Trust me."

Though he was still uncertain, her reassuring words put his mind at ease. That is, until she told him the charge. It was considerably more than he was expecting to pay for underwear, but he relinquished the money without complaint. *At least this ordeal was at an end.* The woman wished him a nice day, and he returned the sentiment.

Out of the store and finally finished with shopping for Olivia, Mitchell recalled the one item he needed to pick up for himself. Attentively on the lookout, he sought out the closest liquor store.

After a tediously long day of accidental death, murder, and paper work, Detective Nick Hagan picked up the folder for the James Friedman case. So far the search for the missing daughter had come up bust, none of the private schools had her on the roster, and she had not returned to the apartment. *Where could she have gone?*

Hagan glanced up at the clock on his office wall. 3:47 p.m. There was just enough time to pursue the only other lead he had at the moment, assuming of course that they did not close early today. Reaching into his shirt pocket, he fished out the business card he'd acquired from the personal effects of the late James Friedman. The card listed two offices, one in Manhattan and the other, presumably a satellite location, in Pittsburgh. Hagan dialed the local number and a woman's voice answered on the second ring.

"Friedman Financial," she greeted coldly.

"Good afternoon. I'm Detective Nick Hagan," he said, adopting her no-nonsense attitude. "I'm involved in an investigation and wondering if you might answer some questions regarding James Friedman."

There was silence on the other end of the phone.

"Mr. Friedman is currently out of the office," she replied. "I'd be happy to take your name and number and have him call you back."

Nick rubbed his temples; it was looking like this would take a while.

"I'm aware that he's not at the office," he noted curtly. "I just need to gather some information."

"What sort of information?"

"Did James Friedman have any family other than his daughter?"

The woman audibly cleared her throat into the receiver.

"I'm sorry, sir, but I can't give out any private information about Mr. Friedman. If you would like to call back tomorrow, I'm sure…"

"Perhaps I could speak with his secretary?" Nick interrupted.

There was another grunting noise into the phone, followed by more silence.

"I'm afraid she's gone for the day."

"I see… ," muttered Nick. "Is there anyone there other than his secretary who might have knowledge of his personal life?"

"Sir, we're kind of busy here, so if it's not related to business…"

"I assure you that it's very important."

"I'm sure it is," she said dismissively. "But like I told you before, we can't give out…"

"Look!" shouted Nick into the phone. "I don't have time for this kindergarten nonsense. Let me speak with your manager."

"Well there's no need to get snippy," she scolded.

"I wasn't being…did you say *snippy*?"

"It means rude," she explained testily.

"I know what it means!"

"There's no need to shout."

Nick rubbed his hand over his face.

"Just connect me with your manager!"

"Sir, I'm going to have to ask you to calm down," she declared defensively.

Hagan was just about to say something else when he overheard another voice enter the conversation on the other end of the line. The two muffled voices spoke back and forth, neither making progress against the other. He couldn't tell what was being said, but after another moment, a male voice came on the phone.

"Hello?" spoke the new voice.

"Oh, thank god!" said Nick in frustration. "Can I please speak with Mr. Friedman's secretary?"

"Who is this?"

"Detective Nick Hagan, I'm with the Pittsburgh Bureau of Police."

"The police? Is everything alright?"

"I'm afraid not. I was trying to get some information regarding James Friedman. I asked to be transferred to his secretary."

"Well, Christine left early today. I think she had a dentist appointment," the man said apologetically.

Dismay came over Nick as he prepared himself for the same runaround he'd gotten from the receptionist. Before he could inquire further, the man continued.

"But if you just needed some information about James Friedman, I'd be happy to answer any questions you have."

"You would?" asked Nick disbelievingly.

"Sure. Jim and I've known each other more than twenty years."

"That would be great," said Nick, glad to be freed from the receptionist.

"Alright. I'm going to put you on hold for a second while they transfer the call to my office."

Nick heard the man make the request to the receptionist, along with bits and pieces of the disagreement that followed. There was a faint clicking noise as the phone went to hold. After a minute of solitude, the man picked up the other end.

"Are you still there, Detective?"

"I'm here."

"Oh good," the man said with relief. "I was worried that maybe she hung up on you in spite. Sorry about that by the way. We had to let go some of our office staff a few weeks ago and poor Delores has had to work extra hard until we find replacements. She's been a bit cranky because of it."

"No worries," said Nick cordially. "I guess even the investment tycoons are not immune to economic turmoil."

"Well, we had to make some layoffs over the summer, but this was actually over embezzlement."

"Oh… ," said Nick, feeling quite foolish.

"So what can I help you with, Detective?"

"Well, first, with whom am I speaking?"

"My name is Joseph Harper. I'm the senior vice-president of Friedman Financial."

"Ok," responded Nick while taking notes. "How long have you known Mr. Friedman?"

"Oh…I'd say about twenty-five years."

"Does Mr. Friedman have a wife?"

"He did. Sadly she passed away a couple years ago."

"Sorry to hear that. Was he dating anybody that you knew of?"

Harper paused on the other end.

"I'm sorry to interrupt you, Detective, but can I ask what this is about?"

In an effort not to alienate the single cooperative member of the firm, Nick decided to share his information. He let out a mournful sigh.

"I hate to have to be the one to tell you this, but the body of James Friedman was discovered this morning."

"The body? You mean…he's dead?"

"I'm afraid so."

The line went quiet for a time.

"Do they know what happened?"

"We're sorting out the details, but first we're trying to notify the next of kin. Did Friedman have any siblings?"

Harper made several noises into the phone as he regained his composure.

"Well, there was David, but he and his wife were killed in a car accident, maybe five or six years ago."

"I see. Any other siblings?"

"Not that I am aware of."

"What about his parents?"

"Deceased."

"Did Mr. Friedman have any other family?"

"Yes. He and his wife had a daughter. I believe her name is Cecelia."

"Uh huh," said Nick, pretending to take notes. "Do you know if she was theirs by birth or if she was adopted?"

Harper hesitated.

"Why would you think she was adopted?" he inquired suspiciously.

"Just protocol," said Hagan. "I have to ask."

Harper said nothing else, so Nick decided to move on.

"Do you know where she is?"

"I'm sure she was staying with Jim. He's been very protective of her since Elaine passed away. I don't think he's let her out of his sight the whole time."

"That's understandable," empathized Nick. "But she wasn't at his apartment, is there any other place that she might be staying? A friend's house maybe?"

"Jim never mentioned anything like that to me. I never really conversed with his daughter. She was always very quiet."

"I see. Do you know what she looks like?"

"Let's see…Short, skinny, I think she has blond hair."

"Do you know about how old?"

"Um…I'm not quite sure, but if I had to guess, I would say ten or eleven. But like I said, I'm not really sure."

"Ok. Well, we're trying to locate her. Seeing as she doesn't seem to have any other family or friends in the area, she may try to get in touch with someone at the company. If she contacts you, would you give me a call?"

"Not a problem. What's your phone number?"

Nick gave it to him.

"Alright. Sorry I couldn't be more help," said Harper.

"You've been very helpful. Hopefully she'll turn up soon."

"One can only hope. Good luck with your investigation."

"Thank you, and thank you for all your help."

Nick was just about to hang up the phone when he heard the sound of Harper's voice call out to him.

"I almost forgot," said Harper when he'd brought the phone back to his ear. "Jim had a private family lawyer that he kept on retainer. He might be able to help you as well."

Harper gave him the phone number.

"I'll warn you, he can be a little…poignant, but I assure you he's a great guy. I'll let him know that you'll be contacting him."

Nick said his goodbyes to Harper, and hung up the phone. Though he learned a little more about James Friedman, he felt no closer to finding the girl now than when they were standing on the roof. Still seeking answers, Nick lifted the receiver again. He was halfway through dialing the number for the lawyer when Doug entered the room.

"How's it going in here?" he asked boisterously.

Nick startled. He hung up the phone and turned to his partner.

"Hey, Doug. Any luck tracking down the girl?"

Doug shook his head.

"No one has reported seeing her. I've got someone at the apartment in case she comes back, and I sent people to check at hospitals and morgues."

Nick nodded solemnly at the last word.

"Anything from the crime scene guys?"

Doug flashed him a smile.

"Fingerprints," he said smugly.

"Really?"

"Yep," said Doug, laying a folder on the desk for Nick to read. "Twenty-seven unique sets."

Nick groaned loudly.

"That's worse than having none." grumbled Hagan. "Why so many?"

Doug shrugged.

"Judging by his attire, he was at some sort of social event before he died. Maybe a lot of pats on the back from old friends? Or maybe his chauffer was late, and he had to take the train."

Nick smiled.

"Anything on your end?" asked Doug.

Nick shrugged.

"Mostly verifying what we already know. I'm still waiting on the tox screen and autopsy report."

"Did you find any family?"

"Just her. There was a brother and sister-in-law, but they're both deceased. There's nobody else as far as I can tell. I got the number for Friedman's lawyer, so maybe he'll have more information about family members in the will."

Doug nodded.

"Anything on adoption?"

"The guy at the firm didn't say, but I could tell he was withholding something."

"You thinking conspiracy then?"

"Maybe… I'll let you know once I speak to the lawyer about beneficiaries. All I know is that they found a wallet in James Friedman's pocket that had $1,500 in a secret compartment. If he'd been attacked by a complete stranger, why leave the wallet and solid gold wristwatch? Hell, even the guy's shoes looked like they were worth something."

"I see your point."

"So if not robbery, I figure it's got to be murder or accident."

"What about kidnapping?"

Nick raised an eyebrow at him.

"If they were planning on kidnapping him, I'd say they failed."

"Not him, the girl. What if they planned on nabbing her and then demanding ransom from Friedman? The guy was loaded; surely he'd pay a lot of money to have his only daughter returned to him."

Nick thought about what Harper said about Friedman being very protective of the girl. Then he noticed the overeager look of excitement on his partner's face.

"Easy tiger," he chastised playfully. "I know how you get with conspiracies."

"So what now?" asked Doug.

"Here's the plan: I'll call the lawyer, and you go find that missing girl. We'll meet back here in ten minutes for a celebratory coffee."

CHAPTER 8

The absence of yellow caution tape over the elevator doors was a comforting sight to Mitchell after his exhausting day of shopping. For whatever reason, wandering through malls and department stores took a greater toll on his energy than hours of manual labor. His legs were like wet noodles from the walking, each footstep reverberating pain from his feet up to his knees. The bags had grown so heavy in his arms that just pressing the elevator button felt like a chore. As the lift trundled upward, his stomach rumbled, reminding him how physically draining the trip had been.

Stepping off the elevator, he recalled how tired Olivia was when he left that morning. Even sleeping on the king-size bed had not fully rejuvenated her system from the previous day's taxing adventures and she returned to slumber after seeing him off. Carefully inserting the key into the lock, he vowed to keep quiet in case she was still napping.

On entering, Mitchell was accosted by the energetic chords of Abba blasting from the living room of his apartment. He marveled at the soundproof qualities of the building as he closed the door behind him, subconsciously maintaining his muffled presence. Following the sound of the music, he peered into the darkened living room. Seeing no movement, he glanced toward the kitchen.

It was there that he spotted Olivia, completely oblivious to his entrance, happily scrubbing away at the dishes in the sink. Lost in her own world, she softly sang along with the music, her hips gyrating back and forth to the beat. As he stood watching her gracefully swaying, he temporarily forgot all the aches in his own joints. There was something enchantingly beautiful about her movements. Maybe it was the carefree way she tossed her hair side-to-side, or the way she seemed to sync the motions of the sponge with the notes playing in the background, or perhaps it was that she did it all while being unabashedly underdressed, but he could not tear his eyes away. Not wanting to disturb her peaceful reverie, Mitchell simply waited and watched.

Time became a distant concept, and he was unsure how long he'd been standing there when she finally shut off the water. Stepping from the sink, Olivia dried her hands with a towel hanging on the oven door. When she turned around, her eyes found his, her face lighting up like a child on Christmas morning.

"You're back," she said gleefully.

She moved to where he stood, wrapping her arms around his midsection in a warm, affectionate hug. With her body pressed against his, he could feel the moisture of splashed faucet water pass from her body through his clothing. Mitchell delicately placed his free hand across her naked back, hesitantly returning the friendly gesture. Olivia responded to his touch by pushing her face deeper into his torso. Mitchell gazed down at her smiling face, her eyes closed as she nuzzled his stomach. Holding herself to him for another moment, she let out a contented sigh.

When she pulled back, Mitchell noticed a dollop of soap suds that lingered just below her chin line. *What a messy dishwasher*, he mused to himself. She was soaked. It looked as though she had been playing with a garden hose, water still dripping down the entire anterior portion of her body. The frothy moisture pooled on her bare chest, trickled across her soft abdomen, and flowed downwards over her...

"I picked up the things you need," he spoke suddenly, using the bags to obscure his vision. Mitchell could already feel the heat spreading throughout his face.

Olivia motioned for him to set the bags on the island. Mitchell did as he was instructed, glad to be free of the cumbersome burden. As the weight fell from his fingertips, Mitchell felt a downward tug on his elbow. Even with him tilting sideways, she was forced to stand on tiptoes to kiss him softly on the cheek.

"Thank you," she whispered into his ear.

Olivia turned to the bags, pretending not to see the abrupt change in Mitchell's complexion. Sifting through the assortment of items, she found her special shampoo and set it on the counter, keen to restore her hair to its normal shine. Browsing through the clothing, she mentally checked off the list she'd given Mitchell, abruptly ceasing when her eyes found the Victoria's Secret bag. Unsure what to think, she turned back to Mitchell.

"I'll sort through these bags later," she said. "What do you want to do for dinner?"

"I'm not really up for cooking tonight," he said tiredly. "How about we order a pizza?"

"Pizza sounds good."

"What do you like on yours?"

As she pondered, Mitchell sensed an impending debate. Pizza toppings had been an issue of contention with Evelyn all through their short marriage. Whereas he enjoyed the more exotic cuisine, she had reserved herself to cheese, extra-cheese, and the occasional mushroom. She had called it a "sensitive palate," though Mitchell suspected she was just a picky eater.

"Do you like ham and pineapple?" asked Olivia.

"That'll work," said Mitchell with a sigh of relief, not bothering to mention that she had opted for his favorite combination.

"Excellent. I'm going to take a shower before the food arrives," she said, clutching her bottle of shampoo as though it were a precious treasure.

Mitchell gestured to the accumulation of soapy water plastered across her front.

"With all that soap, you're still not feeling clean?" he joked.

Olivia paused, a sly smile spreading across her lips. She raised her hand, making small circles on his chest with her forefinger. Olivia gazed longingly up at him before flashing a flirtatious grin.

"Maybe I'm just feeling extra dirty tonight," she teased.

Turning from him, she made her way toward the bathroom, swishing her behind with every step, leaving Mitchell's jaw to rest upon the floor.

The water in the shower grew cold quickly, not surprising considering how much I used getting all the dishes clean. I didn't mind too much though, what little hot water there had been was enough for me to clear that disgusting dishwater from my body and make my hair feel luxuriously soft again. Besides, I was eager to see what was in the bags on the counter.

Though I easily could have picked out my own clothing if I wanted to, adding a few details where I'd intentionally skimped, I needed to know, for my own sake, how Mitchell felt about me. Despite my excitement, it was mostly with apprehension that I pondered what I might find in those bags. When he made his selections today, had Mitchell thought about me as a woman or as a child?

I thought about the Victoria's Secret bag I'd seen amongst the lot. I had never been in any of their stores before, but I'd heard about some of the outfits they sold, and it set me on edge to think someone had gone shopping there on my behalf. As much as I wanted to be regarded the way my age should dictate, there was a fine line between being treated as an adult and being treated like a sexual plaything. I refused to be the latter, even if it meant having to find myself a new residence.

Turning off the water, I dried thoroughly in the tub before stepping on the raggedy bath mat. Gazing in the mirror, I raised both hands behind my head and struck a pose. Though it was the same body I had that morning, tonight it seemed different, as though I'd gone through a personal metamorphosis. Mitchell had gazed upon my naked form and blushed. I never had that effect on anyone before, and it made me feel attractive in a way that only another person's desire can.

Grabbing the towel I used to dry myself, I wrapped it around my waist, tying it off at the edge. Unhappy with this look, I draped my hair over the left shoulder, concealing the exposed breast. Still not satisfied, I tried it the other way, covering the right one instead. I shook my head with discontent. Parting the hair, I let it fall half on one side and half on the other. That did it. Giving myself one last look, I nervously emerged from the bathroom.

Looking into the kitchen, I found Mitchell seated at one of the island stools. He had his head propped up on the palm of his hand, both eyes closed, his body moving rhythmically up and down as he breathed.

"Mitchell?" I called out gently.

His eyes flickered awake, though they took a moment to adjust. Mitchell glanced in my direction before giving me his undivided attention. His eyes went wide as his mouth hung limply open.

"Could I get you to do me a favor?"

He raised his eyes inquisitively at me.

"Could you take the bags and place them in on the bed?"

Mitchell nodded, grunting as he pulled himself off the barstool. He carried the cargo to its destination, making rustling noises as they settled on top of the bed. With his task complete, Mitchell turned to where I was standing near the doorway.

"Thank you," I said, moving beside the bed next to where he deposited my new belongings.

Mitchell continued to stand at attention, as though awaiting his next command. His eyes flickered between watching me and glancing at the wall as he tried his best to ignore my nakedness. After a few seconds of awkward silence, I shot him the most provocative smile I could muster.

"Would you like to help me get dressed?" I asked coyly.

Mitchell's eyes grew wide, his speech stammered to match his flustered state.

"I, uh…right…sorry," he managed, quickly backing out of the room, closing the door as he went. I felt guilty about tormenting him like that, but it was so much fun watching him squirm. Reaching for the first bag, I began dumping the contents onto the bed, sorting them into distinct piles.

In total, there were six shirts, three pairs of jeans, two pairs of shoes, a package of socks, a pair of sweatpants, a tank top, a light blue sleep shirt, and a dark gray wool winter coat that looked as though it were big enough to cover my entire body instead of just my torso. Thankfully, none of the apparel featured cartoon characters, cutesy designs or childish phrases.

I turned my attention to the remaining bag, its double-striped pink design seeming more ominous than what was probably intended. Perhaps I was thinking too hard about it, but I felt that the contents of this particular bag would determine if there was any hope of a relationship between me and the man I'd grown to desire. With nervous anticipation, I reached into the bag.

When my hand touched something soft, I latched onto it, pulling it slowly from the container. Holding my breath, I gave one last tug, exposing it to the light of the bedroom. In my hand was a pair of turquoise colored panties, a small bow was stitched across the top. I felt my face shrivel at the sight of the saccharine adornment. It was definitely not something I would have chosen for myself.

Sliding on the panties, I turned to the mirror to see how they looked. My opinion of the bow changed instantly. Though the effect was to be cute, it was not in any way to be confused with juvenile. The fabric clung tightly to my hips, exaggerating each curve and crevice as I admired them from different angles. The light color of the material matched my fair skin, accentuating the tender flesh. The bow that I'd found so cloyingly childish hung low enough that it made me think of unwrapping gifts on Christmas morning.

"Hmmm…" I thought aloud, wondering if they made such a design.

Feeling smugly satisfied with how the first pair looked, I eagerly returned to the bag, pulling out each new pair one by one. Though I refrained from actually donning them, I envisioned how they might uniquely express my feminine features. Until today, I never imagined that my boyish frame could be capable of anything even remotely attractive. Even at twenty-three years old, I had only been referred to as cute, adorable, or even darling. Yet, in this moment, I was none of those things. Tonight I was not a girl, but a woman, alluring and downright sexy.

The sound of a doorbell tore me away from my musings.

"That must be the food," I thought to myself.

Peering into the bottom of the bag, I could see one last garment and a piece of paper that I assumed must be the receipt. Lifting the item from the bag, I examined the pleasant looking striped brassiere. I appreciated the sentiment, but it was definitely not something I was going to need. I returned it to the bag, planning to exchange it for something more relevant when I got the chance.

"Hmmm… ," I muttered to myself, remembering my vision about unwrapping presents.

Plucking the tags from the sleep shirt, I slipped it overhead. The velvety material felt wonderful as it brushed across my bare skin. I checked myself in the mirror quickly before emerging from the bedroom.

In the kitchen, Mitchell was drying plates from the dish drainer. As I approached, he glanced in my direction. His eyes scanned me up and down, and then up again.

"That looks very nice on you," he commented pleasantly.

I skipped over to where he stood and wrapped my arms around his waist. I rested my head against his broad back as I hugged him from behind.

"Thank you," I replied happily. I wanted to ask him what he thought about my new panties, but another kind of hunger had started to drain my playful spirit.

After we finished eating, Olivia curled up beside me on the couch. I had grown accustomed to her touch, though I was still mindful of keeping our individual parts separated.

"Really?" she challenged. "Thanksgiving?"

"Why not? Food, family, and football. What could be better than that?"

"Boys...," she said with a disapproving roll of the eyes.

"Well, what about you?" I asked.

Olivia shrugged.

"If I had to pick something, I'd probably say Halloween."

"It's the free candy isn't it?"

She cracked a smile, but shook her head.

"No. I just enjoy the history behind the holiday more than some of the others." she explained. "Besides, I've never been trick-or-treating."

"Never?"

"Maybe when I was very young. It's possible that my birth parents took me, and I don't remember it. We never did anything like that at the orphanage, and my foster parents didn't approve of 'pagan festivals'," she said holding up finger quotes.

"Wow. I was raised Catholic, and your parents sound strict."

"Foster parents," she corrected quickly. "And not really. It was only over very specific things. Violent movies were acceptable but ones featuring sex were a definite no-no. We were free to read whatever we wanted, except literature about witches, wizards, and magic. Can you believe they confiscated the copy of Harry Potter I'd gotten from the library?"

"You're kidding..."

"Nope. I had to read the entire series in secret."

"In secret? Like flashlight under the covers kind of secret?"

"Nothing that high-tech," she said, a sly smile creeping across her lips. "All I had to do was put a religious book cover over it, and they assumed I must be reading scripture like a good little girl should."

"Nice," I replied with a chuckle.

"But the point is that I never should have had to do that. There's been enough books written about banning books that they shouldn't have tried to quell my reading habits. It's repugnant that so many parents think the best way to educate their children is to deny them access to opposing viewpoints."

I nodded in agreement.

"Sometimes it's hard to reason with unreasonable people."

"I guess," she said with a heavy sigh. "It's your turn by the way."

I thought for a moment.

"How about your favorite animal?"

Olivia pondered her answer.

"Probably the okapi."

"The what?"

"Okapi. It's like a cross between a giraffe and a zebra."

"I've never even heard of that," I said, pulling out my phone. Doing a quick search on the wireless connection, I found a picture of one of the strangest animals I'd ever seen in my life. "Huh...weird."

"I know, right?" she said gleefully. "I like unusual creatures, the stranger the better. Have you ever heard of a narwhal?"

I hadn't, but the Internet was superb at curing my ignorance.

"Is that a horn on its head?" I asked disbelievingly.

"Actually it's a tooth, but I think it's still pretty neat."

I had to admit that it was pretty neat and not just because of the political influences sitting beside me. I slid the phone away.

"What about you?" she asked.

"I don't think my teeth grow like that," I replied.

She rolled her eyes.

"What's your favorite animal?"

"Oh…right," I said sheepishly. "I'm kind of a dog person."

Olivia tilted her head to the side and gave me a glare of disapproval.

"A dog? That's it?"

"What? I can't like dogs?"

"Not a wolf? Or an African wild dog? Maybe even a dingo?"

"No. Just a dog."

Olivia sighed audibly.

"You have to at least give a breed."

"German shepherd," I replied quickly.

She gave a consenting shrug.

"Ok. That works," she said with approval. "What was your favorite subject in school?"

"History. Is yours some kind of science?"

Olivia nodded.

"Zoology. Though history was a close second or third."

"I don't think they offered that at my high school. Is that part of the standard curriculum?"

"I have no idea. I was homeschooled for most of the higher level classes. The Friedmans were quite concerned about my education. They even hired me a private tutor at one point."

Something stirred in my mind.

"Did you say 'Friedmans'?"

"Yes. Mr. James and his wife Mrs. Elaine. I thought I mentioned them."

Putting the pieces together, I visualized the fetid corpse back on the roof.

"You did," I said, shaking off the dreadful thoughts. "I must have blanked for a moment. Didn't you say they passed away a few years ago?"

Olivia eyed me curiously.

"Mrs. Elaine died back in 2008. I don't think Mr. James ever fully recovered from her passing. He was never the same after that. I guess it's hard when you've been married to someone for a long time."

I nodded empathetically, though my stomach was doing backflips. Her adopted father met his end on the same rooftop where I woke up yesterday morning. Had I been somehow responsible for his demise? Olivia spoke beside me and it barely registered in my mind.

"What was that?"

"I said that it's your turn again," she reiterated with concern. "Are you feeling alright? You look a little pale."

"I'm fine," I assured her. "I guess I'm still a bit wiped out from all the walking today."

Olivia continued to regard me with sympathetic eyes, but made no move to conclude our little game. I wasn't sure what this activity was meant to prove other than how different the two of us were.

"Favorite sport?"

Olivia shook her head.

"I'm not a big sports fan," she said. "You like football, right?"

I nodded.

"Favorite candy bar?" she asked on her turn.

"Well, I know it's not technically a candy bar, but they sell it in the same section of the store so I consider it one. Reese's."

She flashed a smile at me.

"Mine, too," she said.

A match? I couldn't believe it.

"Favorite ice cream flavor?" I asked, wondering if we could maintain momentum.

Olivia touched her tongue to her upper lip.

"Chocolate fudge moose tracks," she stated gleefully. "But anything chocolate will do."

She gave me an inquisitive look.

"Definitely anything chocolate." I said in agreement.

Olivia seemed to be pondering her next question.

"Favorite television show?"

I didn't even need to think about that one.

"Firefly."

Her eyes sparkled with excitement.

"I love that show," she squealed.

Olivia lifted her feet from the floor, crossing them beneath her on the couch. Focusing her attention on me, we discussed our favorite characters, favorite episodes, and how much we wished they'd done a second season. Mostly we agreed about everything, except that she seemed to enjoy the doctor character more than I. Overall it was a welcome distraction from the morbid thoughts plaguing my brain.

After about an hour of nonstop discussion, Olivia glanced up at the clock. She stretched her arms overhead, letting loose a loud yawn.

"I think it's about time for bed," she said sleepily.

I looked at the clock.

"It's not quite eight yet," I protested.

Olivia bit her lip, her eyes checking the time again.

"One more round," she acceded.

I wanted to object, but her eyes made it clear I wouldn't win that argument. Despite my disinterest a little while ago, our energetic conversation over the last hour made me suddenly *want to know everything about my new companion. Realizing that she was tired and that we could pick this up tomorrow night, I decided to keep it simple. I meant to ask her about favorites foods, but when I gazed upon those adolescent features another question came to mind.*

"How old are you?" I asked.

She shot me a look of surprise.

"What?" she asked, a hint of nervousness entering her voice.

Pushing through my own trepidation, I asked her again.

"How old are you?"

It was clear by her facial expression that she was pondering some major decision, but of what I did not know.

"That's not how this game is played," she said.

"You don't have to answer if you don't want to," I offered.

Again she hesitated.

"Why do you want to know?"

It was a valid question, but it still took me a moment to gather my thoughts.

"Because I'm curious," I explained directly. "It's like your mind and body don't match up. When we talk, it's as if we're on the same intellectual wavelength, but then when I look at you, you don't look my age. Does that make sense?"

Olivia hung her head. Pulling her legs from their crossed position, she sat on her knees, gazing downward as she rested her haunches on her calves. When she finally looked back up, her eyes were watery, as though she might burst into tears.

"I want to tell you," she said. "But I'm afraid that you won't believe me if I do."

I felt myself giving her a quizzical look.

"Why wouldn't I believe you?"

"Because sometimes the lie is easier than the truth."

Somehow I understood what she meant, but was just as clueless at the same time. I reached out my hand and gently patted her knee.

"I'll believe you no matter what," I assured her. "I promise."

Olivia sat quietly for a moment, inhaling deeply a few times, gathering her courage. With a single forced exhalation, she released all the pent up anxiety that had been building up inside her.

"I'm twenty-three," she spoke hastily, her eyes watching me intently for my response.

I had to admit, it did seem rather implausible. I fully expected her to be older than she appeared, but twenty-three? I was a year into my master's program at that age. How could she be that old and still look that young? Hormones? Malnourishment? Growing up in an orphanage probably carried its share of setbacks in the nutrition department. Could it really be that simple?

No matter the cause, no matter the reason, her limited physical maturity did not match her impressive mental acumen. But which was the truth and which the falsehood? Was it my eyes that deceived me or was it the words she spoke? Which of us was the liar? I thought about my explanation to Abigail and what Olivia thought of my deception. It didn't take a rocket scientist to figure out which of us was the more honest.

"I believe you," I said.

Olivia looked at me with sanguine reverence, those blue sapphires radiating with joy as a single teardrop flowed down her cheek.

"You do?" she asked with a sniffle.

I gave her knee a reassuring squeeze before pulling my hand away.

"Of course. Why wouldn't I?"

Olivia wiped her cheek with the palm of her hand.

"I'm sorry," she said. "It's just...you're the first person to believe me when I've told the truth. Most people assume that it's some strange game I like to play or that I'm telling a joke they don't understand."

"Not even your adoptive parents?"

Olivia shook her head.

"I'm not sure what the proper way to ask this is, but what causes...or how come..."

"Why do I look like this?" she said, finishing my question.

I nodded.

"I have no idea," she said with a head shake. "It's just the way I've always been; the way I probably always will be."

She gave a solemn sigh and a silence developed between the two of us. After a long moment, she smiled at me.

"Ok. My turn," she said.

I had completely forgotten we were still playing.

"I want you to close your eyes," she instructed.

I cocked an eyebrow at her.

"Why?"

"Just do it."

"You know, commands aren't the same thing as questions," I said jovially.

She scooted closer, placing one hand over my eyes like a blindfold.

"Fine," I conceded. "Now what?"

"What do you see when you look at me?"

I turned my head toward her voice.

"The inside of your hand."

Olivia let out a quiet chuckle.

"Seriously, what do you see?"

I heaved a sigh.

"Do I really need to be blindfolded for this?"

"Yes," she said authoritatively. "It will keep you from being...distracted."

"You mean keep me from looking at you?"

"Something like that."

"How am I supposed to tell you what I see when I look at you when I can't look at you?"

"There's more to a person than just their appearance," she explained.

"I see...so you want me to tell you what I think about you when I'm thinking about you?"

"But I don't want you to tell me about what I look like. I could stand in front of a mirror for that."

I gave an appreciative head nod.

"This is a very interesting idea you have," I complimented.

"Thank you."

"There's just one problem though."

"Oh yeah? What's that?"

"Even if I can't see you, I can still remember what you look like."

For a moment, nothing happened.

"Ow," I exclaimed as I felt one of my arm hairs being plucked out.

"Sorry, had to distract you from thinking about my body," she teased. "It was for your own good."

"I thought you said the point of the blindfold was to keep me from being distracted."

"Well, I guess it wasn't doing the trick. I had to improvise."

"Some improvisation," I mocked. "It hasn't stopped me from thinking about how you look though."

I felt another pain in my arm.

"Will you stop that?" I pleaded.

"I would answer the question if I were you," threatened Olivia playfully. "There are a lot more hairs where that one came from."

"Okay, fine. Just no more hair pulling."

"I'm sorry," she said, gently rubbing the area she'd assaulted. "Do you want me to kiss it and make it better?"

Before I could say anything, I felt her soft lips press against my forearm.

"You're very kindhearted," I stated abruptly, hoping to keep myself from blushing.

"Thanks, but I was kind of the one who inflicted the injury."

"No...you asked what I see when I look at you...I see a kind-hearted person."

There was a pause.

"What else?" she asked eagerly.

"I see someone who's not afraid to speak her mind."

"Is that all?"

"You're very imaginative. I don't think I've ever met anyone who sees the world quite the way you do."

Olivia said nothing so I decided to continue.

"You're creative, and witty, and brilliant..."

"You think I'm 'brilliant'?"

"Are you kidding? How many other people even know what an otaki is off the top of their head?"

"Okapi," she corrected.

"Exactly my point. And it's not even just biology. You know tons of stuff about philosophy and history, and who knows what else."

I wasn't sure if I should say it, but I was feeling on a roll and couldn't stop myself.

"Plus, you have the most beautiful blue eyes I've ever seen. Looking at you is like gazing into a gem mine filled with sparkling..."

I never got to finish that thought as a pair of soft lips pressed against mine. They opened slightly, latching ever so gently onto my upper lip. I could taste a sweetness on her that was as enticing as nectar. Losing control of my inhibitions, I felt myself lean forward, returning to her the same passionate kiss that she bestowed on me.

After a few more seconds, Olivia placed her free hand on my chest, pulling herself away from our embrace. I tried to follow her with my lips, but she tenderly pushed me away. There was movement beside me and I felt her body lean close to mine. Olivia lifted her hand from my eyes, and I gazed upwards into those gorgeous sapphires.

"Tell me... ," she said seductively. "Do you like what you see?"

Moving my gaze away from those deep blue eyes, I focused on the adolescent features of her face. In spite of everything that she said, despite our inflamed gesture a moment ago, and even though I didn't want to admit it, I could still see the childish aspects of her young form. Olivia had been right about one thing: the lie definitely seemed easier than the tribulations that came with the truth.

Still catching my breath, I peered upwards into those starry blue orbs and smiled.

CHAPTER 9

It wasn't long thereafter that Olivia slipped off to bed, leaving me with a lot to consider. I believed her when she told me her age, but ultimately that wasn't the only thing on my mind. There was no denying what she wanted, but how could I provide it when I couldn't get passed her young physique? What was I supposed to do, blindfold myself every time we kissed? What kind of life would that be for either of us?

I shut off the hot water. Usually a relaxing shower was all I needed to clear my head, but not tonight apparently. I was halfway through drying when I heard the sound of the deadbolt click open. I hurriedly pulled on my shorts and t-shirt before stepping into the hallway to intercept the intruder. On seeing the figure standing by the entrance, I glanced up at the clock, not expecting to have any company this late at night.

"What are you doing here?" I demanded.

"What do you mean what am I doing here?" she asked with incredulous acrimony. "I told you I'd be coming by after work."

I searched my memory but came up empty.

"No you didn't."

"I did so."

"I think I'd remember if you'd told me you were coming over, Abigail."

"Well, I did. I even left you a voice message."

I moved to the kitchen island, picking up the phone from where I'd laid it prior to my shower.

"There are no messages here."

"Well, I called."

"Are you sure you dialed the right number?"

Abigail folded her arms in front of her, clearly not in the mood for bickering.

"Regardless, I'm here now."

I set the phone back down on the counter.

"So what do you want?" I asked.

"I'm taking the girl down to the police station."

I felt a tightening in my chest.

"Why?"

Abigail narrowed her eyes at me.

"So that they can try to find her real parents. Lord knows she's better off with them than in this trash heap."

"You don't know that," I said defensively, though I wished I hadn't.

Abigail glared at me suspiciously before giving a patronizing shake of the head.

"You can't keep her Mitchell. She's not a pet."

"I know that."

"Just because you found her doesn't make you responsible for her."

"I know that, too."

Abigail pursed her lips together tight enough that they changed colors.

"You have no business trying to raise an eleven-year-old."

"She's older than..."

"She might have told you that she was thirteen or fourteen, but girls lie about their age, Mitchell. Trust me, I know."

I knew that if she wouldn't believe those ages, I would be wasting my time trying to convince her of what Olivia told me. I decided to keep quiet.

"If you're done arguing, I'd like to get going."

"Now?"

"Yes, 'now'. The sooner we get her to the police station, the sooner we can get this whole thing straightened out."

I struggled to find the argument that would keep her from taking Olivia away.

"But it's nine o'clock at night."

"And?"

"And she's sleeping."

"So, wake her up."

"Come on, Abigail. She's not hurting anything, just let her sleep. I can take her to the station tomorrow."

"You mean like you could have done today?"

I let out a heavy sigh.

"Look...even if you get her down there tonight, chances are that the people who handle these kinds of cases will already be at home. She may have to wait until morning before anybody arrives. Do you really want to drag her from a nice comfortable bed just to force her to sleep at the police station?"

Abigail paused to consider this, though I could tell how much it aggravated her that I might have a point.

"Fine," she said testily. "Just make sure she's ready at 10. I have a client at 11:30 for whom I can't be late."

"Not a problem," I said pleasantly. "We'll be ready to go when you get here."

"We? I don't think so, Mitch."

"Geezus, Abigail. I'm the one who found her. Don't you think I should have a say in what happens to her?"

"No I don't. As far as I'm concerned, you've already involved yourself too much with that girl. It's time to take a step back and let the professionals handle it."

"I just want to make sure she ends up someplace safe. Is that too much to ask?"

"It's none of your concern what happens to her. Seriously Mitchell, there are hundreds of little girls just like her in the system. You can't save them all."

"But I might be able to help this one."

She shook her head.

"When did you become such a Samaritan all of a sudden?"

"When did YOU become such a frigid b...?"

"Don't you dare call me that! Don't you dare," she yelled, jabbing her finger at me. "Do you have any idea how many hours I spend each week trying to help children like her with problems at home? And some of them come from really twisted and broken households."

"It must be such a burden to get paid to help people."

"I'll have you know that a lot of it is pro bono work, thank you very much."

"So what's the problem with me wanting to help out for a change?"

Abigail nearly growled with exacerbation.

"Fine! Come along if you want to, but if I smell even a hint of alcohol on your breath I'm leaving you here. Got it?"

I glared at Abigail over the underhanded insult.

"Got it," I replied between clenched teeth.

"Good!" she stated harshly. "Then I'll see both of you in the morning."

With that she turned on her heel and stormed out of the apartment. The door slammed violently in her wake to emphasize that she had won the last word. With enough force to inflict pain on myself, I locked the deadbolt behind her in defiance of her insidious interference in my affairs. When I looked back in the apartment, Olivia was standing in the doorway to the bedroom.

"Didn't go so well, did it?"

I was halfway through shaking my head when her presence brought me back to the conversation with Abigail. I retrieved the phone from the kitchen island and scrolled to my recent calls. Earlier that afternoon I had gotten a call from Abigail's number, but it hadn't registered in my missed calls when I'd checked the phone before.

"You knew she was coming over didn't you?"

Olivia looked down at the floor.

"You deleted her message?"

Olivia nodded solemnly.

"Why would you do that?" I demanded.

She came across the kitchen, wrapping her arms around me.

"I'm sorry. I panicked. I didn't know what else to do."

I shook my head in frustration.

"Are you angry?" she asked fretfully.

I inhaled deeply, trying my best to maintain the rage inside me, but it was impossible to stay mad at her.

"Of course not," I said amicably.

I reached my arm around her back, returning the affectionate embrace. After a reasonable period of apology, I set the phone on the island and placed a hand on each of her shoulders. I gently pushed her out of the hug so that I could look her square in the face.

"Look... ," I began, "We're in this together, or not at all. Understand? There can be no secrets between us. Not telling me that Abigail was coming over was like throwing me to the wolves. I could have been ready for her. Instead, I froze up."

Olivia nodded appreciatively.

"If it makes you feel better, I think you did a great job."

I shook my head in disagreement.

"I should have told her the truth. If I had you wouldn't be forced to the police station tomorrow."

Olivia gave me a sympathetic smile.

"Would she have believed you if you had?"

I thought about it, and shook my head.

"So no harm done, right?" she said reassuringly.

I exhaled with relief.

"I guess not."

Reaching out my hand, I pulled out one of the stools from beneath the island.

"Here, have a seat," I instructed. "We have some things to discuss."

As Olivia climbed the stool, I went into the bedroom and retrieved a piece of printer paper and a pen from the computer desk. Returning to the kitchen, I laid them down in front of her.

"First things first," I said, "I want you to write something down for me."

"What is it?" she asked, readying herself with the pen.

I cleared my throat, enunciating every syllable as I spoke.

"I will not delete voice messages from Mitchell's phone."

Olivia cocked an eyebrow at me.

"No wait... ," I interrupted, remembering the other functions on the device. "I will not delete ANYTHING from Mitchell's phone."

Olivia continued to glare incredulously at me.

"You can't be serious... ," she declared skeptically.

I reached over and tapped the paper with my forefinger.

"Ten times. Let's go."

Olivia stared at me defiantly for another moment before putting pen to paper.

"Is this what you wanted to discuss with me?"

"No. I just figured we needed to lay down a few ground rules first."

I opened the fridge, desperately wanting anything to take the edge off after my confrontation with Abigail. Remembering my promise to be sober, I begrudgingly grabbed the orange juice instead, hoping the biting flavor might help do the trick.

"Would you like some?" I asked, holding the carton up for her to see.

"Sure, I'll have a glass," she said warmly before returning to her assignment.

"I was thinking about tomorrow," I said.

"And?"

"And I think we should make sure our stories match," I replied, pulling two glasses from the cupboard.

"You don't want to just tell them the truth?" she asked.

"It's a little late for that now. If we tell them anything different than what we told Abigail…"

"What YOU told Abigail." she corrected.

"…Then she's likely to call us out on it in front of the police officers. I think that could get messy."

"I seem to recall someone mentioning something about that before," she stated smugly.

"Yeah…yeah…yeah," I muttered, pouring the juice into the glass.

After putting the carton away, I carried the glasses to the island and set them down on the countertop. I slid one across the surface to Olivia.

"Thank you," she said. "I've finished by the way."

"Excellent," I replied, lifting the paper up to my face.

I scrunched my nose in confusion as I looked at the doodle on the page.

"What is this?"

"It's a turtle," she said pleased with herself. Her eyebrows were raised as though to challenge me, both arms folded defiantly across her chest.

"Fine," I remarked, carrying the picture to the refrigerator. I slipped the piece of paper beneath a magnet. "I don't want you deleting my messages any more than you would want me to destroy your turtle. So can you at least TRY to not erase my stuff?"

"Alright," she said with appeasement. "I'll try."

"Good, that's all I wanted."

Returning to the island, I lifted my juice from the countertop.

"So what's the game plan?" I asked.

Olivia raised her glass in the air as though to toast.

"Here's to confounding our enemies," she said, a sly twinkle in her eye.

I clanked my glass against hers.

"…And to delighting our friends," I responded, completing the quote.

I upturned my glass, finishing off its contents in a series of gulps, all the while wishing that it had been bourbon.

"Hello?"

"Hey. It's me. I just pulled into the parking lot."

"Okay. We'll be right down," Mitchell replied as Abigail gave him the coordinates.

Setting down the phone, Mitchell gazed over at Olivia who had already donned the winter coat he bought for her. This morning she had been the first to rise, helping to drag him lethargically from the couch. Ironically enough, the girl who insisted on wearing as little clothing as possible helped him to pick out something to wear.

"Are you ready?" He asked, feeling somewhat pretentious in the navy blue pinstripe suit she selected for him. Olivia said it would help with his image, whatever that meant, but he was only too overjoyed to wear anything that would help their day go smoother.

"As long as it's not forever," she commented sadly.

Taking her by the hand, they exited the apartment, heading joylessly toward the elevators. Mitchell had walked these narrow corridors every day since the start of his trial separation from Evelyn, and they had never felt as gloomy as they did right now. The only consolation for this depressing atmosphere was the feel of Olivia's tender fingers entwined with his.

Thus it was with great anguish that he was forced to relinquish their hold as they entered the car park. He knew that any affection he displayed toward his young companion would only further Abigail's wrath, something he wanted to avoid very much.

Up ahead he spotted the familiar emblem of her gray sedan. Holding the door open for Olivia, she slid behind the driver's seat. Before entering on the passenger's side, Mitchell held down the adjustment button until the leather seat came to a halt in its rearmost position. Even with the chair all the way back, both of his legs grazed the panel as he climbed inside. Mitchell wondered how short the European manufacturers must be if they considered this vehicle a luxury.

Abigail glared menacingly in her rearview mirror at the small girl positioned behind her. Though Olivia had spent much of the last two days with minimal clothing or none at all, it was Abigail's ominous stare that suddenly made her feel naked.

"Glad to see you wearing something more appropriate than my brother's t-shirt," said Abigail, casting her intimidating leer at Mitchell and another at his attire.

Olivia wore a pair of her new jeans with a teal, crocheted, knit top. Although it was her size, the fabric hung loosely off her shoulders. Even with its enthusiastic chest allotment, Olivia loved the color, pattern, and feel of the shirt against her skin. Unfortunately, the day's events seemed to dictate that she wear the irritating and unnecessary bra, which detracted from the comfort of the shirt.

The drive downtown was filled with aggressive accelerations and heavy braking. Each sudden stop caused Mitchell to wince with pain as his knees slammed into the dashboard. In the backseat, Olivia fought off the motion sickness the haphazard driving was causing. She let her gaze fall to the floor, partially to alleviate the discomfort, but mostly to avoid the constant evil eye Abigail was giving her through the mirror's reflection. Olivia wondered if this was how Frodo felt on his journey to Mount Doom.

When they arrived at the police station, Abigail was quick to emerge from the car. Throwing open the rear door, she made motioning gestures with her hands.

"Come on," she ordered. "I haven't got all day."

Olivia stepped out of the car, feeling resentful at being barked at.

Sorry we had to inconvenience you like this, thought Olivia bitterly.

Shutting the car door forcefully, Abigail thrust her hand toward Olivia.

"Here. Take my hand."

Olivia looked over at Mitchell, who gave a subtle shrug of the shoulders. Reluctantly, Olivia complied, and the three of them trekked up the sidewalk to the police station.

Inside, the noise was almost deafening. Officers rushed through the corridors, handcuffed prisoners belligerently demanded this or that, and the phones never seemed to silence. Sensing Olivia's anxiety, Mitchell placed a comforting hand on her shoulder, all the while scanning their surroundings for potential hazards.

The lone woman at the front desk stepped away, leaving a vacancy in the line. Abigail surged forward with such ferocity that the officer on duty leaned away from her advancing form. He watched with concern as a fragile looking girl was dragged along in the wake. The girl hung her head but seemed to be otherwise unharmed by the forceful jerking motion. The officer focused his attention back on the irate woman before him.

"What seems to be the trouble?" he asked nervously.

Abigail tilted her head to the side, gesturing toward the small girl by her side.

"We're here to file a report on this girl," she stated.

"What girl?" questioned the officer.

Abigail almost snarled at him.

"What do you mean 'what girl'?! This girl right here!" she shouted, tugging upwards on Olivia's arm to indicate to whom she was referring.

The officer squinted at Abigail, as though trying to decide if she was being serious. He leaned over the counter, peering at Olivia as though she were a harmless infant. Olivia slowly lifted her gaze, greeting him with a shy smile. The officer looked to Mitchell for an explanation but got none. Twice as confused as when he'd began, he turned his quizzical stare on Abigail.

"What's she done?" he asked with more curiosity than concern.

Abigail shook her head with agitation, distressing at the amount of time this misunderstanding was draining from her day.

"It's not like that," she said harshly. "My brother found her."

The officer glanced at Mitchell again.

"Found her doing what?"

"She wasn't *doing* anything," screamed Abigail. "He just found her."

The officer eyed Abigail suspiciously before trying another approach.

"What is it that you would like us to do?"

Abigail sighed loudly to express her frustration.

"I want you to file a missing persons report," she snapped. "You know? In case anybody is looking for her."

The officer's face registered with acknowledgement.

"Oh…I get it now," he said pleasantly. He gestured to a row of chairs against the far wall. "Why don't you all have a seat over there while I contact our child services personnel?"

Abigail glanced at the waiting area with disdain.

"We're kind of in a hurry," she said.

"I understand," the officer stated patiently, "but we're a little swamped this morning, and it will be a few minutes before I can get someone to review your case."

Abigail glanced anxiously at her watch.

"How long is this going to take?" she demanded.

"Hopefully not too long," he said, reaching for the phone on his desk. "I'll have someone down here as soon as possible."

When Abigail did not budge, he held his hand over the mouthpiece.

"I promise I'll do everything I can to hurry this along," he said encouragingly.

Abigail was not convinced, but followed his direction anyway, never noticing the look he gave to his coworker behind her back. The three of them took adjacent seats, Abigail wedging herself between the other two. She may have lost the battle with the front desk, but the war was not over, and soon she would be rid of this brat for good.

After a good sixty seconds of sitting, Abigail hopped up like she'd been launched from a springboard. The officer at the front desk, having just laid down his receiver, was able to spot her before she pounced on him. Mitchell thought he saw the man wince at she neared. He felt a sense of sympathy for the officer when she started in with the hand motions.

Mitchell glanced down at the pile of magazines that rested beside him. Sifting through the periodicals, he passed over several topics including automotive, housekeeping, and fitness to find a discarded newspaper from March. Flipping open toward the back, he found a half completed Sudoku. Without a pen at his disposal, he attempted to solve the puzzle in his head. Mitchell thought he was doing fairly well in this endeavor, even discovering where the previous challenger had gone astray, when Abigail returned to her seat, breaking his concentration as she landed forcefully in the chair beside him.

"He says it'll only be a few more minutes," relayed Abigail. "Someone will be along shortly."

Mitchell feigned interest, though he felt he'd already been privy to this conversation. Despite her heartening words, Abigail was soon back to anxiously shifting in her seat and repetitiously checking the time. Mitchell tried to return to his problem, but soon gave up, too distracted by the vibrations of Abigail's leg pressed against his own.

When a few minutes became ten, Olivia stood from her seat and began to unfasten her coat; the slight morning chill had been replaced by more balmy temperatures. She handed the coat to Mitchell to hold while she explored the reading materials in another section of the waiting room. Mitchell kept an eye on her movements, though he was just as wary of the actions of the people about her. He felt a tug on his shirtsleeve.

"Hey... ," whispered Abigail. "Where did she get that coat? It looks brand new."

"It is brand new," replied Mitchell nonchalantly. "I bought it for her."

"You bought her a coat?" she asked with disbelief.

Mitchell shrugged his shoulders.

"She didn't have one," he answered in earnest.

"Don't get smart with me," she scolded in a hushed voice. "That coat must've cost at least $300 or $400."

Only if you bought it brand name from a department store, he thought.

"And how much did your coat cost?"

"That's not the point," she said defensively. "You barely know that girl. Why would you spend that kind of money on her?"

"What's the big deal? It's been chilly the last few nights, and it will only get worse the closer we get to winter. She needs a coat."

"If she made do without one for this long, what would a few more days hurt?"

"It's Pittsburgh, Abigail!" he reproached. A few pairs of eyes glanced in his direction before he resumed their muted exchange. "Maybe not today, maybe not tomorrow, but she will eventually need a coat."

"But that doesn't mean you had to be the one to get it for her."

"What would you have me do? Let her run around naked?"

Abigail was just about to respond when a man clad in uniform approached. His light brown hair was trimmed tightly in military style with no facial adornment to match. Above his right eye was a faint scar, faded from years of fewer foolish decisions. The officer glared sharply at everything he looked at, making his prior injury all the more fearsome. Even when compared with Abigail, the man was on the shorter side; his skinny build looked as though he counted calories by the week instead of the day.

"Excuse me," he began politely. "Are you the couple who found the child?"

"We're not a couple," said Abigail quickly. "We're brother and sister."

The man stared at her as though he couldn't care less; his inflection indicative of the impatience he had at having to repeat himself.

"Did you find a child or not?"

"Yes. We found a child," said Abigail. "She's over there."

The man turned toward Olivia. She was standing beside the far magazine pile, a copy of *National Geographic* in her grasp. Mitchell thought how bittersweet it must be to finally find something worth reading among the scarce assortment, only to be carted away before you could peruse its pages. She dropped it solemnly back on top of the others.

"I'm Officer Henry Jensen," he said without offering a handshake to any of them. "Could you all follow me this way?"

The three of them followed him with Abigail taking the lead. She clutched firmly to Olivia's feeble wrist, her grip tight enough to ensure the girl could not break free. The awkward angle caused a painful numbness to traverse up and down her tiny arm. Olivia grimaced from the pain but did not cry out; she was not going to give her tormentor that satisfaction.

Coming to the end of the hallway, Jensen motioned to a room and they entered. Abigail took the seat closest to the desk, forcing Olivia into the chair beside her. Mitchell chose to remain standing, taking the far corner so he and Olivia could see each other.

Jensen closed the door behind them before plopping down in the worn computer chair. Typing quickly on the keyboard, he accessed what appeared to be some sort of database, at least from where Mitchell was standing. Using the mouse to position into the correct box, Jensen prepared his fingers along the home row.

"What's your name?" he asked.

"Abigail Parker. I'm a psychiatrist and youth counselor."

The officer rolled his eyes before pointing directly at Olivia.

"Oh. Her name is Olivia."

"Olivia what?"

Abigail turned to Olivia and nudged her hard, as if trying to force her to speak. Olivia rubbed her arm attempting to lessen the soreness. The officer shot a look at Abigail.

"Olivia Morgan," she said.

The officer entered the name into his computer and the search engine yielded a single result. In 2002, an Olivia Morgan had gone missing from the Love on High Home for Children in eastern Pennsylvania. Skimming through the digital report, the girl was described to be of blond hair, skinny, and around sixteen years of age. Jensen glanced over at Olivia and shook his head.

"Sorry," he said. "There doesn't seem to be a missing child by that name in the system."

Jensen began to type again without uttering a word. After a few seconds, Abigail piped up impatiently.

"Could we file a report saying we found her at least?"

He did not look up at her, holding up a finger instead, indicating for her to wait. After several more key strokes, he looked over at Olivia.

"How old are you?" he asked.

Mitchell could feel himself holding his breath, anxiously awaiting Olivia's response.

"I'm twenty-three," she answered.

Mitchell let out a sigh of relief. Her honesty over her age might be the catalyst that put all of this trouble behind them. His relief was short-lived however as he spotted Jensen's unamused face.

"Young lady," he began sternly, "it's been an intense morning here at the station, and everybody is very busy. We could get through this much faster if you knock off the nonsense. Got it?"

Olivia's shoulders sagged in response to the scolding. Mitchell, unpleased by the treatment she was getting from the officer, took a step in his direction.

"I'm sorry," said Olivia quickly. "It won't happen again."

Mitchell gave her a questioning look, and she found his gaze. Maintaining eye contact, she shook her head subtly while mouthing the word *no*. Mitchell reluctantly gave in, taking a step backward to his initial position.

"Apology accepted," said Jensen amiably before returning his hands to the keyboard. "How old are you?"

Still maintaining her gaze with Mitchell, she cocked her eyebrows at him, as if to say I told you so.

"I'm eleven," she said.

Jensen nodded his approval at her cooperation, typing her age into the system.

"Date of birth?"

"September twentieth."

Mitchell committed the date to memory. It was just a little over two weeks away.

"What year?"

Olivia paused for a moment.

"Ninety-eight."

Jensen entered the new information before glancing over at Abigail.

"You both came across her. Is that right?"

Abigail was about to speak when Mitchell cut her off.

"Actually, it was I who found her," he said.

"And what is your name?"

"Mitchell Flynn," he enunciated.

Jensen gathered some personal information about Mitchell before continuing with his interrogation.

"When did you find the child?"

"Early Monday morning."

"Do you remember about what time?"

"Maybe about one or two," he lied.

"What were you doing when you found her?"

"I was on my way home. She was lying on the ground behind a dumpster down by The T."

Olivia shifted uncomfortably in her seat, but said nothing.

"What were you doing out so late, Mr. Flynn?"

"Excuse me?"

Jensen swiveled around in his chair to focus his attention on Mitchell.

"Where were you coming back from when you encountered the girl?"

Mitchell glanced over at Olivia who nervously stared right back. It was a question that they had not anticipated. He looked back at Jensen.

"Why do you need to know that?" asked Mitchell.

Jensen folded his arms across his chest.

"Is there a problem, Mr. Flynn?"

Mitchell stared down the officer's hardened gaze. He had absolutely no idea where he was at one o'clock Monday morning, but he possessed no interest in telling Jensen about the rooftop situation. Mitchell began formulating a story about how he'd been out late at the apartment of a woman he'd met at a bar last week.

"There's no problem," he replied submissively.

"Good. Glad to hear it," said Jensen gruffly. "Now tell me where you were that morning."

Mitchell opened his mouth to speak, but closed it again when he caught a glimpse of Olivia out of the corner of his eye. With her watching him, he could not bring himself to utter the falsehood he made up for the officer. It wasn't that he thought he might get in trouble with her for dishonesty again, although he probably would have. It wasn't that Abigail would ask him a bunch of follow up questions that would inevitably poke holes in his story. It wasn't even how much the mention of another woman might upset his frail companion. It was the fact that Olivia's presence was beginning to have a profound effect on his life, and what he wanted to do with it.

"I was out getting drunk," said Mitchell.

All at once he felt six eyes staring at him in surprise.

"What was that?" questioned Jensen with disbelief.

Mitchell glanced sideways at Olivia, her face still contorted from the shock of his confession. She neither moved nor blinked as he waited for her response. Just when he began to grow wary of how she would react, Olivia smiled at him, nodding her head to express both encouragement and adoration.

"I said I was out drinking," repeated Mitchell, focusing his full attention on the officer. "I was walking home when I found her."

Jensen continued to gawk at him another moment before shaking off his stunned silence with a jerk of the head.

"Ok," he said with astonishment. "I'll just put down that you were catching the game over at the sports bar. That work for you?"

Mitchell shrugged his shoulders as Jensen returned to his computer monitor. As he typed, Mitchell and Olivia exchanged reassuring glances with each other, though the efforts were mostly in vain as they both nervously anticipated an incoming barrage of questions. Oddly enough, the next inquiry came from Abigail.

"How much longer will this take?" she asked impatiently. "I have an appointment at 11:30."

Jensen glanced up at the clock. It was 10:45 already.

"There's only a little more I have to get through," he assured her. "Shouldn't be too long."

Though the man spoke with forthright authority, Mitchell doubted his sincerity. After a few more minutes of typing, he looked over at Olivia.

"What are your parents' names?"

Olivia shook her head.

"You don't have any parents?" Jensen asked with a hint of skepticism.

Olivia hung her head. Unsure what to think, Jensen peered over at Abigail. When she seemed just as clueless as him, he sought answers from Mitchell, who only shook his head.

"Oh," said Jensen, his voice sounding more compassionate than it had at any other point so far today. "I'm sorry to hear that. Do you have a foster family that you stay with?"

Olivia hesitated and the officer was quick to read her body language.

"What are their names?" he asked.

Again, Olivia shook her head.

"C'mon sweetheart," he urged. "You can tell me. I promise that they won't be in any trouble if you tell me."

Olivia shook her head once more and Jensen exhaled in frustration.

"Why don't you want to tell me?" he asked.

Olivia raised her head and looked straight into his eyes.

"Because I don't want to go back."

Jensen swallowed hard, his voice drastically softer when he spoke again.

"Why don't you want to go back?"

When Olivia did not respond, he motioned to Abigail and Mitchell.

"We're going to step out into the hallway for just a second." he explained to Olivia. "I promise it won't be for long. Are you going to be alright while we're gone?"

Olivia resented the patronizing tone he took with her, but nodded anyway.

Jensen led the others out of the office, closing the door behind him as they exited. Lowering his voice, he turned first to Abigail.

"That girl in there…"

"Olivia," interjected Mitchell.

"Olivia…she ever mention a foster family to either one of you? Or maybe why she ran away?"

"What makes you think she ran away?" asked Abigail.

Jensen pointed his finger at Mitchell instead. He thought about everything that Olivia had said in the last two days about her home life and decided to say nothing. If Olivia wanted to tell people about her situation, that was her business, not his.

"She only mentioned to me that her birth parents were gone," he said. "She didn't mention anything about running away."

Jensen turned back to Abigail.

"You mentioned being a shrink, right? For kids?"

"A psychiatrist," she corrected. "And yes, I deal with adolescent clients."

"Would you be willing to go in there and maybe…"

"Oh, she won't talk to me. I'm the one who's been trying to send her home, remember?"

Jensen thought about the brutish way she handled the child and wondered if there might not be another reason for the girl's unwillingness to cooperate.

"Well that settles it," said Jensen. "I'll page Dr. Faust. Give her ten minutes with the girl, and she'll know every bit of her history."

"Who's Dr. Faust?" chimed Mitchell.

"She's a counselor down at CPS who specializes in abuse cases."

Mitchell must have looked concerned because Jensen patted him reassuringly on the shoulder.

"Don't worry. Dr. Faust is great at her job. You'll see."

Without another word, Jensen disappeared around the corner, leaving Mitchell alone with Abigail. She glanced down at her watch.

"I have to run and meet my client," she said. "Will you be alright handling the rest of this by yourself?"

Mitchell was delighted at the prospect of getting a reprieve from her scouring eyes and meddling hands.

"We should be fine," He replied.

Abigail moved forward as though to hug him, hesitated, and placed her hand on his arm instead. Her tender squeeze was like the cold grip of a mechanical vice. The sympathetic way she rubbed his arm might as well have been done using sandpaper. Every time he felt her touch it was like someone was pouring lemon juice into a fresh wound.

"It's all for the best," she told him. "Everything will work out just as it's supposed to. Trust me."

With that, she relinquished her hold on him and departed down the corridor. Watching her leave, Mitchell wondered what would happen if he attempted to walk along that same hallway with Olivia in tow. *Would they stop him? Was it busy enough that they wouldn't even notice?*

He turned back to the office window, peering through the pane at those gorgeous blue eyes staring back at him. Somehow Mitchell was not surprised that she had been eavesdropping, it was *her* life on the line after all. With a smile, Olivia placed a hand on the vacant seat beside her, gesturing toward it with a tilt of the head.

Mitchell heaved a great sigh.

There are moments in our lives where we must make choices that will forever alter our existence. Despite the potential outcomes in question, being dragged to such a crossroads feels no different than being hauled off to the gallows. Nothing is more ominous than one's fate.

To the left fork, I could give in to my whimsical desires, running the great risk that Olivia was only an illusion; a façade of adult makeup on a child's face. And to the right, I faced the everlasting torment of abandoning the only kindred soul I had met since my life fell into decline. A man cannot escape his destiny forever, but I intended to idly linger at this intersection for as long as I could.

I entered the office and turned the shades closed before taking the seat beside Olivia. In the darkened room I cradled her in my arms, alleviating her fears and quelling my doubts, until the door creaked open and the black silhouette of circumstance threatened to drive us apart forever.

CHAPTER 10

Olivia sat alone in an insincerely decorated room. Though the colorful furniture and cartoon pictures were supposed to elicit peace in those unfortunate enough to be privy to them, all they did was remind her of the impending calamity she faced. Of course, it might have been a more serene environment if Olivia cared for clowns.

Despite the creepy faces plastered on the wall, the thing that bothered her most right now was her separation from Mitchell. Even if his presence could not prevent what happened here today, at least it would alleviate some of her anxiety. She had to admit that part of her wanted desperately for him to scoop her in his arms and make a daring escape from the police station. She could never have asked him to abandon his whole life on account of her, but she had no intention of going long without him either.

The door opened to reveal a rather portly woman adorned in a gray pants suit that did little to flatter her physique. She wore her dark hair in a tight bun on top of her head. Attached to a cord around her neck was a pair of bifocals that bounced recklessly against her chest as she tediously maneuvered across the vast room. The woman walked with a guarded gait, carefully monitoring every step as though she were afraid of falling, perhaps a realistic response to some recent unpleasant experience. She never once looked up from the floor until she was within arm's reach of Olivia.

"Hello, dear. My name is Doctor Sharon Faust," she said, extending her right arm toward Olivia and clutching a yellow legal pad against her chest with the other.

"I'm Olivia," she replied, taking hold of the hand in front of her.

Dr. Faust relinquished her grip and took the seat opposite Olivia. Using the two armrests, she carefully lowered herself into the chair, making a sound of relief as her butt made contact with the cushion. Though the woman appeared to be of less than average height, she was still a full head higher than Olivia sitting down; an effect that Olivia suspected had been created on purpose.

"Officer Jensen asked me to talk with you, " said Dr. Faust after getting herself situated. "Do you mind if I ask you a few questions?"

Go ahead, it's not like you're invading my privacy or anything…

"I suppose not," replied Olivia politely.

"Excellent. I'm just going to be taking a few notes while we talk. I hope you don't mind."

Before Olivia could respond, the woman proceeded with the first question.

"First of all, what is your full name, sweetheart?"

Olivia grimaced at the use of the pet name. Only children and lovers got called *sweetheart*, and she was pretty certain she wasn't dating Dr. Faust.

"Olivia Morgan."

Dr. Faust started taking notes.

"Good. And where are you from, Olivia?"

"Originally? Connecticut."

"My, that's quite a distance for one so young," she said with irritating affability.

Olivia groaned silently to herself. The condescending tone that was being applied against her had already begun to grate on her last nerve. Still, it was of vital importance that these exchanges end without adding any further complications to an already delicate situation. Swallowing her pride, Olivia steeled herself for the inevitable utterance of that most pivotal question. She didn't have to wait long before Dr. Faust dropped it on her.

"And how old are you, Olivia?"

Here we go again…

"I'm twenty-three," she said earnestly.

Doctor Faust pulled her bifocals forward and peered over them down at Olivia. The small girl squirmed under her gaze. Faust said nothing, only made a long series of notes in her book that Olivia could only assume were not the numbers two and three.

"That was the same age you told Officer Jensen, was it not?" she asked while studying the file in front of her.

"It was," stated Olivia with a head nod.

Dr. Faust glanced up at her, a sympathetic smile on her lips.

"I bet most people don't believe you when you tell them that."

Olivia hung her head.

"No…they don't."

Dr. Faust removed her bifocals and beamed brightly at her.

"Well, I do," she said cheerfully.

Olivia looked up at her with astonishment.

"You do?"

Dr. Faust nodded.

"I believe that you are much older than what people might assume based on your physical appearance."

Maybe there was some hope to be had after all.

"Yes, that's it," Olivia squealed excitedly.

Dr. Faust gave an appreciative head nod before continuing.

"It's actually not that uncommon."

"It's not?" she asked with disbelief. "I thought I was the only one."

"Oh, no," assured Faust. "There are thousands if not millions of girls who have gone through exactly what you've gone through, experienced everything that you've experienced. I've dealt with many such cases myself."

"You have?"

"Oh, yes," she declared. "You see, Olivia, sometimes adults forget what it was like to be a young person. They forget the hurt of being treated like a child. Do people often talk down to you?"

"All the time." she responded, leaning slightly forward in her chair.

"Why do you think they do that?"

"It's because I'm small."

Dr. Faust jotted something down on her legal pad.

"You know something Olivia, I think you're right. But just because you're smaller than other people, doesn't mean that you are any less significant. Right?"

"Right," she agreed enthusiastically.

"But once in a while we find someone who treats us like we want to be treated. They make us feel good because they seem genuinely interested in who we are on the inside rather than what we look like on the outside."

Olivia felt her temperature rise just thinking about Mitchell.

"Was there ever anybody like that for you? Someone you would hang out with that made you feel just a little bit more...like an *adult*?"

Olivia opened her mouth to speak, but hesitated before answering. Every fiber of her being wanted to scream out *yes*, but something was wrong. She could sense the subtle change in atmosphere. There was something to the way that Dr. Faust had used the word *adult* that implied something far more sinister.

"What do you mean?" she asked.

"I mean," began Dr. Faust gingerly, "perhaps there is, or was, someone in your life who made you feel special. Someone you felt completely comfortable being yourself around, maybe someone with whom you felt you could confide all of your secrets. Maybe this person asked you to do...*things* with him or her that you wouldn't have normally wanted to do, but felt okay because it was with this special person?"

Olivia suddenly realized where this was going.

"Are you talking about Mit...Mister Flynn?" she asked, quickly correcting herself with the name.

Dr. Faust raised an eyebrow at her.

"Did Mr. Flynn ever ask you to..."

"NO!" she said sternly.

Dr. Faust startled at her outburst.

"It's not like that," Olivia asserted though less forcefully than before. "He took me in, fed me, gave me a place to sleep…if not for him I'd be…"

Olivia shuddered at the thought.

"I'm sorry," said Dr. Faust, holding up her hands submissively. "I did not mean to imply any wrongdoing on the part of Mr. Flynn."

Olivia glared at her. It was clear by the insinuations made against Mitchell that Dr. Faust had never really thought about her as anything but a child, incapable of making those kinds of decisions on her own. *How dare she treat such a sincere display of affection as if it were a mere act of depravity?*

"Officer Jensen mentioned that Mr. Flynn found you behind a dumpster a couple days ago," said Dr. Faust, looking to change the subject.

Olivia forced an exhale, releasing her anger as she did so.

"That's right. I think it was early Monday morning."

"Officer Jensen also said that he thinks you may have run away from home."

Olivia gave her a blank stare. Dr. Faust decided to try another tactic.

"Those are lovely clothes you're wearing. They look new."

"Thank you," she said genially. "Mr. Flynn bought them for me. Aren't they wonderful?"

"Yes. They're quite pretty," Dr. Faust replied absently.

"There's more like this back at his apartment," she said proudly.

"I see," stated Dr. Faust. "And what's the living arrangement like there? Do you get your own room?"

"Actually there's only one bedroom, so Mr. Flynn's been sleeping on the couch. It was nice of him to let me have the bed, but I think we should switch. It can't be good for a man of his stature to be sleeping on such a tiny bed."

"I suppose not," said Dr. Faust between notes. "So, how do you feel about staying at Mr. Flynn's place? Is it…*comfortable* there?"

Olivia smiled.

"I love it there. It's a bit messy, but at least it feels *safe*."

Dr. Faust nodded at the inflection on the word, scribbling something into her notes.

"Was there something that happened at your old home that made it feel not so *safe*?"

Olivia narrowed her eyes at Dr. Faust.

"To be honest, it hadn't really felt like *home* for a while now," she answered tentatively.

"I'm sorry to hear that. Did something happen between you and your parents?"

Olivia shook her head.

"My birth parents died when I was pretty young. I had been staying with a foster family for a few years when…"

Olivia abruptly stopped, letting silence envelop the room. She hung her head to gaze on the floor.

"When what, Olivia? What happened at the foster home?"

Again, Olivia shook her head. Dr. Faust leaned over and placed her hand gently upon Olivia's.

"It's ok," she said. "You don't have to talk about it if you don't want to."

Olivia patted the hand of Dr. Faust and felt an affectionate squeeze in response.

"What were your foster parents' names?"

Olivia raised her head.

"If I tell you where I came from, you might try to send me back there."

"I promise we wouldn't put you in harm's way, Olivia."

She shook her head.

"I'm not going back," she stated. "That's all there is to it."

Olivia dropped her head again and let out a pitiful sniffle. A few seconds passed, and Dr. Faust pulled her hand away. She scribbled a few more notes on her legal pad and slipped the pen into her pocket.

"I'm going to go have a quick word with Officer Jensen," she said as she rose from her chair. "Are you going to be alright for a few minutes?"

"Could I have some water?" she asked. "Please?"

Dr. Faust smiled at her.

"Certainly, dear. I'll go get you some right now."

After she returned with the water, Dr. Faust was off again, leaving Olivia alone once more. Standing from her seat, Olivia began to pace the room nervously while her fate was discussed in a nearby corridor of the building.

During their discussion, Olivia had realized that Dr. Faust shared the same opinion as everybody else she'd encountered. She saw Olivia as acting older than her age rather than someone who was genuinely older. Still, it had been a mostly pleasant conversation and under different circumstances Olivia felt as though she might have come to befriend the jovial psychiatrist.

And yet, the words of the kind therapist had created doubts about her own significance in the eyes of the man she loved. Olivia relived all the moments of the last forty-eight hours, second-guessing every detail. *What if she had imagined their emotional connection? What if she was just another child to him after all? Worse still, what if he'd actually come around on the idea of the two of them together, only to be pushed away again by the unsettling words of Dr. Faust?*

Olivia did her best to shake the unending voices in her head, but they held fast to her mind, like leeches adhering to tender flesh.

Back in the small dark office, the two men listened intently as Dr. Faust recanted what she gleaned from her conversation with Olivia.

"You say she definitely shows signs of abuse?" asked Jensen.

Dr. Faust nodded solemnly.

"I'm afraid so," she said. "I'm not sure to what extent, but all of the warning signs are there."

"Did she mention where her foster home was located?"

"She did not."

"What about the names of her foster parents?"

"Nope."

"Nothing?"

"Nothing. She's too afraid we'll send her back."

Jensen grunted.

"Even after you assured her that we wouldn't?"

"To be honest, after whatever happened at the last foster home, I don't think she trusts being placed back in the system at all."

"So what would she have us do with her?"

Dr. Faust shrugged.

"I know what I would want if I was in her shoes, but good luck trying to petition the court for emancipation without the legal guardians present."

Jensen grunted again.

"You know if it was up to me I'd already be arresting the bastards. Not bothering to fill out a report when she'd run away would be suspect enough even without her testimony. Still, you know how tricky some of these cases can get."

This response bothered Mitchell.

"You're not actually considering sending her back there are you?" he demanded.

The two looked at him with surprise, as though they'd forgotten he was standing there. Jensen glanced over at Dr. Faust.

"We understand that this whole situation must be difficult for you," she began, "seeing as you are the one who found her, but these matters must be handled within the confines of legality, which means they can sometimes take a while to sort out. You understand, right?"

"I don't think I do," responded Mitchell callously.

"What my colleague is trying to say is that we really only have temporary jurisdiction in these types of cases. If it looks like there is a need for it, an officer can place a child into protective custody, but only for a limited amount of time. After that, it's up to the courts to decide where she goes."

"Unfortunately, once this foster family finds out about her case, they may attempt to retain custody. I doubt that they'll succeed, especially with testimony from the child, but we should be prepared for a lengthy legal battle."

Mitchell sighed with despair.

"Where will she stay while these matters are being sorted out?"

Jensen gestured to Dr. Faust.

"Well, once a police officer deems it necessary to place the child into protective custody…"

"Check," said Jensen, holding up his hand in response.

"Then the child is turned over to Child Protective Services. We are in charge of determining where to place temporary custody of the child. Usually it's granted to a family member."

"What if she has no living relatives?" asked Mitchell.

Dr. Faust let out a sigh, bracing herself for impact.

"There are foster families that specialize in temporary relief."

"Great!" he exclaimed sarcastically. "Let's just send her right back to the place she ran away from."

Mitchell placed both hands on his hips, shaking his head with frustration.

"So what happens now?" he asked.

Jensen flashed a look at Dr. Faust before rising from his desk.

"Well, we would like to thank you and your sister for doing your civic duty today," said Jensen, extending his arm toward Mitchell. "Most people probably would have ignored that poor girl, but you stopped to help. That showed amazing character."

"Thanks," responded Mitchell, taking hold of the officer's hand.

"But I'm sure that you've got other important places to be. We can handle it from here."

Mitchell peered down at the man passively trying to remove him from the office. Standing tall in this tiny space next to the scrawny police officer and the diminutive psychiatrist made him feel all the more colossal. He wondered how far he might get if he attempted to push these two aside and make a mad dash with Olivia in his arms. He thought the plan futile at best once he remembered what building he was in.

Turning his gaze from the officer, he looked at Dr. Faust, who seemed to be monitoring his actions closely. She turned her attention to Jensen.

"Could you give us a minute, Henry?"

Jensen glared at her suspiciously, but nodded nonetheless.

"Sure thing," he replied. "It's just about time to put in a lunch order anyway. Did you want anything?"

"Are you going to the normal place?" she asked.

"That was the plan."

"Then I'll have my usual."

"One Reuben extra sauce coming right up," he said with friendly demeanor. "Don't grill this boy too hard, Sharon."

"Hmmm," she replied with a chuckle.

After he left the room, Mitchell raised a questioning eyebrow at Dr. Faust.

"We work a lot of cases together," she explained.

Mitchell nodded in response, though he felt there might be more to the story than she was telling. Dr. Faust motioned to one of the chairs in the room.

"Have a seat, Mr. Flynn. Looking up at you is starting to strain my neck," she said with a smile.

Mitchell did as he was instructed, and Dr. Faust took the seat beside him.

"You seem to be rather heavily invested in that girl," she said.

"What do you mean?" he asked without looking at her.

The image of the expensive winter coat flashed through her mind.

"I mean," she began, "most people would not have bought a random stranger such expensive clothing. You've known her barely two days, and you purchased several hundred dollars' worth of attire."

"She needed clothing and had no money. What was I supposed to do?"

"You've been trying to fight the entire system on her behalf all afternoon."

"That's because the system is lousy."

"You seem gung-ho on sticking around until we've settled every last detail about her case."

Mitchell focused his eyes on Dr. Faust.

"It's because she's my responsibility. I am the one who found her, fed her, clothed her, cared for her. It would be unfair for me to abandon Olivia before I found her a suitable home."

Dr. Faust listened intently at all of his explanations. She couldn't be certain, but she felt his using Olivia's name meant that he had already formed an emotional bond with the girl, just as she so obviously had grown attached to him.

"Do you have children, Mr. Flynn?"

He shook his head.

"No. My ex-wife and I were thinking about having children before we got divorced. It was probably for the best that we never had any."

"Since your separation, have you ever thought about adoption?"

Again, Mitchell shook his head.

Typical man she thought. Never any inclination toward fatherhood until faced with the prospect. Now that he experienced the joys of having a child, he was enthusiastic about the idea, but didn't fully understand his feelings yet.

"Mr. Flynn, it seems to me that your heart is in the right place in wanting to find a nice home for the girl."

"Olivia," he corrected.

"Right…Olivia. But Olivia is not like other girls."

You can say that again, thought Mitchell, though he continued to listen.

"She has been through some sort of abuse, be it physical, psychological, or even *sexual*."

Mitchell felt pangs of guilt building inside him.

"Because Olivia has been subjected to this type of adult behavior, she has developed a defense mechanism whereby she pretends herself to be an adult. I'm sure you've noticed such precocious behaviors yourself. You probably didn't think much about them at the time, but they are warning signs for deeply-rooted, emotional trauma."

Mitchell thought about the deep intellectual conversations they had about Asimov and Plato. *Could she really have just been pretending?*

"When I first asked her how old she was, she told me that she was twenty-three. Can you believe that? Like anybody wouldn't be able to see through that façade."

"Yeah…ridiculous right?" he responded, though deep down he felt ashamed for believing it himself.

"It's of the utmost importance that we don't encourage these behaviors. If we were to indulge her, then she might act out in…*other ways.* Not everybody is as kindhearted as you, Mr. Flynn. Someone might try taking advantage of her naiveté if she places herself in situations beyond her maturity level."

Mitchell nodded absently though his mind was a million miles from the conversation. There was a huge part of him that wanted to believe in Olivia; needed to believe in her. They connected on so many wavelengths that he felt elation like he'd never known before, not even with Evelyn.

And yet, the discussion with Dr. Faust had shaken his faith in Olivia right down to the core. The more his mind whirled, the less real his affection for Olivia seemed to be. *What if it was true that all of Olivia's behaviors were only an act to make her seem more grownup than she really was? How hard would it be for her to learn a few interesting facts to create the illusion? Did that mean he had not simply been showing her kindness and compassion, but had been inadvertently manipulating her vulnerable psyche the whole time? What if Abigail was not the bad guy here, but was only trying to protect him from doing something incredibly stupid? What if everything that he thought was real was just a dream, a fantasy he concocted in his own mind?*

"After everything she's been through, Olivia is going to require a special kind of care and support from whomever we grant custody to. I don't take that decision lightly, Mr. Flynn."

Mitchell swallowed hard.

"I understand."

Dr. Faust stood from her chair and put her hand on his shoulder. Though he didn't much care for this woman, he couldn't help but feel comforted by her gentle touch.

"She trusts you, you know?"

Mitchell nodded.

Perhaps too much, he thought.

"So tell me, Mr. Flynn. Why did you stop to help her?"

Mitchell glanced over at her.

"What do you mean?"

"Well, given the circumstances, you could have just as easily ignored her and boarded the train home. You could have left her where you found her and gone about your life as though it never happened. Instead, you chose to help her. All I want to know is why?"

Mitchell had been dealing with these internal struggles for the last two days. Now that someone expressed them from an outsider's viewpoint, he had to admit, it seemed rather suspect for a man in his thirties to show such interest in the life of a prepubescent girl he knew almost nothing about.

His mind flashed to the image of finding her naked and alone on the unforgiving concrete beneath his trench coat. Remembering how he felt in that moment, he turned to look Dr. Faust in her eyes.

"Because it was the right thing to do," he said.

Dr. Faust peered down at him in stunned silence before finally smiling.

"That's right," she said kindly. "It was the right thing to do."

Mitchell beamed proudly.

"And you want to continue to do what's best for Olivia, don't you?"

Mitchell nodded quickly.

"I do."

"No matter the consequences?"

Mitchell hesitated this time, but nodded nonetheless.

"Good. I'm glad," she stated earnestly. "That's why I want you to pay very close attention to what I'm about to say to you."

Mitchell listened attentively as she explained the plan for Olivia's future. When she had finished, she gestured toward the office door.

"I guess we should go tell Olivia," she said.

Olivia had been alone with her thoughts for nearly forty-five minutes. Their weight pressed firmly down on her with such intensity that she was becoming fatigued. As she continued to pace restlessly back and forth, she contemplated who would be the next person through that door. If it was the police officer, she was off to foster care for sure. If it was Dr. Faust, she gave herself fifty-fifty. And if it was Mitchell…

Olivia felt herself blush.

She was glad that thoughts of him could still affect her heart rate. Over the course of the last few hours, her faith in Mitchell had waxed and waned so many times that she began doubting her feelings for him altogether. Even worse, she began to doubt his feelings for her.

She clutched her face in her hands. The waiting was maddening. She began to think of herself as Schrödinger's cat. *Would her life with Mitchell continue onward or be extinguished inside this menacing clown-filled box?*

Feeling the exhaustion of her constant movement, Olivia sat down in one of the colorful seats. Being situated between the four walls inside a police station brought to her mind the classical Prisoner's Dilemma situation. Olivia found strange solace in knowing that Mitchell would have been exposed to the scenario during his philosophy studies. All they had to do was stick together, and they would get through this unscathed. *After all, wasn't it Mitchell who said they were in this together?*

Olivia thought about Dr. Faust and what she might be telling Mitchell behind closed doors.

Suddenly the chair no longer held comfort but anxiety. She returned to pacing the room like a wolf guarding its lair. She grasped desperately at any idea that might distract her but only came up empty. Her heart raced as panic set in full force. Olivia took in sharp shallow breaths in an effort to regain her composure. It seemed to be working until the door creaked open, and her breath stopped altogether.

Olivia halted mid-pace, not moving a single muscle. She stared intently at the doorway, waiting for the light of the room to shine on the shadowy figure. At first, all she could see was dark hair, then a nose, and at last an eye that peered at her through the opening. After seeing her standing there, the door pushed inward, revealing the identity of her mysterious intruder.

It was Mitchell.

Olivia could hardly contain her excitement. She desperately wanted to run to him but her feet were simply not cooperating. A single teardrop ran down her left cheek as she smiled warmly at him. Her savior had once again battled tooth and claw against her opposition and prevailed. Everything was going to be alright.

She continued to smile at him, but Mitchell was not smiling back. His face carried a look far too sullen for that. She was about to ask what was going on when Dr. Faust stepped into the room behind Mitchell. Olivia's heart sank. Dr. Faust had gotten to him after all.

Olivia felt an agonizing pain building inside her chest. Her mouth hung limply open as she looked between Mitchell and Dr. Faust in despair. Her jaw trembled as she tried to force herself to speak, but no words were coming out. She longed to scream out to Mitchell; to tell him to take her in his arms and run as fast and as far as his legs would carry them. She wanted to promise him that they could still find a way to be together, in some other place, in some other time. But in her heart she knew it would all be a lie, a pipedream, something that only ever happened in stories that parents tell their children. This was not some fantasy land, and they were not in some long forgotten time. This was real life and everything she desired in these last few days had ultimately come to an end.

Olivia focused her gaze down at the floor, a lump forming in her throat making it more difficult to breathe. Her fingernails dug into her palms as she clenched both fists by her sides. Olivia's whole body shook from the effort of fighting back tears, but she was losing the battle and the dam threatened to break wide open at any moment.

"Are you ready?" asked Mitchell.

Olivia pulled her gaze from the floor to find Mitchell grinning contentedly back at her. *How could he be smiling at a time like this? Didn't he understand what was happening?* She glanced at Dr. Faust in her confusion.

"Mr. Flynn has agreed to accept temporary protective custody over you while we get all of this straightened out," explained Dr. Faust. "That is, if it's alright with you."

Olivia turned back to Mitchell, her eyes wide with shock.

"Come on," he said. "It's time to go home."

Joy overwhelmed Olivia's small body and she rushed forward into his powerful arms. He lifted her from the floor with ease, ensnaring her in an affectionate embrace. Unable to hold back any longer, two salty streams flowed freely from Olivia's closed eyelids, moistening his broad neck as she nuzzled against him.

Dr. Faust looked curiously at this sudden display, her emotions ranging between bewilderment and happiness. After considering the proper response to witnessing such a scene, Dr. Faust chose to smile.

CHAPTER 11

With Mitchell leading the way, they strolled out the front doors of the police station into the warm glow of afternoon sun. Feeling insecure about their newfound freedom, he extended his stride and hastened their footsteps. The brisk pace caused her to pant and sweat, but Olivia was delighted to be creating space between them and the ominous concrete structure behind them.

When they were sufficiently far away not to be subjected to eavesdropping bluecoats, she reached out to take Mitchell's hand. As if from a hot flame he recoiled from her touch, leaving her addled and forcing a dour tone on an otherwise victorious occasion. Not wishing to be denied, she entwined her arm with his elbow instead, holding fast when he attempted to pull away. It was not the type of all-embracing affectionate comfort that she craved at the moment, but at least it was something. Noting the tension in his muscles, she decided not to press the issue any further until they got someplace where she could explain everything to him.

Olivia thought about the business card tucked safely away in her back pocket. Dr. Faust had slipped it to her before they left the station, insisting that Olivia contact her day or night with any problems or concerns that might arise. Though she appreciated the advantage of being able to call someone for assistance, Olivia doubted she would ever need help from the therapist as long as she had Mitchell by her side.

Olivia turned to Mitchell; his discomfort had already started to fade.

"When did you say that Dr. Faust would be coming by?" she asked.

"Friday morning at 11:00 sharp," he stated, doing his best to mimic the instructions of the psychiatrist.

"And we'll be all good if we pass this little inspection of hers?"

"Not exactly," replied Mitchell. "Apparently this is only temporary until either they can find your legal guardians or get a court to review your case."

"I see," she uttered glumly.

"Cheer up," he said with a smile. "It's not her fault that they can't grant legal custody for longer than three days without court approval."

Olivia did the math in her head.

"So she'll be back on Saturday to collect me?" she asked with grim disappointment. "Or does it count from Friday since that's when she's coming to check on the apartment?"

Mitchell shot her a smug grin.

"That's the beauty of it," he said. "Apparently weekends and holidays don't count."

She pulled closer to him.

"I suppose we should make the most of it then," she said.

Olivia thought about how Dr. Faust had scheduled their appointment on Friday, probably aware that Monday was Labor Day, giving them almost a week together before the courts would have to intervene. She smiled with the knowledge that Dr. Faust was far too smart for those bonus days to have been a complete coincidence. Perhaps there was something to having a personal case worker after all.

"Are you hungry?" asked Mitchell.

Olivia felt the pangs in her stomach that she had been ignoring.

"I could eat," she said.

"What type of food do you want?"

Olivia was pleased to be given the opportunity to express her preference. Over the course of the last few years, it was a rare occasion when someone sought her input about anything, even something as mundane as what to have for lunch. She gave it considerable thought.

"Can I have whatever I want?" she asked.

Mitchell eyed her suspiciously.

"As long as it's within reason," he replied, a hint of apprehension in his voice.

She smiled.

"Is there a Chinese place around here?"

"There's bound to be I suppose."

"Let's go there then."

Mitchell gazed down at her with surprise.

"You can have anything you want and you want *Chinese*?" he asked questioningly.

She nodded.

"Mr. James didn't care much for Asian cuisine, so I didn't get a chance to eat it very often."

Mitchell inwardly grimaced at the mention of the rooftop resident.

"Well it's fine by me," he said agreeably, pulling out his phone to search for nearby locations.

They continued to walk down the street, Mitchell doing his best to maintain distance between the two of them while Olivia's efforts were focused on just the opposite. It wasn't long before they came across a place and made their way inside, Mitchell making sure to hold the door for his small companion.

The inside of the restaurant was decorated with an assortment of dragons and Chinese characters. The tables were wood with black tops, and the chairs were padded metal. Soft ambient lighting matched perfectly with the serene, almost mystical, music playing in the background. A young waitress approached them, her height considerably closer to that of Olivia than Mitchell.

"Just two?" she asked with a heavy accent.

Mitchell nodded, and she led them to a small table in the back corner.

"Anything to drink?"

"Do you have hot tea?" Mitchell asked.

The woman nodded with a smile before turning to Olivia.

"Hot tea sounds good," she said.

The hostess gave a subtle bow before disappearing into the kitchen, allowing them to look over the menu. Olivia glanced at hers for nearly half a second before closing it again. Mitchell raised an eyebrow at her.

"You already know what you want?" he asked with disbelief.

"Yep," she said bouncing joyfully in her seat. "I'm getting the steamed dumplings."

Mitchell glanced up and down the menu.

"I don't even see dumplings," he stated.

"They're under the 'Appetizers' section."

He checked again.

"And that's *all* you want?"

She shrugged.

"I'm not as big as you," she said. "It doesn't take as much to fill me."

Mitchell peered at her over the top of his menu.

"That's certainly an understatement. I could easily hide you beneath my coat."

"Then you should have smuggled me out of the police station," she said playfully.

"I was tempted, believe me."

"You were?" she asked with surprise.

Mitchell felt slightly embarrassed at this confession.

"Hey, I didn't want to be there any more than you," he declared defensively. "I was doing my best to get us out of there as quickly as possible."

"Then what took you so long?" she asked with a sly smile.

Mitchell rolled his eyes.

"It only took me a few minutes to convince Dr. Faust," he asserted. "I spent the rest of the time in the restroom. You wouldn't believe the line there."

"Hmmm…" she said folding her arms.

"Fine. Next time I'll just push past a couple dozen armed guards, shouldn't be too much of a problem."

The server returned with their beverages, steam rising from the container in puffy clouds. Mitchell sighed contentedly. There was nothing quite like the soothing properties of a nice cup of hot tea, nor anything quite as disappointing as when it came lukewarm. She set two ceramic glasses on the table, a mug for Olivia and a thimble for Mitchell.

The server pulled out her notepad.

"Do you know what you want?" she asked Mitchell first.

"I should be good if you start with her first," he replied, gesturing toward Olivia.

It took Olivia a few seconds to respond. She was not used to ordering for herself, finding the prospect pleasing, but daunting at the same time.

"May I have the steamed dumplings, please," she said, handing her menu to the server.

"Is that all?" asked the waitress.

Olivia nodded.

"Ok," said the young woman jotting the order on her pad. "And for you, sir?"

"A bowl of hot and sour soup and the Mongolian beef," he responded. "Also, the chicken curry lunch special and an order of spring rolls, please."

"Ok," she said taking his menu. "It'll be right out."

As she walked away, Mitchell turned his gaze back to Olivia. She stared at him with both eyes wide with surprise.

"What? I'm bigger than you, remember?"

Olivia shook her head in amusement. With the menu gone, she focused her attention on the placemat in front of her. The red and gold bordered sheet was filled with elaborate drawings of animals and their respective descriptions within the Chinese zodiac. Olivia was pleased to be under the year of the tiger but didn't see herself as particularly aggressive or courageous.

"What are you?" she asked.

Mitchell scanned the dates.

"The horse."

Olivia found the entry.

"*Popular and attractive to the opposite sex...*" she teased. Lifting her head Olivia studied the outline of his muscular physique through his tight fitting dress shirt, biting her lip delicately as her mind drifted to dangerous places.

Definitely.

"Yeah...yeah...yeah..." he replied. "What's yours?"

Reading the passage for the tiger, Mitchell was disappointed to discover that both of the birthdates Olivia gave the officer fell under that single entry. Despite this minor setback, Mitchell continued through the text with the prospect of gleaning some hidden insight to his small companion. Although he did not entirely agree with the information as it might pertain to Olivia, there was a particular line near the end that caught his eye.

Mitchell had never been much for astrology in any of its many forms, but it was suddenly hard to ignore the fact that both entries paired the tiger and the horse as being romantically suited for one another. He raised his eyes to Olivia. It was clear by her flushed face and convivial expression that she had read the same section. Before he could say anything, Mitchell noticed a sensation along his inner ankle that felt very similar to…

"What's your other sign?" he asked quickly in an octave higher than his normal voice.

Olivia moved her shoeless foot a little higher until the velvety material rubbed gently just beneath his knee. She flashed him a lascivious smile.

"I'm a Virgo," she said with full sultry intonation. She peered down at her body before flicking those enticing sapphires at him. "What about you?"

Mitchell swallowed hard; he could feel his heart beating inside his chest.

"I'm…uh…I'm a Capricorn," he replied, moving his leg away from her seductive caress.

Olivia chuckled inwardly at his bashfulness before transitioning back to a serious demeanor.

"We need a plan, Mitchell."

"A plan for what?" he asked nervously.

"For when Dr. Faust comes by on Friday, of course," she said coyly.

Mitchell stared at her blankly.

"Oh, right," he said finally. "What kind of plan are you thinking?"

"Well, the way I see it, the first thing we need to take care of is getting our apartment straightened up."

"Is it *our apartment* already?" interjected Mitchell.

Olivia flashed him her pearly whites before continuing.

"I can take care of that part, but there's going to be some things you'll need to look into. We've been lucky so far but we need to continue to make a good impression, especially if we have to go to court."

"Like what?" asked Mitchell as he reached for the teapot.

Olivia hesitated before continuing.

"You need a job," she said.

Mitchell's body tensed.

"No I don't," he responded brashly, the steam coming off the pot matching the heat rising off him. "I've got enough saved up to get us by, at least for a while."

Olivia exhaled slowly.

"I know that," she said empathetically. "But the courts will want to see that you're a functioning member of society. That means having a job."

Mitchell grunted as he poured the tea.

"What would you have me do?" he asked angrily. "Go back to teaching and deal with those vacant stares all day? No, thank you."

Olivia sighed.

"I would never ask you to do anything that makes you unhappy," she said. "Why don't you head down to the unemployment office in the morning? Surely there's got to be *something* that you enjoy doing."

"What if the only jobs they have available are scrubbing toilets?" he demanded, pushing a cup of steaming beverage in her direction.

Olivia shrugged.

"It only has to be for a couple weeks. I'm sure Dr. Faust already has the ball rolling on a court hearing. After that, you can quit if you want to. Besides, scrubbing toilets isn't so bad. Can you imagine having to be the guy who feeds the sharks down at the aquarium?"

"I guess, " muttered Mitchell halfheartedly.

Olivia reached across the table and placed her hand on the underside of his chin, lifting up so that she could look into his eyes.

"Do it for me," she said softly.

Mitchell gazed into those sparkling blue sapphires tucked away in that adolescent face and wondered at what age women learned to implement that particular wile.

"Okay," he sighed, lifting his tiny cup between his thumb and forefinger. "For you."

Olivia wrapped her fingers around her own cup.

"For us," she toasted.

Mitchell nodded in agreement, clanking his glass quietly against hers.

The server returned, setting the bowl of soup down in front of Mitchell. He thanked her, and she nodded politely before departing. Mitchell leaned his head close to the bowl and inhaled deeply, sighing contentedly at the pleasant aroma.

"Would you like to try some?" he asked.

Olivia hesitated.

"What's it taste like?" she asked.

"It's hot and sour soup," he stated matter-of-factly.

Olivia looked at him blankly.

"Here," he said, pushing the bowl toward her. "Try some."

Olivia retrieved her spoon from the silverware wrap, unfolding the napkin and draping it across her lap. She dipped the utensil into the soup, pushing it away from her as she lifted it from the hot liquid. Holding her free hand beneath the spoon, she blew softly across the surface before letting it slip past her lips. She swished it back and forth in her mouth, carefully analyzing the taste and enjoying the spicy tinge as it hit the back of her throat. She felt her spirits rejuvenated from the inside out as it coursed through her esophagus.

"That's very good," she said.

Mitchell smiled before pulling the bowl closer to his side of the table.

"I was just thinking..." he began as he lifted his own spoon.

"Shall I call emergency services?" she asked, dipping her utensil into his soup once again.

Mitchell glared at her with mock disapproval. She ignored his chastisements, capturing a third spoonful of warm broth under his watchful eye.

"As I was saying," he continued, "expectations go both ways."

Olivia gave him a puzzled look.

"What do you mean?"

"I mean, if as a good citizen, I'm supposed to be looking for a job, then what are *you* supposed to be doing all day?"

"I said I would handle the housecleaning," she said defensively. "I can also cook if you want me to."

"That's not what I'm getting at," he explained. "I'm not looking for a job because we need money; I'm doing it because it will help our chances with Dr. Faust."

"And?"

"And she's going to want to see that certain…arrangements have been made on your behalf."

"What sort of arrangements?" she asked suspiciously.

Mitchell sighed deeply, wondering if there was a more delicate way to broach the subject.

"Do you know what *truancy* means?" he asked gently.

Olivia suddenly realized where this was going.

"Absolutely not!" she protested.

"Hey…all I'm saying is that normal little girls don't stay at home all day cleaning house."

"I don't care what *normal little girls* do," she asserted indignantly. "I am NOT going to school!"

"Look…it's only for a couple weeks. Surely…"

"I don't care if it's for one day. Do you have any idea how *boring* high school was for me? And now you want me to go back there? I couldn't imagine a worse hell."

"We could always try the middle school," he suggested.

Olivia graciously declined the offer.

"Ow…" exclaimed Mitchell, rubbing the now sore spot along his shinbone.

She glared defiantly at him.

"And what did *you* learn today in school?" she taunted.

Mitchell sighed with exasperation.

"Fine. Have it your way," he conceded. "What do you want me to tell Dr. Faust when she asks me what school you will be attending?"

Olivia narrowed her gaze at him but her features quickly softened.

"You might have a point," she said, looking down at the table with chagrin. Her eyes flickered back and forth as she contemplated the dilemma in her mind. After a few seconds, both eyes went wide at the discovery of a particular revelation.

"Didn't you use to be a teacher?" she asked.

This time it was Mitchell's eyes that went wide.

"I don't like where this is going," he objected.

"Oh come on." she urged. "Plenty of kids get homeschooled these days. Plus, it's not like you would actually have to teach me anything."

"Aren't there special requirements for homeschooling?"

"I'm sure we can check that online. I'm pretty confident that I can pass whatever state exam they throw at us."

"I don't know…"

"I'll tell you what. If you agree to the homeschooling plan, I promise to wear a plaid miniskirt and stockings to all of your classes."

Mitchell's face went beet red.

"Olivia!" he scolded in a hush voice.

"What?" she asked innocently. "You've never had a schoolgirl fantasy?"

Mitchell checked over his shoulder to make sure that no one had heard her.

"Ok, fine," he said with annoyance. "But don't blame me when you get held after class for flirting with the teacher."

Olivia smiled suggestively at him.

"Does that mean I get to pass you naughty notes?" she teased, just in time to redden his face before the server returned with their entrees.

Mitchell took the comments about his complexion in stride, thanking the waitress and glaring at Olivia. Once again, Mitchell shared his food with Olivia, though she was not so generous with her dumplings.

"What else?" he asked between bites.

"Make sure that if she asks you about living arrangements that you tell her that you've been considering moving to a bigger apartment."

"Why?" asked Mitchell.

"So that you can accommodate an extra person living with you," she said.

"I mean, why do we need a bigger apartment? Isn't the place big enough?"

"Yes…but it's not about the space. It's the fact that there's only one bedroom. Dr. Faust has already asked me about sleeping arrangements which means that it's something she's going to be focused on."

"She asked you about sleeping arrangements?" he asked with surprise. "What did you tell her?"

"I told her the truth; that I've been sleeping in the bedroom and you've been on the couch. I may have mentioned that we were considering swapping because of your size."

"I'm comfortable sleeping on the couch," he asserted.

Hopefully not too comfortable, thought Olivia.

"Regardless, I think that she finds the whole thing a bit…suspicious."

Mitchell nodded.

"Alright. I'll tell her that I've been looking," he agreed. "How do you think of this stuff anyhow?"

"I've…dealt with these people before," she said.

Mitchell studied her a moment before an arm came into view.

"You can pay at the front when you're ready," said their server, setting down the check tray.

Olivia reached for one of the two fortune cookies, broke off an edge, and began to crunch as she read. Mitchell followed suit, although setting the pieces of cookie aside on his plate instead.

"What does yours say?" he asked.

"You will be asked to step up in new ways," she read, giving a short groan afterwards. "Is yours any better?"

Mitchell looked down at his slip of paper.

"Anything is possible with a willing heart."

Olivia felt heat rising to her face.

One can only hope, she thought.

"Are you ready?" he asked, reaching for his coat.

"There's just one more thing…" she said.

Mitchell raised a quizzical eyebrow at her.

"What is it?" he asked worriedly.

Olivia peered at him across the table and spoke as nonchalantly as if her request were as normal as asking for the time.

"I want a key."

Detective Nick Hagan sat fastidiously working through paperwork when Doug walked through the door. Nick took a quick peek at the clock before addressing his partner. It was shortly before 4:00.

"Find out anything?" he asked.

"I did actually," replied Doug, tossing a folder on the desk.

Nick gave him a confused look.

"There is no record of James Friedman or Elaine Prescott ever having had a child."

Nick raised an eyebrow in response as he opened the folder before him.

"Then who's the girl staying with him?" he asked.

"I knew you'd ask," Doug said with a smile, "so I did some snooping around."

"And?"

Doug stuck out his chest proudly.

"Cecelia Friedman: daughter of David Friedman and his wife, Julia Valerio."

Nick skimmed through the pages of the folder.

"Friedman's brother?"

Doug nodded.

"It appears that Elaine Friedman filed paperwork to legally adopt Cecelia after the death of James' brother. Naturally, with James Friedman's assets, the court agreed to grant custody."

Nick found the paperwork regarding the adoption of Cecelia by James and Elaine Friedman. He flipped through the rest of the documents quickly, but did not find what he was searching for.

"Where's the birth certificate?" he asked.

Doug shrugged his shoulders.

"There wasn't one."

"How can there be no birth certificate?" demanded Nick.

"That's where the plot thickens," said Doug. "Cecelia Friedman was not the daughter of David and Julia Friedman. They adopted her."

"You're kidding."

Doug shook his head. He pointed to the folder.

"They adopted Cecelia Collingwood in March of 2004."

"That was a little over six years ago, shortly before they were killed in a car accident."

"I looked into that, too. Your contact at Friedman Financial was a little off on his dates. According to the death certificates, the two passed away on July fifteenth of 2006. Only four years ago."

Nick found the death certificates in the folder and considered this new information.

"Do you think he had any reason to lie?"

"I doubt it," said Doug. "From what you told me, he wasn't keeping very close tabs on the Friedman family. He probably just didn't remember."

Nick nodded. Going through the papers, he selected one and removed it from the folder.

"The orphanage seems to have been in eastern New York. Why go all that way just to adopt a child?"

"Well, David Friedman was living up that way at the time. He had to relocate quite frequently for his job."

"What type of work did he do?"

"David Friedman was a software architect."

Hagan looked at him with confusion.

"A what?"

Doug was about to answer honestly when he remembered with whom he was speaking.

"He did stuff with computers for major corporations," he explained.

"Oh...ok," responded Nick absently. He focused intently on the paper in his hand.

"How old did their neighbor say Cecelia Friedman was?"

"Around eleven or twelve. Why?"

"The orphanage has an estimated birth date around 1995. That would make her fifteen today."

"So the woman got it wrong. She said she wasn't quite sure."

"Yes. But how could you possibly confuse a fifteen-year-old girl with an eleven-year-old girl? It's like night and day."

"Maybe she was a late bloomer," suggested Werner.

"Hmmm..." muttered Hagan with uncertainty. He rubbed his fingers along his chin, thinking deeply about the information. His concentration was broken by Werner.

"Did you get the tox-screen back yet?"

Nick nodded. He scrounged through the papers on his desk. He held one up for his partner to read.

"Blood alcohol was point two one," said Hagan as he handed the paper over.

Doug made a whistling noise.

"With a BAC like that, he was lucky not to have fallen off the roof."

"With a BAC like that, he was lucky to make it to the roof."

Werner reviewed the rest of the report. Nothing else was out of the ordinary. He handed the paper back to Hagan.

"So, you think it was an accident, then?" he asked.

Nick shook his head.

"I'm not ruling out foul play until we locate the girl."

"You think she might be involved?" asked Doug. "Offed him for the insurance money?"

Nick chuckled. That was Doug, always the conspiracy nut.

"I think if she had something to gain from his death, she'd have come forward by now."

Doug nodded in agreement.

"You think that maybe they had a falling out then?"

Nick considered this a moment before his mind drifted back to the earlier conversation.

"Did you find a birth certificate for Cecelia Collingwood?" he asked.

A smirk crossed Doug's face.

"Nope."

"You seem pleased by that," said Nick questioningly.

"You're going to love this," he began. "There's no record of a Cecelia Collingwood matching that age description."

"Meaning?"

"Meaning that she changed her name *to* Cecelia Collingwood. And do you know why someone so young would change their name?"

"I don't, but I'm sure you're eager to tell me what theory you've cooked up..."

"Adoption," interrupted Doug.

"But you just said she'd been adopted by..."

"Before that," he explained.

Nick blinked with shock.

"Are you saying that you think she was adopted by someone before being adopted by the Friedmans?"

"Bingo."

Hagan leaned back in his chair.

"Man…I hope for the sake of that poor girl that isn't the case. Can you imagine the tragedy of losing your parents, not once, but three times?"

Nick glanced over at Doug whose gaze held firm.

"But that's exactly what happened isn't it?" he asked sadly.

"I'm afraid so," said Doug. "Although it's just a theory at this point, I'm fairly confident that's what we'll find at the other end of the rabbit hole."

Nick shook his head, unable to make sense of it all.

"Do you know where she lived before?"

"Still working on that," said Doug. "I called the orphanage, and they said she was dropped off after being picked up for truancy."

"And nobody came looking for her?"

Doug shook his head sullenly.

"Any luck with missing persons?" asked Doug, hoping to change the subject.

"One of the local stations picked up a girl, but they said her name was Olivia something," lamented Hagan. "Just another lost child whose parents abandoned her…"

Doug wanted to say something reassuring, but nothing came to mind.

"Did you get a chance to talk with Friedman's lawyer?"

Nick rose from his chair and grabbed his coat.

"I'll call him later or maybe tomorrow," he said. "Right now I need a break."

Doug nodded.

"You wanna grab a bite with me?" asked Hagan. "We can check out the orphanages later."

"Sounds good to me. I've barely seen sunlight today."

"Any preferences?"

"Hey, as long as you're paying, I could go for whatever."

Nick pondered.

"When was the last time you had Chinese?"

The hardware store attendant handed Mitchell the key.

"Four dollars twenty-eight cents," he said.

Mitchell handed the young clerk a five and received his change. He turned and placed the key gingerly into Olivia's small, outstretched palm. She clutched it firmly in her hand before slipping it snugly into the tight pocket of her jeans.

"Ready to go home?" he asked her.

She nodded weakly. The day's excitement had taken its toll, and a full belly further added to her sleepiness. Olivia looped her arm in his, and they began the long trek back to the apartment. As they walked, her steps declined in speed, and she placed her heavy head against his stout arm. Monitoring her lagging pace, Mitchell came to a sudden halt.

"Here," he said gently.

Kneeling on the sidewalk beside her, Mitchell assisted her up onto his back, manually wrapping her small arms around his neck. He secured her legs tightly against his flanks before rising from the cement. Once again, Mitchell was stunned by the light weight of her tiny frame. As they progressed, his ambulation generated gentle, rocking motions which quickly lulled Olivia to sleep. Long before they arrived home, Mitchell could feel the pool of moisture that accumulated near her open mouth, but found himself not the slightest bit repulsed.

Back in the warm comfort of the apartment, Mitchell carried his small charge to the bedroom. Bending low he let her arms slip from his neck, lowering her gently on the bed. Turning to face her, he met the soul penetrating gaze of those deep blue eyes. Though he might have imagined it, he could have sworn he saw her smile change from withdrawn to inviting.

"I'm tired," she spoke weakly. "Could you help me with my clothes?"

There was something to the inflection in her voice that disinclined me to offer my assistance. Torn between the cumbersome warnings of a squat psychiatrist and the hidden motives suppressed deep within this petite girl, I found myself drawn to the safer path. Still, I had already seen her in various stages of undress, what could it hurt to be involved in the process?

I slipped the shoes off her tiny feet and slid them beneath the bed. The socks came off just as easily, and I began a pile on the floor beside the footwear. I reached for her t-shirt, generating a timid coo from Olivia as my fingers accidentally grazed her bare abdomen. I pulled upwards, letting the garment slip from her body and added it to the socks.

Taking a deep breath to steady my hands, I extended downwards toward the button on her jeans. Tugging gently on the garment, I managed to undo the clasp. As my finger touched the zipper, she squirmed beneath me, causing my hand to slide away from its mark. Olivia's breathing grew erratic as I made contact with sensitive terrain.

"Sorry," I whispered before continuing.

Having more luck with the zipper on the second try, I slipped my thumbs into the belt loops along her waist. This time I advanced with more care, gracefully avoiding any further missteps on my part. When the jeans pulled free I caught a glimpse of her undergarments, and the tender topography that lay beneath. Quickly averting my gaze, I placed the jeans on the growing mound beside me.

With the outer garments removed, I looked back to Olivia. She smiled bashfully down at me before casting her eyes upon the striped brassiere. Olivia peered at me again, this time biting her lip as though from nervousness.

Following the signal, I reached around her midsection and grabbed hold of the rear clasps. Maintaining constant eye contact with Olivia, I undid the fastening, letting the fabric fall free of her shoulders. Without peeking at her bare body, I tossed the soft material into the pile with the others.

As I turned back to Olivia, I felt two hands take hold of the back of my neck. She leaned forward, guiding her lips toward my own. At the last moment, I turned my face away from hers, letting her kiss land on my cheek instead.

"Thank you," she said softly into my ear.

I gave an appreciative nod, maneuvering myself out of the crouching position. My joints groaned as I rose to my feet. I lifted the blankets, and Olivia curled into a fetal position beneath. Tucking her warmly under the comforter, I bent forward and kissed her gently on the forehead.

"Sleep well."

As I pulled away from her, our eyes locked. Though my heart urged me to her side, thoughts of the day's events continued to drive a wedge between us, ensuring that I could only love her from a distance.

CHAPTER 12

Olivia awoke from her nap shortly after six o'clock, wasting no time in dragging herself from the comfort of the bed. It had been a mostly restful slumber, but there was far too much on her mind to remain idly between the sheets. Not wanting to bother getting dressed again, Olivia pulled on her sleepshirt before exiting the bedroom.

She found Mitchell in the kitchen hovering above a steaming pot and periodically stirring its contents. He looked in her direction when he noticed the soft padding of bare feet on the linoleum.

"I decided to make some pasta. Would you like some?" he asked.

Olivia approached behind him, wrapping her arms affectionately around his abdomen. Letting her head rest against him, she closed her eyes and listened to the sounds of him breathing. After a few seconds, he looked at her over his shoulder.

"Careful," he said worriedly. "I don't want you to get burned."

Olivia gave him one last squeeze before stepping away, lifting herself on one of the stools next to the island. Olivia watched absently as Mitchell finished preparing the food, all the while pondering how best to broach the subject on her mind.

"Would you like a plate or a bowl?" asked Mitchell abruptly.

Olivia broke her gaze from the spot on the island countertop where she'd been staring to see that the meal was ready. Despite her attention being focused on other issues, Olivia was troubled over how easily she had drifted out.

"Whichever," she replied.

With a little more fiddling in the kitchen, Mitchell placed a plate on the table in front of her before sitting along the adjacent edge of the dining area. Olivia looked at the abundant quantity of noodles piled high on her dish. It was clear that Mitchell had not fully acclimated to her dietary allotments. She lifted her fork to the plate, but mostly just pushed the pile back and forth lethargically.

Olivia looked from her food to Mitchell. Though he was in the closest seat, he still seemed very far away from her. With his nose to the grindstone, Mitchell recklessly attacked the linguine in front of him, the sides of his mouth bathed in pasta sauce. She was in awe of his appetite, surprised that he could eat anything after the meal they had back at the restaurant.

"How is it?" he asked between bites.

Olivia looked down at the untouched entrée before her. She couldn't have cared less about the taste of the pasta right now.

"It's delicious," she said.

The rest of the meal passed in silence, the only sounds coming from the muffled noises of Mitchell's intense mastication. Both of them continued to focus at their plates, neither making the effort to reach out to the other. When they had finished eating, Mitchell carried the plates to the sink.

As he cleared and stored the remnants of dinner, Olivia sat alone at the island. She clasped both hands firmly together in a vain attempt to quell her nervous fidgeting. And yet, the image of her interlocking fingers only further reminded her of what it was she did not possess. Olivia shook her head, dispersing the dreadful feelings of insecurity.

This is ridiculous, she thought to herself.

Olivia waited for Mitchell to finish drying his hands before moving to his flank. She said nothing to answer his inquisitive stare, only reached out to take his hand. Pushing through his resistance, Olivia led him from the kitchen to the living room couch. Olivia turned in her seat so she could face him directly.

"Mitchell, " she began timidly, "Do you still want me around?"

Mitchell, who had been inspecting a particularly interesting bit of debris on the floor, glanced suddenly in her direction.

"What?"

"It's okay if you don't. People change their minds."

"Why would you think I wouldn't want you around?" he interrupted.

Olivia let out a heart wrenching sigh.

"It's just that you've been ignoring me all night."

"I haven't been…"

He cut himself short when Olivia gave him a look that solidified the truth. Mitchell thought about all the words of advice that Dr. Faust had given him regarding Olivia. Surely there had to be a better middle ground than this current behavior.

"I'm sorry," he said, averting his gaze in shame. "I guess I'm just a little stressed is all. It's been a long day."

"I understand," she empathized, "But that doesn't make it okay to shut me out. We're in this together, remember?"

Mitchell continued to avoid eye contact, his head drooping like a scolded dog. It had not been her intention to harrow his emotions, and she would have sought to comfort these grievances if not for a thought that suddenly came to mind.

"What did Dr. Faust say to you?" she demanded.

Mitchell looked up quickly, though his massive frame seemed to shrink beneath her watchful gaze.

"What do you mean?" he asked nervously.

Olivia folded her arms.

"You have been acting differently toward me ever since we left the police station. Surely it couldn't have been anything from the police officer, and I've already heard what Abigail has to say about me, so that only leaves Dr. Faust."

Thoughts of the intense conversation at the police station ran through his head. Mitchell recalled how the psychiatrist explained about Olivia's adult façade, her history with abuse, and even how Mitchell should conduct himself in the presence of his small companion. He remembered that part most of all.

"It was nothing," explained Mitchell. "We mostly talked about court stuff and how temporary custody works."

"Uh-huh…" replied Olivia dismissively. "What else did you talk about?"

"That was it," he said, quickening the tempo in his speech. "We might have discussed our favorite sports teams. As you probably remember, I've been a home team fan since I was a boy, but not Dr. Faust. Would you believe…?"

"Mitchell!" she intervened, her tone like a sword slicing through his rambling.

He groaned audibly, protesting any situation that placed him between two competing female viewpoints.

"Come on, Mitchell. Tell me," she urged soothingly. "I promise I won't be mad."

Mitchell seriously doubted that, but being aware that there was absolutely no chance of victory in a situation such as this, he chose to surrender sooner rather than later.

"She said you were a bit mature for your age," said Mitchell, paying special attention not to use the word precocious.

"And?" pressed Olivia.

Mitchell exhaled deeply.

"And she thinks that might be a side effect from abuse."

Olivia stared at him wide-eyed. It didn't take a professional to read the hurt written across her face.

"I see," she uttered mournfully. Olivia turned her gaze to the coffee table, her lips pursed tightly together as if fighting against some long forgotten memory. Her eyes watered, and Mitchell watched as a teardrop rolled down her cheek.

"You have to give her credit for one thing," she began, wiping away the tear with the back of her hand, "Dr. Faust really knows how to find the rough spots."

Mitchell raised an eyebrow at her.

"You mean…?"

Olivia shook her head.

"No. It wasn't *me* that got abused. At least, not really."

Olivia's head sagged; chin nearly resting against her sternum. Mitchell slid closer, wrapping his arm around her shoulders, seeking to provide comfort in any way he could.

"Look…you don't have to talk about it if you don't want to."

Olivia shook her head.

"It's fine," she said. "I don't mind, as long as it's with you."

Olivia remained quiet, inhaling long, slow breaths.

"I'm not sure exactly where to start," she admitted.

"How about from the beginning? That's usually a good place."

"Should I start with the Big Bang or can I fast-forward up to the age of the dinosaurs?"

"Some of us have to be up early tomorrow to go look for a job," he pointed out. "Why don't we skip ahead to the good parts? I hear that 1986 was a good year."

Olivia smiled to herself. Even if Mitchell continued to carry his own brand of uncertainties, he was continuing to give her the benefit of the doubt, which was more than anyone else seemed to allow her.

She leaned close to him and placed a gentle kiss on the underside of his chin. Mitchell did not even flinch at this affectionate gesture, nor did he try to pull away. She withdrew her lips, sliding downwards to find a comfortable spot where she could rest her head. Wrapped in the strong embrace of his muscular arms, Olivia snuggled against his broad torso and recanted for him the story of her life.

I was born Olivia Josephine Morgan, the only child of my aging parents Tom and Christine. Like many of their professional colleagues, my parents decided to wait until they had acquired some degree of financial security before trying to start a family. Perhaps they were a bit overly cautious because I was born into a six-bedroom house, with a massive backyard in an esteemed neighborhood on waterfront property in Connecticut.

I never really knew what my parents did for a living, perhaps I was too young to be concerned about such things. All I remember is that their jobs required a lot of traveling, and I was often left alone with my nanny, Winifred, although I generally referred to her as Aunt Winnie. For the most part, it was a picturesque childhood, beautiful home, loving parents, and an adorable cocker spaniel named Oscar. I loved that dog, and we spent many summer afternoons romping around the yard and chasing insects down by the embankment.

Then one day, when I was around seven, Aunt Winnie came to tell me that my parents had been involved in a dreadful incident overseas. She described a political dispute I did not understand, that erupted in a town I could not pronounce, in some far-off country I had never heard of. All I knew is that my parents had gone away and would never come home again.

Shortly after, some relatives whom I had never met came to live with me at the house. At first, I was excited because they had a daughter, and I thought we could become really good friends. As it turned out, these so-called family members were nothing more than con artists looking to turn a profit off my parents' demise. Once they had secured the deed to the house, I was sent away to live at the orphanage.

Up to that point I had always been considered a shy girl, but after the loss of my mother and father I was all but a recluse with other children. Most days, I hid in the library where stories of distant lands and fantastical creatures helped me forget about life's tragedies.

It was there that I met Melissa, a girl my age with jet black hair and an even darker sense of humor. She enjoyed reading tales about abandoned princesses being heroically rescued from their various forms of imprisonment. Despite her outgoing personality and pugnacious attitude, the two of us were very much alike. I think that's why we ended up becoming so close.

We spent every waking moment together. The two of us would wander the woods near the orphanage pretending we were lost explorers. At meals, Melissa would encourage us to behave like royalty, holding our pinkies up as we sipped water from our glasses. Sometimes after lights out, she would crawl into my bunk, and we would read ghost stories by flashlight. When we got in trouble for sneaking out to see the new comet, Melissa and I were side-by-side scrubbing the kitchen.

A few months following our punishment, after we had both turned ten, a minister and his wife came to adopt a child. I had long since abandoned hope of ever leaving that crummy orphanage, but Melissa always thought about finding a family to call her own. With each new prospect who came through the door, she was right there to greet them - prim, polite, and with a smile that would warm even the most bitter of hearts. Naturally, Melissa's charismatic charm and vibrant outlook was a perfect match for the young couple. They began to fill out paperwork that very day. And who could blame them? Melissa was everything anybody could ever have wanted in a daughter.

I remember being ecstatic that Melissa had finally gotten her wish. We even snuck some snacks from the kitchen to celebrate. I know that it must seem a bittersweet victory, but I was genuinely happy for my friend. Still, when the day came for her to leave, it took all of my willpower not to burst into tears. Looking back, I think I was pretending to be strong for her, as if being stoic would prevent her from feeling guilty about leaving. If the shoe were on the other foot, I'm sure I would need lots of encouragement and assurance that it was indeed okay to go.

But that's not what happened. When the family arrived to take Melissa to her new home, they pulled me aside to tell me the most wonderful news. To this day, I don't know how she managed to convince them, but Melissa told her new parents that she couldn't stand the thought of being separated from me, so they agreed to adopt us both. Not since the death of my parents had anyone ever stood up for me like that. That was the greatest day of my life. It wasn't just that Melissa and I were staying together, or that we were bidding farewell to those miserable dormitories, or even that we had found ourselves loving parents, it was that heading to the same home meant we would no longer be friends, but sisters.

I found out later that Mr. Jonathan and Miss Rachel had been missionaries in Africa for the last few summers, and their work overseas had rekindled their love for children. Through the years prior to our adoption, the two of them had tried to have a baby, each attempt ending in a miscarriage. I'm sure it saddened Miss Rachel that she was never able to have her own, but to their credit, I always felt that the two of them loved Melissa and me as though we were their true children.

Melissa and I continued to be inseparable, right down to sharing a bedroom. We sat next to one another in all of our classes, we ate all of our meals together, and we sometimes swapped clothes. Melissa continued to sneak into my bed, though we talked less of scary stories and more about the boys in class we thought were cute. The change in our pillow talk assured me that life was getting better for both of us.

Things took a sudden turn the summer we both hit thirteen. Like many of the girls in our class, Melissa started having her calendar days. They would come on so intense that I would have to carry her books to class and perform extra chores at home. I didn't mind though, I was happy to help. It didn't make me particularly eager to grow up though.

When Melissa started to develop in other ways, the boys at school took notice. The more others paid attention to our bodies, the more self-conscious we became. At least once a week Melissa and I would measure her progress in front of the bathroom mirror. Afterwards she would bolster my spirits, assuring me that my time would eventually come. I remember sometimes being jealous of the girls in my class, but never of Melissa. She was my sister after all, and I wanted the best for her.

The guys were not the only ones who observed the changes with Melissa's body and eventually came The Talk. Mr. Jonathan and Miss Rachel sat us down one night to go over the birds and the bees. As with most adults, they showed up for the lecture long after we had already been exposed to the information by our peers, making the discussion all the more awkward.

And yet, their lengthy exposition contained very little of anatomy or physiology but dealt mostly in the realms of faith and morality. For them, sex was clearly bad, as was anything that resembled or mimicked it. Kissing was also not allowed, with special ground rules being applied for when and how boys might be present in the house. Strangely, Mr. Jonathan talked of Melissa's cycles with the same contempt and loathing he held for sexual activity. Even though I was still fairly young, I felt that there was something degrading and unfair about shaming her for something that was only natural.

When they finished talking, I expected there to be some sort of question and answer session, but instead Mr. Jonathan pulled out these rings. He said that they were intended to help keep us "pure", whatever that meant. Apparently many of the girls in his congregation were wearing them, and it would help set a good example for the others if Melissa and I would wear them as well. Melissa agreed and I followed her in solidarity, though it was mostly a moot point with me. I never had to worry about sex because none of the boys ever showed an interest in me.

When summer came around again, Miss Rachel decided to return to mission work. The trip she had in mind would keep her out of the country for nearly the entire summer with her coming home the week before we headed back to school. Mr. Jonathan agreed to remain stateside and make sure we were well looked after. I have often wondered if things would have turned out differently if Miss Rachel had never left.

It wasn't long after his wife departed on her travels that Mr. Jonathan began making advances toward Melissa. They were subtle at first; an overly affectionate hug, rubbing her back as she sat beside him on the couch, a peck on the lips instead of on the cheek. Slowly it progressed until one night he came to our room after we were in bed.

Neither of our foster parents had ever come to check on us before and it probably should have set off some warning bells, but we were too young to understand what was happening. He called for Melissa, asking for her to speak with him in private. Though it was late, she followed him, and Mr. Jonathan closed the bedroom door behind them. I remember lying awake for what seemed like forever for them to return.

Melissa was alone when she came back, her face contorted as if trying to make sense of whatever had happened during her absence. Her pajama top lay open, unbuttoned down to the navel, the fabric lying precariously against her bosom. From the safety of my warm bed I could see parts of her bare chest and knew it strange for her not to be wearing a bra.

As if in a daze, she shut the door, double-checking to make sure that the knob had latched. Turning to face the dark room, Melissa crossed her arms in front of her chest, shrouding her nakedness the way someone might shield themselves on a brisk, windy day. She stared a long time at her empty bed before sliding beneath the sheets next to me.

I remember Melissa wrapping her arms tightly around my torso, grip like a vice, her head firmly resting on my shoulder. With her as the big spoon and I, the little one, we lay cuddled in each other's arms, neither of us wanting to address the issue. When I finally got the nerve to speak, Melissa only shook her head, and then her entire body began to quake uncontrollably. Eventually the tears subsided, and she drifted off to sleep, still clutching me for support.

The next morning was like the events of the preceding night had never happened. Mr. Jonathan was up early to make breakfast, his chipper demeanor an irritating pretense for concealing the iniquities better left unsaid. If it had been up to me, we would have gone immediately to the police and had him locked away, but Melissa convinced me to wait until Miss Rachel returned. I think the way Melissa saw it was that as long as we stayed put, we at least had each other, but there was no telling where we might end up, or even if we'd remain together if the authorities intervened without our foster mother there. And so we waited.

When Mr. Jonathan came for her again, Melissa defiantly refused. She had always been the stronger of the two of us, and not just physically. But her adolescent willpower was no match for his adult strength. As he started violently pulling her from the bed, I tried my best to defend her. What little resistance I could muster had absolutely no impact on his large frame. I never saw him swing, just felt the impact against the side of my face. When I regained consciousness, Melissa was with me; her clothing torn open to expose her olive skin. She squinted through her left eye as her cheek was red and swollen. When I asked what happened, she only shook her head with amusement. Apparently my own face looked much worse.

In the morning, Mr. Jonathan explained to us that we were his children and we would do as we were told. He threatened to do depraved things to Melissa if I ever said anything to anybody, and he told her that I would be beaten mercilessly if she did not comply. I was willing to risk another thrashing to go for help, but Melissa convinced me that it was only for three more weeks, and we could hold out until then.

So every night Mr. Jonathan would drag Melissa from her bed and take her into his bedroom. I never asked her what went on behind those closed doors, but I watched the sadness in her eyes grow a little more each day. Every night when I would rock her to sleep in my arms, I felt pangs of guilt that he always ignored my flesh. To be honest, I understood why he favored her to me, but that didn't make it any more justified.

Why should my sister, so vibrant and full of life, be subjected to such deplorable behavior that ultimately extinguished her inner light? It should have been me instead. The first time he laid his grimy fingers on me, Melissa would have cut them off. She would have exposed his every sin in front of all his friends, parishioners, and every single news station that would run the story. And yet, she had absolutely no willpower left to fight when it was her own body on the line. I wanted so much to help my sister, but I was a coward. Even as I wished to alleviate her suffering, if only for a single night, when that door opened I would become afraid, silently hoping that he would overlook me another night.

Eventually came that magical day when Miss Rachel came home. I was so relieved to see her that I could have tackled her with a hug as she crossed the threshold to the front door. Unfortunately, that display of emotion would have to wait, for Mr. Jonathan was there to greet her as well, preventing me from divulging his dirty little secret.

It took me some time before I managed to be alone with Miss Rachel, but at last I was able to speak with her in private. I confided in her everything that had been going on while she was away. When I finished, I breathed a sigh of relief knowing that Miss Rachel would set everything right and send that miserable wretch to pay for his crimes.

Instead, she called me a liar. She told me that there was no way that Mr. Jonathan would ever do anything of the sort and that Melissa probably made the whole thing up to get attention. At first I was shocked, and that quickly escalated into outrage. How could she not believe me? Why would I make up such a story? Miss Rachel continued to deny my claim, saying that even if it had been happening, it was definitely Melissa who had instigated the events, not her perfect husband, and that I shouldn't be so quick to make outlandish accusations.

From then on I seethed every time we were forced to sit through his sermons about the decline of morality in our society. Melissa was still urged to wear that damn ring he'd given her. When people saw that symbol, they were reminded of the upstanding preacher who taught abstinence before marriage to his entire congregation. I no longer wore mine, refusing to be associated with the circle of lies which allowed an innocent girl to get raped every night by the very man who was supposed to be her greatest advocate.

And then there was Miss Rachel. For all her empathy and compassion for the mistreated youth abroad, she had allowed her children to fall prey to a predator in her own home. So *many times I wanted to tear down that church from the inside out; to denounce their pastor as a child rapist and his wife as the enabling hypocrite who supported him. From the stained glass to the pulpit, it was all a lie; window dressing to what was probably decades of little African children being molested and abused in the name of the lord and savior.*

For me, the masquerade was over, and it was time to be on my way. I couldn't just sit idly by any longer and wait for what had happened to Melissa to happen to me. When the plan was set, I urged my sister to run away with me. Despite our tragedy-riddled pasts, we found happiness together once; surely we could find it again.

But for some reason, the prospect of having to start all over again was too daunting a burden for Melissa. The unknown seemed to frighten her more than the darkened rooms, groping hands, and chafed orifices. Nothing could have scared me more than the torment she endured almost daily. With only heartache awaiting me if I should stay, I set out for new horizons, terrified and on my own…

"It wasn't your fault, you know."

They both remained speechless long after her narrative ended. Olivia's silence was merely the side effect of fatigue, but for Mitchell it had been a tough story to embrace all at once, especially since he knew it was true. Now that the stillness had been broken, Olivia gazed curiously up at Mitchell from her cushiony position nestled against his chest.

"This world is filled with all sorts of terrible people," he said. "It sounds like your foster father was just another among the multitudes and, under the circumstances, I think you did everything you could for your sister."

Olivia rested her head back down.

"Then why do I feel so bad about it?"

Mitchell wrapped his arm tighter around her torso.

"It's normal to feel regret when something bad happens to someone we care about, but the truth is, you probably would have had the exact same reaction to the situation whether you had been living there or not. And just because it happened while you were staying there doesn't make it your responsibility."

"I guess…" she replied, her voice a little less melancholy than before.

"What happened to Melissa?"

Olivia shook her head.

"I wish I knew. I never saw her again after that day."

"Well did you…?"

"Shhh…" interrupted Olivia. "Please. Just hold me for a while."

Mitchell did as he was instructed, tenderly stroking her soft hair as they enjoyed the calm of their surroundings. When she was ready, Olivia continued her story.

When I ran away, I took only a few sets of clothing and enough food to last less than a week. I suppose I was feeling overly optimistic about what my future could be like after escaping such a horrible place. Mostly through luck, I managed to safely hitchhike to Pennsylvania. Seeing my emaciated form, one of the drivers decided to take me to the local orphanage: The Love on High Home for Children.

I foolishly kept the same name, but fortunately my old family never came looking for me. I suppose they were glad to see the young troublemaker gone.

Though I clearly didn't look it, I was one of the oldest children there. Some of the other girls had begun the transition into puberty. Like my previous stay at an orphanage, I tended to stay to myself. The familiar surroundings made the separation from Melissa all the harder, and I buried my emotions by reading all that I could get my hands on.

Unlike my stay at the foster home, Love on High was associated with a private high school and insisted that we get our education from the special instructors there. We were told that it was for our betterment, but I had a feeling it was so that they could successfully monitor the secular works that might infect the residents. I soon outshone the rest of my peers academically, which is probably part of the reason I was allowed to pursue other interests, even those that weren't strictly of a religious context.

I don't know if it's because the girls were older at the new orphanage, or if the attitudes just change that much from state to state, but my peers were much more clique-oriented. Being the latecomer to the party, I was usually the outcast for all activities at the orphanage, which suited me just fine.

I was not immune to their teasing and taunting, however. Sometimes it was that I was a bookworm who hardly socialized with anyone. Other times, it might be because my world views so vastly differed from theirs. Mostly though, it was because, even at fifteen years old, I showed absolutely no signs of puberty. My flat chest and boyish frame made me stand out from the others, which is the same as a pariah to teenage girls. Our communal showers did little to alleviate their torment, so I often skipped bathing altogether, a move that made me ever the more unpopular.

My time at this orphanage was short-lived however. After about a year and a half, the teasing started to turn into hazing. Rather than simply call me names, the other girls started to play pranks on me. It began harmlessly enough with one of the more developed girls thinking it funny to steal my clothes and towel while I was in the showers, forcing me to walk naked through the hallway. Like usual, no one seemed to pay any attention to my shapeless body.

Since her first attempt had not yielded the type of humiliation that she had been seeking, one girl decided to take it one step further. The next shower day, all the girls got together and tossed my few clothes out onto the lawn, including those back in the room. Because they had been nice enough to leave the sheets on my bed, the only real humiliation I suffered was when the headmistress asked a passing resident why one of the boys was walking around in a toga.

After that, the pranks became increasingly violent, and I knew it was time to move on again. Taking some food from the kitchen, I made off in the middle of the night. Aware that my name might launch me right back to where I had left, I chose a new one based on a character from one of my favorite books: Cecelia Collingwood.

My escape was fleeting to say the least. I was picked up by a police officer the following week for truancy and was once again back at an orphanage. This time though, I told them that I was eight. They would have been hard-pressed to believe my actual age anyway, but at least it kept the older girls from bullying me. Instead, they saw me as cute, and I became like a mascot to them.

Two years went by, and I was finally adopted again. The Friedmans were by far the best family I had lived with since my parents died. Sometimes we would go to the theatre, while other times it might be a simple picnic in the park. Regardless of how busy they were with work, they always made time for me.

At my insistence, they allowed me to do homeschooling. By now, I was far too advanced to learn anything in public school, and I couldn't imagine trying to make friends with people nearly half my age. Naturally, I breezed through the coursework; Mr. David and Miss Julia thought I must have been especially gifted. Life might have been a lot less complicated later if I had just told them the truth back then…

"Why didn't you?" asked Mitchell.

The sound of Mitchell's voice broke her from the reverie. She looked up at him with a puzzled expression.

"Why didn't I *what*?" she asked.

"Why didn't you tell them the truth? Surely they would have believed you."

Olivia shook her head.

"I doubt it. No one has ever believed me before. They've all treated me the same way that Abigail and Dr. Faust did; like I was a child acting out of the ordinary just to get attention. And let's face it, if two therapists who have been trained to listen to people's problems didn't bother to hear me out, then what chance could I have with anybody else?"

Mitchell gave a solemn nod.

"I suppose you might have a point there," he said sadly. "Although…I can't help but wonder…"

Olivia gazed at him expectantly.

"Wonder what?"

"If the best among us is only capable of such superficial notions, does that mean that the bulk of humanity is composed of individuals who might well be just as judgmental as a bunch of elitist teenage girls?"

Olivia let the idea linger a moment.

"Hey Mitchell…"

"Yeah, Olivia?"

"Give it a rest."

CHAPTER 13

Joseph Harper stood before the bathroom sink splashing cold water on his face. Despite years of service to Friedman Financial, he had never gotten over his anxiety at public speaking, not even for the few and familiar members of the board. He thought about the bottle of blue label scotch hidden in his desk and brushed the idea aside. It was always better to utilize that particular resource after a speech, that way he only had to experience the harsh burning sensation once.

He reached into the black toiletry kit he kept at the office solely for such occasions and removed a toothbrush and mouthwash. When he'd finished with those, he pulled out a comb and corrected the patches that had gotten disheveled from the dry heaving. Harper took one last look at himself in the mirror. It was hard to believe how many people had complimented him on his eloquent, oratory skills.

Exiting the bathroom, he headed for his office and deposited the hygiene bag in the lower drawer of his desk. Harper checked his watch. It was ten past nine; he was already running late. Though punctuality was nothing to scoff at, experience taught him that arriving late and departing early from the board meetings kept them from dragging on longer than necessary. Members were far less likely to discuss frivolous topics when you seemed too busy to care.

Harper took his time gathering papers before strolling down the hall toward the boardroom. With all of the inner blinds closed, the area appeared more foreboding than usual, setting his sweat glands into overdrive. It couldn't be helped; it was the only way to ensure privacy. Whereas normally there would be an assistant or two present to help with notes and dispense beverages, today's meeting was top secret, which meant board members only.

Harper pushed open the boardroom door with enough momentum to startle the membership already inside. The low murmur of voices cut off instantly as a dozen pairs of eyes bored into him. Harper was suddenly thankful that he had purged himself already.

"Good morning, gentlemen," he enunciated loudly. "Please take your seats."

The few standing board members took their chairs, and Harper waited for the commotion to die down. He glanced around the room, counting heads to be certain everyone was present. Including the few computer monitors scattered about for the members whose business overseas kept them from being present in person, Harper counted fourteen in total. That meant the only missing person was James Friedman.

"First of all, I want to thank each of you for taking time out of your busy schedules to be here. I know how inconvenient it is for some of you to come all this way, and I appreciate your efforts. We have a lot of important issues to discuss, but I promise to keep it as brief as possible."

The room remained silent as he faced down the intimidating faces staring at him. Harper swallowed hard, pushing past the nervousness.

"Late Tuesday afternoon I received a call from a detective of the Pittsburgh Bureau of Police who informed me that they discovered the deceased body of James Phillip Friedman."

The silence was immediately replaced by boisterous droning panic.

"Gentlemen…gentlemen…one at a time," urged Harper.

"Are they absolutely sure it's James Friedman?" asked the Canadian member.

"Yes. I personally identified the remains yesterday."

"How did he die?" asked one of the computer monitors.

"We'll get through this much quicker if we keep to relevant questions," chastised Harper.

"Why hasn't the death of Mr. Friedman been announced to the public yet?" asked one of the elderly members.

Harper looked up and smiled. In the past, he and Ian Goldman had always been on the same page with corporate issues. It had been a nice change to have someone with moral scruples on the board of directors.

"The detective said that they were still trying to notify the next of kin. He informed me that they were having some difficulties in locating her."

"Who is the next of kin?" asked Goldman.

"His daughter, Cecelia."

"Wasn't she staying with him?"

Harper shrugged.

"I'm not completely sure. I was told she wasn't at his residence."

As Goldman pondered this new information, a voice resounded from the screen hanging on the far wall. The portly face spoke with imperious authority.

"I'm sure we can all agree that the untimely death of Mr. Friedman is a tragedy unparalleled in the history of this company, and he will be sorely missed," said Dorian Abernathy.

There were many head nods throughout the room and a few audible agreements to the talking head. Harper remained skeptical.

"I for one," he went on, "deeply respected James Friedman's business acumen. It's not just anybody who possesses the remarkable foresight necessary to establish an esteemed financial institution such as this from the ground up. For that I applaud his ingenuity."

Joseph Harper restrained his tongue as he quietly fumed at the front of the room. Though the words were amiable, he sensed an underlying motivation for these insincere niceties. He had always had a sharp dislike for Dorian Abernathy, the pompous attitude and pretentious haughty tone grated on his nerves like nails on a chalkboard. Whereas James Friedman was at least a charitable man, Harper saw Abernathy as an ideal portrait of how money could destroy a person from the inside out.

"But I think we can all agree that James Friedman lacked the necessary fortitude to carry this company into the future," continued Abernathy. "Now I'm not saying that he was no longer capable of handling the job, farthest thing from it actually. But even you Harper would have to admit that his performance in the last few months had deteriorated to the point that it was having negative consequences for all our investors."

Harper narrowed his eyes at Abernathy but said nothing.

"I believe that this company will see vast improvements now that the backward thinking minds are no longer here to slow progress. Wouldn't you agree, Mr. Harper?"

A wicked smile formed at the corners of Joseph's mouth and pushed outwards until it bloomed brightly like spring flowers in the meadow.

"Actually, that's the reason I called this board meeting," he said. "With the death of Mr. Friedman, I move to suspend the announcement of our initial public offering until next month."

The room erupted with the sounds of outraged board members. As words like *ridiculous, impossible,* and *out of the question* soared around the room, Harper gleefully watched the reaction of his obese rival, smug in the knowledge that his announcement caused noticeable grief for the greedy bastard. Better still, there was nothing that Abernathy or his many brown-nosers could do to challenge his decision.

"Gentlemen, please!" he said forcefully. "Allow me to finish."

The room grew quiet again, but the angry stares remained.

"With the death of Mr. Friedman, we now have neither an acting president nor a chairman of the board. As senior vice-president, it is my duty to maintain the integrity of investments for our clients, no matter how unpopular those decisions might be. Any public offering we introduce now will be a financial sinkhole because no one will have faith in a company without leadership. If we take a few weeks to regroup, we can regain the confidence of investors and assure a successful IPO."

A wave of commotion filled the room as individual members debated the issue with those sitting beside them. From what he could discern from the conversations, Harper estimated that almost half of the board was in favor of his proposal. He was feeling quite sure of himself until he spotted the devious grin in the big screen monitor.

"I am sure I speak for everyone," began Dorian Abernathy, "when I say that far too much money has been invested in this IPO to delay it even a single day. Regardless of when we make the announcement, we are still going public the last week in October. The sooner we get the word out, the better our profits will be."

The next voice came from Justin Blair.

"I agree wholeheartedly with Mr. Abernathy," he declared. "Why let one man's death interfere with our plans for the future? I say we go ahead with the announcement as scheduled."

Harper felt his opposition growing. He glared with annoyance at the man who seemed to enjoy making a habit of being at odds with him. For every ounce of greed that filled Abernathy's wide load, so too was the junior vice-president filled with ambition. Fortunately, Abernathy's massive posterior provided plenty of room for Blair to stuff his head.

The next voice to speak belonged to Harry Easton.

"Why don't we take a vote on it?" he asked.

Always the diplomat, thought Harper.

"I hate to be the bearer of bad news, gentlemen," he said, "But there might not be a public offering at all."

"Now look!" shouted Abernathy. "You might run the minor day-to-day operations around this place, but *we* make the decisions. You got it? We're in charge! And *we* decided that we are going to start trading shares publicly. There was even a vote, or don't you remember?"

Harper could hardly contain his eagerness at overcoming this blowhard.

"Of course I remember the vote," he said. "But as *you* might recall the vote was mostly by proxy since several board members were not present the day of the vote."

"It shouldn't make any difference *how* the votes were cast as long as we have them recorded, right?" asked Easton.

"Normally you'd be right, but in this case, the official vote was set to take place yesterday morning. Mr. Friedman was planning to be in attendance."

"And?" badgered Blair.

"And…since Mr. Friedman was going to be here, he decided to hold off casting his vote until then."

Harper found himself facing down a sea of bug-eyed faces. It was Ian Goldman that was the first to speak.

"You mean…he never cast his vote?"

"That's exactly what I mean."

"What difference does that make?" demanded Blair. "The rest of us…"

"It doesn't matter," interrupted Easton. "James Friedman owned the majority share by himself. Without *his* vote we don't even meet the minimum requirement for quorum."

"It's like the vote never happened at all," agreed Goldman.

Blair clenched his fist and slammed it on the mahogany table.

"That's unacceptable!" he shouted, wincing at the sudden pain in his hand.

"Perhaps," replied Goldman. "But that's the way it is."

"What if we take another vote?" asked the Canadian member.

"Wouldn't make a difference," said Easton. "We still don't have a majority present."

"But without Friedman, aren't the rest of us here?"

"Yes, but Friedman's shares didn't vanish when he died," explained Goldman. "They belong to his estate now."

"So who's in charge of his estate?"

A dozen eyes descended on Harper.

"Yes," came the insidious voice of Dorian Abernathy. "Tell us Harper, who is the new majority shareholder?"

It had taken Detective Nick Hagan several attempts to get the Friedman family lawyer on the phone. How a lawyer remained so busy when he served only a single client, one who was deceased for that matter, was beyond him. Still, after finally reaching Victor Tchernowitz, it was Hagan who almost prematurely ended their conversation as he nearly dropped the phone from his hand.

"Did you say *all*?"

"That's right," said Victor. "In January of 2007, James came to me to redraft his will. He said it was to make provisions for his newly adopted daughter."

"Cecelia?"

"Yes, that's right. According to the new will, if Elaine passed before him, all of the assets were to be transferred to Cecelia, *to be held in trust, with disbursements made on her behalf for any and all requirements she may possess.*"

"I see…" replied Hagan. "Is that all there is?"

"Hell no! It's filled with pages and pages of legal jargon. Haven't you ever seen a will?!"

"I can't say that I have."

"Well consider yourself lucky. It's mostly inconsequential legal nonsense; a lot of it deals with the provisions of setting up the trust account, which is only really important for the lawyer who manages it."

"So who will manage the trust for her?"

"That would be me, detective. I've managed the Friedman account for a long time, and I doubt there's anyone else out there with my credentials."

"Fair enough. Do you mind if I ask you a couple of questions?"

"Was that not what we were doing?"

"I meant about Cecelia Friedman."

"Oh, I suppose not. I don't know how helpful it'll be though. It's not like we're pen pals or anything."

"I understand. But at this point we could use all the help we can get."

"I'll do my best."

"Do you know where Cecelia liked to hang out? Maybe any friends she had?"

"Has she disappeared?" he asked with concern.

"The police are still searching for her. She's been missing since the day his body was discovered. Possibly before that, we don't know."

"Well that's going to make my job especially difficult, missing client and all..." he reflected out loud. "But no, I don't know any of her friends."

"What about other relatives?"

"None. All deceased."

"Are you sure?"

Victor sighed loudly into the receiver.

"Detective Hagan, I've been James Friedman's personal lawyer for more than twenty years. In that time, I have advised him on issues ranging from taxes to insurance to lawsuits to things best not disclosed to a police detective and all the spaces in between. Do you honestly believe that there is any aspect of James Friedman's personal life that I don't know about?"

"I suppose not," replied Hagan sheepishly.

"Is there anything else, detective?"

"Just one more question. Now don't breathe too much into this, but I want your honest opinion."

"If brutal honesty is what you crave, you've come to the right place."

Nick chuckled.

"The cause of death in this case was a wound to the back of the head, and I was wondering if James Friedman had any enemies."

"Absolutely," he replied quickly. "It's hard to be both rich and famous and not accumulate a few adversaries along the way. Still, I don't know anybody who hated him enough to murder him. That's not really the *modus operandi* for the privileged society."

"What about Cecelia?"

"Is that supposed to be a bad joke?"

"Well, she did have the most to gain from his demise. Perhaps things weren't going well at home?"

"You've been reading too many Agatha Christie novels, detective. You're right that she had the most to gain from his death, especially considering the substantial life insurance policy, but I doubt James ever told her about those things. She never showed an interest in his financial endeavors and, to be quite frank, she's still a child. Why burden her with thoughts of death if you don't have to? It's not like she hasn't suffered enough in that department already."

"Even people who don't have an interest in finances still appreciate the value of money…"

"Are you kidding?! She's the daughter of James Friedman, for Christ's sake. She could have had anything she wanted at the drop of a hat. What could she gain with her father's money that she didn't have already?"

"So Friedman furnished her with lots of gifts I take it?"

"That's the funny thing; Cecelia never cared about material possessions. I guess that's a nice side effect of growing up poor in an orphanage, but it used to drive James crazy around her birthday. Where most girls would have been delighted to be showered with lavish jewelry or fancy clothes or expensive dolls, Cecelia didn't want any of it. She was just as happy reading a book."

"So there were some possessions she cared about?"

"Hah! James would have bought that girl her own Barnes and Noble had she only asked. Instead, do you know what she got?"

"What is that?"

"A library card. Can you believe that? With all the funds in the world at her disposal she still went out and borrowed second hand books. Go figure."

"His daughter?!" demanded Abernathy. "Does she even know the first thing about this company?"

"I'm sure she knows it exists," offered Harper.

"Why did he leave everything to her if she's incapable of running the show?" asked Blair.

"It's his money," chimed Goldman. "If that's what he wanted to do with it, that was his choice."

"It was a poor decision if you ask me," said Blair. "Besides, can we even be sure that this is his real daughter."

"Of course, it's his real daughter. Who else would she be?"

"I'm just saying before today, I didn't even know he had a daughter."

"That's because you never think about anyone but yourself."

"How dare…"

"Gentlemen!" yelled Harper, holding his hands up to cease the bickering. "This isn't helping."

"Sorry," apologized Goldman.

Blair only snorted.

"So where is Cecelia Friedman anyway?" asked Harry Easton.

"I'm not sure. The detective said she'd been missing since they found…since the incident."

Harper felt a twinge of melancholy as he thought about his deceased friend.

"Well gentlemen," he said quietly, "if there are no more questions, I need to get back to work."

Blair gave him an incredulous stare.

"You can't leave. We still have a lot to discuss."

Harper gathered up his belongings and turned to face the junior vice-president.

"We can't proceed with the IPO because there aren't enough votes to carry the motion. We can't hold a new vote because there is no chairman. And we can't vote for a new chairman until quorum is met, which can't happen until we locate Cecelia Friedman. As far as I'm concerned, we're done here."

Harper moved to the glass door and rested his palm on the handle.

"Make sure you close up when you're done," he said to Blair before pushing his way out of the office. Justin Blair slammed his fist down on the closest bit of table, a hollow thud echoing throughout the small room.

"That's just great!" roared Blair. "The fate of the company rests in the hands of some little brat, and no one knows where she is. Meanwhile, the man in charge couldn't care less. How the hell are we supposed to run this company with the two of them in charge?"

"We're not," stated Abernathy.

All heads turned toward the face taking up most of the rear display. His two fat palms were pressed against one another with his thick fingers resting against his second chin. There was a twinkle in his eye as he peered out over the boardroom.

"It's quite clear to me that Joseph Harper is every bit as much a stubborn old fool as James Friedman ever was. There is absolutely no way we can trust that man to run the company."

"What do you propose we do?" asked the Canadian member.

"First of all, how many of you still want to proceed with the IPO announcement as scheduled?"

Though some were hesitant, the majority of the hands in the room eventually went up.

"Excellent," he said, strumming his fingers together as he schemed. "I assure you all that I have a plan to settle this matter once and for all. Until then, I will ask each of you to downplay the death of James Friedman, at least for the time being."

"We can't keep the death of James Friedman a secret from the shareholders," stated Ian Goldman.

"I promise that we will disclose all necessary legal information before the date of our initial public offering. However, we don't want to create widespread pandemonium among shareholders by informing them that our company is currently being managed by some teenage girl we can't even locate. How would that look for our image? In the meantime, we have to make sure that no one finds out about our current situation."

"You mean lie?" asked Goldman suspiciously.

"I don't think we should be doing anything dishonest," said Easton. "Perhaps Harper is right; maybe we should postpone the IPO, at least for now."

Murmurs of assent traveled through the room.

"Gentlemen!" Abernathy shouted with authority. "It's not just my money on the line here. If this IPO fails now, no one in their right mind will ever want to invest in this company again. We all stand to lose millions if that happens. The future of the company lies in the success or failure of our public launch. We can't let our decisions be swayed by personal jitters or individual codes of self-righteous ethics. We need to do what's best for the company."

Abernathy heard the murmuring swing in his favor.

"I agree that the IPO should go on as scheduled," said the Canadian member, "but how do you plan on keeping Friedman's death a secret until then?"

"You let me worry about that," assured Abernathy. "Besides, as of right now, the police are still searching high and low for his missing daughter. Until they locate her, we've no reason to inform the public. It is our *moral responsibility* to allow the police department enough time to notify the next of kin before letting the whole world know about his demise."

"And how long will that take?" demanded Goldman.

Abernathy flashed him a wicked smile.

Hopefully longer than it takes to locate the girl myself.

CHAPTER 14

Olivia stirred awake, grumbling softy in protest at the invasive rays of morning sunlight penetrating through the bedroom window. Her eyelids fluttered in resistance as she attempted to force them to remain open. Despite multiple attempts, grogginess ultimately overcame motivation. Pulling the blankets over her head, she rolled away from the window and buried herself beneath the warmth and darkness of the comforter.

Spreading out over the center of the bed her outstretched arm grazed the vacant section of mattress. Olivia moved her arm up and down seeking out any trace of human presence. Finding none, she opened her eyes. A despondent sigh escaped her lips as she focused on the empty space beside her.

Olivia ran her hand over the sheet, pretending it to be Mitchell's muscular torso. She fondled the fabric with her fingertips as though she were caressing the sparse hairs on his chest. Olivia pulled the adjacent pillow closer and rested her head against it as though she were cuddling against his shoulder. Imagining the weight of the blanket being the force of his arm wrapping around her, Olivia cooed with contentment, a shiver of excitement surging through her tiny system.

Though Olivia found pleasure in this serene position, she yearned for the real thing. *How much longer would Mitchell keep her waiting?*

Mitchell's leg shook with impatience as he sat in the now crowded waiting area. Despite arriving at the unemployment office just as it opened, he was forced to wait more than two hours. At this point, his enthusiasm had been replaced by cynicism and discouragement.

The clipboard of paperwork he filled out would have drained even the most optimistic of spirits. With each page, the questions intensified until they seemed like incoherent dribble. Several times he returned to the front desk for clarification on this or that, only to discover that the receptionist's level of helpfulness oscillated between minor and none at all. Eventually he stopped caring whether the answers were right, just like that chemistry exam in college where he'd bubbled in "c" for every answer.

Perhaps the worst part of waiting was the cramped space. When he arrived, there had been three or four people. Now the entire room was filled with obnoxious individuals all trying to talk above one another. Among the crowd, Mitchell spotted a woman who, judging by the number of children, seemed to be trying to populate the entire planet by herself, a scraggly bearded gentleman who was wearing garments that had probably been to Goodwill more than once, and at least two people who smelled as though they had not bathed all summer. Mitchell shifted uncomfortably in his seat trying to avoid looking at the woman on his left, whose attire could charitably be described as revealing.

Thankfully, he didn't have to wait much longer before a woman in clunky high heels approached him. She led him to a nearby office and closed the door behind them, motioning for Mitchell to take a seat. The sudden quiet was a welcome relief to the maelstrom outside, and for a moment he forgot about the frustrations of the morning.

"What can I do for you today?" asked the woman, taking a seat behind the desk.

"I need a job," he replied jovially.

"I understand," she said, turning to her computer. "What is your full name?"

"Mitchell Flynn."

"What was your previous employment, Mr. Flynn?" she asked while typing.

"I was a teacher."

The woman made a noise that sounded like approval.

"And what was the reason for your leaving?"

Mitchell sighed heavily.

"I was asked to resign."

The woman glanced at him sympathetically, her lips pursed together almost mournfully.

"I'll just put in here that you were laid off," she said helpfully.

Mitchell smiled; *perhaps everything would work out after all.*

"How long have you been unemployed, Mr. Flynn?"

Mitchell pondered.

"About a year."

The woman gritted her teeth.

"That might be a problem," she said.

"What do you mean *problem*?" asked Mitchell with alarm.

"Well you see, Mr. Flynn..." she began, swiveling around in her chair, "we can only process claims a certain amount of time from the date of unemployment. In your particular case, the deadline for filing for benefits has long since passed."

"But I'm not interested in benefits."

"You're not?"

"No. I'm looking for a job."

"Oh...well that's a different story then."

Mitchell breathed a sigh of relief.

"I apologize for the confusion," she said. "Normally when people come here, it's to file for unemployment checks. We don't see a lot of people looking for work."

"I guess I'm a rare breed."

"Indeed. But in all honesty you didn't actually need to bother coming all the way down here just for that. All of our job listings are available on the website."

Mitchell felt something churn in his stomach.

"Excuse me?" he asked with disbelief.

The woman reached for a post-it note from her desk and began jotting down some information.

"It's very easy," she said cordially. "All you have to do is go to our website and create a profile. It takes about five or ten minutes. After that, you can search our entire database of available jobs."

She handed the information to Mitchell. Gripping the piece of paper between his fingertips, Mitchell could discern the information, but all he could think about was the hours he wasted in this horrible place. He exhaled deeply to calm his nerves before slipping the website information into his back pocket.

"I don't suppose there's a computer here that I can use?"

The woman shook her head.

"Sorry, but we don't have any for the public," she said. "If you like, there's a library not too far from here. I'm sure they have some."

Mitchell got directions and quickly headed out the front door, anxious to be away from there before the impulse to lash out overcame his inhibition.

Olivia set her breakfast plate in the sink, satisfied that this morning's load of dishes had cleared out one of the two deep bays. She made a detour at the bathroom to brush her teeth before moving to the bedroom to retrieve some cleaning supplies. Once inside, however, she found herself distracted by the reflection in the bedroom mirror.

It had only been two days since she observed the boyish-looking figure in the reflection, but this morning that image seemed a distant memory. Her blond hair flowed elegantly across her torso like silky strands of golden sun. Her once pale skin now glowed with the hue of creamy buttermilk. Where there had been the frail skeleton of a malnourished child, there now stood a vibrant young woman whose insignificant mosquito bites had developed into enticing shapely mounds. Even if it was just her imagination, Olivia marveled at the changes.

Stepping away from the mirror, she headed to the bag beside the bed which held some of her few material possessions. Reaching inside, she removed the apron that Mitchell purchased for her and tied it around her waist. With the apron in place, Olivia reached underneath and slid the only other garment off her hips, stepping out as it fell to her ankles. Olivia folded the panties neatly and placed them on the bed. With a lot of cleaning to accomplish before tomorrow's visitor, she was not going to risk damaging any of her brand new clothes in the process.

Olivia swept through the apartment like a cyclone. She filled the washing machine with clothes, washed a load of dishes, swept the kitchen floor, wiped the counters, scrubbed the toilet and tub, and put a new load of clothes in the washer. Though the tasks required a great expenditure of energy, the last twenty-four hours filled her with such jubilation that she was functioning almost solely on adrenaline.

She dragged one of the island stools to the living room and propped it beside the closest bookshelf. Paying special attention to balance herself on it, Olivia moved the books from the top shelf and placed them on the upper ledge, making sure to maintain their current order. She was surprised to discover a second row of books behind the first, but continued her task all the same.

Using a dishcloth and household cleaner, she dusted and polished the now empty space. Confident that the vacant section had been completely purged of contaminants, she dried the area with a paper towel before returning the books to their rightful location.

As she wiped down each individual book, Olivia came across a particularly unusual volume. Whereas the rest of the books had been tomes by famous philosophers and great thinkers, this one was a novel by Jane Austen. As she cleaned the cover, the weight shifted unevenly in her hand. Turning it over to dust the pages she found them to be solid.

An artificial book?

Even before prying open the wooden case, Olivia was certain of what lay beneath its cover. She pulled back the lid to reveal an unopened bottle of Irish whiskey. Judging by the amount of dust on the box, the bottle had been stored there a while ago.

Peering down the row of books still to be returned to the shelf, she counted three more famous titles that were likely not what they appeared to be. Sure enough, the first contained another unopened bottle of liquor, though the other two were empty.

Olivia continued to clean the bookshelf, setting each wooden box aside. When she finished with the first shelf, Olivia moved to the other. All in all, she found fifteen of his special hiding spots. Some contained unopened bottles, some were empty, but none had partially drunk bottles, nor had they secreted anything other than alcohol.

Olivia took a seat on the couch and stared at the troublesome stack before her. *It was all happening again. How many men's lives would she have to witness being ruined by this dreadful substance? Mitchell was heading down the same road that had led to Mr. James' demise. How could she rescue him from the same fate?*

The more she thought about it, the simpler her decision became. Olivia grabbed the first few boxes and carried them to the sink. She opened the top cover, removed the vodka bottle and dumped the contents down the drain. She placed the empty bottle in a trash bag designated for recycling and the artificial box in another to be hauled to the dump. She took the next one and repeated the process.

When the last bottle had been dealt with, Olivia began a scavenger hunt for any other hidden treasures. She checked inside the cabinets, in the furniture, under the bed and beneath the kitchen sink. Even as she continued to clean the apartment, Olivia gave due diligence to discovering and disposing of all the intoxicants she found. In spite of the impending argument that would surely ensue from her rogue operation, Olivia carried on, prepared to beg forgiveness, but never for permission.

Justin Blair was startled by the invasive beeping noise filling his corner office. After regaining himself, he reached across the desk and pressed the button on his intercom machine.

"I have Mr. Abernathy on line one," sounded the voice through the speaker.

"Thank you, Emily," he replied.

Blair let out a bleak sigh. The fact that Dorian Abernathy was looking for him was definitely not a good sign. It had always been a chore to be polite to the man, but it was even harder to ignore his money. Blair picked up the receiver.

"Good afternoon. This is Justin Blair."

"Hello, Mr. Blair," greeted Abernathy in a manner far too friendly for his usual decorum. "How are you doing this fine day?"

"I'm just fine, Mr. Abernathy. What can I do for you?"

Justin Blair waited patiently for the sounds of exerted respiration to subside on the other end of the line.

"That was some very unpleasant news at the board meeting this morning..."

"Yes it was," agreed Blair. "First and foremost, I want to apologize to you on behalf of my colleague. I had absolutely no idea he was going to do that, otherwise I would have warned you."

"Oh, I know you had nothing to do with this nonsense," Abernathy said pleasantly. "And there's no need to apologize...water under the bridge, so to speak."

"Yes, sir."

"The important thing is that we work toward a solution to this matter."

"What can we do?" he asked hopelessly. "Without Cecelia Friedman, our hands are tied."

"Come now boy," Abernathy encouraged. "That's the type of backward thinking that got this company into the position it's in now. Leave that defeatist attitude for the James Friedmans and Joseph Harpers of the world. You're far too intelligent and capable to fall in line behind those useless naysayers."

Blair smiled at the praise.

"It has occurred to me," continued Abernathy, "that Joseph Harper has become a massive liability to this company. He is the only one leading the charge against our going public, and he is doing it despite the majority of the board being in favor of the idea. I believe that Mr. Harper has performed admirably for us in the past, but actions speak louder than words, Mr. Blair, and this tells me it's time to bring in some fresh blood. What we really need right now is an ambitious young man who's willing to grab the reins and lead this company into the future. What do you say to that, Mr. Blair?"

Blair felt a tingling sensation in his lower abdomen.

"That sounds exactly like what the company needs, Mr. Abernathy," he said excitedly.

"I'm glad you agree, Mr. Blair. You know, you always were a team player. That's what I've always liked about you, Justin. You never let your personal qualms interfere with business. It's quite a remarkable quality to have, especially when so many of those around you lack such fortitude."

"Thank you, sir."

"Of course, what we need to accomplish first is locating this girl before Harper gets a chance to lay his hooks into her."

"What did you have in mind?"

"I'm sure that the future leader of this company will come up with something, wouldn't you agree?"

Blair felt his pulse quicken

"Yes, sir, Mr. Abernathy."

"Excellent," said Abernathy, audibly licking his lips. "My personal jet touches down back in the states first thing Tuesday. I expect I will have a private meeting with this missing child on Wednesday morning?"

Blair swallowed hard.

"Yes, sir, Mr. Abernathy."

"Good. And Justin…"

"Yes?"

"Try to keep this from reaching the press until after I've had a chance to *discuss things* with little Miss Friedman."

The phone clicked silent.

Justin Blair hung up the receiver and immediately pressed the intercom button; the adrenaline had already begun to surge through his veins.

"Yes, Mr. Blair?"

"Get me a private investigator on the phone, right away."

At one, Olivia took a break from her work to make lunch. Failing to find unexpired jelly, she opted for a plain peanut butter sandwich. With every bite, she strategized her next plan of attack. So far the morning's efforts had proven quite fruitful, and she intended to maintain momentum for as long as she could muster.

She glanced quickly at the clock. Mitchell had been gone a long time now, and it made her wonder if something went awry at the unemployment office. She shook her head. No time to worry about that now. Stuffing the last bite of sandwich into her mouth, she deposited the empty plate in the sink.

The first step was to rotate the laundry. After having to climb over piles of dirty clothes the last couple days, clearing a path in the bedroom gave her a great sense of accomplishment. Carrying the basket to the bedroom, she hung up what seemed to require hanging and folded the rest into drawers, periodically taking the time to hold the freshly washed clothes against her face to absorb their delightful warmth.

Returning to the living room, she glared with disgust at the assortment of debris scattered about. Clearly it was time to start hauling trash down to the garbage chute. After gathering a few items together, Olivia began turning the doorknob before she embarrassingly remembered her modest attire.

Setting the cargo aside, she unfastened her apron and draped it across the back of an island stool. In the bedroom she located her sweatpants and tank top and gave herself a once over in the mirror. The thin white material did little to conceal the features beneath, but she decided to make do. It wasn't like she intended to linger for long outside the apartment.

Leaving the door open, she dragged the bags down the hallway one at a time. Because the chute did not stay open on its own, Olivia struggled to load a bag inside, sometimes being forced to empty half its contents on the floor before she could muster the strength to lift its weight. Olivia was in the middle of fighting with a particularly cumbersome box when an apartment door opened behind her. A woman stepped out and came to her aid. Together they succeeded, both women groaning with the labor.

Olivia turned to face the woman.

"Thank you," she said.

"No problem," replied the woman. "I don't think I've seen you around here before. What's your name?"

Caught between wanting to be honest and worrying about being ratted out to Abigail, Olivia did not feel bold enough to tell her the truth.

"My name is Olivia," she said. "I'm in town visiting my uncle."

"Your uncle?"

"Yeah. He lives at the other end of the hall."

The woman glanced over her shoulder to the open door where Olivia was pointing. As she looked away, Olivia regarded the woman's unique attire. She wore a red and black plaid button-down shirt with a pair of black jeans. Her brown sandals clashed so greatly with the rest of the outfit that it bordered on rebellious. Her hair was short, noticeably less than shoulder-length. The whole ensemble reminded Olivia of a lumberjack, and she felt inspired by the tenacity of such a woman, even if it wasn't this particular individual.

Suddenly the woman's face scrunched up, as though she were trying to make sense of some elusive concept.

"You're *Mitchell's* niece?" she asked inquisitively.

Olivia nodded hesitantly.

The woman narrowed her gaze at Olivia.

"I wasn't aware that Abigail had any children." she stated suspiciously.

Ooops, thought Olivia, inwardly chastising herself over the obvious blunder.

"Oh, Aunt Abby isn't my mother," she replied with a smile. "My parents live in Chicago. They went to Europe on vacation, so I'm staying with Mi…my uncle until they get back."

The woman continued to eye her suspiciously, but dropped her defensive stance.

"I see…"

An awkward pause developed between the two, and Olivia decided to help fill that void.

"So what's *your* name?" she asked pleasantly.

There was another awkward pause as the woman hesitated.

"Harriet," she replied finally.

"It's good to meet you, Harriet," said Olivia. "How long have you lived here?"

"Well I've only lived *here* for about three years, but I moved to Pittsburgh almost a decade ago."

"What caused you to come to Pittsburgh?"

"Initially I came for school, but I dropped out after a couple semesters."

"How come?"

"I wasn't really enjoying it, then I got an opportunity to work for this magazine, and the next thing I knew, I was working full time. That's the way life goes, I guess."

"What were you studying?"

"I was a double-major actually. Communications and biology. I have no idea what I was thinking when I put those two together," she laughed.

"Is the magazine National Geographic?" Olivia asked excitedly.

Harriet shook her head.

"No, nothing that glamorous. Mostly fashion tips and relationship advice."

"Oh," replied Olivia with disappointment. "Do you still work there?"

"No, I quit after about a year and a half. The pay was definitely not worth the humiliation."

"I'm sorry to hear that," said Olivia. "So what do you do now?"

"I'm a writer."

"Oh, neat!" exclaimed Olivia. "What types of things do you write?"

Harriet looked around to make sure that no one could overhear their conversation.

"Mostly romance novels," she said, lowering her voice.

"Anything I might have read?"

Harriet let out a chuckle.

"Probably not," she said. "What I write is not really *appropriate* for a girl your age."

Olivia outwardly maintained her friendly smile, but inwardly she felt the pangs of dismissal, another person treating her as a child. Still, the situation allowed for a certain degree of mischief, which Olivia saw no reason to let pass her by.

"Why not?"

Harriet pursed her lips as she thought of a proper response.

"Well…my books have a tendency of exploring some…*adult situations.*"

"You mean, like they're violent?" asked Olivia, feigning innocence.

Harriet shook her head.

"Not *violent*, really. But there is some bad language and definitely a fair amount of sexual topics."

"Oh, ok," replied Olivia amiably.

Harriet exhaled with relief, as though she'd just avoided stepping on a land mine. Olivia took that as her cue.

"Miss Harriet," she began, "do you mind if I ask you a question?"

"Of course not, Olivia. What is it?"

"Um…What does *sexual* mean?"

Harriet's eyes grew wide, and she nervously glanced down at her wrist, although she was not wearing a watch.

"Oh, look at the time," she commented abruptly. "I really should get back to work."

"Ok," said Olivia cheerfully. "It was nice meeting you."

"And you as well," said Harriet, shutting the apartment door behind her as though it might shield her from further social faux pas.

Pleased by her performance, Olivia turned to stroll back to the apartment, happy to be making friends, but eager to return to work.

CHAPTER 15

Detective Nick Hagan laid the receiver of his phone back in its spot just as his partner Doug entered the room.

"Any luck?" asked Doug.

Nick leaned back in his chair and folded his hands behind his head. His eyes stared vacantly up at the ceiling. Werner had seen this pose many times in the past and knew not to interrupt. Eventually, a smile crossed Hagan's face.

"That was the Love on High Home for Children," he said, gesturing toward the phone.

"I'm glad they went with a nice humble name. I hate it when religious groups put themselves on pedestals."

"If you think that's bad, you try talking to them next time."

"That bad, huh? They say anything interesting?"

"Something about fire and brimstone and a burning bush, but I wasn't paying close attention. Do you suppose they were trying to invite me to a barbecue?"

"I hope not. Last time I left you in charge of a grill I almost had to file a claim on my homeowner's insurance."

"How was I supposed to know the propane tank had a leak?"

"You didn't notice the terrible smell?"

"I thought that was the tofu dogs the vegetarian couple brought. There's something unnatural about fake meat, you know?"

"All joking aside, what happened with the orphanage?"

"So you remember how Cecelia Collingwood was picked up for truancy back in 2002 and was later adopted by the Friedmans from the orphanage?"

"Yeah."

Hagan turned to his computer.

"Apparently there was an Olivia Morgan who had gone missing from the Love on High orphanage one week prior to them nabbing the Collingwood girl."

"And?"

"And I'm thinking that the two might be the same girl."

"Hey, that is something. How old was the Morgan girl?"

"Sixteen."

Doug massaged the bridge of his nose between his thumb and forefinger.

"Don't take this the wrong way, Nick, but I think that sleep deprivation has started to affect your mind."

"Wait, here me out," said Hagan, pressing the print button on his desktop.

Doug made a "go on" motion at him.

"We weren't able to discover a birth certificate for Cecelia Collingwood, and there's no record of her existing prior to being taken in for truancy. Bare minimum, we have to assume that she changed her name to Cecelia sometime between when she left home and was dropped off at the orphanage."

"Uh-huh..." encouraged Doug reluctantly.

"Assuming that she had been adopted, she likely would have at least kept her first name. Now I have searched the records high and low and there have been no missing Cecelia's in any orphanage records or filed in missing persons reports in the two years prior to her discovery."

"Ok."

"What's more is that I checked on the police reports of Olivia Morgan."

"Let me guess," interrupted Doug. "There are no records of Olivia Morgan at any point after she ran away from Love on High."

"That's almost correct," replied Nick eagerly. "There's actually been one police report filed under the name Olivia Morgan since then."

"Really? What was it?"

Hagan reached over to the printer and removed a sheet from the lower tray.

"Do you remember the couple that came in with the girl the other day?"

"Yeah."

Nick handed him the paper he'd printed out.

"Guess what the name of the little girl was?"

Doug read the name on the file.

"You've got to be kidding me?" said Doug incredulously.

"Quite impressive, isn't it?" Nick beamed.

Doug sighed heavily.

"Nick," he began softly, "how old was the Olivia Morgan who ran away from Love on High?"

"Sixteen."

"And that was in 2002?"

"Yep."

Doug shook his head, unsure if there was something he was missing or if his partner had completely lost his mind.

"The dates don't match, Nick. It says here that the Olivia Morgan they picked up yesterday was eleven. The other one would have to be in her twenties now."

"Supposedly."

"And even back in 2002, Olivia Morgan would have been five years older than Cecelia Collingwood. There's no way that they could be the same person. You said it yourself, there's no way to confuse a sixteen-year-old with someone who's eleven."

"Ah…" exclaimed Nick, raising his forefinger dramatically in the air. "But what if Olivia Morgan does indeed look the same now as she did back then?"

"What?" asked Doug in confusion.

"Bear with me here, but what if the first Olivia Morgan, for some reason or another, actually did look eleven years old?"

"Alright, fine. Assuming she did, then what?"

"Then, she changes her name to Cecelia Collingwood. For reasons unbeknownst to science, she continues not to age. She gets adopted by the Friedmans, and then the other Friedmans, before running away again after the death of James Friedman."

Doug remained speechless; staring blankly at his partner.

"After running away again, she is found by this couple. Since a long time has passed, she decides it's okay to go back to being Olivia Morgan. But once again, for reasons unbeknownst to science, her appearance hasn't altered in the slightest since her days at Love on High. She still looks like she's eleven."

"How is that even possible?" asked Doug.

Hagan grinned from ear to ear.

"That's the exciting part. I've figured it out."

"You have?"

Hagan nodded.

"Some people might tell you it's a gypsy curse, while others might say she is an evil hell spawn in disguise, but the truth is even more fascinating than that."

Doug clutched the paper tightly with both hands, following every word with bug-eyed intrigue.

"Which is?"

Hagan did a drum roll on his desk.

"Because…"

Ending the drum solo he raised his hands in the air dramatically.

"She's a vampire!"

Werner took the file in his hand, crumpled it into a ball, and threw it forcefully at his partner's face.

"Dammit Nick!"

Hagan was barely able to shield the incoming projectile due to his raucous laughter.

"What? You love conspiracy theories."

Doug rolled his eyes.

"Yeah…ones that could *actually* happen. Not a bunch of supernatural nonsense."

"Oh c'mon. You have to admit that was pretty clever."

Doug shook his head.

"So you've still got nothing?" he demanded.

"I've got you," Nick said playfully. "What else do I need?"

Doug sighed.

"I'm going to the common to get a coffee. You want anything?"

"Thanks, but I'm good. I'm going to make a few more phone calls to see if we can locate this girl."

Doug nodded but before heading to coffee, he slipped inside his own office. He reached into the bottom drawer of his desk and pulled out a thick black address book. Opening it to the desired page, he dialed the number into his cell phone, connecting to his quarry on the third ring.

At the library, Mitchell applied for several jobs online. Although he was certain that he would never get any of the positions, the effort made him feel as though the day had not been completely wasted.

Stretching both arms high overhead, Mitchell let out a loud yawn that startled his neighbors at the computer station and earned him a few angry glares from the library staff. Interlocking his hands behind his head, he peered at the clock on the wall that read 4:30. This prompted his stomach to rumble.

He was just about to get up when the calendar beneath the clock reminded him that Monday was Labor Day. It had been an exhausting week, not just for him, but for Olivia as well. If there was anybody who could use a holiday, it was both of them. Cracking the joints in his fingers, Mitchell set to work once again on the computer.

It was after 5:00 when Mitchell finally emerged from the library. As he maneuvered down the sidewalk, the cravings for alcohol soon found their way at the forefront of his thoughts. Everything that had been simple about his life seemed to have vanished in the blink of an eye and he longed for that gentle release. He passed by a corner bar and forced himself not to indulge. Mitchell desperately wanted to get back home, and the fastest way was through the liquor store.

"I had to warn you," said Ian Goldman. "It's as though Abernathy has a personal grudge against you."

"You don't say," replied Harper sarcastically.

"I'm serious, Joseph. He's been playing politics all afternoon. He even took the time to call *me*. That's how badly he wants you gone."

Harper exhaled heavily into the phone.

"You know I'm not delaying the IPO just to spite Abernathy right? I really do believe it's the best thing for the company right now."

"I know that, Joseph, and I completely agree with your decision. But Abernathy is making it seem like you have some ulterior motive for the delay. It's only a matter of time before he starts convincing others."

"I see..." replied Harper.

"Look, I'm only saying this as a friend. If Abernathy gets to that girl first, he's going to find a way to take control of this company to allow the IPO to go ahead as scheduled. You and I both know that the short-term profit is little compared to the long-term backslide. We need to find that girl before Abernathy does."

"Hmmm..."

"What is it Joseph?"

"I think I might have an idea that will delay the IPO and take the pressure off of us at the same time."

"What is it?" asked Goldman.

"You've always been a good friend to me, Ian. That's why I don't want to involve you in this plan, just in case the whole thing turns sour. You've got a lot more to lose in this than I do."

"Okay. Just take care of yourself."

"You, too."

"Oh, and Joseph?"

"Yes?"

"Are you going to be around for temple tomorrow night? We're supposed to be having that guest rabbi come to speak."

"I'll be there. At this rate I could use all the help I can get."

Mitchell slowly trudged down the hall to his apartment. The day's tedious tasks had drained him of energy and the extra weight from the bottles in his coat did little to relieve his burden. After the day he had endured, it was looking like another pizza night.

When Mitchell closed the apartment door behind him, he stared in astonishment at the complete change of decor. Everything looked immaculate. The floors had been swept and mopped, every piece of furniture was thoroughly dusted, and everything reeked of the smell of cleansers, which was a welcome surprise to the usual garbage odor.

Mitchell removed his coat and hung it by the door before advancing further into the pristine abode. As he progressed, the innocuous vapors of lemon-scented furniture polish were replaced by the salivating aroma of slow-cooked beef. After taking a moment to enjoy the pleasant fragrances of the kitchen, he continued in search of his small companion.

He found her standing beside the bed, carefully pulling clean laundry from a basket and folding it into neat piles on the bed. She wore the apron he had bought for her, although its red color had been covered in a layer of dust. Quietly approaching behind her, Mitchell wrapped his arm around her in an affectionate hug.

Olivia let the item in her hand fall gracefully onto the bed and returned the embrace by clutching his arm with both of hers. She leaned her head backwards against his chest until she was able to apply a tender kiss on his cheek.

"How did the job search go?" she asked gently.

She felt his body stiffen.

"Not so well," he replied solemnly.

"It's ok," she said reassuringly. "There's always tomorrow."

He nodded, though was clearly not convinced.

"Are you hungry?" she asked.

Again, Mitchell nodded weakly.

"I've got some soup simmering in the pot out there. Why don't you get a hot shower? It should be ready by the time you get out."

Mitchell touched his face to hers before giving one last loving squeeze and pulling away. Taking a seat on the edge of the bed, he removed his shoes and socks, asking Olivia where to put his dirty laundry. She watched him intently as he slowly unbuttoned and removed his shirt, exposing his muscular physique. Olivia bit her lip in lascivious anticipation as Mitchell undid the clasp of his belt.

Sadly, before he removed anymore of his clothes, Mitchell grabbed a clean pair of pants and a shirt and made his way into the bathroom. Resisting the urge to follow, Olivia heard the door close quietly behind him. She took a deep breath to steady her rapid heartbeat and then resumed folding laundry.

Olivia returned to the kitchen stove and stirred the pot. She spooned some of the broth into a ladle, blowing gently across the surface several times before bringing it to her lips. She swished the warm liquid analytically back and forth before deciding to add some more black pepper.

Content with the soup, Olivia looked on the counter for any bags that Mitchell might have brought in. Finding none, she searched the living room. Still not having discovered any special packages, Olivia moved the investigation to his coat. Inside, she discovered two bottles which had not yet been opened.

Taking a moment to make sure that the water was still running in the shower, she slipped quickly back into her sweatpants and tank top. At the end of the long corridor, she tossed the full bottles down the trash chute, only remembering on her way back that they probably should have been dumped out first. Hopefully, the building wasn't old enough to still have an incinerator.

Back inside the apartment, Olivia realized that she could no longer hear running water. Gripped with panic, she moved swiftly to the bedroom, stripping out of her clothes as fast as she could, taking the time to fold them and return them to their original location. Olivia was on her way back to the kitchen when the bathroom door abruptly opened. She stopped dead in her tracks and stared at him like a deer in headlights.

"What are you doing?" Mitchell asked, raising an eyebrow at her.

"I uh..."

"Yes?"

With an idea suddenly coming to mind, Olivia clasped her hands behind her back and craned her neck to gaze innocently up at him.

"I was just hoping to catch a peek," she said with a coy grin.

Mitchell rolled his eyes.

"Sorry to disappoint," he replied.

"Well, dinner is ready," she said. "Why don't you pour us each a bowl? I'm going to slip into some clothes."

"Should I be expecting company then?" he asked suspiciously.

Olivia swung back around, relieved that he hadn't noticed that she'd forgotten to put the apron back on after her endeavor. Keeping her arms behind her, Olivia tilted her head to the side.

"The soup's hot, Mitchell."

"Uh-huh...And?"

Olivia brought a finger to her lip, tenderly ran it down her chin, over her slender neck and across her naked sternum.

"You wouldn't want me to spill any on my sensitive skin now would you?" she teased.

Mitchell found himself glancing away, his face already changing color.

Victor Tchernowitz put down the phone receiver. Although they still had not been able to locate Cecelia Friedman, Joseph Harper seemed to think that if they posted an announcement in the paper, it might cause the girl to come forward. Tchernowitz was unconvinced, but assented since it had been two days since James Friedman's body was found.

Tchernowitz reflected on what he knew about Cecelia Friedman. He had met the girl on a few occasions. She was quiet and small; easily overlooked in any gathering. Even though such functions required formal attire, the dresses she wore were plain, with absolutely no glamour or glitz. Cecelia did not wear jewelry and, at least as far as he knew, she didn't even have her ears pierced. She did not wear glasses, did not have any noticeable birth marks, and certainly did not have any tattoos. Although Victor approved of the last bit, his description so far was looking particularly worthless in helping to locate her.

In his mind, Olivia's most discernable characteristics were not the physical ones. He remembered that she was smart, probably from years devoted to reading. There was that soft spot she had for animals, even the creepy crawly ones. But what stuck out most was that she was kind. After decades of being solidly devoted to the estate of James Friedman, Victor had forgotten that compassion and politeness even existed. *How strange a world it must be that a miserable wretch like James Friedman could ever end up the father of a sweet girl like Olivia.*

And now that she was missing, Victor feared greatly for her safety. *If she had been simply visiting with a friend, wouldn't she have returned by now? If someone had attacked James Friedman and kidnapped her, wouldn't they have sought a ransom? If she was indeed ok, why had she run away?*

Victor had heard stories of wealthy business men with perverse pleasures for which they thought they were above the law. *Perhaps he came after her, and she tried to defend herself. Maybe he was greatly injured in the struggle, and guilt caused her to abscond into the night.*

Victor shook his head.

There was no chance of a girl Cecelia's size ever overpowering the portliness of James Friedman. With no answers to the multitude of questions zigzagging through his mind, Victor focused on the task at hand. Flipping open his laptop, he began typing, deciding that a cash reward might motivate people more than a proper description.

When he finished with the announcement on Cecelia, he began to write an obituary for the late James Friedman. In his many years as an estate lawyer, Victor had been forced to wear many different masks. Tonight, as Victor Tchernowitz summarized the life of his former employer, he wore the most unpleasant of all his faces: the mask of lies.

Mitchell and Olivia sat side by side on the couch, her small frame leaning against his for support. Whereas the meal rejuvenated his depleted spirit, the warm repast soothed an already exhausted Olivia into a peaceful nap. When her head became too heavy, she lowered herself into a fetal position, utilizing Mitchell's massive thigh as a pillow. The rhythmic ebb and flow of her breathing added a tranquil ambiance to the stillness of the apartment.

With Olivia's head resting in his lap, Mitchell gently ran his hand over her back, all the while imagining what life would be like for the two of them. *When you're in love, you want to shout it from the highest rooftops; you want to write songs and poetry chronicling your endless devotion, you want to have romantic getaways in exotic lands and make passionate love on remote beaches, and you want to do it all with the support of your friends and family. How could he ever find true happiness with Olivia when he couldn't even tell his own sister about it? How much of their life together would they have to spend hiding their affection for one another, as though it were something to be ashamed of?*

Mitchell felt himself being dragged toward that impending fork in the river. It was now approaching with such momentum that he would have to choose a direction soon or risk crashing upon the shores of indecision, his fate determined by the actions of those around him. So much of his life he pondered the *what ifs* and *what could have beens* that he ultimately squandered many fruitful opportunities. *Was it possible to find happiness with Olivia if it meant giving up everything else? Wouldn't life be much easier if he ignored his feelings and tried to carry on without her? Why must the road less traveled always be the more perilous journey?*

With the questions continuing to plague his mind, Mitchell fondly remembered the bottles he had stored in his coat. That sweet nectar would surely put an end to the tumultuous whirlwind battering his brain. And yet, as much as he wanted that drink, he couldn't stand the idea of Olivia seeing his inebriation. It didn't matter who else saw, just not her. Besides, she was sleeping, and he refused to move if it meant rousing her from slumber.

Suddenly, his phone lit up, its familiar ominous music tearing through the placid surroundings like a foghorn in the wee hours of the morning. Olivia stirred beneath him, her body tensing as she recognized the eerie tune.

"That's got to be Abigail," he stated, his voice carrying the same joy one reserves for a dental visit. "It was bound to happen sooner or later."

Olivia tightened her grip around his pant leg.

"Let it go to voicemail," she pleaded.

They didn't have to wait long before the ringtone silenced and was replaced by the loud beep of the notification. The message was short, Abigail requesting that he call her back as soon as possible.

"I have to call her," he said. "She's going to be pissed."

Olivia nodded her agreement.

"Wait until I get back. I want to hear what she says."

As Olivia scurried to the bathroom, Mitchell turned and propped his feet up, taking the entire couch. By the time he maneuvered into a comfortable position, preparing for a lengthy argument, the bathroom door opened. Mitchell highlighted the first name on his contacts.

"I'll put it on speaker phone," he said as Olivia drew near.

Seeing Mitchell spread out, she decided to climb on top rather than make him move. She straddled her legs around his midsection and waited for him to press the send button. On the fourth ring, a female voice resounded through the living room.

"Hello?"

"Hey…it's me."

"Oh, hey Mitchell. How are you tonight?"

"I'm good. Was your day alright?"

"Yeah, it was pretty good. Busy, but good."

Mitchell waited for her to go on, readying himself for the storm to come.

"Listen, Mitchell, I want to apologize about yesterday. I'm sorry for leaving you at the police station. I meant to come back soon, but I got so caught up in work and couldn't get away. I should have called last night to make sure you got back okay."

Mitchell and Olivia exchanged confused glances.

"That's alright," he said reassuringly. "These things happen."

"Thanks Mitchell. I know that I wasn't particularly pleasant either. You were going through a lot, and I should have been more sympathetic to your needs rather than just thinking about myself."

Mitchell rested his free hand on his forehead, as though it might relieve his bewilderment.

"Don't worry about it."

"I'm so glad to hear you say that. And look, if you start feeling lonely around the apartment with that girl gone, we can get you a pet hamster or something."

Mitchell gave Olivia a wide-eyed stare. *She doesn't know?*

"I know that this whole ordeal has been pretty rough on you, and I want to do something nice. I'm busy tonight and tomorrow, so how about this weekend we grab lunch, just the two of us? My treat."

"Uh…yeah. That sounds fine."

As they began to discuss restaurants, days and times, Olivia reached down and undid the top button of Mitchell's shirt. He shot her a look of surprise, squirming beneath her to position himself away from her fingers.

"Wha…?" he began.

Olivia put her finger to her lips, *Shhh…*

Mitchell eased back against the couch as Olivia continued to unfasten his shirt. He eyed her intently, hurrying along the phone conversation as best he could. When it ended, Mitchell set the phone down on the edge of the coffee table before looking up at Olivia.

"I guess we dodged a bullet on that one," he said with relief.

"When are you meeting her for lunch?" she asked, untucking the bottom part of his shirt.

"Saturday at noon down at the...what are you doing?"

"You heard her," said Olivia. "She's not coming by tonight."

With that, Olivia finished the last of the buttons.

"What does that have to do with anything?"

"You said it yourself; there's no need to be all dressed up if company's not coming over."

"Well that's not *exactly* what I said."

"Close enough," she argued, rubbing her hands along his bare torso.

Her fingers groping back and forth caused a spark to kindle within him.

"Olivia, I don't think we should..."

Olivia put her finger over his lips. She leaned closer to him, the thin fabric of her shirt grazing against his exposed flesh. With her form now pressed against his own, Mitchell's heart began to race. He could hear the pulse beating in his ears and feel the powerful thumping of the muscles inside his chest. Mitchell tried to calm his nerves by taking slow, shallow breaths, but all it did was leave him feeling lightheaded.

Or was there something else causing that?

"Aren't we supposed to be up early tomorrow?" he offered.

Olivia moved her face so that it hovered inches above his. Those blue sapphires sparkled in the dim lighting of the living room, somehow easing his apprehension. Tilting her head lower, she rubbed her nose against his, nuzzling affectionately before moving her mouth close to his ear.

"Excuses are for little children," she whispered seductively.

She leaned away from him, maintaining her balance by resting her palms against his abdomen. Grabbing the lower edges of her sleepshirt, Olivia raised her arms overhead and discarded it with carefree grace beside the couch.

Perhaps it was merely the dark atmosphere around us, or maybe it was the confident smile Olivia wore as she sat astride my torso, or it could even have been simply that I finally stopped lying to myself about what I wanted, but for whatever reason, all the childish features I saw in her face vanished that night. From that moment on, the little girl from the roof was no more, replaced forever in my mind by the woman whose intelligence, kindness and intrigue had so thoroughly won my heart.

In college, I had been exposed to many axioms, mantras, and aphorisms, but none had stuck with me quite as long or as deeply as the one that came to mind that night: If ever I find myself in a situation where I am both damned if I do and damned if I don't, surely I will be damned if I won't.

With nothing left to restrain me, I pulled Olivia close, embracing her with unequivocal desire, our lips coming together time and time again, long past the tingling sensations, until we finally succumbed to sleep, still wrapped in each other's arms.

CHAPTER 16

Justin Blair strolled into his office with a skip in his step. It was certainly going to be an excellent day. His conversation with Dorian Abernathy assured him that his long awaited promotion had come at last. He cheerfully stepped aboard the elevator and pressed the button.

To his right was a young woman whom he had seen around but had not actually bothered to learn her name. He always presumed that she was the secretary to one of the other executives, and therefore, wasn't that important. Despite his previous prejudice against the woman, his mood was so great on this day that he leaned over and wished her a good morning.

"Good morning to you, too, Mr. Blair," she replied. "How is your day going so far?"

Blair smiled at her.

"I have never felt better in all my life," he said.

The woman seemed taken aback by his answer, but he didn't care right now. Life was good, and everything was only going to get better. He merrily exited the lift, wishing the young woman a good day as he went.

When he arrived inside his office, Emily greeted him with a cup of coffee and the daily newspaper.

"There was a call for you from an Edith Schellman," she said, handing him a note and number.

He looked at her inquisitively.

"Who might that be?" he asked cordially.

"She said she was from the newspaper."

"Ah…she must have more questions regarding the IPO," he muttered quietly to himself. "I'll take care of it. Thank you, Emily."

Blair whistled a carefree tune as he entered the corner office and placed his belongings haphazardly on the desk. He moved to the panoramic view out the window and gazed over the beautiful cityscape. Blair took a long swallow from his coffee mug and smiled. It was such a lovely day.

He sat down in his luxurious office chair, taking time to fondle the expensive leather upholstery. Setting the mug on a ceramic coaster, Blair dialed the number for Edith Schellman. She answered on the first ring, and they exchanged salutations.

"So what can I do for you today, Mrs. Schellman?" he asked, propping his feet on the cherry-stained oak desk. "Is this about the initial public offering?"

"Actually, I had some questions regarding James Friedman."

Blair reached for his coffee mug.

"I'll do my best to answer them," he said, taking a sip from the cup.

"First of all, do you know how he died?"

Blair sputtered coffee all down his white button-down.

"Excuse me?!"

"I was wondering if you knew how he died," she reiterated louder and with more enunciation.

"Who told you James Friedman had died?" he asked in a panic.

"Well, it was in the paper this morning. Didn't you read it?"

Blair hurriedly opened the newspaper and flipped it to the obituaries. Sure enough, covering the entire page was a picture of James Friedman, solemnly smiling back at him. Blair immediately began to shred the paper while uttering expletives that carried through the receiver to Edith.

Olivia clutched her wrist tightly. The fall from the couch had been slight but her land had been awkward. The area had already begun to swell in the few minutes that Mitchell had been absent. He returned carrying a wrap bandage and a sandwich bag filled with ice.

Mitchell took a seat next to her injured arm and tenderly examined the inflamed region. Olivia winced at the pressure.

"Sorry," he muttered.

Mitchell carefully placed the bag of ice across her swollen wrist. She grimaced, though Mitchell couldn't tell if it was from the pain or from the cold. When she stopped gritting her teeth, she looked at him.

"You shouldn't have let me fall," she said.

Mitchell rolled his eyes.

"It's not my fault you were having dreams about skydiving."

She smirked at him.

"It wasn't skydiving I was dreaming about."

"Oh no?" he teased. "Was it flying squirrels again?"

She shook her head.

"No. I was dreaming about riding a horse."

"Really? What kind of horse?"

She leaned her head into his shoulder.

"A large, wild stallion," she whispered playfully into his ear.

Mitchell blushed.

"Too bad he didn't enjoy me riding him," she continued.

"What makes you say that?"

She nudged his side jokingly.

"Because he bumped me off," she said matter-of-factly.

Mitchell lifted the ice bag and peeked beneath. Not satisfied, he returned it to her arm.

"Perhaps you spooked him a little. Not all horses like to ride full gallop straight from the starting gate."

"I don't see why not," she commented. "If I was the horse, I'd want to be ridden hard and put away wet."

"Geezus, Olivia!" exclaimed Mitchell.

She flashed him a coy smile.

"Sorry," she muttered. "Was that crossing the line?"

Mitchell shook his head with mock disapproval.

"And then some."

He lifted the ice bag again. This time, the swelling seemed to have gone down.

"How does that feel?" he asked.

Olivia raised and lowered her forearm.

"It still hurts, but not as much."

Mitchell nodded. He set the ice bag aside and grabbed the bandage.

"Is it too tight?" he asked as he completed the wrap.

Olivia shook her head.

Mitchell nodded and carried the ice to the freezer. While in the kitchen, he grabbed the phone book and carried it, along with his phone, into the bedroom. Olivia could hear him talking but could not make out the words. When he returned to the couch, he had a small piece of paper with him.

"I made you an appointment to see the doctor," he said.

"I don't want to go to the doctor, Mitchell," she said in protest.

He shrugged.

"If you didn't want me to call the doctor, you should have told me."

Olivia shot him an angry look.

"I would have if you had bothered to ask."

Mitchell shrugged again.

"I guess I'll know that for next time," he said, handing over the information.

"Fine," she exclaimed, snatching the paper from him. "It's just a bruise though."

"Better safe than sorry," he replied, moving toward the kitchen.

Olivia followed, watching as Mitchell started the coffee pot.

"Would you like me to cook breakfast?" she asked.

"Don't you think you should be taking it easy?"

Olivia held his gaze.

"No," she said nonchalantly.

Mitchell sighed.

"I'll tell you what…I'll cook a light breakfast and we can go out for lunch."

Olivia shrugged.

"That seems fair," she agreed. "In the meantime, I'll pick out something for you to wear."

Mitchell watched her head toward the bedroom, quietly shaking his head as he reached for a frying pan. When she returned, they switched places, and she managed the frying pan while he got dressed. By the time he came back, she'd finished the eggs.

"I poured you some coffee," she said, pointing to the island.

Mitchell took his seat, delighted that she fixed his coffee the way he likes it.

"Thank you," he said, gesturing with his cup.

Olivia gave him a warm smile as she set plates on the island and took the adjacent chair. As she sat down, Mitchell glanced over at her nearly bare form.

"Don't you think you should consider getting dressed soon?" he asked.

Olivia sipped her coffee.

"It's barely after ten," she said. "I've still got plenty of time."

"Yeah, but aren't you a little cold?"

"I'm comfortable. Why? Is this bothering you?"

Mitchell looked down at his plate.

"It's not that it bothers me, it's just kind of awkward to be sitting here in a suit and tie when you're almost naked. I feel a bit overdressed for the occasion."

Olivia raised an eyebrow at him.

"Would you like me to get changed?"

Mitchell nodded.

"If you don't mind."

"Okay."

Olivia stood from her stool and turned her back to Mitchell. Clasping the top of her waistband, she maneuvered the thin material down her legs, making sure to gyrate her hips the entire descent. When they slid off her feet, she carried the undergarment to Mitchell and draped it delicately across his forearm. His mouth hung loosely open as she retook the stool beside him, taunting him with her eyes and sipping from her mug.

"There's no point in arguing with you is there?"

"No," she stated matter-of-factly. "Not unless you enjoy losing."

"Oh, I may have lost the war," he said, "but I assure you that I am *very* happy with the terms of surrender."

Olivia rose again from her chair, padded softly across the floor, and planted a kiss on his cheek.

"I'm going to get dressed," she said, tussling his hair as she went.

Mitchell swiveled around in his chair to watch her go, never once feeling guilty about stealing a glance.

Dr. Faust arrived a few minutes ahead of schedule with clipboard in hand. As Mitchell invited her across the threshold, she gave a quick look around the place, nodding quiet approval as her pen furiously attacked the paper.

"You have a nice home," she said with a smile.

You should have seen it a few days ago.

"Thank you."

Mitchell directed her to one of the island chairs, and she graciously took a seat, plopping heavily against the padded back. She continued to scribble notes on her legal pad as she spoke. Several times Mitchell tried to sneak a peek at her papers, but the chicken scratch eluded him.

"Would you like some coffee?" he asked. "Or something else to drink?"

"No, thank you," she said with a shake of the head. "I can't stay for long; I have another appointment on the other end of town in less than an hour."

"I see," replied Mitchell, hoping that her short visit was a positive sign.

"How long have you lived here?" she asked.

"In Pittsburgh?"

"Actually, I meant this apartment."

Mitchell thought.

"A few years."

Dr. Faust took a note down on her clipboard, giving another approving nod.

At that moment, Olivia exited the bathroom wearing a pair of brand new jeans and a light blue t-shirt. She waved hello to Dr. Faust before taking a seat beside her.

"Good morning," she said with a smile.

"Good morning, Olivia. Did you sleep well?"

Olivia glanced over at Mitchell.

"Very well. Last night was probably the best night's rest I've had in my whole life."

"I'm glad to hear that," replied Faust, still not looking up from her notes. "And how has everything else been?"

"Fantastic. Mr. Mitchell and I are going out for lunch today. Isn't that exciting?"

Faust nodded absently, finally looking up from her paperwork at Olivia.

"Oh, my. What happened there?" she asked with concern.

Olivia glanced down at her bandaged wrist.

"Oh, that? I fell out of bed."

"You fell out of bed?" she asked suspiciously.

Olivia nodded.

"My foot caught on the blanket as I was standing up and down I went. I can be a little clumsy some times."

"I see...and did you go to the doctor?"

"It just happened this morning. Mr. Mitchell put some ice on it, and it feels much better now."

"She has an appointment with the doctor tomorrow morning." chimed Mitchell. "It was the earliest I could get her in."

Faust nodded her agreement.

"Better safe than sorry, right?" she said.

Mitchell shot Olivia a smug look. She waited until Dr. Faust looked away before narrowing her eyes menacingly at him.

"So how's the job hunt going, Mr. Flynn?"

"Eh, not so good. The economy is kind of in a slump at the moment."

"That's understandable. Have you filed for unemployment?"

Mitchell shook his head.

"No, but I am using the unemployment office's website to look for a job."

"What would you say is your primary source of income?"

"After my last job, I was given a considerable sum as severance pay. I've been living off that plus some money my father left when he passed away."

Dr. Faust made one last footnote before clicking the pen closed and sliding it into the breast pocket of her shirt.

"I also have some things I want to discuss with you," she said, pointing to Olivia. "Preferably in private."

Dr. Faust glanced over at Mitchell.

"By all means," he said, motioning toward the bedroom. "I'll be outside the door if you need me."

"No problem," said Olivia. "Let me get some coffee. Do you want any?"

Dr. Faust raised an eyebrow.

"I'm good," she replied.

Olivia grabbed her mug and headed toward the bedroom. Dr. Faust took a few steps in that direction and paused.

"Make yourself comfortable," she called. "I will be right in."

Olivia nodded and closed the bedroom door. Dr. Faust turned to Mitchell.

"Mr. Flynn, could you get me a glass of water?" she asked politely.

Mitchell nodded, reaching for the pitcher inside the refrigerator. As he handed the glass to her, she stepped in close and spoke in a hushed voice.

"You know, Mr. Flynn, coffee is not really good for a girl her age."

Mitchell shrugged.

"It's not much better for you and me," he said casually.

He could tell by her body posture that this was not the answer she was looking for.

"But, I'll keep it in mind," he said quickly.

Dr. Faust nodded appreciatively before disappearing into the bedroom.

Mitchell escorted Olivia down the sidewalk to the diner, their arms interlocking at the elbows. Their meeting with Dr. Faust had been a resounding success, with the therapist thanking him for the efforts he made in caring for Olivia. Perhaps she would have thought twice before congratulating him if she'd known the truth.

"So what did you two discuss back there?"

"You."

"Me?!"

"Of course. What did you think we'd be talking about?"

"I don't know. Maybe I assumed you'd be chatting about how things were going with you, how you were adjusting, things like that. What did she ask about me?"

"What it is like living with you, and how the job hunt is coming along, and whether or not you are abusing me. You know, the usual stuff."

"She asked if I was abusing you?"

Olivia held up her bandaged wrist.

"I guess it does look a little suspicious," he admitted. "What did you tell her when she asked?"

Olivia shot him a mischievous grin.

"I said you only spanked me when I was being *naughty*."

"I see...does that mean I need to pick up a paddle on the way home?"

"Or you can use your bare hand," she said, nudging him playfully in the side. "I don't mind."

"Uh-huh...I don't suppose she asked you anything else I might need to be aware of?"

Olivia hesitated.

"She may have wanted to know if you'd tried to put your hands on me."

"How is that different from abuse?"

"I meant sexually."

"Oh..." said Mitchell, opening the diner door for her. "And you said?"

Olivia shrugged.

"Nobody's perfect."

Once inside they were led to a booth near the back on the right-hand side of the restaurant. There was a small lunch crowd. Mitchell counted two elderly gentlemen near the entrance, a duo wearing college duds and a lone man who appeared to be in his early forties. Mitchell took the seat facing the wall. The server noted their drink orders and headed off.

"We should do something to celebrate," said Olivia, setting her menu aside.

"Absolutely," agreed Mitchell. "What are we celebrating?"

"My extended stay at your deluxe penthouse apartment," she said cheerfully.

Mitchell raised an eyebrow at her over the top of his menu.

"Let's not count our chickens," he said, returning to the lunch section.

"Oh come on, admit it. We had a major victory today."

"That's true, but if you're going to be allowed to stay, I still need to find a job."

"Don't be such a pessimist," she chastised. "We haven't had the best of luck lately, and we should take some time to appreciate when something goes in our favor."

"Sorry," he muttered. "What would you like to do?"

The server returned with their drinks and Mitchell requested another moment to glance over the menu. When she'd gone again, Olivia spoke up.

"Well, since Monday's a holiday, how about we do something then? Catch a movie? There's bound to be something good playing."

Mitchell shook his head.

"It can't be this weekend."

"Why not?"

"Saturday I have to meet Abigail, and I don't know how long that'll take. Then we have something planned for Sunday."

Olivia looked at him curiously.

"We do?"

Mitchell nodded just as the server came back around. Mitchell put in his order, Olivia eyeing him suspiciously. Recovering from her distraction, she gave the server her selection, thanking her as she returned the menu. When the waitress was out of earshot, Olivia turned back to Mitchell.

"What do we have planned on Sunday?" she demanded.

"I wish I could tell you," he said with a sly smile, "but I've been sworn to secrecy."

Olivia narrowed her eyes at him.

"Just tell me."

Mitchell shook his head.

"Can't. It's a surprise."

Olivia's eyes widened with excitement.

"What kind of surprise?" she asked gleefully.

"You'll have to wait until then," he said.

Olivia folded her arms across her chest and gave him a pouting look. He only chuckled.

"We can do something tonight to celebrate," he offered.

Olivia pondered, her eyes sparkling with delight as an idea came to mind.

"Well, there is one thing I would like to do…"

"Oh yeah? What's that?"

Mitchell felt something brush the inner aspect of his left thigh. Olivia flashed her eyebrows suggestively across the table at him as she continued to run her foot up and down. Mitchell pulled his leg away.

"Don't you think of anything else?"

"I'm twenty-three and still a virgin. What do you think?"

"I think that there's more to life than sex."

"Says the person who's been married. You've probably had sex 100 times already."

Mitchell sighed heavily.

"Look, there's nothing wrong with being a virgin. I was around your age for my first time."

Olivia glared disbelievingly at him.

"Ok, maybe it was a few years before," he admitted. "But just because I was younger doesn't mean you need to rush into it."

"I don't understand why we need to wait. It's not like you haven't done it already. You do like me don't you?"

"Of course."

Olivia hung her head.

"Is it because I'm not attractive?"

"What? Who said you weren't attractive?"

"Well I don't look like other women," she pointed out. "They…"

"I don't care what other women look like," he interrupted.

Mitchell reached across the table and placed a hand on top of hers and the other beneath her chin, lifting it so that he could peer into those deep, blue sapphires.

"Yes, other women might have features that you don't, but do they have velvety blond hair that smells like bliss or eyes so gorgeous that it's like gazing into the heavens?"

A grin began to form at the corners of her mouth.

"And who could ever match that sexy little butt of yours?"

Her lips curled into a full-fledged smile.

"That's better," he said, releasing her chin.

Olivia shifted nervously in her seat.

"If you find me so alluring, then why…?"

"Because even though it wouldn't be my first time, it would still be my first time with *you*. I want our first time together to be special, the culmination of a beautiful day on the beach or a passionate release after an exciting event, not just a quick fling back at my place. You mean so much more to me than that."

Olivia glanced down at the table, her face flushing from emotion.

"It's definitely not me then?" she asked, returning her eyes to his.

"Of course not," said Mitchell, interlocking his fingers with hers. "I love you, Olivia."

Her eyes grew wide and Mitchell quickly realized his blunder.

"I mean…"

But before he could recant his comment, Olivia pulled closer and pressed her mouth to his. Mitchell gave no resistance, and the world slipped away from them. For an endless moment they were caught in ecstasy, two souls weaving together in space, desperately clinging to one another, breathing the same air, sampling the same sweet essence, merging themselves into a single entity.

They were brought crashing back to reality by the sound of shattering glass. Mitchell pulled back, gazing longingly into those entrancing blue orbs, still lost in their Elysium. It wasn't until Olivia forcefully shoved herself away from him that he noticed the unwelcome voyeur. Mitchell swallowed hard as he turned his eyes to the waitress who now stood above a pile of food and broken dishes, hands clenched fiercely by her sides and every bit of her shaking uncontrollably with anger.

CHAPTER 17

The waitress raised a trembling hand, pointing her finger at Mitchell with vicious accusation. Her lips moved but no words formed as her face contorted into an expression of horror usually reserved for tarantulas and scorpions. The two culprits sat perfectly still, neither daring to move, too afraid their actions might set off an irreversible chain reaction.

Olivia's mind revved like a six-liter engine firing on all cylinders, every piston working overtime to come up with a solution. Devising an exit strategy is never an easy matter, especially when standing in the middle of the storm, and yet she managed it all the same, forming a viable explanation in those few fleeting seconds of agonizing silence. Unfortunately, before she could implement her idea, Mitchell spoke, pleading the most self-incriminating statement a man has ever uttered to another human being.

"Wait, I can explain."

The woman suddenly found her voice again, her face like stone, words biting like shards of ice in a blizzard.

"You bastard!" she yelled.

Mitchell rose from the table, holding his hands up defensively, motioning for her to lower her voice.

"Calm down," he pleaded. "It's not what you think."

His movement only made the situation worse; further fueling the woman's rage and causing her to scream more obscenities. Reaching inside her apron she withdrew a leather check holder and launched it at him with all her might. Mitchell groaned in pain as the projectile made contact with his right eye.

Olivia slid from the booth and leapt to his side.

"Are you alright?" she asked in a panic.

Mitchell nodded, still clutching his eye.

"I'm fine. She just surprised me."

"I think we should go," whispered Olivia into his ear.

Mitchell nodded, whipping out his wallet and throwing a few bills haphazardly across the table. When he turned back around, he felt a sharp blow impact the side of his head. He recoiled in pain, gripping the table for support as Olivia let out a shrill cry beside him.

Guided by instinct, he managed to deflect the next incoming strike. Holding his arms defensively above him, he watched as the waitress swung repeatedly with a heavy plastic tray. With her quick speed and his wounded eye, the server was able to connect almost as many times as he was able to block. She shouted defamatory insults with every blow.

"Pervert!...Pedophile!...Scumbag!"

Out of the corner of his good eye, Mitchell could see that an audience was growing. A man approached the commotion, a metallic name badge displayed prominently on a white button-down shirt. Unwilling to enter the fray, the manager called out to the waitress who was still busy pummeling Mitchell with the serving tray.

"What's going on here?" he demanded.

The waitress ceased her assault to answer, though never relinquished her tight grip on her weapon.

"I caught this sleazeball putting his hands on that little girl," she explained.

"That's not what happened!" exclaimed Olivia, her voice drowned out by all the shouting.

Hearing the words from the server, the lone middle-aged man rose from his seat and stepped to the forefront of the fracas. He shoved Olivia aside, holding up both fists as he moved in and took a wild swing at Mitchell. Mitchell managed to dodge the attack, but was clobbered by the tray instead. He sidestepped the next assault by the waitress, but got nicked on the jaw by an incoming fist. Noticing that the two college boys began to make their way over, Mitchell took a step backward to distance himself from the onslaught.

As Olivia stood unprotected nearby, the manager grabbed her by the wrist and dragged her away from the melee.

"Come on. We'll call the police," he told her.

Olivia dug her heels in, but her small frame offered only minimal resistance. She tried to yank her arm free but his grip was firm around her wrist. He responded to her struggles by pulling so hard that Olivia thought her arm might rip from the socket.

"Ow!" she cried out. "You're hurting me."

The man ignored her and continued pulling her toward the back of the restaurant. The closer they got to the door, the more Olivia struggled to break free. Wincing from the bruise forming on her wrist, she swung her arm about desperately, but he did not release her. Terrified of what might happen if the police were called, Olivia tried the only tactic left at her disposal.

"Mitchell!" she shouted above the noise of the restaurant. "Save me!"

Even from far away, those words penetrated deep into his skull, shoving aside all else. Scanning his surroundings, Mitchell centered on Olivia and how she was crying out in pain. The placid, ambient lighting of the restaurant was immediately replaced by a thin veil that bathed everything he saw in a deep red hue. A carnal roar escaped his lips as he steeled himself against his attackers.

When the middle-aged man took another wide swing at him, Mitchell parried the assault, countering with a powerful knee strike to the midsection. With him doubled over in agony, Mitchell grabbed the back of the man's neck and forced his head into the edge of the booth table. The man's body went limp.

Mitchell dodged the incoming tray, grabbing its edges with both hands after it missed his face. Fueled by rage, he ripped the item from her hands and snapped it effortlessly over his knee. Tossing the pieces aside, he stepped forward, causing the waitress to retreat to the far corner of the restaurant.

After a few more steps, he encountered the college students, two young men who fanned out around him. The boy on his left was the first to move, throwing a forceful punch aimed at Mitchell's face. He managed to dodge the haymaker, and the one that followed. On the third, Mitchell ducked low, lifted the boy overhead, and deposited him on top of a nearby table. The young body struck with such force that the table gave way and landed the boy in a broken heap upon the floor.

The second young man, hoping to avenge his fallen comrade, rushed to tackle the larger man's knees. Mitchell easily overcame the momentum, grabbing hold of the youth's neck and arm in a headlock. Mitchell spun clockwise, gathering speed as he swung his assailant around. With one final rotation, Mitchell released his hold and sent him flying into a row of chairs like a human bowling ball.

Departing from the growing mound of bodies, Mitchell headed to the source of his beloved's distress. He located her near the back, grimacing in pain as a man dragged her to and fro. Mitchell pointed his finger menacingly at the manager.

"Let her go!" he growled.

The manager froze in terror as the enraged behemoth stormed toward him. He desperately tried to release his grip on the small girl, but fear had taken over, and he couldn't force himself to let go. Even when Mitchell was close enough to grab his collar, all he managed to do was let out a pathetic whimper.

With his words continuing to go unheeded, Mitchell reared back his free arm and struck the man in the center of his forehead. The grip on Olivia slackened immediately as the manager crumpled to the floor. The matter resolved, the world resumed its normal color, the veil of red fading from Mitchell's vision. Olivia still clutched her wrist tightly, her warm smile a welcome glow of sunshine after his scarlet covered dome of bloodlust.

Olivia released her wrist and held both arms high overhead, flexing her tiny fingers rapidly. Mitchell followed the cue, lifting her lightweight body off the floor and cradling her in his arms as the two absconded from the scene.

Mitchell continued to move as quickly as his legs would carry them. For a moment, it had seemed that all of their freedom had been at stake, and he would not feel safe until they were back in his apartment.

He looked over his shoulder to be sure that neither the patrons nor the staff had followed them. Mitchell slowed his pace to keep from attracting unwanted attention, although his pulse continued to race from the adrenaline coursing through his veins. His heartbeat continued to surge even as he boarded the elevator up to his apartment.

When Mitchell emerged from the lift, he breathed a sigh of relief that they were almost in the clear. Shuffling down the hallway he was startled by a voice calling his name. He reluctantly turned to face his neighbor.

"Hey, Mitchell," called Harriet.

"Good afternoon, Ms. Vilespy," he replied. "How are you today?"

"I'm great," she said enthusiastically. "And please call me Harriet."

Mitchell nodded.

"I would ask if you went on a walk with your niece, but it seems that you are the one doing all the walking," she joked.

Mitchell glanced inquisitively down at Olivia over the word *niece*. She gave a subtle nod.

"We went for a walk after lunch, and she got a little tired so we came back," he explained.

"Oh my," she said worriedly. "Are you doing ok, dear? Feeling sick?"

Olivia shook her head.

"No. I'm fine. I just get tired sometimes. How is your writing going Harriet?"

"It's great. I've gotten through my quota for the day, so I decided to take a break for dessert at the bistro around the corner. You are welcome to join me," she invited.

"Maybe next time," said Mitchell.

"Oh, ok," she said. "Have a wonderful afternoon. I hope you feel better."

"Thanks."

They watched as the elevator door closed before continuing down the hallway. Mitchell set Olivia down to retrieve his keys. After they entered, Mitchell made sure to secure the deadlock before turning his back to the door and leaning heavily against its solid surface for support.

"That was exciting," commented Olivia as she removed her shoes. "Would you like me to make some food?"

Mitchell moved forward, wrapping his massive arms around her in a passionate embrace. Olivia could feel his entire body quivering against her.

"I thought I lost you," he said quietly.

Olivia pulled close, resting her head against his shoulder and patting him gently on the back.

"When that man took you...I..."

"Shhh...It's okay. We're safe now. That's all that matters."

Mitchell shook violently.

"I didn't want to hurt them. It was just...they..."

Olivia rubbed his back soothingly a moment before pulling away.

"I know you didn't mean it," she said, placing her hand on his cheek. "It's not your fault. You did what you had to."

As Mitchell gazed into those starry blue sapphires, something came over him. Caught between the thrill of the day's adventure, the abundance of adrenaline in his system, and the affectionate caress of Olivia's soft fingertips across his face, Mitchell could no longer resist the carnal urges building in his loins.

Olivia cooed softly as Mitchell touched his lips to hers, probing her mouth gently with his tongue. She latched onto his neck with both hands as he lifted her from the floor, her tiny legs wrapping tightly about his midsection. Never breaking their kiss, Mitchell carried her into the bedroom and deposited her gently on the mattress.

Kicking off his loafers, Mitchell positioned himself directly over her, making sure to keep his body weight off her small frame. Mitchell leaned forward to kiss her on the mouth before traveling lower to kiss her chin, her neck, and finally the top of her exposed sternum. He ran his hands delicately over her face, lightly massaging the ears between his fingers.

Moving south he lifted the bottom part of her shirt from its tucked position to expose her bare abdomen. Olivia moaned softly as he planted tender kisses in the region between her belly button and the top of her jeans. Her excited shrills only intensified as his tongue replaced his lips.

Olivia sat up and pulled his head away from her abdomen. As they continued to make out, Olivia undid the buttons on his shirt, helping to push the fabric off his shoulders as the last one came loose. Mitchell slid his hands beneath her t-shirt and pushed it up until it slid overhead, exposing her chest.

Olivia leaned back against the pillows, closing her eyes as Mitchell explored her bare torso. He placed his hands at her waist, ran his fingers up to her navel and retreated back to the top of her jeans. Mitchell continued to move his hands back and forth, pushing higher with every stroke, until Olivia gasped with elation as he touched her bare nipples, her body tensing with the unfamiliar sensations.

After a few more passes, Mitchell reached for the top of her jeans. His hands shook violently as he unfastened the clasp, the images around him growing fuzzy. Shaking off the fatigue, Mitchell managed to undo the fastening, lowering the zipper to expose a pair of blue and yellow lace hipster panties. He gave her glutes a tender squeeze before sliding the jeans the rest of the way off her body.

While down below, Mitchell took hold of the first of her socks and removed it from her foot, planting a tender kiss on its dorsal side before moving to the next. When the second one lay bare, Mitchell lightly tickled the underside. Olivia giggled as she kicked free of the teasing hands and rolled just out of his reach. As she lay on her stomach, Olivia bit her lip seductively and started wiggling her butt enticingly in his direction.

Mitchell grinned at her playfulness, eager to pounce on her.

Without warning, his chest constricted, and his vision blurred. He attempted to shake off the lightheadedness the way he had before, but it was to no avail. He clutched his chest in a vain attempt to slow his heart rate and reduce the pulsing thump inside his head. His breathing grew erratic as he struggled to maintain consciousness. As the world faded to darkness, Mitchell could clearly make out the distant sounds of Olivia calling his name.

Two officers from the city arrived at the mom and pop diner within an hour of the incident. There were already ambulances parked outside the restaurant as they pulled up. They entered through the main entrance and were immediately stunned by the destruction and carnage. It didn't so much look like a family establishment as the scene of a barroom brawl.

Medical professionals had already begun to see to two boys in their late teens, presumably college students based on their attire. Though both were battered and bruised, neither seemed seriously injured. The officers approached with the first of them flashing a badge.

"Good afternoon, gentlemen. I'm Officer Jeffries and this is Officer Price. Can you tell us what happened?"

One boy shook his head at the other, and neither said a word.

"Have it your way," said Jeffries before walking away.

Moving on, they came upon where the middle-aged man lay on the floor. An emergency rescue person was moving a finger to and fro in front of his eyes and analyzing his response with a flashlight. The man seemed like he was going to be alright, but answering basic questions was probably a bit advanced for him right now.

Continuing around the restaurant, they found a waitress sitting at a table in the back. Despite the no smoking sign on the front door, she was puffing away like a locomotive. Unlike the others, she seemed completely unscathed, at least physically.

"Excuse me, ma'am," said Jeffries, "Would you mind telling us what happened here?"

She didn't waste any time.

"Yes. It was all that monster's fault. First, he put his hands on that little girl, and then he assaulted the rest of the patrons. He even attacked Terry."

"Who's Terry?"

"The manager. He's over there," she pointed.

Jeffries followed her finger to a man on the floor. Paramedics were over top of him as well.

"They say he'll be fine, but all he was trying to do was protect that little girl. He didn't deserve to be beaten up for that."

"Where is the little girl?" asked Price.

The woman shrugged her shoulders.

"He made off with her. We tried our best to stop him, but he overpowered us."

The officers looked at each other. They saw the two young men, two waitresses, the middle-aged man and the manager. That was six people against one man, and he managed to fend them off. Certainly this was a very dangerous individual.

"Do you have security cameras?" inquired Jeffries.

The waitress nodded.

"Sure do. Only problem is they don't record. They're mainly a way for the manager to keep an eye on the front end."

"I see. Well, thank you for your time."

The officers made their way to the table of elderly men. With all the commotion that transpired there, they seemed to be rather calm.

"Good afternoon, gentlemen," began Jeffries "Were you two here when all this went down?"

"Yes," replied Andrew, the taller of the two.

"Would you mind answering a few questions for us then?"

"I don't see why not," said Felix.

"From what I've been able to piece together, a fight broke out between a large man and pretty much the rest of the restaurant," stated Jeffries. "The waitress says that he was forcing himself on a young girl, and she intervened. When he overpowered her, other people got involved. The man took out three other patrons and the manager before making off with the girl. Does that sound about right?"

"No," said Andrew quickly.

The officers exchanged glances.

"Care to explain what *did* happen?" asked Price.

"First of all, he wasn't forcing himself on the girl. She was his daughter," stated Andrew.

"His daughter?" asked Jeffries. "Are you sure?"

"Of course we're sure," replied Felix. "We saw the two of them come in together."

"How do you know it was his daughter?" asked Price. "She could have been some girl he just met."

"I doubt that," replied Andrew. "She was very relaxed around him. I think few children are that trusting of adults unless it's their parents."

"I see," replied Jeffries. "What happened next?"

Felix and Andrew looked at each other.

"Well, neither of us actually saw what caused the fuss," said Felix.

"But, we think that he must have been holding her hand or kissed her or something like that. Anyway, the waitress got the wrong impression and started accusing him of being a pedophile," said Andrew.

"He tried to explain to her that she had gotten the wrong idea, but she refused to listen," added Felix.

"And that's when she went after him with the serving tray," said Andrew.

"So he retaliated?" asked Jeffries.

Felix shook his head.

"No. He just stood there and took it. You'd think for a guy as big as he was, he could have easily taken the tray and been done with it. Instead, he tried to reason with her, and she continued to beat him. His little girl tried to intervene to help him."

"But she was small, so they mostly ignored her," said Andrew.

"Well, if he didn't overpower the waitress, what happened next?" asked Jeffries.

"Well, with all the commotion, the other patrons started to get involved," said Felix. "First, the older man and then the boys."

"The big fella put up a strong defense, but it looked like they were going to subdue him with the superior numbers," said Andrew.

"That's when the manager," Felix interjected, pointing to the man lying on the floor, "decided to do something."

"He grabbed the little girl and pulled her away toward the back, " said Andrew.

"Then she called for her daddy to come save her," said Felix. "And that was that."

The officers looked at each other.

"What do you mean by that?" asked Price.

Felix and Andrew glanced with amusement at one another.

"You two don't have children do you?" asked Andrew.

The two officers shook their heads.

"When you do, you'll understand," said Andrew. "Now I have a daughter from the woman I met back in Saigon, and Felix here has three with his ex-wife. I assure you that if a man threatened any of our children the way that foolhardy manager did, we would have skinned him alive."

"Maybe not *that* extreme," said Felix. "But it would have been a lot worse than what happened here."

The officers looked at each other skeptically, but of all the eyewitnesses, these two were the only ones not to have been unconscious or in hysterics, which brought up another interesting point.

"You two seem awfully calm for watching such an event unfold right in front of you," stated Jeffries.

It was Andrew who responded to the inquiry.

"Young man, when you've been to war, nothing else can shake your nerves. We've both woken up with night sweats over memories far worse than anything that happened here today."

The officers nodded in unison.

"So, the girl...did he snatch her up and take her with him, or did she go more or less willingly?" asked Price.

"She was delighted to be reunited with him," said Felix. "She even asked him to carry her. I guess the whole thing was a bit traumatic for one so young."

Price finished taking his notes and closed the notepad. He nodded to Jeffries.

"Well, gentlemen," Jeffries said, "Thank you very much for your time. And thank you for serving our country."

Jeffries reached over and shook Andrew's hand first and then that of Felix, and Price was quick to follow suit. The elderly men nodded appreciatively at the young officers.

Back in the car Jeffries looked over at Price.

"So...what do you think?" he asked.

"I'm inclined to believe the war vets myself," he replied.

Jeffries nodded.

"It's funny how a little misunderstanding can cause so much trouble."

When Mitchell regained consciousness, he found himself on the bed with his head cradled in Olivia's lap. She gently stroked his hair as she peered down at him with distraught eyes. Her melancholy expression transformed to one of relief when she saw him focus on her.

"I was getting worried," she said.

Mitchell let out a low groan.

"What happened?" he asked, touching his hand to his forehead.

"You had an anxiety attack," she stated.

"An anxiety attack? Are you sure?"

"Either that or you're diabetic," she said. "Do diabetics usually clutch their chest before collapsing?"

"Huh..." said Mitchell reflectively.

"Do you always get that excited about seeing a woman naked?"

"I swear that's never happened to me before."

Olivia smiled sweetly.

"I'm sure that's what all men say."

Mitchell took a deep breath.

"We could try again in a little while if you want."

Olivia shook her head.

"I appreciate the sentiment, but if it's all the same to you, I'd rather you survive the night."

"Isn't that supposed to be every man's ideal way to go; arriving and departing simultaneously?"

"I think most men would rather that happen when they were say, ninety years old."

"Yeah, but I was raised Irish Catholic, so I'll get to go to heaven, right?"

Olivia's face hardened.

"Even if you believe that, you'll go to heaven some day, there's no need to try and catch the five o'clock flight."

"What about other religions? I've always been open to converting."

"I see… what do you have in mind?" she asked.

"How about Islam? I hear that you get to wear some really neat hats in that faith."

"Yeah, but they probably don't carry robes in sizes above giant."

"Who needs robes? With seventy-two virgins, I'll have little need to get dressed in the morning."

"You're right. You'll be passed out the whole time."

"Hey. I wasn't *passed out.*"

"I'm just saying, if you pass out from seeing just one virgin, I don't much like your chances with a whole flock of them."

Mitchell pretended to ponder.

"You might have a point, " he said.

"Probably shouldn't go Mormon either; might run into that same problem with the extra wives," she teased.

Mitchell ran through the list.

"What about the Buddhists? I bet I could really pull off the bald look."

Olivia thought for a moment.

"Do you think that inner peace would help you with your anxiety problem?"

"One step at a time, my dear. I have to start with basic meditation."

"I think most men could benefit from a little meditation."

"Do you?"

"Absolutely," she stated. "If men focused on clearing their minds more often, women wouldn't have to fight so hard to empty them before having to fill them with good ideas."

Mitchell smiled.

"There is a drawback of course."

"What is that?" Olivia asked.

Mitchell held up a finger to emphasize his point.

"Some monks, you see, believe in maintaining their spiritual purity through celibacy."

Olivia considered this.

"I'd be fine with that," she said.

"You would?" Mitchell asked with surprise.

"Sure," she stated. "Just as long as you know that if you don't use it, you'll lose it."

Mitchell gulped and looked up at her with wide-eyed trepidation. She gazed down at him defiantly.

"Do you often threaten your boyfriends?" he asked.

"Only when they need a little extra encouragement."

"I see… should I practice sleeping with one eye open?"

"You could, but I'd rather you spent that time practicing not fainting rather than sleeping."

Mitchell exhaled forcefully.

"I really wanted to, you know."

Olivia smiled.

"I know," she said. "I shouldn't have pressured you though. I'm sorry about that."

"That's okay. It was actually quite enjoyable right up until, well, you know."

Olivia nodded.

"I'm also sorry for kissing you."

Mitchell raised an eyebrow at her.

"Back at the restaurant. If I waited until we got back, none of that would have happened."

"It's not your fault."

"But I instigated everything. You got hurt because of *me*. You must have been so scared fighting all those people."

Mitchell shook his head.

"That's not what scared me," he said, reaching for her hand.

Mitchell noticed the bruises on her wrist.

"You're injured," he stated with worry.

"It's not that bad," she said reassuringly. "It barely even hurts."

"I should get…"

Olivia placed a gentle hand on his chest, guiding him to lie back down.

"Just rest for now. You can take a look at it later."

Mitchell nodded before laying his head back in her lap.

"Are you hungry?" she asked.

Mitchell pondered.

"A little," he said.

"Would you like me to get you something?"

Mitchell shook his head.

"I just want to lie like this for a little longer."

Olivia nodded, returning to stroking his hair.

"So…" said Mitchell. "What's your favorite song?"

Andrew and Felix headed back to the retirement village half an hour after being interviewed by the police officers. Today's luncheon had been the most entertaining afternoon that they'd experienced in a long time, but they were both looking forward to the quiet comforts of home.

"Do you suppose that man and his girl will be alright?" asked Felix.

"One can only hope," replied Andrew. "He sure fought hard to protect her."

Felix nodded.

"Would you have fought that hard for me?" he asked.

Andrew grabbed his partner's hand.

"I already have."

CHAPTER 18

Mitchell opened his eyes to the most beautiful sight he'd ever seen. Olivia lay with her arm draped casually across his torso, most of her naked back sticking out above the blanket. Her soft skin glowed under the illumination of the sun's streaming rays, making her look almost angelic as she slept soundly beside him. Her body shifted gracefully with every breath, causing it to glide ever so gently along his bare chest. He raised the blanket a few inches, relieved to find that he was still wearing his shorts, though he was quickly distracted by other sights.

Mitchell lowered the comforter and glanced at the clock to see that it was shortly past eight. He turned back to his tiny companion and rested his head against hers, savoring the delightful fragrance of her silky hair. Mitchell ran his hand up and down her back, enjoying the feel of her smooth skin beneath his fingertips. His gentle caress stirred Olivia to life, her eyes flickering open to reveal those sparkling blue sapphires. She let out a contented sigh and nuzzled her head deeper into his chest.

"You know, we'll soon have to get up," he said.

Olivia let out a quiet murmur of protest.

"No," she said softly, snuggling closer.

Mitchell nudged her lightly with his leg.

"Come on," he encouraged.

Olivia groaned weakly as she slid from beneath the covers and placed her bare feet on the cold floor. Mitchell gazed in fascination as she stretched her arms overhead. His eyes followed every movement, flowing southward to admire her alluring backside. Letting her arms return to her sides, Olivia peered over her shoulder back at him. He quickly raised his head to meet her eyes, though not fast enough to avoid detection.

"Don't stare too long," she teased. "You remember what happened to Icarus when he flew too close to the sun?"

"At least I'm already lying down this time."

"Hey, if I have to be up, you don't get to pass out."

Mitchell shrugged.

"I'll be up in just a second."

Olivia rolled her eyes and strutted to the edge of the bed to retrieve a pair of underwear from her designated drawer. Turning her back to him, Olivia bent forward, exposing all of herself. She maneuvered her slender legs through the holes, taking her time as she raised them to her hips, giving one last playful swish as they fell into place.

"Just a little extra motivation," she said with a sly smile.

Mitchell waited until he heard the bathroom door close before climbing out of bed. He hurriedly threw on some clothes, making sure to tuck in anything that might stick out. By the time Olivia returned from her morning ritual, he was completely dressed, much to her disappointment.

After a quick breakfast, they headed out to their respective outings. Olivia slipped her arm through his as he escorted her to the doctor's office.

"What time is your lunch with Abigail?" she asked.

"Noon."

"Does that mean you'll stick around for my appointment?"

Mitchell shook his head.

"I can stay for a little bit, but I need to take care of something."

"You mean *the surprise*?" she asked excitedly.

Mitchell flashed a grin at her.

"They close at noon today so I need to get it straightened out before I meet Abigail."

"Who closes at noon?"

Mitchell shook his head.

"I'll tell you later," he said. "Wouldn't want to ruin the surprise, would we?"

Olivia smiled but felt anxious about how the interaction might go today.

"What are you going to tell Abigail?" she asked.

Mitchell gazed down at her curiously.

"About what?"

"About us."

Mitchell's face scrunched in agitated concentration.

"I don't know if it'll even come up," he admitted.

"You know we'll have to tell her eventually. The longer we keep it from her, the more upset she'll be when she finds out."

"It's not that simple. Abigail is…complicated. There's no telling how she'll react when I inform her that the girl she tried to get remanded to foster care is back in my apartment, let alone if she finds out we're dating."

Olivia gave his arm a reassuring squeeze.

"I'm sure you'll do whatever's right," she said.

Mitchell nodded.

"I'll let you know how it goes."

They arrived at the building ten minutes before her appointment. Mitchell held the front door open as they stepped inside and navigated the long corridors to the doctor's office suite. Once inside, Mitchell led them to the receptionist area, bending down to one knee to speak through the small sliding window. He was handed a clipboard holding several blank forms. Preliminaries handled, they moved to the waiting area.

Olivia took the clipboard from him.

"You don't need to wait around," she said. "I know you're anxious to go take care of that other thing."

Mitchell glanced at the time on his phone.

"Are you sure you'll be alright?"

"It's just a doctor visit. I'll be fine."

Mitchell nodded as he reached for his wallet. He extracted a large quantity of bills and a folded piece of paper, holding them for her to take.

"For the visit, lunch and a cab ride back to the apartment, if you need one. I wrote down the address and my phone number just in case."

As Olivia reached for the money, Mitchell closed his hand over hers, attempting to be as inconspicuous as possible. They smiled knowingly at one another as they shared their secret embrace. Mitchell pulled away quickly so as not to attract attention.

"I'll see you back at the apartment," he said.

"Have fun with your sister," she replied encouragingly.

Mitchell groaned in response, giving one last wave as he left the doctor's office. When he was out of sight, Olivia carried the unfilled clipboard up to the front desk and rapped lightly on the glass.

"Yes?"

"Sorry to bother you," said Olivia, "But could you tell me your policy on cancelled appointments."

The receptionist cleared her throat.

"Well if it's done at least forty-eight hours before your appointment, there's no penalty. If you miss your appointment after that, we have to charge you."

"Okay," replied Olivia glumly. "Thank you."

If they were going to have to pay for this appointment whether or not she stayed, she might as well go ahead and see the doctor. Olivia exhaled a dismal sigh as she returned to her seat to fill in the paperwork.

Dr. Keith Fisher sat inches from the computer screen frantically updating his fantasy football team. As fortuitous as being the first to draft might seem, in a league of sixteen players, it had been a near death knell for his roster. Worse still, in an absolutely abysmal preseason, both his second pick quarterback and third round wide receiver had gone down to injuries, with one guaranteed to be out the entire year. Though he could still manage to pull off that vital trade before the opener on Thursday, things were looking very grim.

Fisher glanced up at the clock to see that it was already ten past nine. In previous years, he would have used this time to read medical charts for incoming patients, but he couldn't bring himself to care anymore. Nearly every person who walked through the doors was only interested in finding a cheap and legal way to get high. In the last six months, he had written three times as many prescriptions for painkillers and anti-anxiety medications as he had for every other drug combined. *Why bother expending energy to help those degenerate riffraff ruin their lives when he could be just as productive playing around online?*

Besides, he wouldn't have to endure this job much longer. A golfing buddy on the board of directors for Friedman Financial had given him the inside scoop on a surefire investment opportunity. Fisher did not know much about initial public offerings, and he didn't much care to, just as long as his friend could guarantee a sizable profit. He had even traded in his retirement savings and taken out a second mortgage to ensure maximum return. In another month he would be far away from these irksome addicts and enjoying the refreshing taste of daiquiris on a tropical beach somewhere.

Fisher checked the time again. He decided to allow himself another fifteen minutes before having to deal with his first appointment. After all, he deserved as much time away from their nonsense as he could get.

Olivia sat in one of the chairs of the waiting room strategizing her answers to their survey. When one is inclined to tell the truth, the answers come easy, but when lies are needed, one has to think very far ahead of the consequences. With each question, Olivia became more convinced how much different her life was than those around her.

Name. *Who would she be today; the lost orphan girl still seeking her place in the world, or the little rich girl whom everybody overlooked?* She chose to be Olivia, because that's who she wanted to be.

Date of birth. *The girl she once was and appeared to be, or the woman she had developed into? Would they believe her even if she told them the truth? How would they respond if they didn't believe her?* She decided to chance it.

Family medical history. She had no idea. *Did she tell them that she had been an orphan? Would they check on her background information? If she left it blank would that lead to greater suspicion?* In the end, she checked off hay fever for her father, arthritis for her mother, and diabetes for her paternal grandmother. Olivia felt a little guilty about striking them with such diseases, but figured they probably wouldn't care too much on the account that they were already dead.

Olivia flipped to the next page and groaned in disdain. Sprawled across the top in bold lettering was the word *pediatric*. Fighting the urge to shred the document, she had to make a new decision. *If they had already branded her a child, would she be able to convince them otherwise? If not, should she go back now and change her answers before anyone had a chance to read them?*

Olivia decided to let it stand and hope for the best. She submitted her documentation to the front desk and returned to her seat in the lobby. *Hopefully Mitchell was having better luck at his luncheon with Abigail.*

Mitchell arrived at the restaurant with time to spare. He walked up to the hostess.

"Excuse me. I'm here to meet with Abigail Parker. Has she arrived?"

"Give me one second," she said, entering information into the computer.

She turned to him and shook her head.

"Sorry," she said. "I don't have any bookings under that name."

Mitchell looked at her with surprise. It wasn't like Abigail to forget to schedule a reservation.

"I do have one here for an *Eric* Parker," she said helpfully.

Mitchell's heart sank.

"I don't suppose that reservation was for three people?" he asked, gritting his teeth.

The woman checked.

"Yes, it is."

Mitchell grunted in response.

"Yeah, that's her," he replied. "Have they been seated yet?"

She checked again.

"No, sir."

"Ok. Thank you very much," he said pleasantly.

"You're welcome," she stated with a smile.

Mitchell took a seat at the waiting area. *Hopefully Olivia was having better luck at the doctor's office.*

A woman in scrubs poked her head through the door and called Olivia's name. She followed the nurse to a station to get her vitals taken before being led to a cramped medical room. The nurse closed the door and motioned for her to take a seat on the sizable table in the center. Olivia had to use the footstool, but she managed the climb up on her own.

Olivia watched as the nurse sat down on a wheeled stool and rolled to the nearby computer. The woman set a clipboard on the counter in such a way as to allow Olivia to see that it was the same paperwork she'd given the receptionist. The nurse copied the information into the system, never batting an eye at the inconsistency of the birth date. Olivia sighed with relief. *Perhaps everyone was too preoccupied to notice such nuances after all.*

"What brings you in here today?" asked the nurse finally.

Olivia told her about the bruised wrist and the swelling. A few more generic questions followed, and the nurse stepped away from the computer.

"The doctor will be in to see you in just a few minutes," she stated cordially before leaving, pulling the door closed.

As Olivia sat alone and bored, she scanned the posters hanging on the walls. It had been almost three years since she had set foot in a doctor's office. Miss Elaine had been the one to handle her medical visits, and after her passing, Mr. James buried himself so deep in work that he barely registered anything else. Olivia was his daughter in name only from that point on.

At twenty past twelve, Abigail entered with her husband in tow.

"Sorry for being late," she said. "There was some heavy traffic."

"It happens," Mitchell replied with a shrug, though he couldn't help but assume that the always-punctual Abigail had been delayed by her appearance-obsessed husband. Mitchell regretfully extended his hand to his brother-in-law. He felt dirty just talking to the man, let alone having to shake hands.

The three exchanged polite salutations before the hostess led them to a table by the window. Abigail claimed the chair facing the entrance while Eric took the seat with the best view of the water. Mitchell resigned himself to one of the chairs overlooking the bleak restaurant décor.

Like in most fine dining restaurants, Mitchell felt uncomfortably out of place. The waiters were dressed in pretentious apparel far more formal than he wore for his classroom lectures. The drinks were unnecessarily served in fine crystal instead of normal glasses; a move that put Mitchell on edge that he might accidentally crush one in his massive hands. The patrons gave out artificial pleasantries to the staff to whom they would not normally have given the time of day.

And yet, it would all have been somewhat forgivable if the entrees came in portions greater than sample size. If they had the audacity to charge dinner prices for lunch items, they could at least make it worth your while. For a man of his stature, two entrees could barely satiate his appetite. A lesser man could probably make do, which is why he assumed Eric loved this place.

Eric Parker married his sister about the same time he started seeing Evelyn. Even then, he thought Eric was a sleazy worm who exploited people's emotions for profit, and time had not altered his impression. Though he did not get along well with Abigail, at least he felt she cared about her patients. There was not the same benefit of doubt attributed to his brother-in-law.

Mitchell rolled his eyes as he scanned the man's overdone outfit. Eric's suit single-handedly cost more than Olivia's entire wardrobe. His hands were decorated with diamond and gold jewelry far in excess of the standard wristwatch and wedding band. Even the car they arrived in was one of Eric's many straight off the line luxury sedans.

"How's teaching been going?" asked Eric.

Mitchell cocked an eyebrow at him.

"I haven't taught in a long time," said Mitchell plainly. "But I'm sure you knew that."

Abigail glared at Mitchell, mouthing the word *behave* in his direction. He reached over and took a swig from his water, hoping the iced beverage might cool his temper.

"So what have you been up to lately?" asked Eric.

Mitchell thought about all the excitement of the last few days.

"Nothing much," he said. "Looking for work."

"Did you apply at the unemployment office?" interjected Abigail.

Mitchell nodded.

"I have. It's apparently a pretty rough time in the economy."

Mitchell took another gulp from his glass, not noticing the grateful expression forming on Abigail's face.

"Well if you're in need of a job," said Eric, "we've been looking to hire teachers for our biblical studies classes."

Abigail clenched her jaw nervously as she looked empathetically over at Mitchell.

"Honey…" she said, placing her hand on Eric's wrist. "I don't think that's the type of thing Mitchell would want to be a part of."

"Nonsense," declared Eric, patting her hand with patronizing pride. "It may not pay well, but it's a wonderful opportunity to expand your résumé. What do you say Mitchell, you interested?"

Silence settled over the table as Mitchell held his tongue.

"I spoke with the people at the police station last night," said Abigail suddenly.

"Oh?" asked Mitchell, trying to conceal his panic.

Abigail nodded.

"I asked them what had happened with the girl you found."

"Wait, what girl?" chimed Eric.

Abigail gave him a dismissive hand gesture, as if to say *I'll tell you later.*

"What did they say?" asked Mitchell nervously.

"Apparently," she continued, "they found a new home for her."

"Really?" he asked disbelievingly. "With whom?"

Abigail hesitated before continuing.

"A couple in Maryland," she said. "They were already in the market for adoption so it is a win-win for everybody."

Mitchell sighed heavily, choosing to look at the table rather than either of his fellow patrons.

"And is she happy there?" he asked.

Abigail smiled at him.

"The officer told me that she is really enjoying herself. They have a large farm and several children in the neighborhood. She has already made friends."

Mitchell nodded.

"I'm glad she's doing alright," commented Mitchell. "Heaven knows what would have happened to her if she had stayed with me."

Mitchell downed the rest of his water in three rapid gulps.

"Excuse me," he said. "I need to slip off to the restroom."

Mitchell stepped away from the table and headed to the back of the restaurant. He didn't actually need to relieve himself, but he couldn't stand the sight of their lying faces. Pushing open the door, Mitchell moved to the sink and splashed himself with cold water. He gazed into the looking glass, contemplating what to do about Olivia.

One thing's for certain, he thought to himself. *If Abigail's not going to be honest with me, then why should I be honest with her?* He would just have to keep his relationship with Olivia a secret for as long as he could.

Dr. Fisher skimmed through the paperwork on the next patient; a young girl with a bruised wrist. Among those he'd seen so far today were the usual pill popper, morbidly obese couch potato who couldn't understand why his cholesterol was so high, and a woman wearing fishnet stockings and a tube top that he was convinced would turn up positive for whatever venereal diseases he tested her. The possibility of an abused child among the lot seemed to fit the bill for what society had degraded to these days.

He opened the door to reveal a sickly-looking blond child sitting on the edge of the medical table. Her smile displayed stained teeth and dental abnormalities. Fisher cringed at the sight of her almost translucent pallor. The girl's flat chest and gaunt physique assured him that she was either prepubescent and malnourished or simply anorexic. His diagnosis shifted immediately from neglected youth to bulimic school girl.

"Good morning," he stated more than greeted. "What brings you here today?"

Olivia explained about the bruised wrist. As she showed him the bandaged arm, Dr. Fisher focused his eyes on the fresh dressing on the other side.

"What's that?" he asked, pointing to the injury from the restaurant.

"Oh," she said in hesitation. "That's unrelated."

Dr. Fisher nodded. His mind drifted to images of adolescents wearing black mascara and attacking their arms with Exacto blades. If this girl was already depressed about her figure, cutting wasn't out of the question.

Fisher took a seat at the computer. As he scanned the data, his eye caught the birth date of 1986. He shook his head angrily. *That damn dyslexic nurse must have put the date in wrong again,* he thought. Fisher looked over at Olivia while he pressed the backspace button and entered 1998 instead. *I'm going to have to fire that woman if she doesn't start paying better attention.*

"Let's take a look," he said, turning back to the emaciated girl.

Olivia grimaced in pain at the unnecessary pressure and rapid movement as he quickly undid the bandage. The doctor seemed to be ignoring her cries as he continued the action unabated. When the wrap came off, he prodded the tender region with his forefinger. Olivia let out a shrill, and he pulled his finger away.

"You seemed to have bruised it pretty badly," he stated. "What were you doing when this happened?"

"I was sleeping on the couch and accidentally rolled off," she explained.

Fisher raised an eyebrow. Either this girl was lying to protect whoever assaulted her or she was suffering from some sort of bone density loss, or possibly both. He smiled to himself, feeling greater confidence in his bulimia hypothesis. He reached over and grabbed a slip of paper from the drawer.

"Well, the good news is it isn't broken," he explained. "It looks like you might have sprained it. I could order an x-ray, but I don't think that it'll reveal anything more than we already know."

Olivia considered his words and nodded, quite certain that such a procedure would be quite expensive without Mr. James' insurance.

"The reason that your wrist bruised like that is because you are suffering from bone density loss. That might be partly hereditary, but I would say that environment and poor diet are contributing factors."

Again, Olivia nodded.

"I want you to take both vitamin D and calcium supplements. They should be available at any pharmacy or grocery store," he said, writing the information on a prescription slip.

As Fisher handed her the piece of paper, he remembered the other bandaged arm. He returned to the pad.

"And here's a prescription for Fluoxetine," he said. "It should help with other issues you're having."

She took the second slip and looked at him inquisitively.

"About how much is this prescription going to cost?" she asked worriedly.

Dr. Fisher sighed.

"You can check with my nurse if you want. We might have some samples available." She smiled back at him.

"Is there anything else?" he asked impatiently.

She shook her head.

"I'll send my nurse to put a fresh wrap on that arm. Stay away from any heavy lifting, and make sure to keep it iced. The swelling should go down in another day or two."

Olivia nodded in response, but he was already halfway out the door.

Mitchell exited the restroom debating whether or not to simply slip away while he had the chance. He resisted the urge and returned to the dining area to rejoin his pleasant company.

Back at the table, the server was taking lunch orders. Mitchell put in his standard order for this type of place, which was the item on the menu he guessed to be of the greatest quantity. Once Mitchell sat down, Eric turned to him.

"Abigail was just telling me about your little house guest."

Mitchell glared angrily at her.

"Was she now?"

Eric didn't seem to realize the sensitive nature of the subject and pressed onward with the zeal of Lord Cardigan and his Light Brigade.

"You know you could have brought her to the church. We have connections with many orphanages. We easily could have found her a safe place."

I would rather jump off the Emlenton Bridge than turn her over to your lot.

"I should have thought of that," Mitchell said pleasantly. "I'll *definitely* consider it next time."

Abigail nudged him beneath the table, and he glanced in her direction. Mitchell had seen that look many times and knew what it meant. It wasn't so much that she wanted them to get along better as it was that she wanted him to pretend.

The salads arrived, and Mitchell was quick to dive in to the food. He never cared much for mixed garden salad, but he was hungry. When he felt another kick from Abigail, he turned to Eric.

"So, I hear you have another book coming out," Mitchell stated.

"Ah, yes," began Eric, his face lighting up with enthusiasm. "It will be released in November, just in time for the Christmas rush."

"Expecting a lot of sales on this one?"

"One can only hope," he said. "The last one sold almost two million copies. It would be great if we came close to that this time."

"What's the topic of this one?" asked Mitchell.

"It's about inspiring the love of Jesus in others by doing good works in your community. It's just like in the passage…"

Mitchell drifted away from the conversation. It was hard to take serious a man whose congregation spent more money on constructing a weekly clubhouse than many regions had to fund hospitals. The money spent on the giant cross alone could have fed and clothed dozens of families who were currently without work. The only consolation for Mitchell was that the church resided outside the city limits of his beloved Pittsburgh.

"Fascinating," commented Mitchell as he heard a break in the monologue.

Eric smiled, obviously pleased with himself.

"You know," he said, "I'm doing a sermon tomorrow morning on some of the topics covered in the upcoming book. If you want, you could join us for the service."

The salad turned to ash in Mitchell's mouth.

"I'd love to," lied Mitchell, "but I've been feeling under the weather the last few days, and I'll just take it easy tomorrow."

"Ok," said Eric with disappointment. "Maybe next time?"

Mitchell nodded, though he certainly had no desire to follow through.

Olivia sat perfectly still as the nurse wound the new bandage around her wrist. She was thankful that she showed more compassion than the doctor.

"There, all set," she said pleasantly.

Olivia spun her wrist around, testing that the gauze would stay put.

"Thank you," she said.

The nurse looked over at the other bandage.

"Do you want me to do that one as well?"

Olivia paused.

"You can if you want," Olivia stated with a smile.

The nurse smiled back, carefully unraveling the dressing.

"What's your name?" asked Olivia.

"Joann,"

"Pleased to meet you Joann. My name's Olivia."

The nurse nodded.

"I know. It is on your chart."

"Oh yeah," she replied, feeling somewhat silly at the oversight. "How long have you worked here?"

The nurse paused for a second. She removed the bandage to find the area only slightly inflamed. Olivia was glad to see the swelling had gone down. The nurse pulled out some antibiotic ointment and squeezed some on the affected region.

"About ten years," she replied.

"Oh wow. You must really like it here."

Joann shrugged.

"The pay is decent; can't ask for more than that these days."

Olivia nodded appreciatively, though she couldn't comment one way or the other.

"All done," Joann declared.

Olivia looked down at the fresh bandage with delight.

"Thank you so much."

"Is there anything else I can do for you?"

"Well, Dr. Fisher wanted me to fill a prescription, but he thinks there may be samples available."

"What is the medication?" asked Joann.

Olivia showed her the slip of paper.

"Yes. We received samples a few days ago. I'll make sure to get you some before you go."

"Thank you so much. And do you know where the closest pharmacy is?"

Joann gave her instructions on how to get there.

"Anything else?" asked Joann cheerfully.

"There is one more place I need to go. Maybe you know how to get there?"

"Where is that, dear?"

Olivia told her.

"Why do you want to go there?" Joann asked with surprise.

Olivia smiled.

"I want to pick up a gift for someone."

Having finished their entrees, the trio sat in idle silence. Mitchell was relieved that the afternoon's outing would soon end. He couldn't wait to get home to Olivia.

When the server asked if they were ready for the check, Abigail ordered a cup of coffee. Mitchell got a sinking feeling in his stomach. The beverage indicated that there was still something she wanted to talk about, and it must have been intense since she brought Eric along. Mitchell assured the server that he was good with his water. As the waiter disappeared, Mitchell looked over at Abigail.

"What?" he asked coarsely.

"I didn't say anything," she insisted innocently.

Mitchell shot her a look.

"I know you, Abigail. Just tell me what it is you wanted to talk about."

Abigail took in a deep breath and exhaled slowly as if focusing her energy for the tribulations that were about to unfold.

"Mitchell," she began, reaching her hand across the table to his. "I've been watching you deteriorate over the last year. You barely leave the house except to get food. You live in filth, and you often smell like you haven't bathed in days."

Mitchell pulled his hand away from hers, noticing how she tensed from his withdrawal. Though she was his sister, and the touch had not been menacing, his intimacy with Olivia these last few days made hand-holding seem like a sacred act between the two of them. He didn't want to share it with anyone.

"What's your point?" he asked tersely.

Abigail sighed.

"I'm your sister, and you know that I want what's best for you, right?"

Mitchell forced an exhale to demonstrate his distaste for the conversation so far. He nodded for her to go on.

"I think that most of your recent lifestyle has to do with depression over Evelyn leaving you. Rather than deal with the issue properly, you've been self-medicating."

It was hard for Mitchell to argue, especially since Abigail's psychology background made her feel like she could psychoanalyze any situation, regardless of its truth.

"Therefore," she continued, "I think you should consider going to rehab."

There's the rub, thought Mitchell, *the entire underlying purpose for today's meeting. Abigail had not cared about his feelings regarding Olivia. She did not want to make peace with him over the horrible way she treated his new companion. Abigail didn't even want to just hang out as brother and sister like they used to before Eric. No, today's luncheon was just another way she could criticize him.*

"I'm not going to rehab!" he shouted, his voice carrying through the restaurant.

"Please don't be angry," she pleaded. "I was just…"

Mitchell didn't bother to hear any more. He gathered his coat and stormed out of the restaurant, muttering to himself the whole way. *How dare she tell him to go to rehab?! If he wanted to drink, that was his choice, and no one else's. It wasn't like his drinking hurt anybody, except maybe himself, and if he wasn't bothered by that fact, then she definitely had no reason to try and interfere.*

By the time he made it to the parking lot, Mitchell convinced himself that getting completely trashed on the various liquids scattered throughout his apartment would be a good way to show Abigail once and for all who was in control of his life.

CHAPTER 19

I stood before the bedroom mirror admiring my new purchase. Exchanging the unnecessary bra with something more alluring was a good decision. I couldn't wait to show Mitchell; it was his gift, too, after all.

Placing the items carefully back in the bag, I put it in a safe hiding spot in the rear of the closet until the right moment arrived. I already had an idea for the perfect time to unleash this special present.

Taking up today's clothing from the pile on the bed, I quickly dressed back into blue jeans and t-shirt. I wasn't sure how Mitchell's outing with Abigail had gone, but if it had been successful, there was a possibility that she might come over afterward. In spite of everything that had happened so far, I still held hope in my heart that we might get passed our differences and become like sisters. That outcome would be very unlikely though, if she walked through the front door and found me naked in her brother's apartment again.

I moved to the kitchen to get some water. Checking the wall clock in the living room, I was surprised to find that it was already pushing two o'clock. I wondered what was keeping Mitchell as I turned on the tap. With my glass filled, I carried it into the bedroom and placed it next to my pills on the bedside stand. After extracting one pill from each of three bottles, I reached for the water again.

Raising it to my lips, I heard the front door open and slam shut, the reverberating clash of wood sending a chill down my spine. It was clear that today's luncheon had not gone well. I cringed again as another loud crash came from the bathroom a few seconds later. It had definitely not been a good day for Mitchell.

I struggled to get the three pills down quickly, finally succeeding as the bathroom door opened again. I set the glass down, deciding that next time I would try taking them one at a time. As I sat waiting for Mitchell to enter, I heard the faint sounds of rummaging in the kitchen. Though shocked that he hadn't come looking for me, I chose not to breathe too much into it. After all, it had probably been stressful dealing with Abigail through an entire meal.

When I exited the bedroom, I completely intended to give Mitchell an affectionate hug to help calm his nerves. Instead, I found him squatting beneath the kitchen sink frantically scrounging through the assortment of cleaning products. I knew what was he was after, but he would not find it. I had already solved this eventuality.

Mitchell stood from his hunkering position, leaving the doors wide open and the bottles of cleanser scattered on the linoleum. One by one, he threw open the cabinets and shoved aside canned goods and other nonperishables hoping to reveal any remnant of his previous stash.

Shaking his head in exasperation, Mitchell carried his search to the bathroom sink, the bedroom closet, the lowest level of the chest of drawers, behind the television stand, and finally to the bookshelf. Knocking the front row of books out of the way, he scanned the titles for his secret compartments only to find empty spaces where they had been hidden. Mitchell stared in bewilderment at this disappearance, as though he were unsure if they existed in the first place.

He turned in my direction, his eyes focusing as though noticing me for the first time. I watched his face change from confusion to conviction in a flash as he narrowed his eyes at me. Mitchell approached with such speed that I felt afraid, then somewhat relieved that he stopped a few feet short of reaching me.

"What did you do?!" he demanded.

With great apprehension, I took a step forward, reaching out my hand to his. Mitchell did not recoil, but I could feel the resistance to my touch. He was like a wounded animal, too disoriented to understand his surroundings, too guarded to allow even a cherished friend past his protective layers. When I tried to put my arm around him, Mitchell pulled away completely.

"Please understand…," I pleaded, "I had to."

Mitchell's face hardened, a hollow stare coming from dead eyes. He shook his head with contempt and turned away from me to resume the hunt, futilely hoping that I missed one relic of his former supply. When the bookshelves were cleared, he cast an angry sideways glance in my direction.

His face lit up when he remembered the bottles in his coat pockets. He turned out the pockets entirely, realizing with dismay that they were gone as well. Lacking the motivation to search anymore, Mitchell sat down on the floor, clutching his face in his palms. His body shook violently with tremors.

I walked over and placed my hand tenderly on his shoulder, doing my best to comfort him.

"I'm sorry, Mitchell. I didn't know what else to do."

He refused to look at me, but at least he didn't try to pull away. Beneath even the most iridescent of veneers, all men have their darker side waiting to be exposed. For some, the stain runs deep, contaminating everything from the inside out. But for others, hidden behind a black hole of fear, anger and resentment is an inner flame uncorrupted by the horrors of the world. Buried somewhere in the crumbling colossus before me, struggling to overthrow those inner demons, was the man I'd grown to love.

I knelt beside him, my mind drifting to the cold, decomposing body that could still be all alone on that unforgiving rooftop. Though his life had been extinguished in that terrible place, Mr. James had died long before his final expiration. Many tales have been told about how alcohol can transform a man into a hideous beast, a monster ravaging through the lives of all those he encounters. And yet, as real as that statement can be, it falls far short of the terrifying truth. Alcohol is like an unbridled divorce lawyer; the longer you cling to it, the more it takes from you, until finally there is nothing left.

Unsurprisingly, Mr. James had always been the breadwinner in our household, but it was his wife who managed the affairs. She planned all of their social functions, managed the hired help, handled his personal schedule, and even picked out his suit each morning. After she died, it was difficult for him to even roll out of bed.

It wasn't long after her death that he started having a drink in the evening to help him cope with the loss. One drink progressed into two and so on until he found himself intoxicated every night. He was what many would call a "functioning drunk" because he always showed up for work the next day. I was shocked that he could even stand up in the mornings considering the way he drank at night.

As his drinking developed, so too did his paranoia. Mr. James began to associate me with his wife's passing, and later with his brother's. He couldn't figure out how, but he was convinced that the girl who never aged had plotted the deaths of everyone he cared about. In the eyes of the public, I was his beloved and devoted daughter, but in private, I was a "witch" who had cursed him and his family. I tried to remember him as the man he had been rather than the monster he had become, but memories are quick to fade.

On Sunday night, the drink had entirely taken over, convincing him that the only way to be free of the demon haunting his life was to take matters into his own hands. Judgment passed, he came to my room while I was asleep and dragged me naked from the bed. I tried to resist his pull, but I was no match for his overwhelming size.

It's funny; when Miss Elaine was alive, he barely had time to pay me a moment's notice. Without her, I suddenly became the center of his attention.

I was broken away from my thoughts by Mitchell stirring beside me. His head was raised, and he was staring longingly at the small cabinet above the refrigerator. As if mentally linked, we both came to the same grisly realization.

I had missed one!

Leaping to my feet, I attempted to stop him, but he was too strong and his movement too quick for my resistance. He stormed to the kitchen and threw open the cabinet, a look of joy crossing his face when he saw that the contents still remained. Mitchell reached inside and withdrew a longneck bottle of clear liquid. Hope fell away, and I could feel tears of frustration starting to form.

NO! I screamed inside my head. This was no time to feel sorry for myself, I had to act, now, while there was still time.

I quickly crossed the distance between us. Mitchell's size prevented me from reaching the bottle, so he managed to get it opened without any interference. Holding the container high in the air, he tilted the opening toward his lips. With no better plan of attack, I put my hand over his mouth.

Mitchell gave me a look of surprise as he lowered the bottle to prevent any accidental spill. When he tried to step away, I moved forward, covering his mouth again, this time with my other hand. Mitchell knocked my hand away and took another step backward. I lunged forward to continue my attack.

Mitchell's next retreat sent him hard against the kitchen wall. I grimaced at the resounding thud of his head making contact with the drywall. He winced in pain, raising his free hand to the now sore spot on the back of his skull.

The arm holding the bottle dropped in response to this distraction, and I sensed an opportunity. Latching onto the bottle with both hands, I yanked for all I was worth, hoping to pry it from his grasp. Even with his dazed state, Mitchell maintained a vicelike grip on the bottle. I tugged again. This time it moved closer to me, but still he did not relinquish his hold.

Mitchell regained himself from the sudden impact, shaking his head as if to dislodge the staggering effects. With one hand, he pulled the bottle toward himself, dragging me along with it. As the bottle progressed to its destination, I could sense imminent defeat.

So there I stood, overlooking the precipice, my beloved forcing himself ever closer to the edge onward into oblivion, with me being the only impediment left standing in his way. Many would have let him fall to his doom; if he was so hell bent on destroying his life, then just let him, I suppose. Certainly my frustrations with him were leaning me in that direction.

And yet, I loved him too much to give up without a fight. It wasn't just that he saved my life or that he bought me nice clothes or even that he was my first real kiss. Mitchell treated me as an adult, an equal, someone he could turn to in his time of need and confide his deepest secrets. He had been the only man I had taken to my bed, and though things had not gone well in that department, I still wanted to be with him. After all the turmoil that we endured this week, I knew we could conquer any other obstacles, no matter how severe they might seem.

So how do I solve this one? Mitchell rescued me in my time of need, and I felt that I owed him that much, or at least to try. As the bottle closed in on his lips, I knew it was now or never. How could I save the man that I loved? How could I possibly stop him when he was so much bigger and stronger than I? What do you do to prevent an outcome for which there is no tomorrow?

Whatever it takes.

I jumped into the air, pressing all of my body weight on his arm. He tried to resist at first, but the bottle fell before reaching his lips. Mitchell's body lurched forward, and the bottle came within my grasp. I yanked hard on it with both hands, and it almost came loose.

My victory was short-lived for he quickly regained his balance, making an effort to retract the bottle. I looked from the bottle to Mitchell and back to the bottle. Out of options, I knew only one other way to keep his lips off of it.

Biting the bullet, I leaned forward and engulfed the opening with my mouth, locking my lips around the neck to keep it from accidentally slipping out. I gripped the bottle firmly in both hands in case he tried to pull away again.

As I held the bottle in that precarious position, the acrid fumes rose upward, burning the inside of my nostrils. I shut my eyes tightly, gagging from the horrible taste filling my mouth, thankful that at least I didn't have to smell it. I had often heard that liquor was an acquired taste, but if the vapors were this strong, how could anybody stomach drinking the foul beverage?

I held that position for so long that I began to feel self-conscious. It had been a pointless strategy to say the least; there was no way I could possibly stay like this forever. I thought about Mitchell. How silly this must look to him, like a child holding their breath to get their way. What would his reaction be? Anger? Amusement? At least he had stopped fighting me for it, if only for a few seconds. Maybe there was hope of him pausing long enough to listen to reason? Hesitantly, I opened my eyes.

Mitchell was looking down at me with eyes wide and jaw hanging limply open. He no longer looked angry, but I struggled to assess his current emotion. Was it surprise? Was it confusion? And then I recognized the expression from yesterday's failed festivities.

It suddenly occurred to me what it must look like; me holding the bottle between my lips. There we stood, unmoving, just staring into each other's eyes as I contemplated my next action. Maintaining eye contact with Mitchell, I lowered my head so that a little more of the bottle's neck slid into my mouth.

Mitchell gasped softly above me. I felt his grip on the bottle slacken with my movement. I caved my cheeks around the thick glass and slowly moved my head upwards, allowing the bottle to slide out of my mouth. Continuing to look Mitchell in the eyes, I licked around the outer rim of the bottle and slid my tongue inside the opening. After a few more licks, I lowered my mouth over the bottle again.

I continued this pattern a few more times until Mitchell released his grip altogether. I pulled the bottle away from his hands and held it securely against my chest just in case he went for it again. Knowing that I probably couldn't get away with dumping it out right in front of him, I set the bottle on the countertop behind me, glad to finally be free of that awful taste.

When I turned back to Mitchell the vacant expression from before had vanished. It was as if he were suddenly aware of his surroundings again, almost like the past few minutes had never happened. His eyes followed my every movement with passionate intrigue, just as they had the night before. It was only when he realized I was looking at him that he averted his eyes in shame.

I felt sympathy for his distress and went to him, hoping to apply comfort in whatever way I could. When I took his head in my hands, he didn't try to fight, even allowing his gaze to be directed down at me. Sadly, we only held eye contact for a moment before he looked down at the floor. When he spoke his words were muted, full of guilt, and yet, sober.

"I'm sorry," he said. "I don't know what I was thinking."

"Alcohol tends to have that effect on people." I said curtly.

Mitchell gave a humble nod.

"I promise I'll..."

"Don't promise me anything," I said, letting my anger get the best of me. "I've had enough broken promises to last a lifetime, and I am so damn sick and tired of all the excuses. 'Oh, I know I should be wearing my seatbelt but it just doesn't feel that comfortable' or 'I know I said I'd quit smoking but it's been a long day so I'll give it up tomorrow'. Well you know what, sometimes tomorrow doesn't come."

I pulled away from him.

"I can't stop you from doing what you're going to do, but I can promise you that I won't stick around to watch you kill yourself. I've done that too much already. And I...I just can't do it anymore."

I turned away from him but I didn't get very far before I felt his hand close around my wrist. Without resisting, I let him pull me into his waiting arms. Mitchell's entire body quaked as he held me close.

"I'm sorry..." he began, blubbering a slew of pleas and apologies, none of which I wanted to hear right now. I knew that it had been a rough week, and I was aware that there had been a fight with Abigail, but I didn't care. All I wanted was for him to be safe from harm, and that meant not drinking.

"You really had me scared," I said softly, the fury gone from my voice.

Mitchell rubbed my back.

"I know," he said solemnly. "Can you forgive me?"

I leaned back in our embrace so that I could finally look him in the eyes. Where they normally were soft with compassion, right now they only carried sorrow and regret. Gazing into those pitiful puppy dog eyes, I suddenly had the impulse to laugh.

"You're an idiot, you know that?" I chuckled before pushing my lips to his.

After a few seconds, Mitchell broke away.

"So...are you okay?" he asked.

I smiled up at him, stroking his cheek gently with my hand.

"Yeah, we're good, just don't let it happen again."

Our mouths came together; my hands clasped around Mitchell's neck as his caressed my lower back, bodies falling together against the wall. I pressed myself deeper into his flesh until something firm probed my midsection. I separated from Mitchell, staring downwards in shock at the effect I was having on him.

"I guess you really enjoyed the show, huh?" I teased, causing Mitchell's face to go red with embarrassment.

I glanced over my shoulder at the liquor bottle on the counter still slick with my saliva and an idea formed in my mind. I turned back to Mitchell, biting my lip with excitement as I shot him a wicked smile.

"Come on," I urged, taking him by the hand.

"Where are we going?"

"It'll be fun, I promise."

With that, I led him into the bedroom.

Behind those closed doors, Mitchell and I engaged in a pastime I had never even thought of participating in before. It wasn't the type of activity they taught in school, and it was definitely not something I would have been comfortable discussing with my legal guardians, but somehow it came naturally, as though nothing I did could ever be as venerable or as honest as what we did together between the sheets.

I'm not entirely certain what I was expecting to see when those boxer shorts came off, but I was definitely caught off guard. Despite it being bigger and having a lot more hair than I imagined, I think that it was actually the strange topography that made me so apprehensive about the task ahead of me. Even after having ample time to explore its unique contours with my eyes, hands, and tongue, I still had huge misgivings about putting it in my mouth.

Eventually I overcame my fears and settled into a steady, relaxing rhythm. This being my first time, I was nervous about getting it right, but Mitchell's moans of pleasure from above assured me that I had nothing to worry about. I shut my eyes to keep myself from getting dizzy, which had the added benefit of allowing me to better appreciate the distinct texture and flavor.

After a few minutes, Mitchell reached his hand down to mine, interlocking the fingers in a tacit display of affection. Just knowing that he was enjoying my efforts filled me with passionate enthusiasm, and I continued with increased voracity. Each time I went down, I slid just a little bit more of him inside, the salty tang intensifying with every passing stroke. Mitchell squirmed beneath me in a fit of frenzy as his erratic breathing escalated into full-blown panting. Mitchell's body suddenly tensed, his warm member expanding rapidly and forcing my tiny mouth to stretch wider. Feeling it twitch between my lips, I was overwhelmed by an intoxicating blend of trepidation and triumph as I realized what was about to come.

While Mitchell experienced wave after wave of euphoria, I struggled to keep from drowning in the billowing seas. With every rising swell another powerful stream of thick brine would splash the inside of my mouth, forcing its way down my throat. Several times I gagged as my head bobbed frantically up and down along the top. Desperately gasping for oxygen, I clung firmly to Mitchell's hand as though it were a lifeline, hoping that his encouragement would help carry me through the final surges.

At long last, the storm subsided, the ocean returning to a state of calm. Mitchell tilted his head against the pillows, for some reason taking longer to catch his breath than I. Still not quite sure how these things worked, I lowered myself down again, trying to match my movements to the rise and fall of Mitchell's chest. Sadly, I was only down there a few more seconds before he urged me upward, lavishing me with affectionate kisses, completely unabated by the seawater still running down my cheek.

After getting cleaned up, Mitchell succumbed to an unexpected nap. While he slumbered beside me, I rested my head lightly against his stomach, listening to the sounds of his breathing. Even as I lay there, my lips still tingling from friction, my jaw aching from exhaustion, there was a huge part of me that beamed with lascivious pride knowing that it was I who had caused such ecstasy. Pulling the sheets over his naked form, I curled up next to Mitchell, all the while wondering how long it would take him to fully recharge.

CHAPTER 20

I lay in bed gazing up at the ceiling, fingers interlaced behind my head, feeling more relaxed than I'd felt in a very long time. I sensed movement and turned my attention to the sleeping figure draped across my torso. Her soft hair tickled my skin as she repositioned a few inches higher, nuzzling a cheek affectionately against my chest. With eyes closed she ran her tongue over her lips, a tantalizing reminder of our earlier escapade.

Olivia had entered my life in a whirlwind of mystery and chaos, completely uprooting everything that had been constant or stable in my daily routine. It was hard to believe that so much trouble could come from a package that small. And yet, I couldn't imagine being any happier than I was right now. Any doubts I had about our relationship were gone, dispelled the moment I let that bottle slip from my grasp. Hand in hand, we crossed the point of no return, a realization that placated my fears and strangely invigorated them at the same time.

I resumed staring vacantly upward.

Alcohol had always been my refuge, my guaranteed release from the misery of existence. There was more to it than that, however. Yes, I drank to drown out my sorrows, but I also did it to celebrate major events and minor victories. I drank when I wanted to be the life of the party, and I drank when all I could muster was sulking in the corner. I drank for motivation, and I drank for procrastination. I drank when there was tons of work to be done, and I drank when there was nothing to do. I drank when it was raining, I drank when it was snowing, and I drank when there were blue skies all around. Mostly I just drank. It was as much a part of my identity as my height or my hair color. How could I possibly give it up?

And yet, somehow, I would have to. The events of this afternoon had proven to me beyond any shadow of a doubt that my consumption was causing negative consequences to

STEVE WEST
196

those around me. It had definitely been an issue of contention with Olivia if she bothered to clear out my entire backup supply. How much longer would she stick around if she had to constantly fight to keep a bottle out of my hand? In all fairness, I considered myself quite lucky that she hadn't left already.

Plainly something had to be done, but what? I sifted through the possibilities at my disposal. My first thought was therapy, but I quickly dismissed the notion. The idea of spending fifty minutes with someone as myopic as Abigail made me physically ill. Besides, the agitation alone would probably drive me to drink again.

The next brainstorm I had was to see a doctor. Unfortunately, they were likely to be just as narrow-minded as a shrink. At least with the psychiatrists, they would want to get to the root of the problem before dolling out medicine like a candy machine. What good would it do if I quit the alcohol but found myself pill popping instead? Why exchange one addiction for another?

I could hear Abigail's voice in the back of mind urging me into rehab. I shook my head to discharge the irritating drone of her incessant nagging. In the past, I would have protested because they didn't let you drink coffee, or that their bed times were too early, or even simply that Abigail had been the one to suggest it. Now though, I had a legitimate reason not to let myself be confined in those unsightly stone corridors. Olivia needed looking after, and I couldn't very well do that locked away.

Wondering how other people handle this conundrum, my mind drifted to a coworker from back at school who'd been court ordered to attend special meetings after a DUI. I cringed at the notion, recoiling from the possibility like a moth around a burning flame. There was absolutely no way I'd subject myself to the spiritual hoopla of those religious nuts.

That's when I remembered Olivia and how hurt she had been by my obsession, by my neglect, and most of all by me. If she had walked out last night, wouldn't I have gone after her, done whatever it took to get her back? Then why was I hesitating now, especially over something that required such minimal effort? If I didn't like it, or if it didn't seem like it was going to work for me, then no big deal, all I had to do was come home and try something different. It was that simple.

With begrudging willingness, I quietly slipped from the bed, making sure not to disturb Olivia as I went.

Mitchell stood in the abandoned parking lot nervously anticipating what lay inside the red brick building before him. In spite of the exorbitant number of invitations from his brother-in-law, Mitchell refused to enter any house of worship since his wedding day. Ever since abandoning the faith of his youth, churches seemed to have an inherent sinister quality about them, as though he might be the victim of some gruesome horror movie massacre just for crossing the threshold.

Mitchell double-checked the address on his phone to make sure that this was the place. Although there were several fixtures illuminating the exterior, he failed to see even a single light coming from inside the dark structure. Mitchell wondered if he should take this as a sign to scrap the plan and head back home.

Swallowing his anxiety, Mitchell pushed open the main door, pausing near the entrance. Dull fluorescent lights flickered dimly in the corridor, helping to guide him to a nearby bulletin board. Scanning the list of weekly events, Mitchell located the appropriate room number and made his way upstairs. On the second floor, he came across two men talking boisterously in the hallway.

"Did I tell you that I drafted him in my fantasy league?" asked the shorter of the two men.

"Nice," commented the second man. "Did you have to give up a first round pick for that?"

The shorter man shook his head.

"Third actually."

"Third?! How the hell did you manage that?"

"Easy. There are only eight people in my league."

The taller man glared at him.

"That's so unfair," he protested. "Why are you in such a small group anyway?"

"Not as many people work in my office," the shorter man shrugged. "We even had to recruit one of the guy's brothers to join."

"You're lucky then. Mine's with the folks down at the plant. We had so many that we divided into two groups of twelve, which wouldn't be so bad if everyone wasn't so gung-ho on grabbing the quarterbacks. I drew number three, and he was still gone before I could get to him."

The two men stopped speaking as Mitchell stepped from the shadows. The taller man took a reflexive step backward while the shorter man gazed upward, smiling warmly at the new arrival.

"I see the new security's arrived," he jested.

The shorter man took a step forward and extended his hand to Mitchell.

"I'm Carl," he greeted. "You here for the meeting?"

Mitchell clasped the outstretched hand.

"Mitchell," he replied, unsure how introductions meshed with anonymity. "And yes, I am."

"Excellent," chimed the other man. "My name's Ed, by the way."

Mitchell shook hands with the second fellow.

"Is this your first meeting?" asked Carl.

Mitchell nodded.

"Should have guessed that when you showed up half an hour early," he stated. "Let me show you around."

Mitchell followed Carl into a room. Long, white tables were positioned in the center with chairs around the perimeter. From where Mitchell stood, he could see several papers, a couple baskets, a box of colorful coins and other bits of debris.

Passing by the communal layout, Carl led him to a table at the back of the room. Stacked on top were two large coffee dispensers, one designated regular and the other decaf. Beside the canisters were the usual mixings of sugar, sugar substitutes and creamer. Further down the line were packages of cookies, candies and pastries, all open and ready to be devoured. Cups, plates and utensils were neatly stacked at the far end as well.

"Help yourself," said Ed. "It's usually a pretty small group here on Saturday night."

Mitchell nodded, though he only went for coffee.

"So what do you do, Mitchell?" asked Carl.

"What do you mean?"

"What kind of work do you do?"

Mitchell hesitated.

"I used to be a teacher."

"Were you fired?" asked Ed, tactful as muddy boots at a black-tie function.

Mitchell cocked an eyebrow at him.

"Technically, I resigned."

"Because they were going to fire you otherwise, right?" probed Ed.

Mitchell inhaled deeply before nodding his head.

"I understand," said Ed, strangely sympathetic. "I used to work for the Bureau of Fire until I backed a truck into one of the garage doors. Once they found out I'd been drinking on the job, that was it."

"Sorry to hear that," said Mitchell. "Is that what brought you here?"

Ed chuckled.

"I drank five more years after that. I can be kind of hard-headed."

"I see..." replied Mitchell. "So what do you do now?"

"Waste management," he said.

"Oh..."

"It's not so bad," Ed explained. "It sure beats having to pick up trash on the side of the highway in an orange jumper."

"I suppose," said Mitchell.

"So what brought you down here tonight?" asked Ed.

Carl spoke up before Mitchell could respond.

"A woman," he said.

They both turned to him in surprise.

"How did you know that?" demanded Mitchell.

Carl gave him a shrug.

"I've been around a long time," he said.

Mitchell wanted to inquire further but was interrupted by the sound of approaching shoes. He turned to see a burly gentleman wearing the traditional Pittsburgh black and gold. The man had short, reddish hair and a two-day stubble on his chin. When he drew near, the faint aroma of cigarette smoke permeated the air.

"Looks like Josh is here," said Carl. "Guess we can finally have a meeting."

The new arrival held out his hand.

"How's it going, Carl?" he asked.

"Good. How's Josh doing?"

"Full of sunshine and rainbows," he said sarcastically. "Thanks for setting up by the way."

"No problem."

Josh turned his attention to Mitchell.

"Welcome," he greeted, holding out his hand. "Josh."

Mitchell returned the gesture.

"Is this your first meeting?" asked Josh.

"Yes."

"Glad you're here," he said. "Did you remember to bring your permission slip?"

Mitchell gave him a panicked expression.

"Josh..." said Carl in a chastising tone.

"What?" he asked innocently, moving to the coffee pots.

"He was joking about the permission slip," assured Carl. "He just likes to mess with the newcomers."

Mitchell nodded.

"Do you get a lot of new people showing up?" he asked.

"A few," said Ed. "Though we'll be getting even less if Josh keeps scaring them away."

"Oh, whatever," griped Josh.

Josh stirred his cup and returned to the small circle of men.

"So, are you in charge here?" asked Mitchell when he came back.

Ed and Carl exchanged glances before bursting into laughter.

"Heaven help us," replied Ed.

"I'm just the chairperson," clarified Josh. "I'm in charge of making sure the place is set up and ready to go before we start. The chairperson is also in charge of leading the meeting."

"How do you decide who chairs the meetings?" inquired Mitchell.

"We take turns," explained Carl. "That way everybody gets a chance to do a little service work."

"That is, if Dictator Josh allows it," joked Ed.

"Anyway..." stated Josh dismissively.

As it neared the start time, more people showed up. With every new person, there would be another round of handshakes, with some hugs thrown in for good measure. Everybody seemed to know everyone else, which would have normally made Mitchell feel like an outcast, except that they all seemed to want to talk to him. It was like being at a family reunion.

When the time came to take their seats, Josh took the chair at the head of the collection of tables. Ed and Carl took spots near the front with Josh. Mitchell followed suit, fascinated how everyone seemed to just know where they were supposed to sit, as though there had been a committee on assigned seating the week prior.

As the meeting progressed, Mitchell listened intently to the stories and experiences. When people shared, there were nods of heads, claps of applause, and even the occasional unnerving laughter. Though he did not fully understand or even agree with everything he heard, there was definitely a strong sense of community, as though these strangers were more of a family than anything he had ever known with Abigail.

Mitchell didn't understand how a group of individuals united only by tragic circumstances could remain so honest, open and cheerful with one another, but he planned on sticking around long enough to find out.

After another half hour of sleep, Olivia stirred in the bed. She cuddled against the soft pillow for a few more seconds before realizing that she was the solitary occupant on the large mattress. Olivia reached out for Mitchell, her hand caressing the empty sheets still warm from his presence. She raised her head and gazed toward the open bedroom door.

"Mitchell?" she called out, getting no response.

Sliding out of bed, Olivia padded to the communal area, only to discover a vacant apartment. Just when she was beginning to panic, she spotted a handwritten note on the kitchen island. As she read, Olivia picked up the open container of liquor and began to pour its contents down the garbage disposal.

"*Dear Olivia,*" it began, "*sorry I didn't tell you I was leaving, you looked so peaceful that I didn't want to disturb you. Anyway, I've gone to pick up a few supplies for tomorrow and run an errand. Will let you know how it went when I get back. See you soon. Love, Mitchell.*"

Olivia rinsed out the bottle and set it on the counter. She continued to read the note.

"*P.S. Here is a list of some hiding places that you might have missed when you swept the apartment. Feel free to deal with them; I don't want any temptations lying around.*"

Olivia smiled to herself as she looked over the list. After reading the last line, she folded the paper twice and tossed it in the trash can. Her work might have ended, but Mitchell would still have a long way to go. She opened the refrigerator in search of comfort food that would help ease him into the tough journey ahead.

As the meeting ended, the group stood around the room holding hands. They recited a statement Mitchell did not know, followed by one whose words he knew all too well. After their recitation, the crowd broke into smaller sections, some went to clean, others to smoke, but most just stood around talking.

"Hey there, big guy," said Carl. "Can you give me a hand with these pots?"

Mitchell nodded and carried the large canisters to the kitchen area on the far side of the room, but it was Carl who did the cleaning.

"I really like what you shared," he said.

"Uh, thanks." Mitchell replied with surprise.

Carl nodded.

"It's nice to see a newcomer who is as open and willing as you seem to be. Most of us had a long way to go when we first came in."

Mitchell nodded, appreciating the compliment.

"How long have you been coming?" Mitchell asked.

Carl took a deep breath.

"Thirty-six years," he replied finally.

"Thirty-six years?!" exclaimed Mitchell. "How do you manage that?"

Carl maintained an aura of calm as he continued to clean the insides of the coffee containers.

"One day at a time," he said plainly. "That's all any of us ever get."

Mitchell didn't fully understand the cryptic speaking, but he was impressed nonetheless. This man had been sober longer than he'd been alive.

When Carl finished cleaning the canisters, he dried his hands and turned back to Mitchell.

"Have they gotten you a Big Book yet?" he asked.

"A what?" replied Mitchell.

Carl motioned for him to follow, and they walked to a nearby cabinet. From inside, Carl retrieved a heavy looking, yellow and blue hardback book and handed it to Mitchell.

"Here. You should read this. We sell them for cost, but if you can't pay now, just drop the money in the basket when you can."

Mitchell flipped the pages of the massive text.

"You want me to read *all* of this?" he asked incredulously.

"Well, just start with the first 164 pages. That really outlines the program. The stories in the back are good to read whenever."

Mitchell nodded. Actually, 164 pages wasn't that much compared to his nightly reading regimen in college.

"You should get yourself a sponsor as well," stated Carl, closing the literature cabinet.

Mitchell looked inquisitively at him.

"I don't really understand some of the things about this program," he said. "What exactly is a sponsor?"

"A sponsor is someone who helps you work through the steps. He'll explain anything you have trouble understanding and help guide you in the right direction when you let him," Carl explained patiently.

Mitchell pondered for a moment.

"Then, will you be my sponsor?"

Carl seemed taken aback, but smiled nonetheless.

"I'm always happy to be of service," he stated.

"So, is that a yes?" inquired Mitchell.

Carl nodded, moving to a stand filled with pamphlets stacked in organized rows. Taking one from the rack, he pulled a pen from his shirt pocket and wrote on the back before handing it to Mitchell.

"Here is a meeting list," he said. "I wrote my phone number on the back. I want you to call me daily and let me know how you're doing."

Mitchell took the paper from him with a respectful nod.

"Anything else?" Mitchell asked.

"Yeah…" Carl said with a smile. "Don't drink."

Olivia knelt in the corner scrolling through the songs on the iPod hoping to create the perfect playlist to coincide with her special surprise for Mitchell. Where most people chose songs good for driving or working out, she focused on selections of a far more eccentric nature. After making her choices, Olivia returned the device to its usual place, trusting that her changes wouldn't be noticed until the time was right.

Standing from her squatted position, she stole a glance at the living room clock. By now Mitchell had been gone nearly two hours, and Olivia was growing concerned. *Where was he? What was he doing? Why had he snuck off like a thief in the night?*

Worrying about it certainly isn't going to help, she reminded herself.

Deciding that the best way to kill time was to remain active, Olivia set about accomplishing some household chores until he returned. She scrubbed the dinner dishes, wiped the counters and cleaned surfaces that had been splashed with grease. Before taking the trash out, Olivia retrieved her clothes from the morning and quickly slipped them on. She was halfway through tying the bag when the front door opened, and Mitchell announced his arrival.

Leaving the bag lying on the floor, she ran to greet him. Before he was able to get his coat off, Olivia plowed into him from behind, wrapping her arms lovingly around his midsection. Miraculously able to maintain his balance from the sudden attack, Mitchell rotated in her direction so that he could return the embrace.

After a few seconds he lifted his gaze toward the kitchen.

"What's that smell?" he asked, his nostrils flaring above her.

Olivia shot him a blank stare.

"Maybe it's the hamburgers," she said, more as a question than a statement. "They're keeping warm on a tray in the oven."

Mitchell nodded.

"Smells wonderful," he replied.

Regardless of whether the aroma was coming from the food or not, Olivia smiled.

"Thank you," she said cordially.

Mitchell slid from her arms, smiling fondly into those deep blue sapphires as he ran his fingers through her hair. He surveyed Olivia's body up and down again, his brow furrowing as he pondered what had changed in her appearance. When he finally realized what was different about her, Mitchell's eyes went wide with concern, the color quickly draining from his face.

"Where are you going?" he asked anxiously.

Olivia gave him a curious look, raising her finger in the direction of the trash chute. "I was just heading to…"

Mitchell suddenly moved forward, clasping her outstretched hand in his.

"Please don't go," he begged her.

Olivia raised her eyebrows in surprise.

"What are you…?"

"I'm sorry about what happened earlier," he said in a panicked tone.

"I know," she said softly. "I'm not upset about it."

"It was a moment of weakness," he continued, his tempo intensifying.

Olivia squeezed his hand affectionately.

"It's ok, Mitchell. Really, I'm fine."

Mitchell stared at her with glazed eyes, as though not hearing her words.

"I know I haven't really done anything in the past to deal with the problem, but I assure you that I'm seriously trying this time. I'm even seeking help and everything. That's actually where I went tonight…"

"Mitchell…" Olivia calmly tried to interject.

"I met this guy down there, and he's agreed to sponsor me. I'm not entirely certain what that entails, but he's pretty confident that I can stay sober as long as I work a good program. He said to go to meetings, which I will. And then there's this book that he gave me. It's kind of big, but it has these different stories in it that help…"

"Mitchell…" Olivia attempted again, this time with a louder voice.

"And now that we've gotten rid of all the bottles, I know I can beat this. I know I shouldn't have put anything ahead of you, especially when I said we're in this together, but I won't let it happen again. I'll do whatever it takes to make it right, just please don't leave. I'll…"

Olivia covered his mouth with her hand.

"I'm not going anywhere," she stated in exasperation.

Mitchell sighed heavily, her words finally sinking in.

"You're not?" he asked, seeking reassurance.

"Of course not," she exclaimed. "Why would I leave you?"

Mitchell seemed to relax a little bit.

"It's just...what about those?" he inquired, gesturing toward her attire.

Olivia glanced down before rolling her eyes at him.

"For the love of...my clothes?! Really?!" she demanded incredulously. "That's what this is about?!"

Mitchell sheepishly turned his attention to the floor.

"You only bother getting dressed when you have to go outside," he explained.

Olivia placed a tender hand beneath his chin, gently raising his head to meet her grin.

"I was just taking the trash out, you crazy man," she smiled. "Or would you rather I be naked for that?"

Mitchell smiled hopefully at her.

"So...you're not leaving?"

Olivia kissed him on the cheek.

"I'm staying right here," she assured him. "In fact, since you're here, would you mind taking the garbage out?"

Mitchell nodded, following her to the kitchen. With one hand, he lifted the heavy bag from the floor and began to carry it out of the apartment.

"Oh, and Mitchell?" called Olivia from behind him.

He turned to gaze at her, an inquisitive look upon his face.

"When you get back," she said, undoing the fastening on her jeans, "If I'm not wearing clothes, you don't get to either."

CHAPTER 21

Mitchell felt déjà vu as he awoke to sunlight streaming through the bedroom window. Olivia lay in her usual position, head resting on his chest, snuggled closely by his side. Out of curiosity, Mitchell lifted the blanket and peered beneath. He was clad and she was not, all seemed right with the world.

Mitchell caressed up and down her back, beginning at the top and slowly traveling downward. After a few strokes, his hand passed over her bare behind, and he gave it a gentle squeeze. Olivia squirmed in his grip; her sensitive regions still not acclimated to another's touch. Her eyes flickered open, and she tilted up to look at him, light reflecting off the blue irises like sunshine over tropical waters.

"You know," she said softly, "in some cultures, it might be considered inappropriate to fondle a woman in her sleep."

Mitchell quickly pulled his hand a few inches higher.

"Sorry," he muttered. "I couldn't help myself."

Olivia reached behind and guided his hand back down.

"What a bunch of prudes," she teased, draping her leg across his.

Mitchell resumed his light petting as Olivia fell back into dormancy. He was very much enjoying the relaxing satisfaction of having her nearby when his stomach emitted a low rumbling sound. After glancing at the clock, Mitchell decided that they should get a move on if they were going to have any chance of getting there by lunchtime.

"Ok. Rise and shine," he said softly, giving her a gentle shake.

Olivia groaned.

"Do you think it wise to wake a sleeping tiger?" she asked with eyes still closed.

"What exactly are you going to do, pounce on me?" he asked tauntingly.

"And swallow you whole," she threatened, playfully raking his chest with her fingertips.

"Oh no, not that briar patch over there," he teased. "But seriously, it's time to get up."

Olivia pressed her head deeper into his chest.

"I'm pretty sure that you are mistaken."

Mitchell smiled as he ran his fingers through her hair.

"Look, you can stay in bed a little while longer if you want, but I need to start getting ready."

Olivia rubbed her leg along his, trying to entice him to stay.

"Do you really need to slip off to one of those meetings right now?" she protested.

"Probably," he said, "But that's not where I'm going."

"It's not?"

"No. Don't you remember? We have something special planned for today."

Olivia opened her eyes.

"That's right," she said with excitement. "I had completely forgotten about the surprise you were planning. So what is it?"

Mitchell shook his head and shrugged.

"You know, it's the funniest thing," he said, "I can't remember."

Olivia shifted so that she was lying entirely on top of him.

"Come on, tell me."

Mitchell wrapped his arms around Olivia, holding tight to keep her from sliding off.

"I'll tell you on the way," he assured her.

Olivia made a pouting face.

"You know, Mr. Flynn, we have ways of making you talk."

Mitchell smiled up at her, chuckling at the reference.

"Sorry," he said, running his fingers through her hair. "But my lips are sealed."

Mitchell leaned forward, passionately joining his mouth with hers.

When the timer went off, Mitchell extracted the hot pan from the oven. He tested the texture by probing it with his finger before shutting off the stove. Grabbing a knife from the drawer, he began covering the cinnamon rolls in generous heaps of frosting. Halfway through, he reached into his front pocket and extracted something small and slid it across the island to Olivia.

"The first part of your surprise," he explained.

Olivia examined it carefully.

"What is it?"

"A key."

Olivia glared disapprovingly at him.

"I can see that," she said. "What's it a key to?"

Mitchell beamed at her.

"A 2009 Silverado." he stated, clearly pleased with himself.

Olivia searched her memory.

"A car?"

"Well, technically a truck, but yes."

Olivia looked at him with surprise.

"You bought a truck?"

Mitchell shook his head.

"No. I *rented* a truck. They tend to be cheaper that way."

"Why did you rent a truck?"

Mitchell carried two plates over and took the seat beside her.

"Because it's too far to walk."

"Does that mean we'll be leaving the city?"

"That's not a problem is it?" he asked with concern.

"Nope," she said with a smile. "In fact, I think it'll be nice to get away for a while. Where are we going anyway?"

"So many questions…" he commented dismissively.

"Well, do I need to pack for this trip?"

"I've already taken care of that," he said. "I need to make one last stop on the way out of town for some food supplies, but that's it."

"What about a change of clothes?"

"It's only going to be a day trip, so you should be fine with whatever you have on."

Olivia raised her eyebrows at him before clearing her throat.

"Ah-hem," she said, gesturing toward her nakedness.

"Ok, yes, you'll have to put on something first."

"You never know," she said innocently. "We could be going to a nudist resort."

"I suppose that's true," he admitted. "But I figured you might want to try something different."

"Fair enough," she said, pushing away her plate. "I'm going to go get dressed so I'll be ready to go."

When she emerged from the bedroom, Mitchell gathered up the supplies, leaving her in charge of managing the doors along the way. In the parking lot, Mitchell directed her to the proper vehicle. Olivia manually unlocked the side for him, and Mitchell deposited his cargo in the back seat.

Closing the rear door, Mitchell went around to the passenger side and held it open for his tiny companion. Olivia had never ridden in a truck before, and the height of the seats seemed like a daunting challenge. Leaning her head inside, she carefully examined the interior.

"There's only one seat," she observed.

Mitchell nodded.

"That's pretty common on trucks," he explained. "It's called bench seating."

Mitchell made a gesture with his arms.

"Are you ready?" he asked.

Olivia nodded.

Mitchell lifted her from the ground and placed her delicately in the cab of the truck. Satisfied that she was secure, he walked back to the driver's side.

"So why did you get a truck anyway?" she asked when he climbed inside.

Mitchell gestured to Olivia for the keys as he closed the door.

"Three reasons," he explained, reaching for his seat belt. "First, trucks are bigger. When you're my size, most vehicles are not very comfortable for long periods of time, and that's if I can get in them at all. Secondly, this vehicle has four-wheel drive, which might come in handy for where we're going."

Mitchell stuck the key in the ignition slot and started the engine. As it warmed up, he fiddled with the dials on the steering wheel and dashboard, trying to get a clear idea for where everything was.

"What's the third reason?" asked Olivia.

Mitchell completed his preflight operations and shot Olivia a sly smile. He patted the empty seat between them. Following his lead, Olivia slid closer to him, fastening herself in with the middle belt. Mitchell wrapped his arm around her as they ventured east out of the city.

The pickup truck passed through the state park entrance around one o'clock. Mitchell drove the vehicle to the main registration area and checked them in before heading by the boat concession for a bundle of firewood and down the precarious road toward their campsite. He parked the truck in the proper space and exited the vehicle. Olivia slid toward him, and he lifted her from the cab and set her down on the soft soil. She was ecstatic about being here, and to Mitchell it looked like she was vibrating.

"Come on," she said, taking him by the hand.

Mitchell barely had a chance to lock the truck before they were off.

With her leading the way, they wandered along nature trails in the park, Olivia pausing several times to point out distinct bird sounds and fauna that she spotted. She showed him interesting plant species and explained how some were used in homeopathic medicine. Mitchell was impressed by her knowledge, although he was apprehensive about touching anything else in the forest after she identified poison ivy.

As they walked, Olivia took Mitchell by the hand. The sheer multitude of people in the park made Mitchell nervous to be affectionate in public; the restaurant incident was still fresh on his mind. And yet, few people gave them a second glance. Perhaps they just assumed he and she were parent and child, or perhaps they figured a wild environment dictated a little overprotection, or perhaps they simply didn't care. Either way, Mitchell soon forgot about others in the park or what they thought about him and her and focused on having a good time with Olivia. On one of the more deserted trails, he pulled her behind the trunk of a large tree and passionately kissed her beneath its protective branches.

After several hours of hiking, they returned to their campsite, weary from all the walking. Mitchell retrieved sandwiches from one of the bags, and they picnicked on the tailgate of the truck. He offered her a choice between a cheesesteak and a hoagie, with Olivia opting for the one with greater variety. After finishing their meal, Olivia rested against his shoulder, peering through the trees at the sand encampment in the distance.

"If I had known they had a beach, I would have packed a swimsuit," she commented.

Mitchell nodded; *it was kind of an oddity for a landlocked section of the state.*

"Well it's not like you knew we were coming here," said Mitchell. "Besides, do you even own a swimsuit?"

Olivia shrugged.

"I suppose not," she said.

Mitchell stood from his seat and carried the trash to the nearest receptacle. On his return, he stuck his head inside the truck. Finding what he was looking for, Mitchell carried it to where Olivia still sat.

"What do you think?" he asked, holding the items for her to see.

Olivia looked at Mitchell. Draped over his left arm was a blue tank top, in his right hand he held a pair of matching bikini bottoms. It took Olivia a moment to realize that the two went together as swimwear. She leaped from the tailgate and took the top from his outstretched arm. Olivia ran her fingers over the material, holding its velvety texture affectionately against her face. She looked up at Mitchell with an elated smile.

"It's perfect," she exclaimed.

Mitchell nodded at her satisfaction, relieved that he'd been able to find a swimsuit in her size this late in the season.

"Can we go?" she asked eagerly.

"Ok," agreed Mitchell.

Olivia nearly jumped with glee at his approval. She reached down and clasped the lower parts of her t-shirt. Olivia began to pull the garment overhead when Mitchell darted out his hand to stop her. She looked at him with confusion.

"You should change over in that building," he said gesturing.

Olivia followed his finger to a building with two restroom signs, one on either side of the building. She looked back at him, biting her lip in embarrassment.

"Sorry," she said. "I forgot."

Mitchell rolled his eyes.

"Well, go on. I'll be right behind you."

Inside the restroom, Olivia undressed, swiftly donning the blue, two-piece swimsuit. Even though the task went quickly, Olivia lingered in the stall until she heard the other occupant leave. Once the coast was clear, Olivia emerged from her cubicle and moved to the mirror.

Though her body was pale, the fabric perfectly accented the color of her eyes, the blond hair an excellent contrast to the entire ensemble. Where most bikini tops easily slid out of place on her, this one clung to her thin frame, making her seem petite and perky, instead of flat-chested and childish. Olivia spun around. The bikini bottom adhered alluringly to her backside, nearly exposing the upper crevice. She merrily wiggled her butt back and forth in the mirror, delighting in her sexiness.

Her mind turned to Mitchell. *He really can be quite marvelous when he wants to be. I hope he enjoys the present I got for him as much as I like this.*

The bathroom door opened and Olivia darted outside, fearful that she'd already been caught in her reverie. Away from the building, she found Mitchell waiting for her, two towels draped over his left shoulder. She took hold of his free arm, and they headed toward the beach.

As they walked, Mitchell began to notice several eyes gazing awkwardly in their direction. The late afternoon sun bathed the forest in a romantic summer glow, making their minor affections and meager adornments all the more scandalous. Mitchell lowered his head.

"I don't think we should hold hands until we're back at the camp," he whispered.

Olivia looked at him with hurt eyes.

"Why not?" she asked.

"We're starting to attract unwanted attention," he said, glancing around them.

Olivia followed his gaze, spotting several onlookers who averted their eyes as soon as they were caught rubbernecking. She wanted to tell Mitchell to ignore them; that their love was just as true as anybody else's. And yet, she knew that truth was seldom of importance to a mob. She sadly withdrew her hand from his.

As her fingers pulled away, Mitchell immediately regretted bringing it up. It was as though a part of him had slipped away; that a fragment of his soul had somehow disappeared. *What right did these people have to judge their love? Why should their affections be treated as less significant just because of how they looked?* Mitchell bent down again.

"We can hold hands in the water," he offered.

Olivia thought about it.

"Race you to the beach," she challenged.

The two young lovers bolted toward the water. Together they hurdled a fallen tree, ducked a low hanging vine, and whizzed by a slow moving couple. Though neither wanted to arrive without the other, it was Olivia whose foot touched sand first.

"Beat you," she said, panting for breath.

Mitchell took her hand, and they entered the water as one. Beneath the protective covering of blue, they held hands, frolicked and played; delighting in the joy of being alive. Mitchell splashed, Olivia made waves, and together they cried out in rebellious happiness. When they emerged from the water, Olivia openly clung to him and Mitchell to her. No one would interfere with their love on this night.

Back at the camp, Mitchell started a fire as Olivia slipped out of her wet apparel. After he shed his own, the two hung the swimsuits by the warmth of the fire as they sat on the edge of the truck admiring the beautiful sunset.

When the sun finished its final descent, Mitchell retrieved the last few items from his food purchase. Hunkering by the fire, he began to organize small piles.

"What're you doing?" asked Olivia.

"S'mores," he said cheerfully. "You can't have a proper campfire without them."

Olivia's interest piqued further.

"I've never had those before," she stated.

Mitchell raised an eyebrow at her.

"Really?"

She just shook her head.

Mitchell took a large marshmallow and placed it on the end of a skewer. He handed it to Olivia and instructed her to hold it near the fire until it turned light brown. Mitchell readied the graham crackers and chocolate. When the time came, Mitchell took the skewer from Olivia and slid the marshmallow between the crackers. He handed the complete concoction to her.

"Be careful, it's hot," he said.

She nodded, taking the delectable dessert from him. Blowing a few times across the middle, she bit into the treat. A moan of ecstasy escaped her lips.

"That's amazing," she uttered, her pupils losing focus.

Mitchell smiled before preparing the next round. The two sat enjoying the campfire snack. With food in their bellies, chocolate coursing through their veins and love beating in their hearts, the young lovers cuddled together beside the fire.

When the fire was nearly out, Mitchell unrolled a sleeping bag and pillow in the bed of the truck. He closed the tailgate for privacy as they lay together. He helped Olivia over the top and set her gently in the bed.

Mitchell crawled into the sleeping bag first, removing his shirt as he did so. Using the side of the truck bed as cover, Olivia slid out of her jeans before getting in next to Mitchell. Under the security of the sleeping bag, Olivia slipped her shirt overhead. With a little more squirming, she removed her underwear and put them under the pillow for safekeeping. Finally settled, Olivia laid her head against Mitchell's broad shoulder as he wrapped his massive arm snugly around her.

The fire continued to die down until the two were covered in darkness. As much as Mitchell enjoyed his beloved Pittsburgh, there were some things that one could not experience properly within the city limits. One was stars. There was the planetarium, but for Mitchell, it wasn't the same.

Olivia pointed out constellations. There were the two dippers, Draco, Aquila, and of course, Capricornus. Mitchell learned many of these when he studied astronomy as an elective in college and probably could have recited them from memory, but there was something about her enthusiastic explanations that made him want to listen instead.

After a time, Olivia grew quiet and laid her head against his shoulder, peering into his eyes.

"Thank you for a wonderful day," she said.

Mitchell nuzzled her forehead with his.

"Thank you for sharing it with me."

Tucked together beneath the stars of Capricornus as Virgo reigns in the sky, two ardent lovers, a man of the first house and a woman from the second, came upon a star-crossed path. There is no greater feeling in all the world than the joy of knowing that you've finally found that special someone with whom you were always meant to be. And yet, far easier it is to have loved and lost, than to have triumphed, against impossible odds, only to be damned anyway...

CHAPTER 22

It was only 7:30 when I stepped off the elevator, Olivia asleep in my arms. Neither of us managed to get much rest last night, and the effects definitely showed. Living in a city, there is always a low rumble, a white noise that drowns out the little nuances of the night. In the quiet of the forest, however, every chirp of the cricket, every croak of the frog and every hoot of the owl cuts through the silence like a megaphone. With each passing hour, a new series of critters would emerge with strange noises to disrupt our otherwise peaceful slumber. When the first rays of morning sunlight shown on the horizon, I eagerly packed up the camp and headed for home.

Being careful not to wake my sleeping charge, I nudged open the apartment door. Once inside, I carried Olivia to the bedroom and delicately laid her beneath the top sheet. Starting with the shoes, I worked on disrobing her, the process going much smoother than back at the campsite where I struggled to dress her beneath the concealment of the sleeping bag.

After the final article had been removed, I gazed down at her naked beauty, not with lust, but with awe. It was hard to believe that only a week had passed since I met her, alone and exposed on the harsh surface of the roof. I still remember her body trembling from the cold as I carried her to this exact spot. She seemed so pale and fragile compared to the vibrant and passionate woman I'd grown to love. In spite of everything that transpired around us, Olivia remained true to herself; kind, compassionate and honest, able to master emotions that I could hardly muster.

Indeed, I was the one who was changing. I'd dealt with the side effects of blackout drinking for so long that the mere possibility of existing for another thirty years living like this made me constantly think about ways of simply not being at all. And yet, my obsession for oblivion had been replaced by an even greater desire. No longer did I fear what tomorrow might bring, nor did I feel the crushing dismay of yesterday's defeats. Whatever I won or lost along the way didn't matter anymore. Olivia had given me a will to live, and I intended to enjoy every second of it.

I leaned forward and placed a gentle kiss on her lips, Olivia's mouth subconsciously reacting to my touch. In that moment, there were so many things I could have been accomplishing, from unloading the truck to reading the massive text from Carl. Instead, I quietly closed the bedroom door and began to undress, no longer concerned about concealing anything from my beloved. Sliding into bed beside Olivia, I drifted off to sleep, completely unaware that today was Monday.

Abigail swiped her credit card through the machine, not bothering to see the final price. With the success of Eric's books, financial worries had become more of a momentary annoyance rather than an actual concern. These days, it seemed to be in vast supply; no matter how much she spent, there was always plenty.

And that was the reason she continued to look after her younger brother. Perhaps it was her protective nature. Abigail always felt a need to take care of him; to make sure he was safe. When he lost his job, she was there to offer money. After six months of unemployment, when his drinking really began to spiral, she offered to drive him to and from the counselor's office. When that did not pan out, she insisted on going grocery shopping for him in an effort to quell his drinking and assure him a proper diet. So every Monday, she delivered food and other necessities to his apartment.

But that was all about to change. Saturday's events had solidified in her mind that shielding Mitchell from himself was a lost cause. Every time she aided him with supplies and money, she was only enabling his destructive behavior and further delaying the day when he would finally hit rock bottom. She was not sure how much Mitchell had left from his severance pay, but maybe when it dried up, so might he.

Abigail thanked the cashier and wheeled the cart full of groceries to her car. She could already feel her emotions beginning to run over. In her mind, when Mitchell walked out on lunch, it was like he was walking out on her. Her constant pestering about becoming sober had apparently driven a wedge between them. Though it pained her, Abigail knew she had to do what was best for her and would eventually be best for Mitchell as well.

Driving to his apartment, she anticipated the argument that they were sure to have. Mitchell had not shown much gratitude for the effort she put into keeping him healthy, and she sometimes felt that he resented it. Being blessed financially gave Abigail a sense of duty to help those around her, but unfortunately, there were always those who saw acts of charity as a way to demonstrate superiority over others. Though Mitchell probably resisted her for similar reasons, she felt that it was primarily driven from his hatred for her husband's profession.

When she arrived at his complex, she found a parking spot near the entrance. Abigail quickly unloaded the bags and locked the car. By the time she stepped off the elevator, Abigail was already feeling weighed down by the burdensome groceries. Eager to finally be free of her hefty cargo, Abigail doubled her walking pace down the hallway, only to be accosted by a most unwelcome interruption.

"Hey, Abigail. Long time, no see," called out a friendly voice.

Abigail emitted a groan of annoyance as she turned to face Mitchell's overly enthusiastic neighbor. As usual, the strange woman was dressed in the most unsightly garb Abigail had ever seen. The garish assortment of colors made her look more like a throwback from the eighties than a modern day, professional woman. Even her jewelry was gaudy and mismatched, clanking loudly as she approached.

"Hello, Harriet," replied Abigail coldly. "How are you doing?"

"I'm wonderful," she said.

I'll bet you are, thought Abigail, crinkling her nose at the ubiquitous odor filling her nostrils, hoping it to be patchouli and nothing more.

"And how are you today?"

"I'm fine," said Abigail, noisily shifting the bags in her hands.

"That's great," said Harriet cheerfully. "I am just about to go for a quick stroll to clear my head. It really helps get my mind centered again when I'm having writer's block."

"Uh-huh."

"You know you're welcome to join me if you want."

"I really can't, Harriet. I've got a lot to get done today."

"Oh, ok," she said with a smile. "Maybe next time."

"Sure," Abigail said dismissively.

Harriet beamed at her.

"By the way, I really enjoyed meeting your niece the other day."

Abigail raised an eyebrow at her.

"My *what*?"

Harriet tilted her head in confusion.

"Your niece," she reiterated. "You know...Olivia."

"Oh..." said Abigail, realizing the misunderstanding. "That girl you saw around here the other day, she's actually not my niece."

Harriet considered this a moment.

"I see..." she uttered, her tone far more morose than before. "I know it's none of my business, but I don't think you should treat her any differently just because she's not blood related."

Abigail's head twitched subtly side-to-side, her eyes narrowing on the strange woman as she failed to comprehend her meaning.

"I'm sorry?"

"It's okay, dear. I suppose we all have our prejudices; we're only human after all. All I was saying is just because she's adopted doesn't make her any less your family."

Abigail suddenly felt as though she'd gotten off at the wrong stop.

"You don't understand," she explained. "We're not related."

Harriet took a step forward and placed her hand on Abigail's arm, giving her a reassuring smile as she squeezed gently near the elbow.

"I understand more than you think," she said. "You see, my cousin and his partner adopted a child not too long ago. Now my family is not the most conservative, but they were still bogged down by the idea of a traditional..."

Abigail could barely focus on the words, her mind racing to come up with a way to clarify the mix-up. After a few seconds, she simply gave up, accepting that it would be easier to just go along with it than to prolong this conversation any longer.

"You're right," she said. "I shouldn't have been so quick to judge."

Harriet halted the exposition, her eyes wide with surprise. They regained their usual softness as she nodded, clearly impressed by the sudden change of heart.

"I'm glad to hear that," she said with a smile.

"Well, I really should be getting along," said Abigail, desperately wanting to be free of this conversation.

"Oh, ok. Well, it was good talking with you. Hope you have a wonderful day!"

"You, too," Abigail replied.

When the woman was out of sight, Abigail exhaled forcefully from frustration, her head shaking back and forth. Without looking back, Abigail walked to Mitchell's apartment door. Setting half the groceries on the floor to free a hand, she fished the key out of her purse.

Taking hold of the doorknob, Abigail inhaled deeply, bracing herself for olfactory impact. Though she had long since gotten over the messiness of her brother's apartment, she had never managed to acclimate to the horrid stench that lingered inside. There was something about the combination of mildewed clothing, stale beer and three-week-old pizza that turned her stomach. Reassuring herself that this was the last time she would make this trip, Abigail turned the handle.

Nothing could have prepared her for what she saw behind that apartment door. The pigsty she'd trudged through only last week was no more, somehow transformed into an immaculate abode. Where there had been piles of trash polluting the living room floor, now there was empty space, the wood shining brilliantly from being mopped. Across the room she could read the covers of the books, which had been caked in dust for months. Even the pervasive smell of festering, forgotten food had been replaced by a pleasing, lemon-scented fragrance that made it enjoyable to breathe.

She carried the bags into the kitchen, relieved to be free of their cumbersome burden. Continuing to gaze around, she could see that the dishes had been cleaned and put away, the counters scrubbed clear of dirt and debris, and the inside of the refrigerator was clean for a change. Abigail opened the oven door and peered inside, stunned to see that it too had been restored to its former shine.

Humming softly to herself, Abigail removed her jacket and carried it to the wall hanger near the entrance. Still preoccupied with admiring the changes, Abigail accidentally knocked Mitchell's coat off the hook, causing a resounding thud as it impacted the floor. As she bent to scoop it up, she noticed a thick, yellow and blue hardback book sticking out from one of the pockets. Curiosity piqued, she reached inside, haphazardly returning the coat to its rightful place.

As her fingers skimmed along the top, the bold writing on the front had a bewildering effect on her. *Could it be true? Had Mitchell finally quit drinking after all this time?* She opened the cover and began flipping through the pages, relishing its tangible surfaces, delighting in its sobering words. A smile formed on her lips as she hugged the book to her chest. *It was all too good to be true.*

And yet, wasn't this what she had been pushing him toward from the get-go. All of those times she nagged him about moderation, negotiated with him to get a job, and pleaded for him to take better care of himself finally paid off. Perhaps he had been listening to her on Saturday when she mentioned rehab. Maybe just hearing that word from her lips was the necessary catalyst for him to realize how bad things had gotten. Regardless of why, it was plainly clear that Mitchell was taking the vital first steps on the road to recovery, and it was all because of her.

Book still grasped in her arms, Abigail moved toward the bedroom, eagerly wanting to throw open the door and envelop her sleeping brother in a caring hug, to tell him how proud she was of him. Halfway there though, she stopped short, resisting the temptation.

I'll let him sleep a little bit longer; she thought to herself, *he deserves the extra rest.* With that, Abigail went back to the kitchen to unload the rest of the groceries, hurrying the task along so that she could sooner go congratulate her brother.

Mitchell was jostled awake by the sound of a cabinet slamming in the kitchen. He was annoyed that someone would disturb his restful slumber after only a short nap. As the fog of sleep dissipated, Mitchell came to the realization that Olivia must have gotten hungry and gone to make something to eat. With her being so far away from him, Mitchell felt an urge to get up himself, but last night's sleeplessness left him too exhausted to move.

Closing his eyes, Mitchell rolled back onto his side, draping his arm delicately around Olivia. Pulling closer, he laid his head on the pillow above hers; quietly savoring the fragrances he'd grown to love. Listening to the sounds of her rhythmic breathing lulled Mitchell back to unconsciousness.

Just when he was about to nod off again, another crashing sound came from the kitchen. His eyes opened slightly as he pondered whether or not to see what she was up to in there. When his eyes focused on Olivia beside him, Mitchell sensed something was amiss, but his mind only whirred like the first try on a pull start mower. And then, synapses firing all at once, like a minefield of mental agitation, Mitchell suddenly became aware of who was in his kitchen.

Abigail!

Panic settled over him like a storm cloud signaling impending calamity. Mitchell assumed that his sister would find out about him and Olivia sooner or later, but their current situation constituted one of the absolute worst scenarios for her to make that discovery.

Mitchell desperately considered every idea on how to escape their current circumstance, and he came up empty. *If he pretended to be asleep, there was nothing stopping Abigail from strolling right on in and catching them lying in bed together. If he went out to meet her, she might still spot Olivia bundled beneath the sheets. If he closed the bedroom door behind him, Abigail was sure to be suspicious and ask him who was back there.* In fact, the only feasible strategy he could come up with was to hide.

He placed his hand on Olivia's shoulder and rocked her vigorously.

"Olivia," he called in a hoarse whisper. "Olivia, wake up."

She stirred slightly, giving a groggy moan of discontent. Out in the kitchen, Mitchell heard the sound of plastic bags being gathered up. Soon Abigail would come looking for him.

"Wake up," he whispered again, this time with more trepidation.

Olivia gazed at him through sleepy eyes.

"What is it?" she asked.

Mitchell wanted to hide her in the closet, figuring it to be the safest place for her, but judging by the approaching footsteps, they didn't have that kind of time.

"I need you to duck your head beneath the sheets," he said.

Olivia shot him a look of annoyance.

"You know I don't mind doing it for you," she said, "but couldn't you have at least waited until I woke up?"

Mitchell's face flushed with embarrassment.

"No. Listen," he pleaded, pointing to the kitchen. "Abigail is out there."

Olivia looked at him blankly and then her eyes grew wide with alarm. In unison, they turned toward the sound of a creaking board on the other side of the door. Without another moment's hesitation, Olivia disappeared underneath the blanket. Mitchell could feel Olivia wrapping around his left leg, resting her head along his inner thigh to help obscure her lumpy form. Mitchell raised his right knee to conceal her as well.

Olivia had barely settled into place when Mitchell heard the sound of someone latching onto the doorknob, sweat forming on his brow as he watched it turn.

Abigail peered around the edge of the door as she opened it.

"Mitchell?" she called out faintly.

"Wait, Abigail," he responded, his voice trembling as he spoke. "Don't come in here."

She paused at the entrance.

"Are you dressed?"

There was a pause.

"It's not that," he said. "It's just…I'm not feeling well and I'd rather you not see me like this."

Abigail had seen her brother sick many times over the last few years, and he had never denied her entry, not even when he was suffering from the terrible side effects of a hangover. Full of worry, Abigail poked her head around the edge of the door.

"Are you alright?"

"I'm fine," he said, holding up his hand as if to ward her from the room. "Just please stay out."

Abigail quickly withdrew her head. In the brief instant that she got to look at her brother she could tell he was in great pain, the color completely drained from his features, a look on his face as though he might vomit at a moment's notice. The book in his coat pocket had clued her in on what she might see in the bedroom, but even with the added preparation she had not expected the throes of detox to be quite so intense. She could only imagine the hells he was enduring beyond that door.

In his foolhardy desire to nap unclad beside his beloved, Mitchell opened himself up to a very precarious position. With Olivia's hair draped delicately over his lap, every time she breathed the velvety strands would glide gently across his tender flesh. Combined with the warm air of her exhalations, Mitchell was finding it difficult to concentrate on the conversation. His struggle to resist the urges growing inside him resulted in strained inhalation and a pervasive feeling of nausea, and yet, the frenzy still remained.

"Is there anything I can do for you?" Abigail called from beyond the door.

Mitchell took a ragged breath.

"I'll be fine," he gasped. "Just…need…rest."

There was a long pause.

"Ok," she replied apprehensively. "I brought food."

Again there was a pause.

"There's orange juice. It's supposed to help with...you know."

Mitchell was unsure what his sister meant by the last comment. Before he could respond, Olivia shifted, her silky skin rubbing against him. Mitchell's panting intensified, his body shaking from the sensation. The door moved slightly ajar, but Abigail did not look inside.

"Are you sure you're alright?" she asked with concern.

"I'm already feeling better," he said.

Abigail let out a heavy sigh.

"Ok," she replied apprehensively. "Make sure to call if you need something."

The door closed a few inches and stopped.

"And Mitch..."

"Hmmm?"

Abigail inhaled deeply before continuing.

"I want you to know that I'm proud of you."

Mitchell was too stunned to respond, watching speechlessly as the bedroom door closed behind her with an audible clicking noise. He listened intently to the sounds of Abigail gathering her belongings and moving toward the front door. Mitchell exhaled a sigh of relief when he heard the deadbolt locking into place.

After a few seconds, he lifted the edge of the blanket and peered underneath at Olivia.

"I guess you can come out now," he said with a grin.

Olivia crawled out from her hiding place and positioned herself atop his chest.

"Tell me something," she said, propping up on her elbows.

"What's that?" he asked.

Olivia smiled wickedly down at him, playfully teasing his bare flesh with the side of her foot.

"Do you always get that excited seeing your sister?"

CHAPTER 23

Mitchell hung up the phone and placed it on the coffee table. It had been part of his obligation to Carl, and he was being diligent about making this work. He looked at the clock and saw it to be after nine.

Olivia and he spent much of the day in bed after their terrible scare with Abigail. When one's life seems to be at an end, fear takes over, and adrenaline surges through the bloodstream like salmon moving upstream. Mitchell's heartbeat had raced, causing a stirring in his loins of such immense intensity that he had pounced at Olivia like a hungry lion. She had given him no resistance, the appetite of the hunter no match for that of its prey. Together they tumbled to and fro across the bed, devouring each other in fits of fiery passion. And when that pivotal moment arrived, where they were between one being and separate entities, that lustful drug dissipated, and the two collapsed exhausted against each other.

Mitchell wanted more than anything to take her in that moment, but the weariness of life can only be overcome by sweet rest. Though fatigue had prevented them from connecting like countless lovers before them, they were united in a bond stronger than any created by recreational pastime. Olivia and Mitchell lay as one, existing only for each other.

Mitchell recreated the event over and over in his mind, longing for the time when they might once again give themselves over to those carnal yearnings. His reverie was suddenly broken by the sound of her voice.

"How did it go?" she asked him, gesturing toward the phone.

"I'm not sure," he replied. "He almost seemed surprised that I called."

Olivia nodded.

"Maybe it takes some people longer to read through the book," she suggested.

"He wants me to meet him tomorrow night to discuss what I've read so far."

"Are you going to go?"

Mitchell pondered the question.

"Well, I suppose that depends."

"On?"

"On you."

Olivia crossed her arms and glared at him.

"Why do you need *my* permission?" she demanded.

Mitchell suddenly felt defensive.

"I just thought that maybe you wouldn't like being left alone."

Olivia took a step toward him, never letting up on her gaze.

"You think I can't be left alone here? Don't think I can take care of myself?"

Mitchell shifted uneasily on the couch, not enjoying where this conversation was headed.

"I didn't say that. I just...I thought you would be upset if I didn't discuss it with you first," he explained.

Olivia took another step closer, now standing directly in front of him. Even with Mitchell seated, she was only about eye level, which consequently made it easier to maintain her hard stare. After holding the menacing look another few seconds, Olivia reached out her hands, cupping the undersides of his face and planted a tender kiss upon his lips.

"You know you're quite cute when you're nervous," she teased.

Realizing that she'd been having a go at him, Mitchell crossed his arms, returning to her the same stern gaze she'd given to him.

"That's not funny," he said without amusement.

Olivia clasped her hands behind.

"I'm sorry," she said, innocently fluttering her eyes at him.

Mitchell rolled his eyes at the gesture.

"Are you really sorry?" he asked, feigning chastisement.

"Of course," she replied. "You're so much cuter when you're pouting."

Mitchell unexpectedly lunged forward, gingerly wrapping his fingers around her wrist. Olivia let out an excited shrill as he pulled her to him and tossed her playfully on the adjacent section of couch. With Olivia lying on her back, Mitchell maneuvered his fingers back and forth, eliciting squeals of protest as he tickled the sensitive spots around her torso. Olivia squirmed beneath his touch, shoving his hands away as she struggled to break free. Her body suddenly seized as Mitchell's fingertips accidentally brushed along the top of her breast.

Mitchell retracted his hand in alarm.

"Are you okay?"

Olivia nodded, pulling herself free nonetheless.

"I think I want to get a shower," she said.

Mitchell continued to look at her worriedly.

"Oh…alright," he said, wondering if he'd gone too far with the game.

Olivia patted his thigh reassuringly as she stood from the couch.

"It feels a little chilly in here tonight," she pointed out. "Do you mind if I wear your robe when I get out."

Mitchell raised an eyebrow at her, before letting out a quiet snicker.

"You're welcome to it, I suppose, but I doubt it'll fit. There's a fleece blanket in the closet if you want to try that instead," he offered.

Olivia considered this.

"Yes, I think that will work quite nicely."

While sprawled across the couch, I read more of the massive text I'd acquired from Carl. Whereas the first half of the book was a droning nightmare of detailed instructions, the stories in the back carried their own interesting and unique flavor. Several times I found myself chuckling out loud at unfortunate misdeeds, especially when I had made some of the exact same, foolish decisions. Regardless of whether the narrators were male or female, old or young, rich or poor, I felt a sense of fellowship with each and every one knowing that they faced the same trials and tribulations as I, and they turned their lives around.

Olivia entered the living room, donning the warm blanket like a cloak, concealing all but her face and feet. It was quite an odd sight to see her covered in such a manner, a complete contrast to her usual welcoming personality. With my interest in the book suddenly evaporated, I marked my spot and set it aside.

"Do you mind if I put on some music?" she asked.

"No, go right ahead."

Olivia moved to the iPod station, quickly scrolling through the device until she located whatever it was she was looking for. From the moment the music began, it was like Olivia was in a hypnotic trance. It began with her feet lightly tapping on the hardwood floor, spread to her ankles, and traveled upwards until her hips were in full rhythmic sway. Her golden hair swished to and fro as she lost herself in the entrancing melody, dancing harmoniously in the soft illumination of the living room.

Intrigued by her motions, I pushed myself up to a seated position for a better view. There was something so inherently alluring about this brazen display of femininity that I simply couldn't tear my eyes away. With unbridled fascination, I followed every graceful movement of her supple body, fixated on each accidental leg flash, and focused with intense satisfaction on all the sensual gyrations of her elegant figure. I remained captivated even as the final notes trailed off and Olivia came to a stop in front of the television.

After her little performance, I clapped my hands softly together to show my appreciation, only to have Olivia turn her back to me and bundle the fleece around her like a shroud. This sudden shift toward propriety was making me very nervous. She had been quick to depart after the event on the couch, even asking for my robe to cover herself with. Had I done something to upset her? Was she now uncomfortable being around me? I didn't have to wait long before I got my answer.

When the next song began, Olivia raised the edges of the blanket out to the sides, like an eagle about to take flight. With each rising note she lifted her arms a little higher, bit by bit exposing the tender flesh on the back of her legs. As the opening crescendo reached its peak and petered out so too did Olivia's arms descend, allowing the soft fleece to fall from her hands and expose the secret she'd been hiding all along.

Olivia was clad in a scarlet demi bra, its tight fitting material displaying cleavage where before none had existed. Its elegant floral lace design perfectly accented her supple, delicate features, yet at the same time doing very little to conceal the enticing treasures beneath. The scenery only got better when she spun around to reveal a matching pair of side tie panties that clung snugly to her cute behind, riding low to give a subtle preview of what was still to come.

Olivia continued to prance back and forth across the living room, her movements growing more provocative with every passing note. Olivia smiled seductively at me whenever her hands touched the velvety lace. She let out moans of pleasure as her fingertips traipsed delicately across her bare abdomen. I could feel the heat rising as my heart pounded inside my chest.

When the music ended, Olivia focused her gaze on me, ardent passion blazing in those starry eyes. Fueled by a lascivious appetite, Olivia forced herself on my lap, determined to quell the ravenous cravings of sexual famine. Firmly latching to the back of my neck, she rocked vigorously back and forth, grinding our parts together in zealous repetition. She pressed her mouth to mine, biting down softly on the lower lip as she lost herself to the frenzy.

I wrapped my arms around her back, holding her tightly against me as we savored the throes of desire. Olivia took my hand and slid it lower until my fingers were entwined in the thin strands of her sexy new underwear. Olivia lifted her head away for only a second to speak.

"Are you ready to open your present?" she asked, her lips on mine before I had a chance to respond.

Mitchell carried me across the threshold, kicking the door shut as we entered. Butterflies plagued my stomach as we moved closer to the bed. We had been nearing this precipice since we met, but now that it finally arrived, I was feeling a bit nervous. And yet, I couldn't imagine a better way to end the night.

Mitchell climbed on the mattress with me cradled against his massive torso. Loosening my grip on his neck, my legs gradually slid from around his midsection, and I slumped softly against the comforter. Mitchell leaned forward until his face hovered just over mine. I placed my hand against the side of his face, the apprehension fading away as I gazed into his reassuring eyes.

Our lips embraced as Mitchell's fingertips explored my near naked form. Though he had seen me without clothes before, I still felt warmth in my cheeks when he undid the fastening on my top and smiled at my exposed breasts. I cooed with excitement as his finger ran the length of my sternum, tickling my sensitive navel and loosening the strand below. I trembled when his hand made contact with my bare mound, instinctively grabbing his arm in response.

Mitchell peered at me with concern.

"Please..." I gasped. "Don't tease me anymore."

He chuckled softly, leaning back to begin undoing his shirt. After struggling with the first button, frustration overcame him, and he ripped the shirt from his body. I heard the rain of buttons scatter across the room as he tossed it haphazardly to the side. I reached for him, running my hands along the muscle lines across his torso, his open display of manly prowess further kindling the fire that was growing inside me.

Mitchell slid his hands to his belt and unfastened the lever. He hastily pulled free of his pants, kicking them off the edge of the bed. His shorts quickly followed, and I felt the rigid member graze the inside of my thigh as it popped free of its confinement. I swallowed hard remembering its capacity for growth.

"Be gentle," I pleaded anxiously.

Mitchell nodded, returning to his position just above me. With one hand he touched my face, cradling my cheek affectionately in his palm. The other hand went lower, guiding the tip up and down across my sensitive folds. I shook with delight at every pass, clutching tightly to the sheets beside me.

Mitchell suddenly stopped, placing the tip at the entrance. He looked down at me, waiting for my permission before continuing. I took hold of the hand on my cheek, interlacing my fingers with his. I squeezed firmly, gathering courage for what came next. I nodded, urging him to go on.

His lips touched mine just before gently pushing forward. I moaned softly into his open mouth as I felt him press onward, though his progress abruptly halted just beyond the entry. It was as if a wall had been erected for the sole purpose of hindering our love. Going slowly, he continued to push against the wall until I winced in pain.

"Are you alright?" he asked, sliding himself back out.

I unclenched my jaw and tried to breathe normally. The sensation had been agonizing to say the least, but I didn't want him to know, worried that he might insist on stopping. I heard about this problem during the first time and some talked about persevering through the discomfort until it started to feel good. I wasn't certain if it would work or not, but I wasn't about to give up already. I gripped the sheets tightly; motioning for Mitchell to try again.

He seemed unsure as well, but my reassurance gave him the courage to continue. He pushed forward until he made contact with the wall again. Mitchell looked at me and I nodded. The pain returned, more intense this time. I held the sheets firmly in my fists as he continued to push, but still the wall refused to yield to his advances. When it became too much, I screamed out, tears forming in my eyes.

"I'm sorry" Mitchell said quickly. "I didn't mean to hurt you."

After a few more seconds, the aching subsided. I relinquished my hold on the sheets and took his head in my hands.

"It's not your fault," I told him with a smile. "You're much bigger than I, so this might take a few tries."

Mitchell nodded, though he still looked away in shame.

"Let's switch places," I suggested.

I wrapped my hands about the nape of his neck and guided him from atop me onto his back. Despite our change in position, the wall continued to resist our attempts. With each effort, the region became increasingly sensitive, every thrust aching worse than the one before. Treating it like an adhesive bandage, I decided to give it all I had in one powerful plunge. I counted to three in my head and then went for it.

I immediately cried out from the excruciating pain. Its increasing intensity frightened me, thoughts of blood and being torn in half only heightening those fears. Mitchell lifted my body to the safety of his cradling arms, supporting me as best he could through wave after wave of blinding torture. I sobbed openly against his chest, fiercely shaking as I struggled to keep from blacking out.

Slowly the torment subsided, and my tears of pain were replaced by those of frustration. For me, it would have been worth the momentary soreness, no matter how great, if we could only be together as one. And yet, even with my foolish act of bravado, the wall remained intact.

CHAPTER 24

I lay in bed for almost an hour after Mitchell left for his morning recovery meeting, feeling somewhat depressed about the tragic fiasco from last night. Needless to say, the prospect of never being able to have a proper physical relationship put a damper on an otherwise beautiful morning. Nevertheless, the sun's powerful rays streaming brilliantly through the window reminded me that I couldn't sulk beneath the sheets forever.

Determined to find a solution to the problem, I swung my legs over the side of the bed and tried to stand up. Suddenly lightheaded, I sat down on the edge of the mattress to regain my equilibrium. These episodes were becoming more frequent. The first had been on Saturday while Mitchell was away at his meeting, then there'd been two while we're were camping, at least four yesterday, including a near fall during my dance routine, and now another one this morning. I didn't tell Mitchell, figuring it to be just a passing thing, but now that it developed into something more, it would be downright foolish to hold back any longer.

My second attempt going better than the first, I headed for the bathroom, steadying myself on anything nearby just in case. Fortunately, I managed to get through my entire morning routine without incident.

Going back to the bedroom, I grabbed a couple of pillows and fashioned myself a comfortable place in front of the mirror. Until yesterday I had never given much thought to what went on below. Due to the fact that I wasn't driven to bouts of self-discovery and because I didn't have the catamenial burdens to contend with, the only time I ever noticed it was when I was scrubbing in the shower. Even Mitchell was more knowledgeable in that area than I was.

Holding open the flaps I was able to peer inside, an action I instantly regretted. Being able to see my own internal tissues would have been disgusting enough without the added benefit of a slimy coating across the inside. The strange coloration made the already foreign region all the more alien, as though it were not actually a part of me at all. The minute muscle contractions were sickening, and I suddenly found myself feeling nauseated.

Still, it could have been a lot worse. For one thing there were no signs of physical trauma anywhere. I was expecting to find major hemorrhaging, or at the very least a few serious bruises, but there wasn't even any swelling. I had emerged completely unscathed from yesterday's unpleasantness, other than a wounded ego of course.

And yet, as uplifting as it was to know that I had not suffered a major injury, I was no closer to discovering the source of our dilemma than when I'd first begun. Perhaps it was the distance I had to sit away from the mirror, or maybe it was a bad angle, or even poor lighting, but I just couldn't manage to get clear look inside.

Gritting my teeth, I pushed my forefinger past the opening. Despite the tingling sensation this elicited, I reflexively winced as the squishy flesh compressed around my distal joint. Ignoring its sultry feel, I probed deeper until my finger made contact with the meddlesome barrier. It was still a little sore to the touch, but not nearly as much as last night. Though I spent several minutes inspecting the region through gentle palpation, all I discovered was what we already knew, that it was firm and impenetrable. Unable to discern a way around the impediment, I decided to abandon the task for now, hoping that Mitchell might have better luck later.

As I stood from my crouched position, my stomach rumbled, reminding me that it had been a while since I'd had anything to eat. Stopping off at the bathroom, I gave my hands a thorough scrubbing, twice, before moving toward breakfast. Locating the loaf of bread, I slid two slices from the package and put them in the toaster.

While they cooked, I returned to the bedroom to straighten up my mess. I plucked the pillows from the floor and returned them to the head of the mattress, tucking the sheets around the edges. With that complete, I gathered the discarded clothing from last night and tossed them in the closet hamper. I felt a twinge of melancholy as my fingers touched the scarlet lace, but I quickly pushed those emotions aside, returning the delicate material to its original bag and placing it beside the dresser. If I'd only known how much trouble was to come from that small package, I definitely would have taken the time to hide it better.

Hearing the toaster pop, I headed back to the kitchen. Nearing the appliance, my vision suddenly clouded over and my legs wobbled beneath me. I desperately reached out for something to latch onto, but my hand glided vainly over the surface of the island. Pain coursed through my head as I struck hard against the linoleum. I made a single futile attempt to get back up before quietly slipping into unconsciousness, imagining the faint sounds of someone calling my name...

Justin Blair anxiously shook his leg up and down, hoping that the rapid movement might somehow cause the phone on his desk to ring. It had been five days since he found out about the demise of James Friedman and still he had not been able to locate the missing girl. He checked his watch, for perhaps the fiftieth time that morning, knowing all too well that Dorian Abernathy's private jet would be touching down in just a few hours. Blair gave a despondent sigh; he could already feel his promotion slipping away.

He reached across his desk and pressed the intercom button.

"Emily?"

"Yes, Mr. Blair?"

"Have I had any new messages?"

There was a pause on the other end.

"Not since the last time, sir."

Blair sighed with disappointment.

"Ok. Thank you."

Stepping away from the desk, Blair began to pace the room. He stopped in front of the large, panoramic window and gazed down at the city with disdain. Blair had never much cared for Pittsburgh, it was far too slow for his liking, but he didn't dare leave until the matter with Cecelia Friedman was settled.

He let out a heavy sigh.

Somewhere below him were three private detectives scouring every nook and cranny for any sign of the child. He paid each of them a pretty penny, and still they'd come up short. Blair checked his watch again, wishing that he'd hired a dozen more when he had the chance.

Olivia slowly opened her eyes to the innocuous ambiance of a whitewashed room. The walls were white, the floors were white, the sheets were white, the blinds were white, and even the curtains, which were supposed to bring highlight to the room, were white. The reflective nature of the color only intensified the light streaming through the windows, allowing her to better see the unadulterated gloriousness of white. The whole ensemble was not so much peaceful, as it was boring.

Olivia felt a hand on hers and turned to see Mitchell standing beside her.

"Finally," he said with relief. "I was getting worried."

"Where are we?" she asked weakly.

"The hospital. You fainted back at the apartment."

Olivia nodded, already aware of that last bit of information. She attempted to push herself into a seated position, only to be thwarted by the onset of a skull rending headache.

"Easy," said Mitchell. "You bumped your head pretty badly when you went down."

He helped lift her to an upright stance, maneuvering the pillows behind her for support.

"Is that comfortable?" he asked.

Olivia nodded.

"Thank you," she said softly.

Olivia leaned her head back again, relieved that the throbbing pressure was subsiding. She gave Mitchell a forlorn smile, holding out her hand inviting him to take it.

"What are we going to do, Mitchell?" she asked, interlocking her fingers with his.

Mitchell affectionately squeezed back.

"I think we should start by safety proofing the apartment," he said. "Otherwise, we might be spending a lot more afternoons here."

She gave a glum smile.

"We're quite the combination aren't we? You who collapses when we try to have sex and me who faints when we don't get to."

"I guess all couples have their problems. We're doing alright though, all things considered."

She raised a questioning eyebrow at him.

"What?" he asked. "We have a lot of things to consider."

"Speaking of which, do they know what happened?"

Mitchell shook his head.

"They've been waiting for you to wake up. Someone will probably be in soon to check on you."

Olivia nodded, eyes falling to her bandaged wrist.

"I haven't taken my medication yet," she said worriedly.

Mitchell peered down at her injuries.

"I'll swing by the apartment just as soon as we talk to the doctor. I want to be here for the prognosis."

Curious herself, Olivia reached up to the sore spot on the side of her head, feeling a wet bandage and a layer of gauze wrapped around her head.

"How do I look?" she asked, pointing toward the bandage.

Mitchell flashed her an encouraging smile. He glanced over his shoulder to make sure the coast was clear.

"Beautiful," he said, planting a gentle kiss against her lips.

Olivia passionately pulled him toward her. Though she did not want a repeat of the restaurant incident, there was something exciting about making out in public.

Justin Blair sat at his office chair mindlessly flipping through the rolodex, futilely searching for a way to distract himself from the torment of waiting. Pacing had not helped, nor had fiddling with random debris on his desk or playing solitaire on his computer. He was in the middle of considering raiding the bottle that Harper kept in his office when the phone rang. Forgetting about the alcohol, Blair dove for the receiver.

"Friedman Financial, Blair speaking," he blurted out quickly.

"Aye, and dis be, Tully," came a heavily accented voice on the other end.

Blair's heart skipped a beat in excitement. Of the three investigators, Tully was certainly the one he had the least confidence in, but at this point he was glad to hear anything at all.

"Oi may 'av found' yer missin' treasure," said Tully.

"You found the girl?" clarified Blair.

"Aye. Down at de 'ospital. She be called otherwise, but wus definitely 'er."

"What do you mean 'otherwise'?"

"Waat, ye daft? It wus not de name yer gave me."

"What do you mean it wasn't the name I gave you?"

"Jist waat oi said. Dis girl's name wus Olivia."

Blair felt a headache coming on.

"If the names didn't match, what makes you think it's the same girl?" he asked in a patronizing tone.

Tully took a deep breath, exhaling with frustration.

"Cause, she be de seem as de lass in de picture."

Blair leaned forward in his seat.

"Are you're sure it's her?"

"Aye. Positive."

Blair stood up, reaching for his coat.

"Excellent, I'll be right down. Which hospital is it?"

"Well, thar's a problem," said Tully.

Blair stopped dead in his tracks.

"What kind of a problem?" he demanded.

"Big wan."

"*How* big?" asked Blair, his voice growing louder.

"Aboyt six eight or six nine." replied Tully after some consideration.

Blair rubbed his temples. Thick accents did not complement his patience.

"What are you talking about?"

"De lass, she 'as a paddy wi' 'er."

"A what?"

"A paddy. Yer nu, a gentleman."

"So what?"

"Well…He seems rayle protective over 'er, might not take too kindly ter yer speakin' ter 'er. Dare might be trouble."

"I thought you people enjoyed a good fight."

"Aye. Us Oirishmen love a gran' brawl, but dis ain't no normal lad yer see, 'tis a bleedin bear. Oi'm al' aboyt the millin', but not so much on the dyin', if yer git me drift."

Blair glared angrily at the phone; comforted that Tully could not see him do it.

"Alright, fine. I'll be down shortly. Give me directions."

Blair slammed the receiver down on the phone. Dealing with Tully had been an exercise in frustration, but the man had just saved his chances with Abernathy. Blair quickly departed the office, apprehensive about what he would discover at the hospital.

Detective Nick Hagan was sitting behind his desk when his partner Doug Werner burst into his office.

"Grab your coat," Werner said tersely.

Hagan quickly rose from his chair, donning the jacket as he walked. The two were out of the office and halfway down the hallway when Nick turned to Doug.

"Where are we going?" he asked.

"You remember that Friedman girl we've been looking for?"

Nick's mind wandered to visions of bloody corpses, dead eyes and unmarked graves. There were days when even closing his eyes would conjure the terrifying memories of those poor forgotten souls he discovered throughout his career. The images of children left lying on abandoned streets haunted him most of all.

"Is she…?" he asked worriedly.

Doug shook his head.

"No. Someone reported seeing her at the hospital this morning. We're heading there now, before she gets discharged."

"If she was admitted, how come our informant didn't call us? Don't we still have someone stationed down there?"

"Apparently, she checked it under a pseudonym." replied Doug.

Nick raised an eyebrow at him.

"Why go by a fake name at the hospital?"

Doug shook his head.

"No idea. But we should find out soon enough."

Nick nodded as the two climbed into the car and strapped on their seatbelts. From the passenger seat, Nick turned down the blaring pop music.

"So if she checked in with a different name, how did they know it was her?"

Doug beamed with a self-satisfied grin.

"The person who reported finding her is a private detective; an old friend of yours I believe."

Nick shot him a look of disdain.

"You don't mean...?"

"Aye. Good ol' Keegan Tully." joked Doug in an imitation accent.

Hagan groaned.

"Let me guess, there's a reward?"

"Naturally."

"Of course, there is. Why else would a fine, upstanding gentleman like Tully get involved?"

"He's definitely looking to make bank on this find," said Doug.

"Off a police reward?" asked Nick with surprise. "Surely, we can't be offering that much to find her."

"We're not the only ones looking for her."

Nick raised an eyebrow at him.

"What have you heard?"

"Not much really. But I made a courtesy call to that lawyer who's been looking for her. You know, the one who was in charge of her adopted father's estate?"

"The Russian guy?"

"Yeah, him. Seems like there's some major issues with settling the estate in her absence, so he's offered a reward as well. Pretty hefty one, too."

"How much?"

"Apparently it's for fifty grand."

Nick made a whistling noise.

"It seems like we're in the wrong business," he said.

"Anyway," continued Doug, "when I called him this morning, he thanked me for the heads up, but mentioned that someone had already informed him."

"Really? Who?"

"Someone with a thick Irish accent."

"Awesome," said Hagan sarcastically.

The two pulled into a parking spot at the hospital and proceeded toward the entrance.

"What's the name we're looking for?" asked Hagan.

"Can't remember. I just know she's on the third floor. It shouldn't be too hard to locate Tully once we're up there."

"Especially if we track him by smell," said Nick.

Not paying attention to where he was going, Hagan ran headlong into a human wall; knocked aside as easily as if he were a ragdoll.

"Excuse me," said Mitchell apologetically.

"Sorry," mumbled Hagan, quickly moving by to avoid further embarrassment.

When the detectives were beyond earshot, Werner turned to his partner.

"Did you see that...?"

"I saw," interrupted Nick. "Up close and personal."

"You don't suppose that guy was part of the Pittsburgh squad?"

"One can only hope. After last year's abysmal season, we could use all the help we can get."

Werner peered over his shoulder to see if the behemoth was still nearby.

"Man, we should have gotten his autograph."

After riding the elevator to the third floor, the duo stepped off, Hagan quickly spotting Tully down the hallway. Beside the short, inebriated Irishman stood a man wearing a business suit and tie. They were quite possibly the strangest pairing in the entire hospital.

"Looks like he's already cashing in on a third reward," whispered Doug.

Nick exaggerated a groan.

"Repugnant little vermin," he growled. "When Saint Patrick cleared the Emerald Isle of snakes, I wish he hadn't let that one slip through the cracks."

"Does that mean you want to go say *hi*?"

Nick glared at his partner.

"I'd sooner listen to more of that double stepping crap you gave me before."

Doug rolled his eyes.

"Besides, I already know which room it is."

Doug shot him a questioning look.

"That one," he gestured. "Both him and the suit have pointed to it since we got off the elevator."

Werner gave a nod of approval as he reached into his wallet and removed the picture he'd gotten from the Friedman residence. The two stormed into the small hospital room, startling the nurse with their loud movements. A petite blond girl lay in the bed, her eyes wide with surprise.

Doug studied her features for a moment before looking at the picture in his hand. He turned to Hagan.

"That's her alright."

The nurse approached them, her face contorted with disapproval.

"You can't be in here," she said with authority. "Friends and family only."

"I couldn't agree more," said Hagan, shoving his badge in her face. "We're going to need you to wait outside."

Nick gestured to his partner, watching with smug satisfaction as he led her out of the room. Doug waited five seconds after closing the door before striking the wood surface forcefully with the palm of his hand, the sound of receding footsteps echoing from the other side.

Hagan put away his badge and turned to the frightened girl in front of him.

"I'm sorry about that," he said softly. "We didn't want anyone intruding on our conversation."

Olivia looked from one man to the next, unsure whom she should focus her attention on.

"Who are you?"

"I'm Detective Nick Hagan, and this is my partner, Doug Werner. We're with the city's homicide investigations unit."

Olivia tightened her grip on the hospital blanket.

"Are you here to arrest me?" she asked worriedly.

"No, no, no...nothing like that," interjected Doug. "We simply need to ask you a few questions."

She let out a sigh of relief, gently pushing herself into a more upright position.

"What do you want to ask me?"

"First of all," began Nick, "are you Cecelia Friedman, the adopted daughter of James Friedman?"

"Yes," she said. "Or at least I was until last week."

"What happened last week?"

Doug cleared his throat beside him.

"Oh...right," uttered Hagan, hanging his head. "We're, um, very sorry about your loss."

Olivia peered dolefully down at her hands.

"Mr. James was a good man," she said. "Though I wish things had been different between us at the end."

"Was there trouble at home?" inquired Doug.

Olivia exhaled slowly.

"Grief tends to affect everyone differently, but for some reason, Mr. James never got over the death of his wife. When Miss Elaine was alive, the three of us were like a real family. Maybe everything wasn't perfect, but we were happy. After she was gone, he sort of ...changed, and things weren't the same anymore."

"Is that why you ran away?" Hagan asked.

She lifted her gaze, raising her eyebrow questioningly at him.

"You haven't been back to Friedman's condo since the incident," he explained.

Olivia nodded.

"No, I suppose I haven't. But it's not like there was much of a home to go back to."

"Fair enough," replied Hagan. "Where did you go after you left?"

Olivia took a moment to consider her answer.

"A kind man found me and took me into his home. I've been living with him ever since."

"Why didn't he notify the police? Surely he had to know that someone would be looking for you?"

"We did go to the police. Who do you think it was who granted him legal custody?"

The two detectives looked at each other with surprise.

"Did you say that he's been granted legal custody?" questioned Hagan.

Olivia nodded her head.

"Yes, that's right, pending a court decision, of course."

"Who's your case worker?" asked Doug, pulling out his phone.

She told him, and Werner moved away from the conversation, covering his other ear with the palm of his hand. Hagan turned back to Olivia.

"If you checked with the police department, how come there haven't been any records of you in our system?"

She nervously bit down on her lip.

"When I met my new caretaker, I didn't tell him that I was Cecelia Friedman. It didn't seem fair to continue using that moniker after I left, so I chose to go by another name."

Hagan groaned with frustration.

"Why would you do that?" he demanded. "Do you have any idea how long it's taken us to find you because of that little identity swap?!"

Olivia winced at his aggressive tone.

"I'm sorry," she said timidly. "I didn't mean to cause any trouble."

Nick massaged his forehead with his fingertips to help quell the building rage. Despite his aggravation, what bothered him most right now was the guilt of having yelled at this poor girl.

"I take it the name you gave to the police department was the same as the one you told this caretaker of yours?"

Olivia nodded.

"And that's the same one you used to check-in at the hospital?"

"I assume so, but I can't be for certain. I was unconscious when he brought me in."

Hagan looked at the bandage around her head.

"I see…and where is he right now?"

"He went back to the apartment to get my medicine, but he should be back soon."

Doug stepped up beside his partner, slipping the phone back into his pocket.

"I just got off the phone with Sharon Faust," he said.

"And?"

"And she remembers processing a little blond girl, but she says the girl's name wasn't Cecelia."

"We've already established that," uttered Hagan gruffly. "Apparently she thought that using an alias would give her the edge on running away."

Doug nodded appreciatively.

"That was pretty clever actually."

Nick glared at him.

"Don't encourage her. She's caused enough problems as is."

"I'll say. Especially considering what name she used."

"Which is?"

Doug gestured toward the girl in the hospital bed.

"Olivia Morgan," she said.

Hagan stared incredulously at her before turning back to his partner.

"You've got to be kidding me. The girl from the missing persons report?!"

"Yep."

"Under our noses this whole time?!"

"'Fraid so."

"Unbelievable…" muttered Hagan, shaking his head at their unfortunate oversight. He paced angrily back and forth, trying to vent a little steam. Halfway through the third lap he stopped, suddenly remembering the rest of the information that he had on Olivia Morgan. Laying out the events in his mind, Hagan fitted the pieces together like a jigsaw puzzle. Once he had them arranged, he faced Olivia again.

"I have one more question," he stated.

Olivia listened intently as he described the details he knew about her life. She was an orphan who had been adopted by the Friedmans after James' brother died. He was aware that she had left the Love on High orphanage and had not been found again. For one fleeting moment, it was as if someone truly understood her plight.

"So I realized," continued Nick, "that both you and Olivia Morgan were runaways at the same time in nearly the same location, which means that your paths might have crossed along the way. Perhaps you even became friends for a little while. It's only natural when picking an alias to select one that'll be easy to remember…"

Olivia's heart sank. *Despite the extensive research this man had done to find her, even knowing every detail about her life from the past ten years, with dates and facts to guide him along, he still could not see past her youthful appearance to recognize her as the real Olivia. How would she ever live a normal life when she couldn't even convince this man of her identity?*

"No," she said sadly. "I don't know where the real Olivia Morgan is now."

"Oh, well," stated Nick. "It was worth a shot."

He motioned to his partner to indicate that he was out of questions. Doug nodded in agreement.

"We want to thank you for your time," said Nick, holding out his hand. "We hope you feel better soon."

"Thank you," said Olivia cordially. "And you two have a wonderful afternoon."

"Take care," waved Doug.

The two detectives departed, and Doug followed Nick to the nurse's station. Hagan got the attention of the woman behind the counter and flashed his badge at her.

"The girl in that room," he said pointing, "What is she in here for?"

The nurse looked nervously at the detective. She was uncertain if it was appropriate to divulge confidential patient information, but this man did have a badge, so she chose to comply with his authoritative demeanor.

"We're still running tests to find out the cause, but she fainted in her apartment, banging her head up in the process."

"Thank you," he said with a smile.

The two moved toward the elevators.

"What do you think?" asked Doug.

Nick pressed the button and the doors closed.

"I think there's a better chance of me going vegan than that girl overpowering James Friedman," he said.

"I'm with you on that," said Doug, the two of them stepping from the lift.

"In fact, I'm ready to chalk this one up to good, old-fashioned bad luck," said Nick as they walked toward the car.

"How's that?" asked Doug.

"Well, the way I see it, James Friedman was probably pretty distraught about the death of his wife."

"Understandably."

"So it's reasonable to expect that he took special measures to cope with his loss."

"His tox screen definitely pointed to that."

"Meanwhile, the poor girl has to watch her father getting wasted every night. Maybe she tries to help him, and he pushes her away. Maybe she tries to stop him, and he lashes out at her."

Doug contorted his face with concern.

"Anyway," says Nick, opening the passenger door, "The girl finds a way out. Certainly not the ideal situation, placing your trust in a total stranger, but perhaps it beats the alternative."

Doug turned the key, and the engine roared to life.

"When James Friedman found out that his daughter ran away because of him, he panicked. He contacted everyone he knew to find her, maybe even lays out a cash reward."

"And that's how Tully got involved."

Nick groaned.

"Yeah…maybe. After dispatching his search team, Friedman starts getting anxious, the guilt grows in him. He decides to drown his guilt with some booze, a lot of booze. But he still feels that anxiety, so he decides to go have a smoke. Now we have James Friedman, old, fat, probably not well coordinated on a good day, completely drunk, scared, and in the cold, pacing on the roof, trying to coordinate a cigarette and a bottle at the same time, something happens and he loses his footing. Bam! Smashes his head against the concrete and lights out."

Doug pondered the theory for the rest of the car ride to the station. He pulled back into his original spot and turned off the engine.

"Do you think the girl is in any danger?"

Nick shook his head.

"Not really. But if you want, we can keep our guy down at the hospital for a few days to keep an eye on her."

Doug nodded.

"By the way," said Doug as they emerged from the car, "I've got something for you."

"Something for me?" Nick asked suspiciously.

Doug moved to the trunk, opening it to reveal a cardboard package with his home mailing address printed across the top. He handed the unopened container to his partner.

"What is it?"

"Open it," said Doug impatiently.

Nick retrieved the keys from his pocket, using the edge of one to slice through layers of tape. Pulling back the flaps and maneuvering the protective shipping contents out of the way, he was able to see what lay underneath. He looked at his partner, eyes wide with shock.

"How did you get this?" he asked.

"You remember the case we did last fall where we found the woman dead in her house and her two kids missing?"

"I believe so. Where we found them tied up in the basement of her ex?"

Doug nodded.

"Turns out that the woman's father is a medical specialist, and he was very grateful to have his grandsons returned to him alive. When I told him that the man who had rescued his grandchildren couldn't afford proper medical equipment, he jumped at the opportunity to help. It arrived in the mail last night, free of charge."

Nick looked from the box to his partner and back to the box.

"You shouldn't have done that," he said quietly.

"Wouldn't...couldn't...shouldn't... I did," he said flatly. "And you're welcome."

Nick looked at him curiously.

"How did you know the measurements?"

"Easy. I broke into your apartment," Doug said with a grin.

"You broke into my apartment?!" Nick said with alarm.

"Of course. I've been doing it a while now. How else would your precious plants survive?"

Doug turned and began to walk inside. He got a few paces away before turning back to his partner.

"By the way," he said, "I pulled some strings and got you the day off tomorrow. Rest up and be ready to go on Thursday."

Doug turned to continue walking, only to be interrupted again.

"Hey Doug!" yelled Nick across the parking lot.

He peered back to see Hagan holding the box as though it were a precious treasure. Unable to find the right words, Nick finally gave up searching.

"Um...thanks," he said.

Doug nodded his head, resuming the trek inside without another word.

CHAPTER 25

Mitchell stormed from the elevator and out the main entrance of his apartment building. As he hurried down the street, the medicine in his coat pocket bumped against his body, making annoying rattling noises with each step. On top of that, his panting grew louder, every ragged breath a burning reminder of the hindering effects of poor life choices on the body. Mitchell pushed past the fatigue in his lungs, urging himself ever onward. Exhausted and furiously wheezing, he arrived at the bus terminal just in time to see the shuttle pulling away.

He cursed between breaths, staggering toward the nearest bench and plopping heavily on its metallic frame. Mitchell gave several violent hacks as his breathing began to stabilize. He wiped the sweat from his brow with his shirt sleeve, the uprising smell making him wish that he'd put on deodorant before foolishly deciding to run the entire way.

A harsh noise suddenly erupted from inside his coat, kick starting Mitchell's heart back to its erratic state. Fumbling around for the device, he finally got it out of the pocket and pressed the answering button.

"Hello?" he replied.

"Good afternoon," came a female voice. "Is this Mr. Flynn?"

Mitchell recognized the voice but couldn't quite place it.

"Yes it is."

"This is Sharon Faust," the voice said. "How are you?"

"Ah...Dr. Faust. I'm good. And how is your day going?"

"I've got no complaints. How is Olivia?"

Mitchell paused.

"All things considered, I think she's doing very well."

"Good. I'm glad to hear that."

A silence developed between the two of them.

"So…what can I do for you, Dr. Faust?" asked Mitchell eventually.

There was another long pause.

"Well," began Dr. Faust, "There's been a bit of a…development in Olivia's case."

Mitchell felt his chest tighten.

"What kind of development?" he asked, trying not to vocalize his worry.

Dr. Faust sighed before continuing.

"It's complicated," she said. "I got a phone call from a detective a little while ago. Apparently they were investigating the death of a local businessman and have been searching for his missing daughter."

"Uh-huh…" Mitchell replied, urging her to go on.

"Well, it turns out that the missing girl is the same one who has been in your care."

"They're looking for Olivia?" he clarified.

"Yes," she replied. "Only they didn't call her Olivia. They believe her name is Cecelia."

There were more words, but Mitchell got distracted by the sight of an approaching bus. He was relieved to see it was going toward the hospital. He stood from the bench and prepared to board.

"Maybe they had the wrong girl," suggested Mitchell when he detected a gap in the conversation.

"I'm not so sure about that. They seem convinced that the two girls are one in the same. It's possible she gave us a fake name to ensure that she wouldn't be sent some place she didn't want to be."

"I see…" replied Mitchell as he stepped onto the bus. "So what happens now?"

"That depends on how the police want to proceed. I'm still waiting to hear back from the detective."

"If they found whom they were looking for, shouldn't that have ended their investigation?" asked Mitchell.

"That's the thing. They weren't conducting a missing person investigation. They are with the homicide unit."

The word struck Mitchell hard enough to knock him back into the nearest seat. Images of the scene on the roof flashed through his mind in quick succession. The businessman lying unconscious on the cold concrete, the pool of coagulated blood behind his head, the naked body of a girl beneath his coat…

"You mean, they think she killed someone?" he whispered into the phone.

The man seated beside him leered over with concern. Mitchell covered his mouth with his free hand.

"Not necessarily," said Dr. Faust. "It's possible that they just want to make sure that she was okay. Sometimes when one family member dies, the others might be at risk."

"I see…" said Mitchell unconvinced.

"Anyway, I just wanted to give you a heads up on the situation. I don't know exactly what will happen until the detective calls me back, but it's possible that they will want her in police custody until they've solved the case."

With the talk of her being taken away still vibrating across his inner ear, Mitchell felt weightless in his chest. It was as if a part of him had suddenly gone missing, the chasm it left behind a black hole sucking away the rest of existence. His vision blurred, colors faded, he could barely find the strength to breathe. His thoughts whirled together like the florescent mosaic of a kaleidoscope.

Mitchell lost sight of the rest of the conversation. He uttered replies as necessary, but they seemed to come from someone else's lips. Eventually, the voice on the other end went silent.

Mitchell sat for a moment listening to the quiet of the phone as thoughts and emotions battled ferociously inside him. After a time, reality impacted him like a barrage of bricks, though the inner turmoil continued to rage.

He looked at his surroundings and realized that his stop was approaching. Minutes dragged by like hours as he anxiously awaited the sight of the hospital building. His legs shook impatiently as he willed the bus toward its destination. When the door finally opened, Mitchell bolted from the vehicle at a full sprint.

He nearly crashed into the slow responding automatic door, came close to colliding with an unfortunate patient and almost trampled an unlucky orderly. Mitchell skipped the elevator and flew up the stairwell, taking the steps three at a time. His aggressive pace faltered on the third flight, causing him to topple forward. Ignoring the pain of the fall, he ventured forward without hesitation.

Mitchell emerged on the third floor like a monster in a horror movie. A nurse screamed at his sudden appearance behind her, his towering frame casting an ominous dark shadow. He moved beyond her, never slowing to apologize. He located Olivia's room, thrust past the open doorway and rounded the corner to gaze at an empty bed. The sheets still held the form where she had lain, her loose hairs sparsely decorating the pillow, and he could even smell Olivia's sweet scent on the air. And yet, she was gone.

Mitchell held out his hand to steady himself against the wall. A torrent of grief washed over him like an enormous swell upon a forlorn ship. The fatigue of physical exertion, and the exhaustion of emotional calamity overcame him, and he began to go weak in the knees. He leaned his back against the wall to prevent himself from falling.

While maintaining his position against the hard concrete, he suddenly heard the sound of a flushing commode. The noise was followed with running water as Mitchell continued to listen. He looked over to see a door closed beside him. Another moment went by and the faucet went quiet. The door opened, and Olivia stepped into the room, her hospital robe nearly dragging on the floor. She noticed Mitchell standing nearby.

"You're back," she stated joyfully.

Mitchell raced toward her, lifting her gracefully from the floor with one hand. Sweeping his other hand beneath her legs, he cradled her in his massive arms. She looked up to him with surprise and worry.

"Wh…" she began, but didn't get to finish her thought.

Mitchell planted his lips against hers, and she reciprocated in devoted passion. She wrapped her arms around his neck, locking her wrists into place. When they broke their embrace, she looked longingly into his eyes, her face flushed with excitement.

"I'm sorry I was gone so long," he said softly.

She smiled up at him.

"So am I," she said.

Behind him, Mitchell could hear footsteps enter the small room. He turned to face their intruder, a middle-aged nurse in floral patterned scrubs. She looked between the two faces in front of her with bewilderment. Memories of the restaurant scene flashed through Mitchell's mind.

"He thought it would be unwise of me to try walking by myself," said Olivia quickly. "At least until we're sure I won't faint again."

The nurse smiled, nodding in agreement.

"That's probably a good plan," she said. "We've got everything set up for your CT scan. Are you ready to go?"

Olivia looked up at Mitchell.

"Lead the way," he replied.

As Mitchell waited for Olivia to return from her testing, he pulled out his phone and dialed the number. On the third ring, a male voice picked up.

"Hello?" the voice said.

"Hey Carl, it's Mitchell."

"Oh, hey. How's it going?" he asked in a friendly tone.

"It's going well. But, listen, I won't be able to meet you tonight. I'm at the hospital."

"Oh, no. Is everything alright?" he asked with concern.

"We're not sure yet," said Mitchell. "Still waiting to hear back the results of her tests."

"Oh, I see. You're just visiting then?"

"Well, I would say more than visiting, but yes."

"Is it the woman you mentioned?"

Mitchell paused for a moment. Sometimes it was hard to separate the lies from the truth.

"Yes," he replied.

"It feels good to be there for the people you love, doesn't it?" Carl said cordially.

"Yes," he responded after a moment of reflection.

"How far have you made it in the book?" asked Carl.

"I finished it," stated Mitchell proudly.

"Finished?" Carl asked in shock. "All of it?"

"Well, I've got a couple more stories left, but I've gotten through the parts you told me to read."

"The first 164 pages?"

"Plus the doctor's stuff."

"Wow…somebody's been busy."

"Does it usually take people a while to get through it?"

"Depends, everybody has their own progression. Three days is pretty quick though."

"Maybe I'm just a fast reader," offered Mitchell.

"I suppose… You been going to meetings?"

"Yep."

"And not drinking?"

"Still not drinking."

"Huh…" replied Carl. "I'm not entirely certain what to do when someone follows directions."

Mitchell heard a chuckle on the other end.

"Do the other guys you work with not do what you suggest?"

"Most of them do eventually, but many are stubborn and rebellious at first."

"Well…don't get your hopes up," stated Mitchell.

"Believe me, I won't. Other than being in the hospital, is everything else going alright?"

Mitchell pondered.

"Honestly, nothing else has been on my mind since she got admitted."

"Not even thoughts of a drink?"

"Maybe once or twice," he admitted.

"Then you're right where you're supposed to be," Carl said reassuringly.

There was another soft chuckle through the phone.

"So…since we aren't getting together this evening, maybe we could talk a little over the phone?" Carl suggested.

"Sure," replied Mitchell. "She still hasn't gotten back from her latest test."

The two men talked about the book, mostly with Mitchell listening and Carl explaining. For Mitchell, much of the reading had been a blur in his memory until Carl discussed how working the steps had helped him in his own life. The longer he talked to Carl, the more optimistic Mitchell felt about everything, including the hospital visit.

"It seems that you've gotten a firm grasp of the first step. You've definitely accepted that you have a problem, and I admire your willingness to do something about it."

Mitchell smiled at the praise.

"Let's plan on meeting soon to discuss the second step," said Carl.

"Which one is that?"

"The one about a higher power."

Mitchell gave a resounding groan.

"Not a fan of the whole higher power thing?" asked Carl, though in a friendly manner.

"Not really," stated Mitchell.

"That's understandable. A lot of us struggle with that concept for a long time, myself included."

"Oh, I don't *struggle* with it, I'm just not a believer," he replied, a hint of anger in his voice.

"Well, don't worry about it right now," said Carl. "If you don't do the whole bearded guy on a cloud thing, you can always make the meetings your higher power for now."

Mitchell did not respond.

"Alright?" asked Carl.

"Alright," replied Mitchell hesitantly.

"Ok. Well, try to have a good night. I hope everything works out well at the hospital."

"Thank you."

"Call me if you need anything."

"Will do."

"Alright, take care."

"You, too," responded Mitchell.

As Mitchell pressed the disconnect button on his phone, angry thoughts churned in his mind. He had been raised a good Irish catholic, attending mass every Sunday and even taking confirmation. Then, somewhere around high school, all the stories he heard in church had become just that: stories; fables to tell your children to make sure that they behaved. For months, he scoured the Bible in an attempt to make sense of the absurd and farfetched tales that lay within, only to find nothing making sense at all. In the end, he filed away the ten plagues, the two arks and even the king of kings in the same bin he reserved for the Easter Bunny and the Tooth Fairy.

In college, his love for studying the world's religions was reinvigorated. Mitchell remained fascinated with all the subtle nuances and differing myths that each faith held dear, and his master's thesis dealt with the effects of religion on populations in the modern world. And yet, the sense of wonder he felt when reading scripture as a child never came back. It was as if that part of him had been lost forever.

There was something almost magical about the various holy books, and yet, it completely dissipated once it got in the hands of men. Organized religion had been used to justify most of the world's wars, genocides, murders and other senseless acts of violence perpetrated by one man against his brother. No matter how much he tried, Mitchell could never look past these atrocities to see religion, or its followers, as anything but evil, brainwashed, or both. Even his own brother-in-law seemed to be contributing to the madness.

Mitchell took a deep breath and slid the phone into his pocket. Perhaps it was simpler to follow Carl's advice, and not worry about it. There were plenty of other matters to concern himself with instead.

"Ok, well, I just wanted to give you a heads up," said Nick Hagan. "You have a wonderful night, Mr. Tchernowitz."

Nick hung up the receiver on his landline. Rummaging through the stack of papers on his home desk, he discovered the file for the Friedman case. He flipped open the front flap and jotted a note about contacting the lawyer in charge of the Friedman estate.

Setting the pen aside, Hagan read through the entire report. When he finished, he set the file back on his desk and called his partner. On the second ring, Doug picked up.

"Nick. What's up?"

"Hey. I was just finalizing the report for the Friedman case. Do you still have Sharon Faust's number?"

"Yes. Did you need something?"

"It's about the Friedman girl. Since Faust is her caseworker, I figure we should give her a head's up, so she can get the ball rolling."

"True. No need to keep the girl waiting."

"Exactly. Why delay the inevitable."

"Is that it?" asked Doug.

"Yep."

"Alright. I'll let her know so she can start filing the paperwork."

"Thanks, Doug," said Nick. "And thanks again for the other thing."

"You got it, partner."

Nick heard the sound of Werner disconnecting, and he hung up the phone.

Hagan looked excitedly at the box resting next to his bed. It was hard to believe that his partner had the connections to score a CPAP machine before his own insurance could handle it. At least for tonight, Nick could care less if the transaction had been on the up and up. He was looking forward to the rest he so desperately needed.

Nick looked back at the phone. There was just one more phone call to make before he could drift off into the land of fluffy clouds and counting sheep. He picked up the receiver and dialed the number. On the third ring, a female voice answered.

"Hello?" she said.

Hagan took a deep breath.

"Hey, Mom, it's Nick."

Mitchell was sitting on the edge of the hospital bed when Olivia was wheeled through the door. She managed to stand of her own accord from the chair, but her feet quickly left solid ground as Mitchell laid her gently back into the bed. She set her hand beside her, feeling the sheets.

"Thanks for keeping it warm for me," she said with a grin.

Mitchell turned to the nurse with the wheelchair.

"Speaking of warm," he said, "is it possible to get a couple extra blankets? It feels a bit chilly in here."

"Absolutely," the nurse said with a smile. Mitchell watched as she wheeled the chair back into the hallway, disappearing out of sight and out of mind.

"How'd the CT scan go?" Mitchell asked, turning back to Olivia.

"I'm not sure. They won't get the results back until tomorrow."

"Tomorrow? You'd think they wouldn't have to wait in the hospital." he said grumpily.

"I think all the doctors have gone home. It is kind of late," she offered.

"I suppose..." Mitchell yielded. "How do you feel?"

"I'm comfortable. I'd much rather be back home though."

Mitchell nodded.

"Any idea on how long before you'll be released?"

Olivia shook her head.

"The nurse said that they would keep me overnight. She said that even if the CT scan came back clean, they would probably hold me over just to be on the safe side."

"Hmmm..." muttered Mitchell. "Maybe I should have asked that nurse to bring up a cot while she was at it."

Olivia scooted sideways in the bed.

"There's plenty of room here," she said playfully.

Mitchell grinned at the suggestion, leaning forward to kiss her on the lips, but deciding at the last moment that the cheek might be the safer option.

"Unfortunately," he whispered, "there are no locks on these doors."

"You could try setting up a barricade," she suggested.

The nurse returned with two blankets. Mitchell thanked her as she set them on a nearby chair. She flashed a quick smile at him before taking off again. Mitchell grabbed the top blanket from the stack, shaking it out before draping it over his small companion.

"Are you warm enough?" he asked.

Olivia shot him a wicked grin.

"If I say 'no' will you change your mind about the bed?"

Mitchell rolled his eyes. Sitting down next to her on the bed, Mitchell tenderly stroked his fingers across the back of her hand. He thought about the conversation with Dr. Faust and what it might mean for the two of them. He averted her gaze, searching for a gentle way to broach this bit of bad news. Sensing something was off, Olivia reached her hand beneath his chin, redirecting his eyes back to hers. Those brilliant sapphires filled him with feelings of both serenity and sorrow.

"What is it?" she asked.

Mitchell exhaled a mournful sigh.

"I have to tell you something," he said.

A look of concern crossed her face. Before Mitchell could continue, a strange musical noise filled the space between them. Feeling the vibration in his pocket, Mitchell reached inside and pulled out his phone. He looked from the phone to Olivia and back to the phone.

"Sorry," he muttered.

Mitchell pressed the receive button.

"Hello?" he said, holding the phone close enough for Olivia to hear as well.

"Yes, is this Mr. Flynn?"

Mitchell recognized the voice.

"Good evening, Dr. Faust. How are you?"

"I'm doing well," she replied.

Silence fell between them.

"The reason I am calling this evening," she began, "is that I've spoken with one of the detectives involved in the James Friedman case."

Mitchell looked to Olivia. He suddenly regretted not telling her earlier about his conversation with the caseworker.

"Uh-huh?" replied Mitchell.

"It seems that they have decided that the death of James Friedman was most likely an accident."

"I see...and what about Olivia?"

"Well, with the case closed, the detectives feel that Olivia is no longer in any real danger, and should be taken out of protective custody immediately and handed over to her real family."

Mitchell and Olivia exchanged looks of trepidation.

"And when will that happen?" he asked.

"That's the thing...according to the detectives, there are no remaining relatives for either James Friedman or his wife Elaine, so there is no family to turn her over to."

"Then where will she go?"

"Well, the first thing we need to do is take her out of temporary care and find her something a little more permanent."

"You mean like foster care?"

"Precisely."

Olivia promptly snatched the phone out of his hand.

"Hi, Dr. Faust. This is Olivia."

There was a sudden lull on the other end of the line.

"Oh, hello Olivia," she replied. "Have you been listening to this whole conversation?"

"Most of it," she replied. "Mit...Mister Flynn was nice enough to put it on speaker phone for me."

"I see..."

"Anyway," said Olivia, "is it possible for a temporary guardian to become a full-time guardian?"

Another pause.

"I take it you are really enjoying living with Mr. Flynn?"

Olivia winked over at Mitchell.

"It's been the most fun I've had in my entire life," she said.

"I'm glad to hear that," said Dr. Faust. "And Mr. Flynn, are you still there?"

"I'm here," he replied.

"Are you willing to take on that commitment?" she asked.

Mitchell looked at Olivia, taking her hand in his.

"Absolutely," he said with enthusiasm.

"Well, good," said Dr. Faust. "I'll start processing the paperwork first thing tomorrow morning. It might take a few days for everything to go through, and I'll keep you posted."

"Sounds good," said Mitchell.

"Well, you two have a wonderful night, and I will touch bases with you later in the week."

"Ok. Good night."

As the phone disconnected, the two young lovers turned toward each other, their eyes filled with longing. There was a single moment of hesitation before they threw caution to the wind, allowing the feelings of elation to take over. After an entire day of keeping their distance, it was such a relief to finally be embracing once again.

Olivia suddenly pulled away.

"Isn't there something you wanted to tell me?" she asked.

Mitchell let out a hearty chuckle.

"Never mind," he laughed. "Everything seems to have fixed itself."

Later that night, long after the nurses made their final rounds and the hospital had grown still, Olivia and I quietly prepared ourselves for bed. Though the hospital staff had not been particularly keen on the idea of this little sleepover, none of them had been willing to

separate the poor girl from the man they perceived to be her father. Perhaps there were some advantages to her small stature after all.

Following Olivia's advice on barricading, I slid the solitary chair in front of the door. It wouldn't stop anyone from coming in, but it might alert us to their presence. Just to be on the safe side, I set my phone's alarm for five. Hopefully with it being only a few hours away, the night nurses wouldn't stumble in on us while we slept.

Once beneath the sheets, Olivia pressed her bare body against mine, that familiar feeling making it seem like we were actually back at home in our own bed. Engulfing her in my arms, we rejoiced in one another's affections until she fell asleep, her head in its normal resting spot upon my chest.

As I lay awake, staring blankly at the ceiling, my mind wandered back to the earlier conversation with Carl. After the hospital scare, the fear of the detectives and the threat of separation, it was remarkably easy for me to count my blessings. With everything that could have gone awry today but didn't, I suddenly found myself wanting to thank whatever powers existed in the universe for delivering Olivia safely back to me. Though I knew I would not throw my lot in with the religious crowd, the spiritual tranquility I felt from my gratitude that night, whether real or imagined, gave credence to the possibility that there could be something to this higher power nonsense after all.

CHAPTER 26

Victor Lazda was born in the small fishing village of Kolka. The eerie clouds of the Cold War had just settled over the Soviet Union, but were nothing compared to the frozen winds of the Baltic. Every day young men faced the wrath of the sea whilst the politicians warned of the dangers of the capitalist regime beyond the ocean. For Victor, it had all been a red herring; a distraction to make them forget about the turmoil they faced on their own shores. Why be concerned about the threat of nuclear winter when there was actual winter to worry about.

Like his brothers, Victor had tasted the salty air from a young age. His hands were callous before he learned to read, though he had been slow in that department. It was only with the urging of his mother that he bothered at all. What good was an education to a boy who would know only fishing?

His parents were blessed with many children, but none younger than Victor survived to adulthood. One by one, his brothers were claimed by disease, famine and unforgiving icy waters. Victor grew to resent the fisherman's life, knowing that it brought misery, poverty and death. When the moment was right, he abandoned his homeland to seek out new horizons.

Alone, he traveled across Europe, taking jobs as they came. For a time, he was a dockhand in Gdańsk, a grape harvester in the Rhineland, and a busboy in Boulogne before taking up factory work across the channel. It was under the tutelage of his foreman that Victor realized his potential for advancement. He had given up any notions of being anything but a common grunt until his boss ignited a spark of desire; a longing for wealth.

Hopping aboard a freighter, Victor found himself on the other side of the Atlantic, once again involved in menial labor. During the days, he packaged cargo for transport, but in the evenings, he vigorously studied the minutiae of estate and property laws. After six years, Victor Lazda passed the New York state bar exam.

Changing his name to Tchernowitz, Victor secured a position with a young firm. From there, his life drastically changed. He found a wife, had a son, and, through the help of his newly discovered client, James Friedman, began to make more money than he ever thought possible.

But like everything else that happened to him, Victor's happiness had been a passing fancy. His wife, a fantastic divorce lawyer in her own right, left him after three years. Although she accused him of being more devoted to his work than to their marriage, he couldn't help but assume that the physical trainer she was seeing might have had something to do with it. After months battling in the courts, she ended up with the house, the money, and most importantly, his son.

Victor threw himself totally into his job after that. Eventually, his main client became his only client. James Friedman had never been one to share his resources and soon demanded that Tchernowitz either work for him full-time or not at all. Victor didn't care much for James Friedman as a person, but the job was too appetizing to pass up.

Over time, Victor's son found him again. Father and son rekindled a bond severed by years of absence. Happiness once again filled his days. Victor experienced his son's marriage, the birth of his four grandchildren, and the most joyous day of all: the death of his moneygrubbing ex-wife.

Then came the frightening news. David, his beloved son, had been diagnosed with chronic renal disease. Without a kidney transplant, he wasn't expected to survive another year.

Victor looked away from his son's picture and back to the papers on his desk. Finding a suitable donor was the easy part; a small sacrifice to save the life of his only son. Paying for the surgery, however, was proving more difficult.

With the decline in the economy, David had been one of the many who lost his employment, and therefore, his medical insurance. Without coverage, the overwhelming costs of surgery seemed a mountain too steep to overcome. Many would have given up hope, but not Victor. For him, it was just another tribulation in a lifetime of struggles.

Victor glanced back at his son's picture. All those years playing the big shot, the parties, the fancy house and expensive car, they made him lose sight of the important things. Feelings of shame and regret overtook him. When he had been spending money like a Hollywood diva, he should have been setting some aside for the future. Life in the old country taught him that rainy days and high waters are very common, and he had forgotten that lesson with his penthouse lifestyle. Now he was paying the price, and so might his son.

Tchernowitz had sought a loan from James Friedman. Though they were mainly business associates, surely the wealthy investment tycoon would help in his time of need. They had known each other a long time after all. Besides, it would be little different than an advance on payment anyway. Friedman was not so keen to the idea, however, telling him that he didn't like lending money. And that was that. After serving the man faithfully for more than two decades, Victor had not even bothered to go to the funeral.

Victor glanced at the letter from the bank. With recent developments in the real estate market, his house had dropped significantly in value. It was now worth only a little more than what he owed on it. The branch manager seemed almost eager to deny his request for a second mortgage. Tchernowitz wrestled with the idea of selling the house, even if it only generated a small profit. He could always ask to sleep in his son's basement.

He studied the values on his retirement account, the various stocks and bonds, and the equity built up on his life insurance policy. If he liquidated all of his assets, he would still be a couple hundred thousand short of his goal. He put his head in his hands, despairing at the numbers before him. Victor had begun his life with nothing, had grown up with nothing, and might very well finish his life with nothing.

The phone rang beside him.

Must be the detectives again.

Victor reached for the phone.

"Good evening, Victor Tchernowitz speaking," he greeted.

"Hello, Mr. Tchernowitz," came a pompous voice. "This is Dorian Abernathy."

Victor hung up the phone. Though he had been disappointed by James Friedman in the end, Dorian Abernathy was a completely different kind of monster. If Abernathy wanted him, there was a plan in motion, and Victor wanted no part in such ventures. Nothing good ever came from following men like Dorian Abernathy.

The phone rang again. Victor crossed his arms and stared at the ringing device beside him. On the third ring, he took up the receiver and placed it down again. The room grew quiet once more.

Victor continued to stare at the silent phone. Curiosity is an insidious disease that corrupts the mind. The longer it festers, the more it takes over. No man is immune to its clutches, and when the phone rang a third time, Tchernowitz grabbed the receiver.

"What do you want, Abernathy?" he demanded.

"Hey, hey," he replied, attempting to diffuse the anger. "There's no need for hostilities. I believe we can be of assistance to one another."

"You have nothing I want," growled Victor.

"On the contrary, a little bird tells me that you've found yourself in a little financial trouble," he stated, a little too pleasantly.

"Your bird is misinformed," Victor stated quickly.

"Is he?" mocked Abernathy. "Pity. Fixing financial troubles is a specialty of mine, as I'm sure you know."

"I've heard."

"Have you? What is it that James Friedman told you about me?"

"Plenty."

"Malicious lies, I assure you. You see, Friedman never cared much for me, I think he saw too much of himself. Tell me, was James Friedman a pleasure to work with?"

Victor said nothing.

"I thought so. For all his gossip about me, I bet he didn't even pay you a fair salary."

Again, Victor said nothing.

"Let's face it, if he had, you probably wouldn't be in this situation. I bet when he found out about your son, he didn't offer to help."

Victor flinched at the mention of his son.

"How did you know about...?"

"The walls have ears, Mr. Tchernowitz."

"I see... and what do these walls tell you?"

"They tell me that the clock is ticking, Victor. It ticks for both of us, and I need your help just as much as you need mine."

"Why would I want to help you?" asked Victor defiantly.

Abernathy let out a sigh.

"Because, if you do, I will write you a check for five million dollars."

The figure seemed to get caught in his throat. Victor swallowed hard, trying to regain his composure.

"Did you say *five million*?" asked Victor.

It was enough to not only save his son, but pay off the rest of his debts, put some away for the next rainy day and still be able to retire in style.

"That's right. There's just one little catch."

Reality struck back hard. Victor remembered that he was talking to Dorian Abernathy.

"What sort of catch?"

"Well, you know that girl of Friedman's? What is her name, Cindy or something?"

"Cecelia."

"Right, right. She seems to have been the lucky recipient of the Friedman fortune."

"I suppose."

"And that fortune is currently being held in trust?"

"Right."

"A trust managed by you?"

"Yes," replied Victor, still uncertain where this conversation was headed.

"Well, part of the problem is that this little girl now owns a majority stake in Friedman Financial, a company she knows nothing about."

"I suppose you're right about that."

"The company has begun to stagnate in Friedman's absence, and I'm not sure that it will survive in the hands of inexperienced leadership."

"And what do you want me to do about it?"

"Simple. I want you to convince that girl to sell me her stake in the company. I need you because it's your hand that signs the checks, at least until she turns eighteen."

Victor scrunched up his face. There was still something amiss about all this.

"I'm sure the girl would agree to sell to you at market price. Why should she need convincing?"

Abernathy took in a deep, slow breath.

"That's the thing," he began, "I don't want to pay market value on her shares. I want to acquire them at a... significant discount, if you know what I mean."

Victor understood. Dorian Abernathy had not changed one bit, he was still up to his old antics. Abernathy didn't *need* him; Abernathy was *using* him, and paying him off with blood money. Victor would not turn a blind eye to this corruption. He would do what he should have done all along.

"Good night, Abernathy," he said, reaching the phone toward the receiver.

"Wait, wait, wait..." came a distant voice.

Victor hesitated and brought the phone back to his ear.

"Look," continued Abernathy. "It's not like I'm trying to steal her money. She'll still have plenty left over after I buy her out, but paying full value on her shares would be financially detrimental to me. You understand?"

Victor wanted to hang up the phone, but sometimes snakes can be very charming.

"The girl will have more money than she knows what to do with, I'll get control of the shares, the company will prosper, your son will get the surgery he needs, and you won't need to subject yourself to the whims of the likes of James Friedman ever again. It's a win for everybody."

Victor thought for a long time. How could he side with someone like Dorian Abernathy; it was like making a deal with the devil himself. He thought of Cecelia, and how innocent she was in the ways of the business world. The idea of betraying her trust for money made him sick to his stomach. Victor looked at his son's picture on his desk. He looked intently at his son's eyes and how full of life they appeared in the picture. Victor cast his gaze away from the picture and onto the floor in shame.

"Alright," he said softly. "I'll do it."

"Excellent," said Abernathy joyfully. "You won't regret it."

I doubt that.

"When do we talk with Cecelia?" asked Victor.

Abernathy paused.

"We've run into a problem on that end, but don't worry, we're working on something. I think we'll make a move on Thursday."

After signing off with Abernathy, Victor hung up the phone. He looked at his son's picture again. Hopefully, it was worth the price of feeling dead inside, so that his son might live.

It had been another long day filled with tests, scans and needles. Olivia lay in her bed, relieved that she could finally get some rest. She stared in boredom around the room, hoping to discover something of interest. The white room held nothing for her. She sighed heavily in frustration.

I'll make sure to have Mitchell bring something to read if he's going to be out for so long.

Mitchell left for a late afternoon meeting with his new support structure. After watching the drink slowly consume James Friedman, she was happy that Mitchell was taking steps to solve the problem. It was a major inconvenience that it took him away from her. At least they spent most of the day together, even if it was in this bleak place.

Olivia looked up at the television resting idly in the corner. She wondered for a moment if there were any good movies playing, but decided that it wasn't worth the effort. She slumped down into her pillow, hoping to sleep away the time apart from her beloved.

As is oft the case, sleep evaded her when she desired it most. She tossed and turned, rolling onto her sides and stomach, trying to get comfortable. Just when she thought she might be able to drift off, another urge arose, and she stood from the bed.

At first, her legs were wobbly beneath her, and her vision went cloudy. She sat for a moment on the edge of the bed until she reclaimed her bearings. Satisfied that another fainting spell was not imminent, she trudged to the restroom.

When she was done, she tried to stand, but the same feelings of lightheadedness swarmed her. This time, there was a feeling of intense pain at her temples as she attempted to stand up. Her vision darkened once more, and she returned to sitting on the commode.

Tears of frustration filled her eyes.

After a time, her vision cleared, and the headache subsided. She took a piece of toilet tissue and wiped away the tears from her eyes. When her cheeks were dry, she reached over and pulled the emergency chord. Her pride was wounded, but she was otherwise unharmed. There was no need to risk her safety by making another pursuit for the sake of vanity.

As she waited for reinforcements to arrive, she decided not to tell Mitchell of this fiasco. He had enough on his plate without having to worry about this as well.

Mitchell arrived in her room around 6:30, closing the door behind him. In his hand he was clutching his phone. On his face, he wore a broad smile.

"Good news," he said, approaching her bed.

"Oh?" asked Olivia.

"I just got off the phone with Dr. Faust. They've decided to schedule the court date for next Wednesday morning."

Olivia nodded.

"Do you think I'll be released by then?" she asked sadly.

Mitchell slid the phone away and sat beside her on the bed. He rested his hand gently against her cheek.

"Of course," he said reassuringly.

She smiled at him, but her eyes still carried the same gleam of melancholy. Olivia leaned forward; resting her head against his chest as Mitchell lightly stroked her hair.

"Do you think it'll ever get easier?" she asked softly.

"I'm sure all couples have their problems," he whispered back.

"Problems like ours?"

"No, not like ours," he admitted. "But just as significant, if not even worse."

"You think so?"

"Absolutely. Just look at that director and his wife."

"What director?"

"You know, the one who married his adopted daughter," he said. "Surely they've got it worse."

Olivia giggled into his shoulder.

"What?" he asked.

"You know, we have a custody hearing next week," she said. "That's a lot like adoption."

Mitchell suddenly stopped stroking her hair.

"Don't talk like that," he said finally.

"Why?"

"I don't know. It's just…weird."

"It is quite odd, isn't it?" she said. "Most people would opt for engagement, but I guess marriage isn't family enough for you."

"What did I just say?"

"Do you suppose it's because Pittsburgh is so close to West Virginia? Maybe getting into your "daughter's" jeans is in your genes?"

"Olivia…"

"If we get into an argument, is it still considered a 'lover's quarrel' or do we just refer to it as 'daddy issues'?"

"I'm warning you," he said playfully.

Olivia leaned closer until he could feel her hot breath blowing against him, his heart rate quickening as feelings of euphoria surged through his body.

"Am I being a naughty girl?" she teased. "Is 'Daddy' going to have to punish me?"

Mitchell moved his hands to her ribcage and gently tickled her with his fingertips. She squirmed within his playful touch until his hands wrapped around her supple breasts, causing her to convulse in his arms. Olivia pulled back until she was looking into his eyes. When his touch suddenly faltered, she clasped his hands and pressed them back to her chest, firmly holding them in place. She closed her eyes, moving her mouth to his as Mitchell tenderly caressed her subtle bumps.

Olivia wrapped her hands behind his neck and pulled him gently toward her. She kept leaning back until she was flat against the pillow beneath his muscular torso. His fingers continued to explore her body as they passionately made out on the hospital bed. Olivia suddenly forced their lips apart and gazed longingly up at him with those deep blue sapphires.

"Do you remember what you said the other night?" she gasped, gently caressing the side of his face. "About other things we could try…"

Mitchell looked down at her and smiled.

"I remember."

Biting down on her lip, Olivia gracefully slid free of her undergarments before adjusting her hands helplessly behind her head.

"Show me."

Never taking his eyes from hers, Mitchell lifted the hospital gown, placing his right hand delicately upon her abdomen. Moving his fingers lightly back and forth, he slowly worked his way down over her pelvis and across her inner thighs, gently massaging the tender flesh. Olivia's breathing became more erratic with every touch as he closed in on the final destination.

Remembering the pain from the other night, Mitchell watched her intently as he made soft circular motions between his second and third fingers. Blood flowed to her face and chest, adding a rosy pigment to her cheeks and pale breasts. Mitchell could feel the heat rising from her body as she shuddered beneath him. Her tiny eyelids fluttered rapidly as though she were enjoying the most pleasant of dreams.

Olivia let out a moan so soothing that it sounded like the coo of a dove. Mitchell leaned forward, feeling her cries of ecstasy against his lips. Olivia wrapped her arms around his neck, running her fingers through his coarse hair. He increased his tempo below and Olivia latched to him with a vice grip. Her moans became more intense, the tingling sensation making his lips go numb. Olivia rocked back and forth in wavelike rhythm to his strokes. When her body began to quake gently, he knew that she was drawing near.

And suddenly there was a loud knock on the door.

Mitchell pulled away quickly, standing up from the bed. Olivia put her gown back into place, covering herself with the thin hospital blanket. Before either could respond, the door opened, and a young nurse wheeled in a food cart.

"Hey there," she greeted pleasantly. "I've brought your dinner."

She lifted the meal from the cart and held it momentarily while Olivia shifted into a seated position. Maneuvering a tray in place, the nurse set the food down in front of her. She looked at Olivia's flushed face with concern.

"Are you feeling alright, dear?" she asked, placing the back of her hand against Olivia's red forehead. "You're burning up."

Olivia gently pushed the woman's hand away.

"I'm good," she stated. "I was just napping when you came in."

The nurse seemed unconvinced.

"Maybe it's a little warm in here," she offered. "Would you like me to turn the heat down for you?"

"I'm fine, really. There's no need to trouble yourself."

The nurse peered curiously at her.

"Ok," she said. "But if you need anything, just press that button beside the bed and someone will be along. Ok?"

Olivia nodded.

"Thank you," she muttered weakly.

The nurse gave her one last look of concern before turning to Mitchell.

"Make sure you keep an eye on her," she instructed.

Mitchell quietly shut the door after nurse. When he returned to the bedside, Olivia was covering her face with her hands, her cheeks bright red with embarrassment.

"That was close," stated Mitchell.

Olivia giggled into her hands. She peered at him through a gap in her fingers before lowering her hands to reveal a wicked grin.

"It was *really* close," she said. "I was almost there."

She motioned to the tray in front of her.

"Can you set this over there somewhere?" she asked politely.

Mitchell did as he was told.

"Not feeling hungry?" he asked worriedly.

When Mitchell turned back, the blanket was pushed down to its prior position; Olivia's hospital gown had crept upwards to reveal her nearly hairless form. She flashed him a lascivious smile.

"On the contrary," she said. "I'm feeling quite famished."

CHAPTER 27

Mitchell moved to kiss Olivia but she recoiled from his affections.

"What's the matter?" he asked.

Looking into his eyes, Olivia used her palms to gently push him away from her face.

"Can you wash first?" she pleaded, her face contorted in displeasure.

Mitchell raised an eyebrow.

"Are you serious?"

Olivia gritted her teeth, but still couldn't overcome the aversion.

"Please," she requested apologetically.

"It's just you," he groaned with frustration.

"I know but…it's still kind of gross." Olivia grimaced.

"I kissed you after…" he protested.

"Yes, but it's…different."

Mitchell sighed.

"Is it really that big a deal for you?"

Olivia hesitated, and then nodded.

"I'm sorry," she said humbly.

Mitchell rolled his eyes.

"Fine," he said, reluctantly rolling out of the hospital bed. As the sound of running water erupted from the bathroom faucet, Olivia reached beneath her pillow and located her underwear. By the time Mitchell returned, she had secured the garment back in place, covering herself with the flannel blanket. He leaned over and planted a soft kiss on her lips, this time meeting no resistance.

"Thank you," she said.

Mitchell nodded in acquiescence.

"How was the meeting this morning?" she asked, changing the subject.

"It was good," he said. "Carl and I talked afterward."

"And?"

"He wants me to attend this workshop."

"What kind of workshop?"

Mitchell paused to gather his words.

"Something about working through the steps the way they did in the old days. Carl thinks that it'll help get me acquainted with the program quicker."

"Like taking an escalator?" she asked jokingly.

"I'm not sure escalators have twelve steps, but sure."

"When is it?"

"This weekend."

"And how long will you be gone?"

Mitchell thought.

"I'm not quite sure. Carl says that it's pretty intense, but I think I should be back in time for dinner."

She nodded her understanding.

"Does that mean I have your permission?" he asked.

Olivia crossed her arms.

"This is not a dictatorship," she stated defiantly. "If you think you need this, then go."

Mitchell maintained his questioning stare.

"Just know that you'll have to pay tribute for your transgressions," she smirked.

Mitchell relaxed his posture and took a seat beside her on the bed. It was comforting to know that not every comment he made elicited an argument with her the way it had with Evelyn. He placed a tender kiss on the back of her hand before interweaving their fingers together.

"Was there any news in my absence?" he asked.

Olivia shook her head.

"The CT came back negative, which rules out concussion, a stroke and brain cancer. Other than that, they still have no idea. But they are reluctant to let me go home until they figure it out."

"How are you feeling?"

Olivia remembered the fainting spell from the night before.

"Just a little lightheaded every now and again. Nothing major though."

Mitchell nodded.

"Hopefully they'll get it all sorted out soon," he said encouragingly.

Mitchell glanced at his watch. It was just past ten.

"I'll see if I can track down a nurse."

Olivia voiced her agreement and Mitchell moved toward the hallway. He took a single step to the right before colliding with something solid. Mitchell looked on in horror as an elderly gentleman fell to the floor in front of him, knocked backward by the sudden force. Mitchell immediately went to the man's aid, reaching out a hand to help him up.

"Are you ok?" he asked worriedly.

Mitchell pulled the man to his feet, making sure he was steady before releasing his grip.

"I'm sorry about that," he apologized. "I should have been paying better attention to where I was going."

"Dees things 'appen," the man replied. "Nathin' ter git on aboyt."

Mitchell eyed the man curiously. It was hard to believe that such a powerful stench of alcohol could come from someone who wasn't even as tall as Olivia, let alone this early in the morning.

"I suppose not," he said finally.

"Tully," the man said jovially, extending his arm.

"Mitchell," he replied, clasping the outstretched hand.

"Wha ye runnin' ter in such a 'urry?"

"I was looking for a nurse."

"Everytin' be al'roi?"

Mitchell blinked.

"Uh...yes." he replied. "Trying to get an update for my..."

Mitchell gestured to the room, though he was unsure of how to refer to his tiny companion to this complete stranger.

"Aye, oi understan'. You're lookin' oyt for yisser wee lassy."

Mitchell stared blankly at the man.

"Uh...Sure." Mitchell responded, more of a guess than anything.

"Yer are gollier fella. Ye an athlete?"

"No. I played a little racquetball in college, but I wasn't very good at it."

"That's too bad. Yer wud 'av been deadly as a midfielder."

A thought seemed to cross the man's mind, for a sudden smile crossed his face.

"Oi don't reckon yer cud use a job? Me cousin Kelly be needin' a fella loike yer."

It took Mitchell a moment to process what had just been said to him.

"A job?" he asked.

"Aye. Do yer be nadin' wan?"

Mitchell thought about the impending court case.

"Actually, yes. I have been looking for a job."

Tully smiled, showing Mitchell his crooked teeth.

"Oi wus jist aboyt ter go over dat way if yer want ter tag along."

Mitchell hesitated.

"Let me go talk with…" Mitchell gestured toward the room again, but still had not come up with a term for Olivia.

"Sure, sure. Take yer time," Tully said with a wave of his hand.

Mitchell went into the room and explained the strange scenario that occurred in the hospital corridor. She acceded to his plan and bid him ado with a kiss. Mitchell grabbed his coat and followed the man down the hall, never noticing the dark garbed man entering the room behind him.

Victor Tchernowitz walked into the small hospital room, feeling both apprehensive and shameful at what he was about to do. Taking a deep breath, he reminded himself that this was all for David's benefit.

He turned the corner to see the frail body of Cecelia Friedman lying in the hospital bed. Her normally brilliant blond hair was matted and unkempt. Her pale skin looked almost translucent in the harsh reflection of the whitewashed interior. Gazing at her haggard form, Tchernowitz was uncertain whether his son or Friedman's daughter was truly the worse off.

Catching sight of him, the small girl's eyes suddenly lit up.

"Hey. I know you," she said excitedly. "You're Victor Tchernowitz, my father's lawyer."

"I'm surprised you recognize me," he stated, though he was more shocked that she'd gotten his name right.

"Of course, I recognize you," she said with a smile. "You haven't changed much since last we spoke."

"Well, no. But it's not like we've spoken at length to one another."

"I guess not. But I always had a fondness for the name Victor, and you were the first person I met with that name."

"I take it you read it somewhere else then?"

Olivia nodded.

"Can't say I would have picked you to be a Frankenstein fan." he guessed.

"Hugo, actually. I am not much of a horror reader."

"You might have been better off with the horror," he said jokingly. "It might have had a happier ending."

"Especially the last one I read."

"The hunchback?"

Olivia shook her head.

"Les Mis."

Victor gazed at her with both eyebrows upraised.

"Really?"

She nodded.

"Huh...figured that one would've been a little beyond your reading level..."

Olivia shrugged.

"What did you think of it?"

She pondered a moment.

"It was half as uplifting as the title implies."

Victor snorted a chuckle.

"It is that," he laughed.

"But you know..." she continued, "in spite of its depressing themes, I like the main character. In a way, it was almost inspiring the way he always tried to do what was right, even if it wasn't best for him. Like with the man in court. Valjean could have easily thrown the other guy under the bus and walked away a free man. Instead, he refused to sacrifice someone else's life for his own gain. I wish more people had that kind of honor, you know?"

Victor averted his eyes from her gaze, peering absently out the window.

"Yeah..." he muttered in acquiescence. "It would be nice..."

Victor once more felt the pangs of guilt as he thought about his son.

"Is everything alright?" she asked after a long interlude of silence.

Victor shook away his thoughts.

"It is good that you read," he said. "It will help make you smart."

Olivia raised an eyebrow at him.

"I'm glad you think that," she grinned. "You did buy me a book on my birthday after all."

Victor looked at her with confusion.

"Did I?"

Olivia nodded.

"On every birthday, actually. At least since I started living with the Friedmans."

"Well, I'm afraid I can't really take credit for that," he explained apologetically. "You see, I generally send my assistant to do the shopping. I told her that you like to read, and she took care of the rest."

"Still, at least you knew what I like," she said encouragingly.

"There is that, I suppose. So what did Vanessa end up getting for you last year?"

Olivia thought for a moment.

"I think it was The Hunger Games."

Victor nodded.

"And how was that?"

Olivia shrugged unenthusiastically.

"It had interesting artwork on the cover."

Victor let out a hearty laugh.

"Well I'll have to make sure she gets you something better this year," he offered.

His lighthearted laughter made Victor suddenly feel the weight of the briefcase in his hand. Inside its leather compartments were all the documents, account information and contracts necessary to hand control of Friedman Financial over to Dorian Abernathy. All they needed was her signature.

Victor laid the briefcase on the chair near the hospital bed, exposing its contents. He shuffled papers around until he located the Last Will and Testament of James Phillip Friedman. Without closing the lid, he turned to face Olivia.

"As you are aware, I have been your father's family attorney for a number of years, with most of that time being spent as his personal retainer."

Olivia nodded.

"As per the wishes of his will," Victor began, holding up the document, "the entirety of the Friedman estate was placed into trust, with you as the sole beneficiary. Due to the exorbitant value of the trust, three smaller accounts were created to be managed individually within the greater.

"The assets of the first were put into the hands of a firm specializing in real estate, and they manage the lands, properties and funds associated with real property that belonged to your father. The second account deals with the assets of the Friedman Financial group, including all of the shares he held with the company. With the suggestions and guidance of the board of directors, I am overseeing this account personally.

"The third account, which controls the majority of the money, is overseen by a separate financial group that specializes in asset management. Because of the sheer quantity of funds left behind by the late James Friedman, I have instructed them to be extremely conservative in their investment strategies. Even so, they expect to have an annual return goal of around six percent, which isn't bad considering how the market is currently fairing."

Victor set the will aside and began to riffle through his paperwork again. Victor recited different fund names, investment totals, estimated return values and other business terms that Olivia did not understand. He was just about to reach for another stack of papers when he noticed the blank stare on her face.

Victor took a deep breath, this time speaking to her, not with the cold and calculating voice of a lawyer, but in the soothing way a father might talk to his child.

"You have no idea what I'm talking about do you?"

"It is a bit overwhelming" she admitted. "Mr. James never spoke of these things to me."

He nodded in understanding, tossing the papers back inside the briefcase and latching the lid in place. Victor set the luggage on the floor, taking a seat in the now vacant chair.

"Let's take it from the top, shall we?"

Mitchell checked his watch to find that they had been walking more than half an hour with no signs of slowing down. The old man was remarkably spry for his age, and Mitchell laboriously panted as he struggled to keep up with his diminutive guide. With their breakneck pace, he estimated they were two miles from the hospital. Mitchell was suddenly wary of his traveling companion; how much did he really know about the man after all?

"How much farther?" asked Mitchell, trying not to let his concern carry over in his voice.

"Two more blocks, roun' de corner, on der lef," stated Tully curtly.

Mitchell continued to follow, his fists clenched tightly by his sides. He decided to go another couple blocks, but if they hadn't arrived at their destination by then, it would be time to ditch this stranger and return to the hospital, with or without a new job.

After the second block, the older man turned right, rounding the sidewalk counter-clockwise. Tully scurried up the street and stopped abruptly beneath a hanging sign. The wood was splintered, and the outer edges were eroded. It squeaked loudly overhead as the wind blew. As they neared, Mitchell could discern the name O'Conner's, a vestige of clover adorning the display's lower half.

The older man waved toward him and ducked inside the dilapidated building. Mitchell eyed the brick and mortar with the same reservation deckhands might for a ramshackle fishing trawler. Nothing about its exterior seemed inviting, yet Mitchell found himself moving inside despite his trepidations.

Whatever contempt he held for the building itself, the inside only further kindled his disappointment. Mitchell had known his fair share of rundown hole in the wall joints and shoddy dive bars, but those were charitable descriptions to the place he now found himself. Tables were cracked, chairs overturned, and the wood had been stained with what Mitchell hoped was red ale. The wallpaper was discolored from years of cigarette smoke. A foul odor of combination musk and stale beer permeated the room, forcing Mitchell to breathe through his mouth. His shoes stuck to the floor as he crossed the room to where Tully was seated at the bar.

"Is Kelly in?" asked Tully, his accent so thick Mitchell thought he was making an order.

"Aye. E's roun' back checking de kegs," replied the barkeep, looking at Mitchell. "Who's yer frien'?"

"Dis be Mitch. Oi towl 'im dat Kelly cud use 'im for work."

The barkeep glared back at Tully.

"Waat did me owl lad say about offerin' jobs?" he demanded.

"Feller needs a job," stated Tully defensively. "'Sides, jist luk at 'im. Built strong as a 'orse 'e is."

The barkeep looked again at Mitchell, having to gaze up this time due to the change in proximity. He nodded to Tully.

"Everyone needs a job, but oi don't tink 'e's 'iring right now. Might want ter fetch 'im."

Tully disappeared behind the corner, leaving Mitchell alone with this new companion. He didn't mind though; Tully's thick accent was starting to grate on his last nerve.

"What's yer name frien'?" asked the barkeep.

"Mitchell," he stated, though confused why he would ask again.

The man shook his head.

"Yer other name…"

"Flynn," Mitchell replied after a moment's hesitation.

The barkeep reached his hand out to Mitchell.

"Daniel O'Connor," he said proudly. "Folks call me Danny."

"Good to meet you," Mitchell said politely, taking a seat at the bar.

"So 'ow long you know Tully?"

"Half an hour," Mitchell replied with a shrug.

"There might be 'ope for yer after all," Danny said with a laugh. "That Tully's more trouble than e's worth. 'Alf the toime e's only coming 'round when e's low on cash and wants to nurse 'is habit."

Mitchell nodded, knowing exactly what kind of habit.

"What kind of work you lookin' for?" asked Danny.

Mitchell shook his head.

"I just need a job. Work is work."

Danny nodded appreciatively at the answer.

"You want anything to drink?"

Mitchell's mind filled with thoughts of amber liquid pouring into a frosty glass. The fluid repast bubbling enticingly as the foam formed along its surface. He could feel the tingling sensations as it flowed across his tongue, the sweet and bitter taste as it slid down his throat, the refreshing chill as it coursed through his esophagus and the soothing warmth as it entered his gut. He sensed the joyful wave of ecstasy as the alcohol took hold of him once again.

"I'll have water," he replied, shaking off the harmful sway of daydream.

When the glass arrived, he instinctively chugged it down. The quenching power of the water helped alleviate his desire, and Mitchell once again found himself in control of his urges. He placed the glass down heavily on the wooden counter, striking the surface with a loud *thunk*.

He looked back at Danny who was staring at him wide-eyed.

"Looks loike you were thirsty," he joked. "Let me get you some more."

Mitchell handed him the glass, somewhat embarrassed by his display. Hopefully, his strange behavior had not lost him favor with the boss's son. When Danny returned the glass to him, he took a long, slow sip and placed the glass delicately down on the counter.

"Thank you," said Mitchell.

"Not a problem," Danny replied with a smile.

The two men looked to the back of the bar as a loud noise caught their attention. Mitchell listened intently to the sound of two raised voices.

"Absolutely not!" shouted the first man, a voice Mitchell did not recognize.

"Jist do me dis favor, O'Connor. Don't oi 'elp yer whaen yer be needin' it," came a thick accent that could only be Tully.

"Aye, you do. But lately you've been good for nothin' but samplin' me wares."

"Aye, an' waat delicious wares they are, but if yer ask me, ought be somebody protectin' yer investment."

"Oh really?! An' you think that shud be you?"

The two men turned the corner into the main bar area. Mitchell rose from his stool, waiting patiently for them to draw closer. When the new man caught sight of Mitchell, he stopped dead in his tracks.

"Great googly moogly!!" he shouted. "Who are you?"

"'Tis yer paddy oi wus tellin' yer aboyt," explained Tully.

The new man stared blankly at Tully, both eyebrows riding high.

"'Tis him shud be guardin' yer shop, O'Connor," continued Tully. "Naw paddy alive wud dare scrap dis wan 'ere."

O'Connor swallowed hard as he extended his hand toward Mitchell.

"What's yer name wee fella?"

"His name's Flynn," interrupted Danny from behind the counter.

O'Connor turned from his son to Mitchell.

"Or Mitchell, if you prefer," he said with a shrug.

"I don't prefer," replied O'Connor hastily, letting his hand slide from Mitchell's grasp. He raised his finger and pointed it authoritatively at the larger man. "You've got a good Oirish name, be proud of it."

O'Connor glanced at his son behind the bar, getting an affirmative head gesture before turning back to the behemoth in front of him.

"So tell me, Mitchell Flynn," he began, a smile creeping across his face, "When do you think you can start?"

Tchernowitz made a motion toward the hallway and led two other gentlemen into the small hospital room. He closed the door to ensure maximum privacy. By the time he returned to the main area, Dorian Abernathy had already approached the frail girl in the bed, his enormous frame waddling carelessly in her direction.

"Hello, young lady," greeted Abernathy, his inflection as sweet as honey. "My name is Dorian Abernathy; I used to work with your father."

Tchernowitz watched the girl closely. She nodded in understanding, but it was evident by her eye movements that she did not recognize the portly man perched beside her bed. Looking between Abernathy and the young girl, he wondered how strange his loyalties must seem to an outside observer.

"It's such a shame about your father," continued Abernathy. "I always liked him."

Victor had to fight back a snicker.

"Indeed. Your father was a wonderful man," chimed in Blair.

Olivia nodded but said little as the two men continued to sing the praises of the late James Friedman. They told of humorous anecdotes, worthless business ventures and interesting friends that they met along the way. But mostly, the two men talked about how the noble James Friedman brought up his company from nothing, and how it was suddenly in danger of collapse.

"That's why we need your help," said Abernathy. "Without James Friedman, the company is poised to go under."

Her eyes went wide with concern.

"What kind of help could I possibly provide?" she asked.

Victor watched a smile snake its way across Abernathy's sinuous lips.

I've led this poor girl into the serpent's lair... he thought.

"The remaining board members and I feel that the best way to honor your father's memory is to expand his legacy; to make Friedman Financial a global superpower in the world of financial investments."

"Okay…"

"However, we are going to need to make some major changes to the company if we are going to be competitive in the years to come."

Olivia scrunched her face.

"What kind of changes?"

"Oh, don't worry your pretty little head about such boring affairs," he said, patting the top of her hand. "We have it all figured out."

Olivia recoiled from his touch, using the hospital linens to wipe away his slimy palm sweat. There was something off about this man's behavior, but she couldn't quite put her finger on it.

"If you have everything figured out," she began, "then what is it you want from me?"

Abernathy shot her a toothy smile.

"Ah, that," he said dismissively, as though it had somehow eluded his mind. "Your father, when he passed away, was the majority shareholder in Friedman Financial. As I am sure you are aware after speaking with Mr. Tchernowitz, those shares transfer directly to you upon his death."

Olivia nodded, seeming to follow.

"And because our majority shareholder has not been present for our board meetings," interrupted Blair, "the company has not been able to authorize any of the major changes we need to implement."

Olivia's eyes flashed brightly with understanding.

"So you need me to approve the changes?" she asked excitedly.

Abernathy glared menacingly at the junior vice-president.

"Actually, sweetheart," began Abernathy, "the board members feel that it would be better if someone more experienced with the inner workings of Friedman Financial is in charge of those kinds of decisions.

"I see," Olivia replied with disappointment.

"But don't fret," began Blair, already getting a *don't mess this up* look from Abernathy, "the members of the board have decided to make you a generous offer on your shareholdings."

Olivia glanced between the anxious faces of the men on either side of her bed. She felt like an antelope between two lions.

"What kind of offer?" she asked.

Abernathy showed his teeth again.

"That's the great part about it," he said. "The board members have authorized purchasing all the shares of Friedman Financial from you. Control of the company will fall to members of the board, and you'll get a nice-sized check. Everybody wins."

Here it comes, thought Victor. *Just how much would Abernathy attempt to discount the company if he was willing to pay me off just to keep my mouth shut?*

"Well, that seems fair," she said.

Abernathy grinned smugly at his accomplice.

"But just so you know," began Blair, "we won't be able to offer you full market value on your holdings; the economy being what it is and all."

"But if something should happen with the company in the next few months, it won't be your problem," stated Abernathy cheerfully. "There's something to be said for having that kind of peace of mind."

Olivia absorbed the information presented to her.

"That sounds reasonable."

This time it was Blair who beamed at Abernathy.

"But I don't think I can do what you ask," she stated apologetically.

Both of their faces fell.

"Why not?!" demanded Blair.

Olivia shied away from his aggressive tone, pressing back against the pillows to maintain some distance from the man. Finding herself cornered between the austere manner of the junior vice president and the eerily insatiable stares of Dorian Abernathy left her feeling exposed, as though she were openly on display for their entertainment rather than snugly hidden beneath the flannel covering. She looked to Victor for support.

"I don't think I'm actually in control of those decisions," she explained timidly. "Vic…I mean, Mr. Tchernowitz is in charge of managing the trust."

The two men snickered with amusement.

"Of course, he is," agreed Abernathy with a patronizing smile. "But if you tell him that you want to sell your shares, I'm quite certain that he would be willing to take care of it."

Abernathy glared menacingly at the lawyer to drive the point home.

"That's right," said Victor, responding to her questioning glance. "Whatever you want to do, I'll make it happen."

Olivia nodded.

"Well I guess that's it," she stated plainly. "How does this work, then? Do I have to sign something?"

Abernathy ran his tongue over his lower lip.

"First, I think we should agree on a price," he said.

Olivia shrugged.

"I'm sure whatever price is fine. Mr. Tchernowitz knows more about the account than I do and if he thinks it's a reasonable price, then I'm on board. It's what's best for the company after all."

The three men exchanged knowing glances, the sound of cash register chimes almost audible as they rang again and again across their synaptic nerves. And yet, that made this deal seem all the more rotten for Victor. This wasn't a kosher business deal taking place between two knowledgeable parties; it was a butcher coaxing a lamb toward the slaughter.

In his panic about David, he completely lost sight of what was really going on. The real battle wasn't between him and Abernathy over the life of his son, it was between his client and his enemy; an innocent girl facing off against an evil tyrant. *Just because James refused to help my son is no reason to take it out on his daughter. Where did I go wrong if I'm suddenly siding with vermin like Dorian Abernathy?*

Victor shook off the thought. *All I have to do is grit my teeth, close my eyes, and soon this whole thing will be over...*

"How about three and a half million?" asked Abernathy.

"*What?!*" screamed Victor incredulously inside his head. *How dare they insult the memory of James Friedman by trying to purchase his company for less than the blood money they'd offered me?! It was madness. Surely even the naïve little girl would never...*

"That's a lot of money," said Olivia, her eyes wide with surprise. "Was Mr. James' company really worth that much?"

"Well it's a bit higher than we were hoping to go," stated Abernathy, "But since it's all going to James Friedman's heir, I don't think the board will mind my spending a little extra."

Victor clenched his jaw to keep from verbalizing his protestations.

"So...do we have a deal?" asked Abernathy, flashing his teeth at her.

Olivia looked from Abernathy to Blair and then toward Victor at the foot of the bed. Though he stood stoic, inside he was anxiously praying that she denied the offer, or at the very least told him that she needed to think about it. Olivia turned her gaze back to Abernathy, giving him a wary but affirmative smile.

Victor gave a sigh of defeat. What little hope there had been to stop this arrangement was gone. If he tried to interfere now he would be going against Abernathy directly, and the man was not known for his forgiving personality. There was no way to back out without putting his son's life in jeopardy.

And for what?

This girl, though she was my client and the daughter of the man I'd served faithfully for almost twenty-five years, still meant nothing to me. In the grand scheme of everything, she was but a single entity in a world population of seven billion. Why bother even trying to help her when there were so many others dying in the world right now from starvation and disease? After all, she would still have plenty left over after this transaction stole her father's company away. Wasn't that worth something?

Victor watched helplessly as Abernathy extended his arm toward the unsuspecting girl. The guilt and shame returned full force as she lifted her palm from the hospital bed. Victor followed her movements anxiously as an old, calloused hand wrapped around her tiny fingers.

"What the hell do you think you're doing?!" fumed Abernathy, still reaching out his empty palm.

Victor's voice caught in his throat as he peered down at their clasped hands. Even as he felt her soft skin against his own, Victor could not believe what he'd done. Looking to Olivia for guidance, he watched as her face transitioned from confusion into a reassuring smile. With a gentle nod of the head she urged him onward, his courage invigorated by her unwavering support.

"What I should have done in the first place," he stated defiantly.

Abernathy lowered his arm, tightly squeezing his fists by his sides. He scowled threateningly at the aged lawyer, his face contorted with unbridled hatred. His foot slid forward as though to lash out, but Abernathy halted, deterred by the hardened stare of his adversary.

"Think about what you're doing Tchernowitz," he pleaded. "Don't forget our deal."

"The deal's off. I'm not letting you take advantage of this girl."

"And what about your son, hmmm? Are you willing to give up on him as well? Surgery's not cheap, you know."

Victor exhaled forcefully.

"I'll find a way, even if it's not with your blood money."

"How *noble* of you," taunted Abernathy. "Meanwhile your son gets worse. How will you feel when he's six feet under, and it's all your fault?"

"Go to hell you rat bastard!"

Abernathy growled angrily at the insult.

"Fine!" he said between clenched teeth. "Just don't come crawling back to me when it's too late."

Abernathy snapped his fingers at Blair, and the two stormed from the room, the thick door slamming violently behind them.

"Good riddance," said Victor, taking a much needed rest in the chair beside the bed. He gently rubbed his temple in a vain attempt to alleviate the chaos brewing inside.

After a quiet moment between them, Olivia spoke up.

"What just happened?"

Victor responded with a heavy sigh.

"It's complicated," he said softly.

When she persisted, Victor explained the deal he made with Abernathy. He told her everything, from how much he would have been paid to how they used his son's condition to secure his allegiance and how Dorian Abernathy had tried to purchase Friedman Financial for only a fraction of its value. When he finished, Victor hung his head in remorse.

"I guess this means you'll be needing a new lawyer," he stated. "I can make a few phone calls when I get back to the office."

Olivia shook her head.

"I don't think that's necessary," she said. "It seems like you are doing a great job."

Victor looked up from his chair.

"You can't be serious…"

"Of course I'm serious. You're a good man, Victor. Besides, I can't imagine there's anyone out there I want managing my affairs more than you."

Victor gave her a bewildered stare.

"Why would you want *me* in charge? I betrayed your trust."

Olivia sighed.

"Do you honestly expect me to be mad at you for trying to protect your son?"

He pondered a moment before humbly shrugging his shoulders.

"I guess not."

"So you'll stay?"

Victor gazed incredulously at her for a long time.

"Ok," he said finally. "If you want me to stay on, I will."

Olivia beamed brightly at him.

"Thank you, Victor. I don't think I could do this without you."

Victor nodded, rising to his feet.

"So…what would you like me to do first, Miss Friedman?" he asked, standing at attention.

"Please, Victor, call me Olivia."

He eyed her with confusion, but remembered a time long ago when he too had felt a need to be someone different.

"As you wish, Miss…Olivia," he corrected himself.

"Before we begin, I'd like to know exactly how much money we're talking about in this trust, so there's not another repeat of this afternoon."

Victor recited a figure that made her feel as though she'd had a mini-stroke.

"I am wondering," she continued after regaining some composure, "if I can sell my holdings in Mr. James' company from within the trust, does that mean I can spend money that's in the accounts as well?"

"Absolutely," replied Victor. Rummaging through his briefcase he located and withdrew a thick, rectangular box, holding it up for her to see. "These are checks for the main portfolio account. Just say the word, and we can buy whatever you like. Depending on how big a purchase you want to make, we might have to sell some stock first, but it shouldn't take more than a couple days to process."

He handed her the box of checks and explained how the account functioned with the checks, showing her how to fill in the information when she wanted to make a transaction.

"May I have a pen?" she asked when he finished the exposition.

He eyed her suspiciously and handed her one. She quickly filled out the information on the check, being sure to conceal it from him, and folded the slip of paper in half. Olivia thanked him as she handed it back. Victor gazed curiously at her secretive behavior but decided not to pry.

"What's next?" he asked.

Olivia sighed.

"If that man returns wanting to buy my father's company, I think you should sell it to him. He might not be the most upstanding person in the world, but he was definitely right when he implied that I had no business trying to run the day-to-day operations of the company, not that I'd want to of course."

"Ok," replied Victor, reluctant to deal with Abernathy after today's debacle. "How much should we ask for?"

Olivia shrugged.

"Whatever you think is fair," she said. "You've got a better understanding of that sort of thing than I do."

A wicked smile crossed his face.

"I'll take care of it," he assured her.

"Thank you."

"Is there anything else?"

Olivia handed him the folded check, her tiny body shaking with animated excitement.

"I'm sure you'll know what to do with this," she said cheerfully.

Victor raised an eyebrow at her as he took the piece of paper. Carefully sliding the edges apart, he examined the pristine handwriting within. Seeing his name on the top line was a shock to say the least, but not nearly as much as the amount listed beside it. Victor steadied himself against the side of the bed to keep from keeling over.

"What is this?"

"For your son," she said with a radiant smile. "Let me know when it runs out and I'll get you some more."

Victor stared at her in bewilderment. He couldn't believe that she and James Friedman had ever managed to share the same roof. The differences were like night and day.

"I can't accept this," he objected.

Olivia looked crestfallen.

"Why not?"

"Because it's too much. Besides, how can I take money from you after I walked in here today fully intending to rip you off?"

"But you didn't rip me off. In fact, I believe you did exactly the opposite."

"Yes...but I was going to."

"And you didn't. When all was said and done, you did what was right. Why not have a little Samaritan bonus for your efforts?"

"But eight figures?! Even Abernathy was only going to offer me half that."

"And Abernathy is particularly generous with his money, is he?"

Victor was taken aback by the sarcasm.

"Well...no, he's not."

Olivia sighed.

"Look Victor, you're way too hard on yourself. If I had not run away in the first place, we could have had this conversation a week ago. You would have gotten the money for your son's surgery and never have needed to consult with Abernathy in the first place. Why don't we accept equal parts blame in this situation and move on?"

Victor considered this a moment before hesitantly nodding his head.

"Deal?" she asked, extending her pinky finger toward him.

Victor chuckled softly as he entwined his little digit with hers. Slipping the check into his wallet for safekeeping, he withdrew a business card and placed it in her outstretched palm.

"If you need *anything*, just call me and I'll make it happen."

"Thank you," she said, wrapping her arms around him in a friendly hug.

Gathering his belongings, Victor bid her farewell, closing the hospital door quietly in his wake. As he lightheartedly strode toward the elevators, Victor speculated on what the perfect present might be for Olivia's upcoming birthday.

When the nurse came in a little while later, Olivia suddenly recalled that Mitchell left before they got an update on her condition.

"Excuse me," she called to the nurse. "Has the doctor figured out what's wrong yet?"

The news of the trust fund had finally sunken in, and Olivia was excited about prospects for the future. All her life, she had been reading books about faraway places, intriguing adventures and young couples making love beside majestic waterfalls, and now she had the means to experience it. But first things first. She had to be released from the hospital.

The nurse turned to her, biting the inside of her lip.

"I'm sorry," she said. "I'm new here, but I can take your chart to the doctor and see if there are any updates."

Olivia considered the words with uncertainty. *Wasn't she the same nurse who had been on duty the day I was admitted?* Olivia watched as the nurse took up the paperwork, shutting the door behind her.

Though the door had been closed for a lot of her stay, Olivia had not known the nurses to be in favor of such practices. Something was definitely not right. She quickly slid from the bed and stepped on the cold linoleum. She crawled across the floor on her hands and knees, still not confident in her ability to keep from toppling over.

Once at the door, Olivia eased her head against the solid wood, trying to discern the conversations being carried on in the hallway. After a moment, she was able to detect the voice of her messenger.

"…was asking if there's been any progress on her condition."

Olivia heard the voice of a man responding. She recognized it as Dr. Baker's. He had seen her for a combined total of three minutes since her admission.

"Tests still haven't shown anything conclusive," he stated tersely.

"What should I tell the girl?"

"Tell her just that."

"But she…"

"Look!" barked the voice of Dr. Baker. "That girl in there has experienced lightheadedness and fainting with her CT scan indicating no sign of serious physical trauma to the head. She is currently having trouble standing and walking unaided. At least one nurse has reported signs of fever and fatigue. When she was admitted, there were signs of bruising that she acquired prior to the fall. She appears to be small for her age, most likely underweight, and her bone density scan came back low, even though she reports having been on supplements and medication. There's not enough data yet for a proper diagnosis, and I don't want you frightening the poor girl until we're absolutely certain, but for someone her age to show all those symptoms it usually indicates one thing."

"Which is?"

"Leukemia."

The word burned her ears as intense as the toxic venom of a hornet's sting. Over and over it replayed in her mind like the eerie tune of a calliope. The words she gleaned from the conversation from that point on were but distant sounds from a far off place.

Olivia picked herself off the floor and proceeded in somnambulant strides back to the warm protection of her bed. As though from a dream, she watched the nurse return, hearing the soothing voice, but not the words; all the promises of the future falling to the wayside like the discarded petals of the ephemeral flower.

CHAPTER 28

After Mitchell left for his new job, I lay awake in the darkness of my room, just thinking about everything that happened today. The last twenty-four hours had been a whirlwind of polarizing emotions, and I needed time alone to make sense of it all.

On the one hand, Mitchell had secured a job, which made our impending court date seem promising; the detectives who were searching for me called off the investigation; Friedman Financial's board of directors extracted everything they wanted from me, with no signs of needing to harass me in the future; I now had a personal lawyer who was willing to stand up for me in all things financial and legal; with the passing of Mr. James, I found myself in possession of such vast wealth that monetary concerns were no longer an issue; and, most importantly, Mitchell and I still had each other. Things definitely seemed to be going in our favor.

There was, of course, the terrible news from earlier. Even though the nurses weren't using the L-word in my presence, I overheard that tomorrow's round of tests would include a bone marrow examination. Just knowing how seriously they were considering it as a possibility made it all the more real to me, and when I finally fell asleep, it was on a sodden pillowcase.

That night I dreamed of my childhood home. The three story colonial sat comfortably nestled in the midst of a placid suburban neighborhood along the edge of Long Island Sound. Its ivory exterior was complemented by deep blue shutters; large wooden pillars and a white fence adorned the porch around the entrance. The surrounding property was more than two acres of lush, green grass pleasantly shaded by massive branches of a dozen tall elms. I remember spending many summer afternoons racing to and fro with my little cocker spaniel nipping playfully at my heels.

And yet, I was sitting alone on the front stoop, sobbing uncontrollably into my palms. The memories of that day remain distinctive in my mind; one of the few sad events I encountered in the brief time I spent with my birth parents.

My father came to comfort me. He wore his usual blue jeans and topsiders. Today's floral patterned shirt was blue and white, a few buttons undone to reveal a white undershirt. A bushy moustache highlighted that familiar reassuring smile.

"What's the matter, sweetheart?" he asked, taking a seat beside me.

I wiped my cheeks and tried to steady my voice. I always wanted to look brave in front of my father.

"It's Oscar..." I whimpered. "He's run away."

Daddy wrapped his arm around my shoulders. Just having him near made the sadness bearable and soon the tears dried up.

"I'm so worried," I admitted, blotting my eyes with the skirt of my dress. "What if something happens to him?"

Daddy said nothing, taking me by the hand and helping me to my feet. Together we walked along the pathway, following the sidewalk toward the local park.

"Where are we going?" I asked.

He looked down at me with that signature smile of his.

"To get Oscar, of course."

"But we don't know where he is," I protested.

"Maybe so, but wherever he is, I'm sure he's very frightened. You remember how you felt when you got separated from us at the fair last summer?"

I bit my lip and looked down at the ground quickly.

"It's okay to be scared when these situations arise," he explained. "The important thing is that you don't let your fear keep you from doing what's necessary. No matter how scared you feel right now, I'm sure Oscar is even more afraid because he's alone. Do you understand?"

I nodded, feeling somewhat ashamed of my earlier waterworks.

"Come on," he urged, giving my hand an encouraging squeeze. "Let's go find him."

Filled with renewed zeal, we doubled our walking pace, making it to the park in no time. There we found Oscar barking frantically at the swing set.

"Oscar!" I called out excitedly.

His ears perked up and his tail began to wag furiously when he laid eyes on me. The small puppy made a mad dash toward us, helplessly tripping over his own feet. Daddy released my hand, and I scooped the furry brown bundle in my arms. Oscar rewarded me with a slobbery tongue across the face.

"Glad to see you, too," I giggled.

As the three of us journeyed home, Daddy gazed down at me, his voice authoritative, yet gentle at the same time.

"Remember," he said, "no matter how tough a situation might seem, no matter how difficult an obstacle looks to conquer, no matter how much life seems to have you down, it will never get any better as long as you sit idly by mourning the unfairness of it all."

I nodded, his stern words impressing upon me a code of ethics that would follow me the rest of my life.

By doing nothing, nothing changes.

I snapped awake, my father's words still fresh on my mind. The bout of melancholy I faced the night before had dissipated, and I felt ready for the trials of a new day. Daddy was right; I had taken enough time to grieve my unfortunate situation, and now it was time to get up and do something.

Not literally, of course. I was still very much aware of my inability to maneuver on my own even throughout this limited space. I was eager to leave this prison-like room, but didn't want another nasty fall to delay my departure. Reaching to the other side of the bed, I pressed the call button. The unit made a strange noise, and a nurse soon entered my room.

"Did you need something?" she asked politely.

"Yes. I understand that Dr. Baker wants me to have a bone marrow test today."

The nurse gave me a surprised look.

"Who told you that?"

I shrugged.

"The walls aren't that thick. I can sometimes hear you all talking in the hallway."

She suddenly looked uneasy, as though worried about what else I might have gleaned from their conversations.

"I haven't spoken with Dr. Baker about it yet this morning," she said, "But I can check on it for you."

"Thank you. And if it's at all possible, do you think we can go ahead and get it over and done with? There's no point in me just sitting here waiting."

"I suppose not," she replied dismissively. "Is that all then?"

My mind drifted back to the incident from the other night.

"Actually, there is one other thing…"

The nurse gave me an inquisitive stare.

"Would it be possible to speak with a woman doctor?"

She raised her eyebrows with concern.

"Has there been a problem with Doctor Baker?" she asked nervously.

I shook my head.

"Not a female doctor," I corrected, ignoring the implications of her question. "I want to talk with someone who specializes in women's anatomy."

This seemed to confuse her more than the alternative.

"Why?"

I took a deep breath, pondering the proper words to describe my current dilemma. When the optimal explanation eluded me, I blurted out the first thing that came to mind.

"I think my vagina might be broken."

I could tell by her horrified expression that it had been the completely wrong choice of words. Her face turned bright scarlet, and her mouth hung limply open as she stared at me in shock. She blinked several times before finally regaining her composure.

"You know, little girls shouldn't use such language," she scolded.

I let out a groan. Things were definitely off to a flying start so far.

"Why do you think your…you know…why do you think it's broken?"

I rolled my eyes at her puritanical attitude. For some reason, knowing that her prim behavior was driven less by the words and more by their source made it all the more frustrating. Before I could respond, however, a wave seemed to pass over the nurse's face, her eyes flashing with sudden understanding.

"Was there blood involved? You know…down there?" she asked in a hushed tone.

I put my head in my hands. It was all I could do to keep from screaming.

"There's no need to be embarrassed," she said, completely misreading my body language. "It happens to all girls sooner or later. I was about your age when I had my first…'monthly visitor'."

I pulled my hands away from my face. I recalled the day that Melissa found blood in her underwear and how I had tried to comfort her until Miss Elaine came back from the store. We had been told that it was a normal part of life for all young women, but at the same time, being fed adjectives like 'burden' and 'unclean'. I never understood why people treated something so natural with the same contempt they held for a debilitating sickness.

And yet, even now, at nearly twenty-four years of age, I had never endured a single episode. It was one of the many things about my life that clued me in to the fact that I was somehow different from other girls. Where all of my peers at the orphanage had matured into womanhood, I was stuck perpetually in the body of my youth. All of my adult life I wondered why I was so different, and it was not until this hospital stay that I began to suspect it might be due to some dreadful disease.

"Are you okay?" the nurse asked.

I returned to the conversation, shaking off the wistful thoughts.

"It's not bleeding," I assured her.

She tilted her head to the side, as though wondering what else it could be.

"But you were right about me being embarrassed," I lied. "That's why I only want to discuss it with a doctor. That way I'll only have to tell one person."

She gave an understanding nod.

"That makes sense," she said agreeably. "I'll go see if anyone's available to come talk with you."

"Thank you," I replied with a smile.

She moved toward the door, and I quickly called her back.

"I'm sorry" I apologized, trying to sound as pleasant as I could. "But could you give me a hand? I need to use the bathroom."

I lay face down on the table, nervously awaiting the incoming needle. Although I was anxious to discover the cause of my recent medical maladies, the prospect of that long metallic instrument being jammed into my body was making me sick to my stomach.

From what had been explained about the procedure, they were going to apply a local anesthetic by inserting a sharp, painful looking apparatus into my lower back. After numbness settled over the area, they would stick the second device deep into my side until it made contact with my hip, and then apply a corkscrew style force to grind into the hard tissue. The thought of boring into bone, my bone, had been such an alarming concept that I had zoned out the rest.

I thought of Mitchell. He might still be asleep from his late night job, but if he was awake, he had probably already headed to the workshop with Carl. He was likely to be away from my side most of the weekend, and I agreed to it, mostly because I had confidence that a little investment in the beginning could go a long way for the future. I didn't mind giving up a weekend here or there if it meant getting to have him clean and sober the rest of the time.

Those thoughts quickly slipped away as the needle touched my bare skin. I held my breath, gripping the sheets tightly between my tiny fists. Regardless of how much holding Mitchell's hand would have done to actually alleviate the forthcoming pain, I desperately wished he were here. Just having him close would give me an extra ounce of courage.

No such luck.

I winced as the needle pushed past the outer layer of skin, the pointy metal tip driving deeper and deeper into my flesh as though it would never stop. I bit down hard on the pillow in front of me, letting out a groan of agony into its polyester filling. From a place of kindness or mercy, the attendant ejected the soothing serum, and slipped the needle back out again. I was quick to wipe away the newly formed tears before he could see.

"Doing great so far," he said reassuringly. "We'll give that a few minutes to let the medicine do its job before we start the procedure."

The attendant pulled the hospital gown back down, covering my bare back. Fortunately, the sheet was there to keep the rest of me from being exposed. Normally my nakedness was nothing to be concerned about; few people seemed to give me a second glance anyway. But lately, I had begun to view my body as being under joint ownership, and having another man observe my bare physique seemed an affront to Mitchell.

I was still waiting to hear from the nurse about seeing an on duty gynecologist. Instinct told me that something strange was going on below, and I was determined to figure it out. I still didn't know what the bone marrow examination would reveal, but there was one thing I was certain about: there was no way I was going out a virgin.

A few minutes passed, and the attendant returned. A surge of dismay jolted my system at the sight of his gimlet style tool. The fear of impending torment blotted out the rest of my senses so that later all I could recall of what happened next was how little the anesthetic had done to dull the pain.

After the procedure, they brought me back to my room. The nurse from earlier left for her lunch break without informing any of her coworkers of my desire to see someone about my womanly troubles. I paged the nurse's station with the somewhat lofty hope of improving my communication skills.

When a new nurse entered, I quickly learned that her name was Denise, and she was there to help. I decided to take her up on that idealistic offer.

"I want to speak with a gynecologist," I said plainly.

She narrowed her eyes at me, her mouth forming a surprised 'O'.

"Why do you want to see a gynecologist?" she inquired.

Deciding that my approach from before had been a bit haphazard, I chose a new phrase to kick off our adventure.

"I think there might be an issue with my plumbing," I stated. "I want a doctor to check and make sure that everything is working properly."

The nurse raised an eyebrow at me. I clearly hadn't done much better at this second attempt.

"What do you mean "working properly"?" she demanded.

Telling her the truth seemed like a bad idea, so I decided to play at bashful instead.

"I um…would rather just explain it to a doctor if it's alright with you."

Denise furrowed her brow before giving an understanding nod.

"I see…" she began. "Was there blood involved?"

I cringed at the question.

"It's not a period," I explained to her.

She took a step toward the bed and placed her hand atop the thin hospital blanket.

"Well let's take a look," she said helpfully, slowly pulling down on the linens.

"NO!" I shouted reflexively, yanking them from her grasp.

Her eyes went wide with shock, her empty hand still suspended above the bed.

"Sorry," I said, trying to diffuse the situation. "I'm uh…a bit shy."

I tried to force a smile but it did little to remove the tension from the room. Denise took a step back, never taking her eyes off of me. After a few seconds, another woman entered the room.

"Is everything okay?" asked the incoming nurse.

"It's fine, Brenda," Denise informed her. "She just got startled is all."

"What happened?"

Denise forced an exhale, as though my outburst had somehow been a great inconvenience for her.

"She wants to see a gynecologist," she replied dismissively.

Brenda gave me a curious glance.

"Why?"

"Wouldn't tell me," she said, suddenly speaking on my behalf. "I think she might be a little embarrassed."

Brenda held up her hand to silence the other nurse.

"Can you tell me why you want to see a gynecologist?" she asked softly.

I considered my words carefully. I tried being direct and I had tried to play coy, and both methods failed. Third time's the charm I assured myself.

"I just…sense that something's wrong," I replied. "Call it woman's intuition."

It was Brenda's turn to give me a strange look.

"Is this about something that happened in the bathroom?"

"That's a rather vague question," I replied.

Brenda gave me a reassuring smile.

"When you were in the bathroom today, was there blood somewhere you weren't expecting there to be?"

"No."

"Are you sure? It's perfectly normal to get a little scared at the sight of…"

"There was no blood," I repeated. "There's never been any blood there."

Brenda maintained her friendly demeanor.

"And you're worried that there might be something wrong because you aren't bleeding, is that it?"

I shook my head in frustration.

"It's ok. Girls develop differently from one another. If some of your friends have…"

"It has nothing to do with menses!" I asserted. "It's…it's something different."

I took a deep breath.

"Look…I know you mean well, but I would much rather just discuss it with a doctor."

"I understand where you're coming from, I really do," empathized Brenda. "The problem is that the doctors are very busy, and they don't have time to go around seeing every patient. If you let us take a look, or even just explain to us what's going on, we could find out if it's something to worry about and maybe get a doctor to see you sooner."

I hugged my knees to my chest.

"If I wasn't confined to this hospital bed, I would have already tracked down a doctor on my own. Since I really shouldn't be wandering around the hospital without supervision, I would really appreciate your help."

Brenda turned to Denise, her colleague shaking her head in protest.

"Please?" I pleaded.

Brenda eventually gave a heavy sigh.

"Alright," she agreed. "We'll try and page someone, but no promises."

"Thank you," I said, smiling at her compassion.

Brenda nodded in response, but Denise continued to shake her head disapprovingly. She folded her arms across her chest and glared defiantly at the older nurse.

"And who do you suppose I should page?" she demanded.

"Try Dr. Townsend," offered Brenda. "The phone's over there."

Denise stormed across the room, her shoes clacking loudly on the linoleum. Forcefully pressing each button, she input the number and soon a thundering male voice blasted through the speaker.

"Townsend," he answered, his voice as clear as if I were holding the handset myself.

"Yes, hello," replied Denise. "We have a patient on the third floor who would like to see someone regarding her condition."

"What's the condition?" boomed the voice on the other end.

Denise peered over at me and rolled her eyes.

"She says she'll only discuss it with a doctor."

The young nurse nodded affirmatively as Dr. Townsend bellowed something about triage.

"How far along is she?"

Denise grinned smugly in my direction as though his question demonstrated how insignificant my problems really were.

"She's not pregnant."

There were some words spoken which I didn't catch, and Denise eyed me up and down.

"Around eleven or twelve," she said.

He groaned loudly through the speaker and there were some more words exchanged between him and Denise. She covered the receiver with her free hand.

"He wants to know if you've had an infection, or if there've been any signs of inflammation."

I hung my head.

"No," I responded quietly.

Denise relayed the message, almost delighting in the response it drew from the doctor. After another barrage of comments erupted through the speaker, Denise hung the phone back in its cradle.

"Dr. Townsend says he's very busy today. He told me to tell you that if you want, we can take a look at your condition and let him know if it seems like an emergency. Otherwise, he has babies to deliver."

I didn't even bother looking up.

Denise took my silence as surrender and stormed off in a cloud of self-satisfaction. Only when I was certain that she had left did I raise my head to notice Brenda still standing in my room. Her lips were pursed together as she gazed pityingly upon me, her eyes displaying sympathy rather than condescension. Without a word, she moved to the phone and quietly began to dial.

"Hey Sally, is Dr. Moore available?" she asked. "…No, I'll hold."

Brenda shot me an encouraging smile, mindlessly rocking her head back and forth as she waited. After several minutes her face suddenly perked up.

"Hey, Libby. This is Brenda," she said. "…I'm good, and how are you?"

I watched intently, trying to follow along with only half of the conversation.

"Listen, there's a girl up here in general who's been asking to see a gynecologist."

Brenda looked at me.

"Early adolescent," she said. "I know, I know. But she's scared and she wants to talk to someone."

Brenda paused.

"She wouldn't tell me. She did tell us that it's not related to menses. That's right, no blood."

Another pause.

"I understand," replied Brenda. "Thanks Libby."

Brenda hung up the phone and turned to me.

"Dr. Moore says she's a bit busy right now dealing with patients."

I nodded, feeling disheartened.

"She said that she will be up here to talk with you when she gets a chance, but it might be an hour or two."

I felt a smile cross my lips.

"Thank you," I said, holding out my hand to her.

"You're welcome, dear," she said, giving my hand a gentle squeeze before releasing. "Is there anything else you need?"

I shook my head and she departed, giving me one last smile before she left.

Knowing just how vital a first impression can be, I sat in the quiet of my room strategizing on what I would say to the doctor when she arrived. Despite my unsuccessful efforts, I felt optimistic about our encounter. I may not have known what was causing my fainting spells, and I certainly had no clue what terrible calamity led me into everlasting childhood, but I might very well discover the source behind my failed lovemaking attempt with Mitchell, and that prospect alone filled me with almost as much exhilaration as our hospital rendezvous.

It was almost one o'clock when a strange face appeared in my room. Other than the white coat, Dr. Libby Moore was nothing like I was expecting. For starters, she was smiling, a trait that had been all but extinguished from the staff I met thus far. She was about average height and weight. Her long, jet-black hair was pulled into a ponytail that hung gracefully between her shoulder blades. She was not wearing glasses, but had a stethoscope hanging around her neck, a fact that made me suddenly wary of where she might be planning to put that cold, metallic surface.

"Good afternoon," she said pleasantly. "Are you Olivia?"

"I am."

She approached the edge of the bed. Behind her I saw Denise follow her into the room, her face contorted in testy disapproval.

"I'm Dr. Libby Moore," she said with a smile. "Brenda said you want to speak with me."

"Yes, and thank you so much for seeing me on short notice, though I was rather hoping I could speak with you in private," I said, gesturing toward Denise.

"Of course," she replied.

Dr. Moore turned to Denise and motioned in the direction of the hallway. She made a noise of protest, but exited nonetheless; the door shutting loudly behind her. Dr. Moore turned back to me.

"What seems to be the trouble today?" she asked.

I decided to try my original approach; she was a doctor after all.

"I think my vagina is broken."

Dr. Moore seemed quite surprised by my comment.

"You're quite a precocious child, aren't you?"

Honestly, not the response I had been hoping for; it was as if she had two strikes against her as soon as we began.

"Sorry, it's just…I don't know a better way to describe it. I don't really know much about proper terminology for these things."

Dr. Moore smiled reassuringly at me.

"That's quite alright," she said. "I only meant that it was quite a straightforward statement from someone as young as you."

I nodded absently.

"Just to verify what I heard from Brenda," she began, "There was no bleeding, correct?"

"That's right."

"Have you had any menstrual cycles at all?"

I shook my head.

"And how old are you?"

I hesitated. I didn't want to lie to her in case she could actually help me, but I didn't want her to walk away thinking that I was wasting her time either.

"Twelve," I said eventually.

She gave me a confused look, but did not pursue.

"Are you experiencing any pain?"

"No."

"Is there any inflammation?" she asked, moving to simpler terms almost automatically. "That is, any areas of redness or sensitivity?"

"Not that I can tell."

"Any strange smells or discolorations?"

"Well, no discolorations."

She raised an eyebrow.

"What about smells?"

I shrugged.

"I can't smell anything," I said dismissively.

Her eyes widened.

"You mean you can't smell anything coming from down there, or that you can't smell anything at all?"

"Both," I replied.

She nodded, obviously intrigued by this new information.

"Have you always had anosmia?" she asked.

I looked at her blankly.

"Have you always lacked a sense of smell?" she corrected.

"I guess so, as far back as I can remember."

Dr. Moore nodded, her brow furrowing as she considered this new information.

"So tell me what it is that makes you think something is wrong," she continued.

I took a deep breath, concentrating on how to respond. My face must have given something away because she changed tactics immediately.

"Let me try a different way," she said. "What were you doing when you discovered that there might be a problem?"

I looked down at the sheets. Once again I found myself caught between needing to tell her the truth and not being able to on the account of what might happen to Mitchell if I did. Then again, she didn't know Mitchell, and it wasn't like I had to inform her of that particular detail. For all she needed to know he was simply my legal guardian.

"I was trying to have sex with my boyfriend," I admitted, holding my breath for her reaction.

I think I was expecting her to be surprised, maybe confused, perhaps even a bit angry, but instead she just looked sad, as though my statement reflected the depressing reality of her typical workweek.

"Are you sure you should be doing things like that at your age?" she asked.

I sighed with frustration. Though it was a welcome change to Denise's aggressive tactics, her mothering tone had begun to grind on my nerves.

"I don't know," I replied with a shrug. "How old were you for your first time?"

Dr. Moore eyed me intently, as though unsure whether or not to respond. I guess I must have seemed pretty harmless because she didn't hold anything back.

"Not until college," she said.

I nodded, greatly appreciating her apparent honesty.

"And your friends, did they wait until college as well?"

She shook her head.

"No, most of my friends did their fair share of experimenting in high school," she admitted. "But they were still quite a bit older than you are now."

I held my tongue. Despite her stance on youthful sexual indulgence, Dr. Moore had still been younger than I was now when she'd first taken someone to her bed.

"How old is your boyfriend?" she asked.

I wasn't sure if it had been idle curiosity or if she were required by law to ask me that. Still, I knew the statutory laws, and she most definitely would have to report any suspected illegal activity she gleaned from our conversation.

"Same age as me," I replied quickly.

She tilted her head forward, glaring at me incredulously through the upper aspects of her eyes.

"Fine," I pretended to give in. "He's fifteen."

She nodded, apparently satisfied with this new answer.

"And what happened when you two tried to…?" she asked, letting the words dissolve midsentence.

"Nothing," I replied, a little too much disappointment in my voice. "It was like we hit this wall, and it wouldn't go."

Dr. Moore shifted uncomfortably.

"I think you might want to consider that a pretty clear sign that you should be waiting to try such things. Sex isn't healthy for a girl your age."

I pursed my lips together in silent disagreement. Sensing my rebelliousness, she decided to forego the lecture, at least for now.

"Shall we?" she asked, gesturing toward my hips.

I smiled in response, perhaps the only woman in history to be this eager about a pelvic exam. Dr. Moore retrieved a pair of gloves from the nearby cabinet and told me to position myself at the foot of the bed. Using her feet to slide the chair into position, she lifted the hospital gown out of the way. I twitched as latex grazed my sensitive skin.

"You alright?" she asked worriedly.

"I'm fine," I assured her. "Just felt a little awkward."

She raised her head, flashing me an encouraging smile.

"Just try and relax."

With the hospital gown blocking my vision, I couldn't tell what she was doing or looking at.

"Huh…" she said suddenly.

I felt a gentle pressure against the same wall Mitchell and I encountered the other night, though it seemed a lot less painful this time. After three or four palpations, Dr. Moore stood from the chair and began removing her gloves.

"You can slide back under the sheets," she said, tossing the used gloves in the garbage pail and moving toward the sink.

"Did you find anything?" I asked hopefully after covering myself up again.

Dr. Moore finished drying her hands.

"Wait one second," she said, holding up a finger.

She moved quickly to the door and opened it.

"Don't you have work you should be doing?!" she demanded loudly to someone I could not see.

"I was just waiting to see if you need anything," replied Denise, trying to come off as innocent as possible.

Dr. Moore let out an unhappy grunt.

"You can get me the patient's file," she stated curtly.

I could hear the sound of scampering footsteps in the hallway, followed by Dr. Moore thanking the young nurse. She stepped back into the room with me, closing the door behind her. After a few seconds, she abruptly opened the door again and shooed away the eavesdropping nurse.

She quietly closed the door and moved back toward my bed. Her head remained buried in the folder as she paced slowly back and forth. She focused with intense concentration as she cycled through the pages.

"Are you still taking the Fluoxetine?" she asked.

"Yes," I replied.

"Why are you taking it?"

"Dr. Fisher prescribed it to me along with calcium supplements," I explained. "He said it's supposed to help with my low bone density."

Dr. Moore narrowed her eyes at me. I couldn't tell if she was angry or concerned, but she was definitely confused. She shook her head and returned to reading. After the last page, she closed the file and tossed it lightly on the counter.

"Ok," she said enthusiastically. "I think I can help you."

"Really?" I asked excitedly. "You already know what the problem is?"

She nodded with absolute confidence.

"I know a lot more than that," she said. "But first you have to come clean and tell me the truth."

I was suddenly nervous. She knew I was lying about something, but what? Did she know that my boyfriend was not fifteen? Did she suspect Mitchell? Would she try to have him arrested?

"Ok," I agreed, filled with trepidation over what she might ask.

She gave me a hard look.

"Remember…the truth," she reminded me.

I nodded.

"How old are you?"

I delayed, trying to figure out where this was going. She picked up on it immediately.

"Hesitation means you're lying," she stated plainly.

"Twelve," I spat out quickly.

She shook her head with disappointment and quietly approached the bed. She scooted the blankets out of the way and took a seat beside me. Her gaze was stern, somewhat reminiscent of the interrogation down at the police station. Dr. Moore's seriousness suddenly faltered and she looked at me with empathy in her eyes.

"I can't help you if you won't allow me to. Do you understand?"

I didn't really get what she meant, but I nodded anyway.

"Okay."

"Now..." she continued. "How old are you?"

I had been asked that question my entire adult life and, outside of Mitchell, no one had ever even considered the truth as a realistic possibility. I had no reason to believe that the woman doctor would be any different. And yet, as I peered into her soft green eyes, I felt somehow safe; as though she were actually on my side. Throwing caution to the wind, I decided to go for it.

"I'm twenty-three," I said.

"Good." she replied. "That wasn't so hard was it?"

I stared at her in sheer dumbfounded shock. Since the day I first ran away, every single person I met treated me as a child. It was as if people were inherently incapable of seeing beyond the illusion. Now, as if out of the blue, a lone doctor emerged to see me in a whole new light. Was this some kind of trick?

"You really believe me?" I asked, my tone almost sanguine.

"Why wouldn't I?" she said with authority. "I've examined thousands of women, and you're clearly no child."

The confidence with which she declared the statement jolted my system into a state of euphoric enchantment. Losing control of my inhibitions, I reached forward and ensnared her in my arms; hugging her without restraint. At first she flinched, my affection catching her completely off-guard. After a minute, she relaxed, patting my back gently with her hand. Another minute passed and I felt suddenly foolish at my outburst. I pulled away from her, sheepishly wiping the moisture from my eyes.

"Sorry," I muttered. "I just..."

"It's hard when everyone around you treats you like an inferior isn't it?"

I just stared at her blankly, unsure what to say.

"I understand," she said, averting her gaze for a moment. "The other OB/GYN's here have treated me like a residency since I first began working here. After twelve years, you'd think that would change, right?"

She looked back to me. I gave her a supportive smile, but said nothing.

"It's kind of funny, actually. Among my fellow gynecologists, I am the only female here at the hospital. Some might think that being a woman in a field dedicated to female reproduction would give me the edge over the crotchety old men. Instead, they patronize my every decision, as though I were some dumb bimbo off the street."

Dr. Moore gave a disapproving shake of her head.

"Well, what can you do?" she sighed, giving me a reassuring smile.

I patted her hand gently, trying to show my gratitude to her for sharing that with me.

"So what's his name?" she asked.

I felt heat flood my face.

"It's ok. You don't have to tell me," she said. "It must be hard for you two considering your...condition."

I thought of the restaurant incident.

"You could say that."

She nodded with understanding.

"And he's not fifteen is he?" Dr. Moore asked coyly.

I chuckled, shaking my head.

"No. He's a bit older than me."

"Well, I hope everything works out between you two," she said with a smile.

I nodded a 'thank you' and then asked the question that had been consuming the rest of my thoughts.

"How did you know that I wasn't twelve?"

She chortled softly to herself.

"You mean other than the fact that your birthdate of ninety-eight would make you eleven today, not twelve?"

I felt my eyes go wide. I couldn't believe I had made such a silly mistake.

"Besides," she continued, putting her serious doctor's hat back on, "you have a fibrotic hymen."

I felt myself staring blankly back at her. It was a bit embarrassing how little I knew about my own anatomy. Sensing my ignorance, Dr. Moore continued.

"Covering the external vaginal opening, women have a thin membrane which we call the hymen. In adolescent girls, the hymen is usually very elastic and has an opening which becomes enlarged due to tampon usage, pelvic examination or regular physical activity."

I nodded to indicate that I was still following along.

"In your case, you haven't experienced any of that, and the soft tissue of the membrane has hardened over time, making it far less flexible than it should be. It's kind of like when you've been lying in bed for a really long time and your body is stiff as a result."

"Is that normal?" I asked worriedly.

Dr. Moore shrugged her shoulders.

"In most cases, it would have simply been a painful inconvenience during sexual activity. However, the hymen was also imperforate, or very close to it. That is, there was supposed to be a hole, an opening, where menstrual fluid would pass during monthly cycles. In your case, there is no opening."

"Meaning that it really is a wall?"

Dr. Moore nodded.

"I see..." I muttered sadly. "So what happens now?"

"Well, I suppose that's up to you," she began. "I'd recommend surgery. It's a basic outpatient procedure, one that doesn't take very long."

"How much?" I asked.

I watched Dr. Moore's face scrunch in contemplation.

"I'd have to check with the staff in charge of scheduling surgeries. There are different factors: insurance, hospital costs, type of anesthesia, etc. As far as surgeries go, it's not too bad though."

"What happens after that?"

"Everybody responds differently to the surgery, but I'd say after about two weeks you should be good to go."

I could feel my face going red again, and a slight giggle escaped my lips.

"Just take it slowly," she warned. "No need to rush it after all."

"Ok." I agreed, not certain if I'd heed that advice or not.

Dr. Moore stood up and straightened her outfit. Noticing the prescription medication resting on the table beside my bed, she moved in for a closer look. She picked up the bottle, read the label, and slipped the medication into her pocket.

"I'm taking you off these," she said authoritatively. "At least for now."

I made a noise of protest and she held up her hand.

"I'm also going to order some further tests. After we get the results, I'll go over your records and prescribe new medication, hopefully something that'll work better for you."

I eased back into the pillows again, feeling somehow comforted by her confidence. I nodded in agreement.

Dr. Moore glanced at her watch.

"I have to go check on other patients, but I'll be back to see how you're doing. Do you have any other questions before I go?"

"Just one..." I replied quickly. "When can we do the surgery?"

She chuckled at my eagerness.

"Let me make some phone calls," she said.

I suddenly remembered the business card on the nightstand. I reached for it and held it out to Dr. Moore.

"If you need to know any of my financial information, you can call Victor."

"Is Victor your boyfriend?" she asked, taking the card from me.

"No," I said, shaking my head. "Victor's the lawyer in charge of my trust."

Dr. Moore gave me a strange look before slipping the business card into her pocket, tapping the outside to indicate that it was secure.

"Take care, Olivia."

"You, too, Dr. Moore," I replied, smiling back at her.

"Please..." she said. "Call me Libby."

CHAPTER 29

Saturday came and I found myself in a distant ward of the hospital, an intravenous infusion working its way into my arm. I have always found fascinating the difference in circumstances that can occur in a twenty-four hour period. A 300-year reign ending one night in Petrograd, a surge of gender equality one August evening along the banks of Kent, a presidential proclamation made almost 150 years ago. As I laid on the hospital gurney, the anesthetic drugs lulling me into a calm stupor, I reveled in the blessings I acquired since only yesterday.

I don't know if Victor used his financial influence to hurry the procedure along, or if Dr. Moore had more clout at the hospital than she gave herself credit for, but here I was, eagerly awaiting my impending surgery. Either way, it was shaping out to be quite a glorious afternoon.

It was disappointing that Mitchell wasn't here, but to be fair, I hadn't told him about the surgery. There was already enough hope riding on its outcome that I didn't want to pile anymore on top. If everything did not go according to plan, then at least he could walk away unscathed. And if it did go well, then he could join me in the celebration.

That wasn't the only thing I had to feel guilty about either. Even though Mitchell deserved to know the truth, that our time together could be drastically shortened by a few simple words from the oncologist, I still couldn't bring myself to tell him about the leukemia scare. Perhaps I was just being selfish, but if today's procedure was successful, we might finally be able to make love properly, and I didn't want our first time to be marred by feelings of pity. Even so, I made myself a solemn vow that if the bone marrow test came back positive, I wouldn't hide it from him. I would tell him everything right down to the last detail, and then I would ravage his body like there was no tomorrow.

The anesthesiologist pushed through the curtained area and inspected the machines surrounding my gurney before looking at me.

"How are you feeling?" he asked.

Thinking not about the surgery but of what would be coming later, I let out a blissful sigh.

"Wonderful," I said with a smile.

He nodded absently; clearly convinced that it was merely drug-induced euphoria. Right now I couldn't care less what he thought about me, just as long as his medicine didn't leave me comatose.

The next few minutes blurred together as my gurney was wheeled through hospital corridors. More nurses joined the small entourage as we crossed into the surgery ward. The swift arm movements and rapid conversation going on around my bed made me feel a bit anxious. The cart came to a sudden stop inside a large, open space. The anesthesiologist adjusted something behind me, and there was a sudden searing heat erupting near the injection site and working its way up my arm. The strange feeling unnerved even my sedated psyche so that the last thing I felt before passing out was panic…

Dorian Abernathy sat smoking a cigar in the former office of James Friedman, his feet propped disrespectfully atop the mahogany. His acquisition of the company had been a hollow victory to say the least. For months Abernathy had schemed to steal control from Friedman, only to have the man die just before he could put his final plan into action. Nevertheless, the deal was done, and now he could implement the policies he'd wanted to all along.

With the declining economy, many companies were being forced to shut their doors forever, even those that had been around for generations. That's where his brilliant strategy came into play. Once Friedman Financial made its initial public offering, he could begin the process of demolishing the company from the inside out. No one would see it coming; they'd never suspect the owner of such a prestigious company to commit corporate sabotage against himself. The best part was that the more people who invested early on, as they surely would with the hype of the IPO, the greater his reward would be in six months when he had to buy back his shorted stocks at their rock bottom price. The icing on the cake would be getting to witness the death of James Friedman's pride and joy once and for all.

Of course, the profits would have been more substantial if it wasn't for that damn lawyer, he groaned to himself. *Even with his only son's life hanging in the balance, my charitable seven-digit offer had not been enough to overcome Tchernowitz's personal sense of honor. I still had no idea what set him off that day. It didn't make any sense. The business world is no place for morals or ethics and definitely not the forum for such emotional outbursts. All that matters is money, which is exactly what Victor Tchernowitz stole from me.*

Abernathy cringed as he thought about the $93 million he paid the Friedman girl. It might have been a significant price reduction on the true value of the shares, but right now it felt like a worse deal than a timeshare in Baghdad.

"Treacherous kike lawyer…" he growled, forcefully snuffing out the cigar. "I hope his boy dies a slow, agonizing death."

Abernathy glanced at the clock. His first appointment would be walking through the door any moment. He licked his lower lip in joyous anticipation. There was something about the crushing defeat of termination that brought a smidgen of happiness to Abernathy's life. Today's victim was one he'd been looking forward to for a few days now.

The intercom sounded on his desk and he gave the go ahead for his secretary to send the man in. Even before the conversation ended, Abernathy decided that the secretary would need to go as well. *Who needed an old biddy hanging around the office when there were plenty of busty young blondes out there who weren't shy about earning a little overtime pay?*

The door to his office opened, and the vice-president stepped inside. The man wore his typical three-piece suit, the sleek black material radiating with the brilliance of custom tailoring. Even from across the room, Abernathy could sense that new clothes smell.

"Good morning, Mr. Abernathy," he said pleasantly. "Sorry I'm late."

"Oh that's quite all right, my dear boy," Abernathy replied, rising to shake his hand. "I was just sitting here admiring my new office."

"It has a fantastic view," agreed the vice-president.

"That it does," said Abernathy, retaking his seat. "In fact, James Friedman once told me that it was *to die for.*"

Abernathy reached into his desk drawer and retrieved another cigar. Holding the edge beneath his nostrils, he inhaled deeply, savoring the delightful aroma of a Cuban cigar. *Fortunately, there were no trade embargos on Thailand*, he thought to himself. *It was the perfect place to sate those…special appetites.*

"Would you like one?" he offered.

The vice-president held up his palm.

"Thank you, but I don't smoke."

Abernathy scoffed at the man, letting out a condescending chuckle.

"Suit yourself," he said.

Using the edge of the mahogany table to strike a match, Abernathy cropped the tip and lit the end. After a few short puffs, he took a ten-second inhale, blowing smoke across the desk directly in the face of the vice-president, urging the tobacco smell to pervade the man's brand new suit.

"So tell me, how long have you worked at Friedman Financial?"

"A little over ten years."

"That's quite a long time," said Abernathy, taking another long drag on his cigar. "Far too long to be playing second fiddle, if you ask me."

"Indeed it has," replied Justin Blair.

Abernathy nodded with understanding.

"I give you my word that as long as I remain president of this company, you will never again have to kowtow to the likes of Joseph Harper," he assured Blair.

"Thank you, sir," said Blair. "I promise that I'll be the best senior vice-president this company has ever seen."

"On the contrary," continued Abernathy, "we don't really need two vice-presidents, at least not with me in charge. It's about time we started shedding some excess weight, wouldn't you say?"

Blair grinned eagerly from across the desk.

"I couldn't agree more, Mr. Abernathy. It'll be nice to finally see Harper put in his place for once."

"Yes, it will," replied Abernathy, a mischievous smile creeping across his lips. "Of course, if the old dog has outlived his usefulness, one can almost guarantee that the young pup is even less valuable."

The vice-president was like a deer in headlights.

"What?!"

Abernathy grinned at Blair, almost taunting his former associate.

"I'm saying that your services are no longer needed at Friedman Financial."

Blair stared dumbstruck at the portly tyrant behind the desk. After a moment, he let out a weak laugh.

"You almost had me there, Mr. Abernathy," chuckled Blair. "For a second I almost..."

Abernathy's face hardened, and Blair suddenly realized that this was no joke.

"But...we had a deal."

"Did we now? I suppose you brought that contract with you?"

Blair shook his head with disbelief.

"But...I located the girl for you."

"Yes, you did."

"I was the one who came up with the plan to distract her bodyguard so we could have our private meeting."

"That was a very impressive strategy indeed."

"And don't forget that it was I who brokered the deal for you with Tchernowitz, even after he said he would never sell the company to you."

"Yes, and I'm very thankful for that."

"Then...why...?" he asked hopelessly.

Abernathy shrugged.

"It's nothing personal, Justin. I like you and all, but you're really bad for business."

Blair's shoulders sagged with defeat.

"But I..."

"Please have your office cleared out by noon," instructed Abernathy. "We need that space for important staff."

Blair narrowed his eyes in furious anger and Abernathy suddenly realized that perhaps he'd gone too far with the last comment; he didn't know what the man was capable of after all. Blair clenched both fists by his sides and took a step toward the desk. Just when it looked like he might lunge for Abernathy's throat, Blair grabbed the closest item on his desk instead. The item, which happened to be a ceramic coffee mug, sailed through the air and shattered against the far wall. Blair turned around, jamming his finger in Abernathy's face.

"You'll regret this Abernathy! I promise you that!"

Blair stormed out of the office, slamming the door with such force that it caused Friedman's college degree to fall to the floor with a resounding crash. A few seconds later, the secretary poked her head inside.

"Are you alright, Mr. Abernathy?"

"I'm fine. Just a little misunderstanding."

She gazed curiously at him.

"Well, you're next appointment is here. Do you want me to send him in?"

"Give me a few minutes please."

She nodded and disappeared behind the door.

Abernathy swiveled in his desk chair to peer out the office window, still shaken from the encounter with Blair. Of all the people associated with Friedman Financial, Justin Blair had certainly been his favorite. The two were very much alike and, under different circumstances, he imagined that the man would have made an excellent traveling companion. Still, this was business. Besides, he couldn't very well drive Friedman Financial into the ground with an ambitious young man like Blair hanging around.

Though he fancied himself above the law, Dorian Abernathy was well aware that what he intended to do with the company wasn't entirely on the up and up, and should the wrong people catch wind of it, he might find himself in jail for a long time. That's why he needed a scapegoat, and who better than Joseph Harper, his oldest rival. While he sipped daiquiris on his own personal island, Harper could enjoy his retirement in the warm comfort of an iron cell.

Of course, securing the man's loyalty came at a price. Firing Blair assured him that he would have plenty of funds to give Harper a raise, something that would appeal to any man. The worst part would be having to grovel before Harper and apologize for all the years they spent at each other's throats. He hoped that getting rid of Blair would help convince Harper how serious he was about a truce.

Abernathy turned back to his desk and straightened his attire. Reaching into his desk, he removed another cigar and lit it. Putting on his most cordial expression, Abernathy reached over and pressed the intercom button.

"Send him in."

A few seconds later the door swung open and Joseph Harper briskly moved across the room. As he approached, Abernathy sensed something amiss. Where Harper was normally very stoic, his demeanor today was downright joyful, and he wore a broad smile across his face. His usual gray tweed suit had been replaced by casual brown pants, a bright yellow floral patterned shirt and sandals. In the hand he typically carried a briefcase there was a suitcase, one that looked as old and haggard as Harper himself.

"Good morning, Mr. Harper," greeted Abernathy, rising to his feet.

Harper ignored the outstretched hand and instead ripped the lit cigar from Abernathy's mouth, extinguishing the item in the nearby ashtray.

"What are you…?"

"You can't smoke in here," informed Harper. "Or were you out of the country when they passed that law?"

"This is my private office…"

"For now, perhaps, but soon we go public. Might as well get in the habit."

Abernathy glared at Harper, reminding himself that he still needed the man, at least for a few months.

"Why don't you have a seat?" he offered politely.

"No can do. I have a plane to catch," Harper said, gesturing toward the luggage.

"What?!" demanded Abernathy.

"A plane," repeated Harper, this time a little louder. "It's like a car but with wings."

"I know what a plane is," growled Abernathy. "I meant, why are you getting on a plane?"

Harper smiled at him.

"Taking a much needed vacation. I've always wanted to go to Hawaii."

Abernathy groaned with disapproval.

"I see…and how long are you planning to be gone?"

Harper's smile seemed to widen.

"I'd say…forever. The way I see it, what's the point of investing all that money into a retirement account if I never actually retire? Besides, when you're my age, chances are you will never live long enough to spend the money you've got."

Abernathy's eyes went wide.

"You can't leave now," he said, trying to mask the panic in his voice.

"Oh, no? And why is that?" asked Harper with a smile.

"We have an IPO to prepare for! I need you here, not off gallivanting halfway around the world."

"Ah, there's the thing," began Harper. "Truth is I've only come in today so that I could resign in person. That initial public offering thing you mentioned before, that's *your* problem now."

Abernathy rose from his seat.

"How dare you speak that way to me?! You know I ought to…"

"You ought to *what*?" mocked Harper. "Demote me? Fire me? I don't work for you, Abernathy, and I never did."

Harper turned his back on the man and proceeded toward the open office door.

"No one walks out on me!" screamed Abernathy. "Where do you think you're going?!"

Harper paused in the doorway, pivoting to face the bulbous mass behind the desk. Looking at the man he loathed for many years, he wondered how he ever had the energy to care. Reaching into his shirt pocket, he removed a pair of obnoxiously colorful sunglasses and slid them on his face.

"Enjoy the company," he said.

And with that, he was gone.

Sometime after the surgery, I woke up in an unknown part of the hospital, presumably still in the surgery ward. The effects of the anesthetic persisted, and it was difficult to concentrate for long on any specific subject. The room was covered in a thick haze, as though I were still moving through a dream, the colors and outlines of objects blurring together. There was a numbness in my limbs that was akin to the tingling sensation of lying in the wrong position for a long time.

I attempted to raise my hand and succeeded only in twitching my index finger. For some reason, my ineptitude in basic motor function caused hysterical laughter to emanate from my lips. The strange gurgling noise that came out caused someone to come over and check on me.

"Is everything ok?" asked a female voice.

I turned my head to look at the approaching nurse, still grinning happily over my newfound pastime. She seemed perplexed by my strange behavior until I gestured at the finger using my eyes, its sudden movement eliciting another bout of giggles. I smiled at her, hoping that she had been watching.

"That's wonderful dear," she said comfortingly.

My smile broadened.

"I'll let the doctor know that you're awake."

I made a noise similar to "okay" as she departed. I continued to play a few more rounds of my finger game before becoming distracted by some colors on my left. When I became bored with that, I stared vacantly at the ceiling. I was in the middle of making shapes with the holes in the tiles when a face crossed into my field of vision.

"How are we feeling?" asked Dr. Libby.

Forgetting about connecting the dots, I focused my limited attention on her facial features.

"Oooh…pwetty," I managed.

She raised an eyebrow at me.

"Still drugged," she said with a chuckle. "I guess this can wait 'til you're back to normal."

Dr. Libby held up a folder, but I quickly lost interest.

"Are you thirsty?" she asked.

I thought about it.

"Uh-huh."

"I figured you would be," she said. "I'll have one of the nurses bring something to drink. Do you have a preference between juice and ginger ale?"

I thought long about this.

"Warter."

Dr. Libby gave me a sympathetic smile.

"It might be better if you drank something else first," she explained. "It sometimes helps with the postsurgical nausea."

I gave her a pouty face.

"You can have a straw," she said encouragingly.

For some reason this cheered me up.

"Stwall?" I asked excitedly.

"Yes." she said, trying to match my enthusiasm. "It'll help keep you from spilling."

I smiled.

"I like stwall. You bwo in them, and it twickles your nose."

"I suppose it does," she chuckled in response.

I thought about my lips wrapping around the cylindrical plastic.

"It was difrent las time thow…My lips went numb."

Dr. Libby gave me a quizzical look.

"Your lips went numb from sucking through a straw?" she asked.

I shook my head.

"No…From his thingy."

"His 'thingy'?" she inquired.

I started giggling again.

"It was the first time I e'er seen one," I admitted, feeling a bit embarrassed. "I thought it was kinda weird lookin'."

Dr. Libby's eyes suddenly went wide.

"Oh…"

"But I prolly still enjoyt it mor'n he did."

"I see…" she said, her face flushing red.

"Plus it tasted…"

"You really should get some rest," she interrupted, putting her hand gently on my shoulder. "I will check back in a bit to see how you're doing."

I looked into her eyes trying to remember what it was I was about to say. I drew a blank.

"K." I replied cheerfully.

Dr. Libby tucked my arms beneath the warm blanket and wished me sweet dreams. After she left, I tried to resume my game of connect-the-dots, but my mind quickly grew listless and I drifted off to sleep…

Mitchell entered the hospital around lunch time. This workshop was far more intense than he anticipated. So far, he and Carl spent all of last night and this morning following through a workbook and writing down responses or taking notes as Carl saw fit. Even though they were only halfway through the exercises for the day, Mitchell's arm ached with tremendous pain. He grimaced at the thought of the fun-filled afternoon that awaited him tomorrow. At least there would be the comfort of visiting with Olivia, if only for a little while.

He exited the elevator and headed toward her room. Once inside, he could see that she was not in her bed. He checked the bathroom and didn't find her there either. Puzzled by her disappearance, he went to the nurse's station. In the hallway, he encountered a lone nurse walking along the corridor.

"Excuse me," he called to her.

"Can I help you?" she asked when he drew close.

"The girl who is staying in that room," he began, gesturing toward Olivia's room, "Do you know where she is?"

The nurse anxiously looked down at the floor.

"What's the matter?" he asked worriedly.

The nurse glanced over her shoulder at one end of the hallway and then at the other to make sure the coast was clear. When she saw no one, she put a finger to her lips, urging Mitchell to be silent. She led him by the wrist into Olivia's room and shut the door behind them. When she turned around, Mitchell was standing with his arms upraised as though warding himself from an incoming assault.

"What are you doing?" she asked with one eyebrow cocked.

"I was just about to ask you the same thing," he replied.

She shook her head as if to deflect any unintended interpretations to her actions.

"It's about your daughter," she said.

"My daughter?" he asked in confusion, before realizing that she was referring to Olivia.

The nurse nodded and Mitchell's hands descended to his sides.

"I'm not supposed to tell you, but I think there's something you should know."

Mitchell suddenly became fearful.

"Something about Olivia?" he asked.

The nurse nodded.

"The doctor doesn't want her to know. He thinks it will be bad for her morale or something."

Mitchell listened intently as she explained the troubling prognosis so far, and how the doctor was delaying telling Olivia until they had a proper diagnosis.

"Please don't tell anyone that I told you," she begged him. "I could lose my job."

"I promise I won't say a word," he agreed.

She sighed with relief.

"So where is Olivia right now?"

Worry returned to the nurse's face.

"That's the reason I wanted to talk to you. They took her to the surgery ward earlier this morning."

Mitchell felt a tightening in his chest.

"Why?" he asked.

"I'm not sure," she replied. "But I figure it must be bad if they rushed her so quickly. Even Dr. Baker wasn't aware that she'd been whisked away to surgery."

Mitchell held up his hands to silence the flood of unnecessary information.

"Where's the surgery ward?"

"You can't go back there. It's..."

"WHERE?!" he shouted.

The nurse recoiled from his outburst. Mitchell felt ashamed and returned his hands to his sides. A few seconds later the door to the room opened.

"Is everything alright in here?" the incoming nurse asked, looking from the first nurse to Mitchell.

"It's ok. Everything is fine," replied the first nurse.

The second nurse gave Mitchell one last menacing stare to let him know she meant business.

"If he gives you any more trouble, feel free to call security," she said before departing the room, making sure to leave the door ajar.

Mitchell gave a heavy sigh.

"Sorry," he muttered.

The nurse shook her head.

"It's understandable," she said. "I would probably respond the same way if I were in your shoes."

The nurse straightened her outfit before looking back at Mitchell.

"She should be back here after her surgery, barring any...further complications."

Mitchell shuddered at the thought.

"Thank you for talking with me," he said. "I really appreciate it."

"No problem. Just please, don't tell anyone. Not even your daughter."

Mitchell hesitated, and then nodded.

Satisfied, the nurse exited the room and returned to her hospital duties.

After she had gone, Mitchell sat down upon the bed. He wasn't sure if he would tell Olivia the news he heard or not. On the one hand, she deserved to know if something terrible was in the works. Yet, on the other hand, bad news was something that should only be experienced once; might as well wait to tell her until they had the real diagnosis.

Still unsure if that was the proper action, he pulled out his cell phone and dialed Carl. A few short minutes later, he was leaving the hospital and heading to the workshop. He would rush back to Olivia as soon as the workshop closed for the evening, he reassured himself. But for now, he would follow Carl's advice, and accept the things he could not change, even though he felt in his heart that leaving the hospital had been the wrong decision.

I sat in the unfamiliar room, both hands wrapped tightly around a can of ginger ale. It took most of my concentration not to spill it. Even in my hazy mindset, I thought it strange that they brought me soda instead of water to hydrate my system. I wasn't complaining though. The refreshing beverage had already calmed the sickness in my stomach after the medicine wore off.

I was about halfway finished with my drink when three figures came in and stood around the foot of my bed. I recognized Dr. Libby, Brenda and Dr. Baker. My favorite among the three was the first to speak.

"Hi, Olivia," greeted Dr. Libby. "Are you feeling back to normal yet?"

I tilted my head side-to-side.

"Mostly," I replied.

"Do you have any pain?" she asked.

I shifted my hips slightly and then shook my head.

"Not that I can tell," I said. "I am feeling kind of hungry though."

"That's understandable," said Dr. Libby. "We'll see about getting you something to eat."

I nodded, taking another drag on the straw.

"We have some good news," Dr. Libby stated.

I looked up from my soft drink.

"Oh?"

Dr. Libby shot me an eager smile, her cheeks glowing from excitement.

"We may have discovered the source of your troubles."

I gave her a puzzled look, motioning to my gurney.

"I thought that's what we were doing," I said in confusion.

Dr. Libby gave a nervous chuckle, her face going red.

"I'll let Dr. Baker explain," she said, nodding to her right.

Following his cue, Dr. Baker opened the file in his hands.

"Ah, yes," he began, clearing his throat by coughing into his fist. "When we first received you as a patient, we ran a series of diagnostic tests to determine the reason for your recent fainting spell."

I nodded, unsure why he thought I had forgotten the multitude of tests that I had been subjected to.

"Your underweight frame, low bone density and signs of fatigue made me think that there could be a serious medical malady behind these side effects. When your blood work came back negative for antibodies, I figured that it might be an indicator of cancerous cells in the bone marrow instead."

I quickly realized that being well-read had not made me a master of medical jargon, though the mention of cancer sent shivers down my spine.

"Antibodies?" I inquired.

"Antibodies are the body's natural defense against harmful pathogens," explained Dr. Baker. "Often we can diagnose a disease being present because specific antibodies unique to that pathogen are present in the body."

"Ok," I said in limited comprehension.

"Antibodies are secreted by plasma cells, which are a type of white blood cell," continued Dr. Baker. "As with other blood cells, plasma cells come from bone marrow. Since we didn't discover antibodies present in the blood, our next logical step was to analyze your bone marrow."

I felt myself wince at the memory of the painful extraction process.

"And what type of antibodies did you find in the bone marrow?" I asked.

Dr. Baker smiled.

"None," he stated cheerfully. "At least none of the ones that would indicate a serious condition."

I took a moment to consider this influx of information.

"But if there were no antibodies present, doesn't that mean that you still don't know the cause behind my fainting spells?"

Dr. Baker gestured to Dr. Libby.

"After the initial pelvic exam," she began, "I ordered a full endocrine work up. In examining the x-rays from your fall, I was able to make a diagnosis of bone age that did not match your true age."

The way she mentioned my 'true age' made me smile. It reminded me that she believed me; that she was one of few people who were on my side.

"Combining the results of your x-rays and endocrine analysis, along with the presence of amenorrhea, anosmia and low bone density, it didn't take me long to narrow down the culprit."

Dr. Libby took a step toward me, sliding a sheet of paper from her folder.

"Kallman syndrome," she declared proudly.

She handed me a printout detailing the condition.

"It's a congenital form of hypogonadism," she explained.

I moved my eyes from the paper in front of me and gave her a vacant stare.

"It's a somewhat rare medical condition where the body fails to start puberty."

The cogs turned slowly inside my head before finally taking hold. It suddenly dawned on me the significance of what had just been explained to me.

"This isn't about the fainting at all, is it?" I asked. "You've figured out why...why I look like this?"

Dr. Libby beamed ardently in my direction, and then nodded her head.

A tsunami of emotions swept over me. I felt the pangs of mockery from the girls at the orphanage because I didn't look the way they did. I felt the sorrow of many wasted years not understanding why I was different. I felt the neglect as adult after adult swept me out of sight and out of mind. I felt the hope of finally being accepted. I felt the potential for a lifetime of happiness with the man I had come to love. With each added emotion, there was a buildup in pressure behind the floodgates until everything surged forward through the barrier and let loose in a single wave of release.

My body shook violently as the tears streamed unrestrained down my face. I felt the comforting warmth of Dr. Libby's tender hand on my shoulder. My fingers found hers and squeezed affectionately as the rivers continued to run.

"Please give us a minute," Dr. Libby said to her compatriots.

After they had gone, through what seemed like ages of uncontrollable sobbing, the waterworks finally dried up, and I released my grip on Dr. Libby's hand.

"I'm sorry," I said, wiping the tears from my cheeks. "I just..."

"It's ok," she said. "I can't begin to imagine what you've had to go through."

I sniffled audibly as I dried the remaining tears on my hospital blanket.

"What about the fainting spells?" I asked.

Dr. Libby gritted her teeth.

"That happens to be one of the side effects of that medication I confiscated from you."

I gazed at her with surprise. It couldn't really be that simple could it?

"In fact," she continued angrily, "it wasn't even bone density medication at all, which is probably where the confusion came in."

"What was it?"

"An antidepressant."

I raised an eyebrow at her.

"Why would...?"

"Believe me, I'll be sure to find out," she said in a tone that could generously be described as outraged.

I smiled at how protective she had become of me.

"So...what do we do now?" I asked.

Dr. Libby took a deep breath to calm her nerves.

"We'll start you on a combination of hormone replacements for the Kallman syndrome, and some bone formation therapy drugs until we get your bone density back to normal levels."

"That's it?"

Dr. Libby nodded.

"I'll have Brenda work with you tonight and tomorrow to make sure that you are steady on your feet. But other than that, we should be able to discharge you first thing Monday morning."

I couldn't believe that my luck had turned around so quickly. After facing down a potentially lethal diagnosis, I could be leaving the hospital the day after tomorrow. I leaned forward and wrapped her in an affectionate hug.

"Thank you so much," I said. "For everything."

Despite the professional environment, Dr. Libby let herself go, squeezing me tightly in her arms.

"There is some bad news," she said eventually.

I pulled back from our embrace, peering into those mournful eyes.

"What is it?" I asked with concern.

Dr. Libby exhaled a lamenting sigh.

"In many cases of Kallman syndrome, the patient suffers from sterility," she explained. "Oftentimes, we try different types of therapy to overcome various complications, but because it has taken so long to diagnose your condition, there is a high likelihood that, even with fertility treatments, you will never be able to have children of your own."

I looked into her eyes, as if to analyze the truth of her statement. When I realized that she was being genuine, I burst into laughter.

"I'm not joking" she stated.

"I know," I said, calming my laughing fit. "I was worried that it might be something serious."

She gave me an inquisitive stare.

"I take it you're not interested in having children?"

"Well, I might want children," I said, "but if I have any, they'll definitely be adopted. With all the problems associated with overpopulation in the world, it would be irresponsible of me to bring anymore in, especially when there are so many who need good, loving homes."

Dr. Libby smiled at me.

"I guess that resolves that concern."

"And besides," I continued, shooting her a mischievous grin, "now I can have sex as often as I like without any unnecessary consequences."

She gave me a stern look, almost as a forewarning to the lecture to follow.

"I know, I know..."I said, quickly putting up my hand. "I'll be careful."

She nodded. Dr. Libby glanced around the room to make sure we were still alone. She leaned close to me and spoke in a hushed whisper.

"If I were you, I would consider using lubrication for the first few times."

I considered this information and nodded appreciatively.

"Speaking of which..."she said. "The surgery went well, so there shouldn't be the risk of a tear aggravating the region. As long as you feel no pain and there's no blood, then you should be good to go in about two weeks."

I gave a disgruntled sigh.

"That long?" I protested.

She rolled her eyes, laughing at my impatience.

"I would at least give it seven to ten days. Okay?"

"Okay," I agreed begrudgingly.

We embraced one more time before she left. I laid my head on the pillow, my eyelids as heavy as my heart was light. Thinking about Dr. Libby's more lenient abstinence suggestion, I began doing some math in my head. Smiling, I fell into peaceful slumber, silently humming 'happy birthday' to myself.

CHAPTER 30

Mitchell stood before a closed door, its thick framework staring ominously back at him like a sentry barring his entry. He thumped his fist hard against the wood surface, creating a resounding noise that echoed down the hallway. He waited three seconds before knocking again, this time with a little more force. Before he could bring his fist down a third time, the door opened to reveal a robust woman clad only in her nightgown; the cool night air helping to accentuate her firm figure. Mitchell's eyes traced over every inch of her red garment, his mind wandering to memories of the soft ebony skin beneath.

"Hello Evelyn," he said.

She put a hand atop her waist and glowered menacingly at him.

"Watcha doin' here?" she demanded.

Mitchell alternated between looking at her and glancing at the wall beside the door.

"I uh…was just, in the neighborhood and thought I'd drop in."

"Your apartment's on the other end of town," she stated coldly.

"I know, but I had…other business over here. So…you know."

Evelyn leaned forward, flaring her nostrils in his direction.

"Oh, honey," she said with disdain. "You've been drinking again."

Mitchell tucked the hand clutching the bottle behind his back.

"No," he said innocently. "Maybe just some wine…a glass or two…at dinner."

She shook her head.

"How have you been?" asked Mitchell, ignoring her look of disapproval.

She crossed her hands in front of her and leaned against the doorframe.

"Now's not really a good time," she said in a harsh tone.

As if on cue, another voice sounded from inside the apartment.

"Hey, babe. Who you talkin' to?"

Evelyn let out a heavy sigh, continuing to glare unapologetically at Mitchell. Within a few seconds, the door opened more, and a second figure stood there. The man wore baggy shorts and a faded jersey. Mitchell guessed him to be about five seven, and definitely no more than a hundred seventy pounds soaking wet.

"Who's this?" the man asked.

Evelyn looked at Mitchell waiting for him to explain. When he said nothing, she filled in the gaps.

"This is my ex-husband," she uttered abhorrently.

The man suddenly tensed, his fists clenching tightly by his sides. He took a threatening step forward, glaring angrily up at Mitchell as though he were a cobra about to strike. Though his passive nature restrained him from responding in a similar fashion, Mitchell couldn't help but roll his eyes at the man's ridiculous display of machismo. Still, it had become transparently clear that he already overstayed what little welcome he possessed in the first place. He looked back at Evelyn.

"Sorry to have bothered you," he said, his voice coated with defeat.

Mitchell turned back down the hall and headed for the elevators, no longer bothering to conceal the liquor bottle from her vision. He took a long drink from the container, wishing he were already home so that he could get annihilated properly and forget about this foolhardy mission of his.

The doors of the elevator opened and he stepped aboard, pressing the first floor button. Eager to get going, he jabbed the button for the doors to close several times in quick succession, including twice after they already began to shut.

Much to his dismay, when the lift took off, it ascended rather than moving down to the lobby. He held down his floor selection, desperately hoping that the elevator would somehow change its mind. In spite of his protests, the lift continued to trundle upward until it came to a stop on the top floor.

The doors opened to reveal a man anxiously checking his watch. Noticing Mitchell, he politely took a step back, gesturing with his arm to signify that he would wait patiently for Mitchell to exit. Not wanting to look like the sort of idiot who would ride all the way to the top floor when he was heading in the opposite direction, Mitchell reluctantly stepped out. The man gave him one last friendly smile as the elevator doors closed; carrying the stranger in the direction that Mitchell wanted to go.

He waited until the lights above the lift began counting down again before pressing the down button. After all, there was no need to risk hitting the button too early and be forced to face the awkward stare of the man who just left. As he waited for the elevator to return, Mitchell noticed a sign that read *roof access*. Feeling somewhat curious, he wandered away from the lift and walked up the staircase.

Stepping through the metal door, the crisp night air blew across his face, causing him to wince in spite of its refreshing coolness. Looking around, Mitchell could see several rows of heating units, their collaborative effort creating a deep hum that pierced the silence of the otherwise quiet rooftop.

Weaving through the garden of mechanical structures, Mitchell found himself approaching the edge of the roof. In all directions he could see the festive city lights glowing brightly with nocturnal activity. Normally, the hustle and bustle of his beloved city could relieve even his darkest melancholy, but tonight it only reminded him how sad his life had turned out.

Mitchell upturned his bottle, finishing off the last of the brown liquid.

Looking out over the other rooftops, Mitchell thought about what transpired between him and Evelyn. She made it abundantly clear by her dismissive attitude that she wanted absolutely nothing to do with him. *How dare she treat him like that after all their time together? Who was she to judge his behavior? Hadn't she been the one who ran off on their marriage? Wasn't she the one who had given up when things got tough?*

His mind continued to wander, and visions appeared of his zealous brother-in-law, nagging sister, and Evelyn's apparent new boyfriend.

I'll show them, he thought.

Grabbing hold of the bottle by its neck, Mitchell flung the empty container into the night sky, watching it turn end over end as it descended into the street below. Even with the lights reflecting across its glass surface, he lost sight of it halfway through its trajectory. He groaned with disappointment when he didn't even get to hear the sound of shattering glass.

Mitchell peered out over the side of the building, gazing down at the long, steep drop. He imagined the wind swooshing past his face as he hurled faster and faster until he met with a swift and decisive end on the pavement below. *Wasn't that what all this drinking was leading to eventually anyway? Why delay the inevitable?*

He stepped onto the ledge. Mitchell envisioned the faces of all those who had turned their backs on him over the last couple years. He thought about their sorrow and regret at finding him a mangled, bloody corpse in the morning. *That would show them. Teach them all a lesson.*

A loud banging noise erupted behind him, startling him from his pensive thoughts. At the sound of approaching voices, he hopped away from the ledge and tried to conceal himself behind the closest heating unit.

Peeking around the side, he could see two figures approaching from the rooftop entrance. The first was a plump, elderly man, and by the look of his gait, clearly intoxicated. In his right hand, he clutched a bottle still containing a third of its original liquid repast. In his left hand, he grasped the wrist of a small girl that he dragged behind him. Mitchell did a double take when he realized that the girl was completely naked.

"Come on, Witch!" shouted the man in slurred speech. "Let's see if you can fly!"

"No...please..." cried the girl behind him. She struggled to free herself from his grasp, but all her efforts seemed in vain. Mitchell could see tears coursing down her face.

"HEY!" shouted Mitchell, stepping out from behind the heating unit.

Both figures stopped and looked in his direction with surprise.

"Let her go!" he demanded.

The little girl's face lit up with hope, the old man's with contempt.

"This has nothing to do with you," he hollered back.

The old man pulled the girl toward one of the rooftop edges. She continued to resist, her eyes calling to Mitchell for help. Without a moment's hesitation, he ran around the outer perimeter of the metallic structures, cutting them off at the pass. Stepping in front of the shambling duo, he outstretched his arms to prevent them from going by. Mitchell towered over the old man the way a bear might overshadow a chimpanzee.

"LET...HER...GO!" Mitchell growled between clenched teeth.

The old man stopped dead in his tracks, but did not relinquish his hold on the small girl.

"You don't understand," he protested. "This girl is evil."

Ignoring the man's pleas, Mitchell lunged forward, wrapping his massive hand around the old man's throat. His eyes grew wide with fear as he struggled to breathe under the crushing force of Mitchell's strength. Using his free hand, Mitchell took hold of the wrist being used to subdue the girl. The man screamed in pain as Mitchell twisted his arm back until he released his grip on the girl. When she pulled free, Mitchell shoved the old man away, watching with satisfaction as he gasped for air on the concrete.

The girl ran behind Mitchell, clinging to his thick coat.

"Are you alright?" he asked, turning to face her.

She wrapped her arms around his waist in a tight hug.

"It's ok," he said, putting a reassuring hand across her bare shoulders. "I'm not going to let anyone hurt you. I promise."

Mitchell winced in pain as something struck him hard across his right shoulder blade. He wrapped his arms around the girl to shield her from whatever came next. She let out a terrifying shrill just before he felt another incoming blow connect with his exposed midsection. Mitchell saw spots, his heart beating inside his ears as all the oxygen escaped his body in one agonizing breath.

"Quick," he gasped to the small girl. "Hide behind that machine."

Once she was safely out of the way, Mitchell turned to face his assailant. His inebriation was affecting his ability to respond, however, and the next attack struck him hard across his chest. Mitchell staggered backward, the wind once again driven from his system.

Sensing the tide turning in his favor, the old man charged forward. Grasping the liquor bottle with both hands, he swung with incredible force, aiming at Mitchell's head. Mitchell blocked the attack, his left wrist throbbing from the impact. Following up on his momentum, the old man swung again, this time connecting with Mitchell's ribcage, causing him to double over in pain.

Unrelenting in his assault, the old man swung again, this time with all of his might. Mitchell barely managed to get out of the way, feeling a whoosh of air as the bottle moved passed his face. Getting into the rhythm of their dance, Mitchell sidestepped when the old man flailed on the backswing. When he raised the bottle overhead, Mitchell anticipated the arc, easily dodging out of the way. Again and again, Mitchell retreated from the incoming barrage until the back of his heel made contact with the concrete ledge. His balance faltered, and he was able to get a clear view of the frightening drop before regaining his footing.

Returning his gaze to the old man, Mitchell saw a smirk of victory forming on those filth encrusted lips. Out of the corner of his eye, Mitchell saw the small girl cowering behind the heating unit, her face contorted in horror as she helplessly watched the fray unfold. Realizing how much was at stake in this fight, Mitchell clenched his jaw, readying himself for the next attack.

When the old man came at him again, Mitchell deflected the swinging arm, knocking it aside as if shooing away a housefly. With the man thrown off balance, Mitchell raised his massive leg, bent his knee to his chest, and extended until the sole of his foot made contact with the man's sternum. The old man toppled backwards, rolling once heels overhead, coming to rest on his back. The bottle slid from his hand and made a dull clattering sound as it skittered against the side of a nearby heating unit. Mitchell took the opportunity to create some distance between him and the rooftop ledge.

The old man slowly regained himself, putting his hand to his head as he sat upright on the cold concrete. With a loud groan, he pushed himself back to his feet, lurching sideways as he struggled up. Once he steadied himself, he narrowed his eyes menacingly at Mitchell.

A sudden whimper sounded from behind the machinery, and the old man focused his attention on the small girl instead. He rushed forward in a vain attempt to move past the behemoth blocking his path. Mitchell moved with surprising agility to intercept the old man before he could get to the girl. Dropping his shoulder, Mitchell plowed headlong into the oncoming assailant.

The sheer momentum of Mitchell's massive form lifted the man from his feet, driving him back with incredible force. The old man struggled to remain upright, stumbling further back with each footstep. Just when it looked like he might finally regain his balance, his foot landed on top of the liquor bottle. The old man teetered and plummeted toward the edge of a nearby heating unit. There was a soul-sickening crunch as his skull connected with the unforgiving concrete, followed by the eerie sounds of the bottle rolling back and forth across the silent rooftop. Unable to stand the torment, Mitchell grabbed the container and placed it upright next to one of the machines.

Sensing that the danger had passed, the small girl stepped away from the shadows. Though she was still as unadorned, fear completely dissipated from her face, making her seem far less vulnerable than she had a moment ago.

She ran to Mitchell, flinging herself against his chest. Catching the girl in his arms, Mitchell supported her lightweight form with one hand around her back and the other cradled beneath her bare behind. Mitchell ignored the awkwardness of this position as the girl buried her face into his chest, her tiny body shaking as she sobbed uncontrollably. He rubbed her back, trying to soothe her torment with a gentle touch and reassuring words. When the vibrations finally subsided, the girl pulled away, wiping away the tears with the palm of her hand. She gazed up at Mitchell, her blue eyes piercing deep into his soul.

Before either of them could say anything, she leaned into him, firmly planting an affectionate kiss against his lips…

Mitchell awoke from the dream covered in sweat and his heartbeat racing. He took in sharp ragged breaths, trying desperately to calm the wild beast raging inside. His body quaked with thoughts of Olivia. He rolled onto his side, biting down hard on the edge of his pillow until the intense sensations subsided.

As he regained control of that unbridled hormonal rage, Mitchell became entrenched in forlorn melancholy. He longed to feel the warmth of Olivia's supple body, to feel the soft touch of her lips against his. He ran his fingers over the sheets where she normally lay beside him. *If absence makes the heart grow fonder, it could certainly play hell with the rest of the body..*

Yesterday the hospital staff kept her so long in the recovery room that he barely had an opportunity to say hello before going to work. To make matters worse, a nurse was present the whole time, ensuring that the only affection they could attempt mimicked friendship more than sensuality.

Noting an added intensity of sunlight streaming through the bedroom window, Mitchell rolled over to check the clock. He cursed to himself at the time. He had forgotten to set the alarm and now was running late. Tossing the sheets aside, his gloom intensified knowing that his tardy awakening would prevent him from visiting her before joining Carl at the workshop.

Gathering his belongings, Mitchell exited the apartment. He dialed Olivia's room number as he made his way to the elevator, quickly getting a busy signal.

It must have gotten knocked off the cradle, he thought to himself.

As Mitchell turned down the sidewalk, he raised his eyes to the Pittsburgh skyline. *It was strange to think that so much happiness could arise from such dire circumstances. New beginnings from a savage end, two lives saved by a single one lost… Life has its way of being tragically poetic I suppose…*

"Thanks Victor," said Olivia. "I'll see you tomorrow."

She hung up the receiver on the phone. Though her scheduled meeting had its contingencies, Olivia was confident that she would be released from the hospital in the morning.

Since getting up, she had worked with Brenda, per the request of Dr. Libby. Together they walked the corridors with the nurse monitoring her condition to ensure that the episodes of fainting had passed. Luckily, ever since Dr. Libby took her off the old medication, her spells of dizziness dwindled to nothing.

Olivia rolled out of the bed and headed to the bathroom. It was such a relief to be able to maneuver basic, day-to-day activities again without the need for a support team.

When she exited the restroom, she glanced at the clock on the wall, letting out a sigh of disdain. Perhaps the worst part of her hospital stay had been the sheer mind-numbing boredom of it all. She had already spoken with Victor, made a few phone calls, done her exercises with Brenda and finished the books that Mitchell brought over from the apartment, and yet, there were still many hours to go before Mitchell finished with his recovery workshop.

She climbed into the hospital bed, unsure if she would try rereading one of the texts or simply succumb to another late morning nap. Her head was firmly resting against the pillows when a knock sounded on her door. Olivia sat upright, startled by the mostly forgotten social practice ignored by her recent visitors and medical staff.

"How are we doing in here?" asked Brenda cheerfully.

Olivia let out a groan.

"No offense to anybody here, but I can't wait to be back home."

"That's understandable," said Brenda. "I doubt anybody likes being in the hospital."

"I wish there was a book cart here, at least that way I would have something to do."

"There is a rec room down in the residents' ward," offered Brenda. "There's probably not much worth reading, but there might be a deck of cards."

Olivia swung her legs off the edge of the bed.

"Do you think they would mind if I hung out there for a little while?" she asked.

"I doubt it. Hardly anyone uses the space."

Olivia pushed herself from the mattress and moved toward the door.

"Which way is it?"

"I'll take you," said Brenda. "Libby would kill me if I let you wander the halls unsupervised."

Although the rec room had the same banal décor as the rest of the hospital, it was a welcome change from the familiarity of her room. For one thing, the far wall was a series of tall windows, allowing the sunlight to permeate an otherwise depressing excuse for a gaming area. A single shelf held a few recognizable names, though most of the boxes were held together with masking tape. An assortment of tables was scattered throughout the open space. The only occupants were an elderly woman hunkered over a jigsaw puzzle and a lone man staring blankly at a Chinese checker board.

"I'll check on you in about an hour," stated Brenda.

"Thank you," replied Olivia with a smile.

Focusing her attention on the colorful arrangement of marbles, Olivia made her way to the gentleman at the corner table. He didn't bother to look up as she approached.

"Hi," she greeted. "You look like you could use a partner."

The man said nothing, his face contorting as though from frustration.

"Young lady," called a voice behind her.

Olivia gazed over her shoulder at the elderly woman smiling back at her.

"Why don't you give me a hand with this puzzle?" she suggested, patting the empty chair beside her.

Olivia accepted the invitation, glad to have a reason to move away from the man's menacing scowl. After she was seated, the woman leaned in close.

"Leo can be a bit grumpy if his routine gets interrupted," she explained.

"I see...I'm Olivia by the way."

"Ida," she said, reaching for a puzzle piece. "So what brings you to the hospital? Visiting your grandmother?"

"Actually I'm a patient," replied Olivia. "I had a nasty fall about a week ago."

"You poor thing. Are you doing alright now?"

"I think so. It looks like they'll be sending me home tomorrow."

"Well, that's good."

Olivia watched as Ida scanned the puzzle for the proper spot to place her piece. Eventually she gave up, setting it aside with an audible groan.

"This would be so much easier if I were better at geography," she said.

Olivia analyzed the puzzle. The image was a map of the world with all of the individual countries divided into their own irregular shapes, the larger regions broken into smaller sections. Ida had clearly made a lot of progress with the waterways, but other than North America, most of the map remained empty.

"Norway, Sweden, and Finland go across the top of Europe," pointed Olivia. "And beneath Finland are Estonia, Latvia, and Lithuania."

Ida raised an eyebrow at her.

"How can you remember all that?"

Olivia shrugged.

"I find it's easier if you have some kind of mnemonic. For that bit I use Ned Stark of WinterFELL."

Ida gave her another questioning look.

"It's from a book," explained Olivia. "I hear that they might be making it into a TV show soon."

Ida nodded, sliding the Norway piece in place.

"It's funny how much the world has changed," she commented. "A lot of those countries didn't even exist when I was a little girl."

Olivia continued to hunt for the European nations, handing them to Ida as she found them. Reading the names, she was reminded of all the places she always wanted to see but had never been given the opportunity. She envisioned famous museums of Paris, the majestic Black Forest in Germany, delectable desserts made from authentic Swiss chocolate, and a romantic gondola ride for two through the city of Venice.

"So what are you in for?" asked Olivia, reluctantly letting go of the Italy piece.

"C.O.P.D. It's a breathing disorder."

"I'm sorry to hear that."

"Don't be. I never had any interest in sports and certainly there was no chance of me suddenly deciding to take up jogging at my age. Besides, it doesn't really flare up unless I push myself too hard."

"So why are you at the hospital?"

"Well...I had a few close calls when I was still living at home. My children decided that it would be better if I wasn't alone in case it happened again."

"That makes sense."

Ida held up her hand.

"Don't get me wrong," she said, "they're great kids. They come to visit, they call often to see how I'm doing, and they sent flowers on my birthday. But sometimes, I think they worry too much."

A loud groan emanated from the far corner of the room. Olivia looked up to see the old man leaning on his elbows, agonizing over the state of the board.

"We should keep it down," said Ida, leaning in close. "Our conversation may have disturbed him."

"What is he doing?" whispered Olivia.

"Leo used to be a Chinese checker champion," she stated proudly. "Of course, that was back before..."

She tapped the side of her temple.

"It's such a shame," she continued. "When he first came here, his mental faculties had already begun to deteriorate, but you could tell that his mind had once been like a steel trap. He could recall every move from when he won his first championship. Every day since he arrived, he comes down here to replay some of the important matches from his career, hoping that it will slow the progression."

"Is it helping?"

Ida shook her head.

"He's definitely losing the battle. I wish there was more I could do for him."

Olivia placed her hand delicately on top of the older woman's, giving the arthritic hand a reassuring pat.

"Up until a month ago, he would hold my hand as we watched movies. We just sat there, enjoying each other's company. When it was time for bed, Leo would give me a kiss on the cheek before retiring to his own room. I couldn't have asked for a better companion."

Ida lifted her head, her glossy eyes staring wistfully across the room.

"Most days he doesn't even recognize me, just gazes right through the way he does with everyone. But every once in a while, he'll raise his head from that board in my direction, and even though I'm sure he doesn't know who I am, somewhere deep inside he remembers the affection we had for one another, and he smiles."

Ida's body shook as she inhaled a raspy breath.

"It just goes to show that you're never too old to start making memories."

She turned to Olivia.

"Or too young."

Mitchell hit the ground running as he leapt from the bus. His absence from Olivia had been heart wrenching to the point of causing him physical pain. It had been a full day since he had last seen her…spoken to her…touched her. Now that the workshop was complete, that would all change.

The last few days had been mostly a blur, but he felt more at peace, as though the intense work was having a profound effect on his emotional stability. But no matter how much he thought about the steps, the traditions or passages they had read from the Big Book, all that came to mind was Olivia.

Too impatient to wait, Mitchell skipped the trundling elevator and began taking the steps three at a time. His stomach rumbled fiercely as he ascended, not having eaten anything since lunch. His back cried in pain at the exertion, hours in an uncomfortable chair taking their toll on his physique. His eyes were sore from hours upon hours of reading. His hands hurt from the fatigue of countless pages of writing.

That all slipped away as he turned the corner to her room and set his eyes on his sleeping beloved. She seemed so peaceful curled up on her side; it was almost a shame to wake her. Placing his massive hand gently on her shoulder, he coaxed her face away from the pillow. He leaned over and planted a tender kiss upon her lips and pulled away.

Her eyelids flickered open, those deep blue sapphires peering up at him. A flash of awareness preceded a jubilant smile.

"Mitchell!" she cried out, pouncing on him like a hungry leopard.

He wrapped his arms about her back, and she around his neck. With graceful ease, he lifted her from the bed, tucking his right hand beneath her for support. She latched tightly onto him, their lips interlocking as her hips ground softly into his torso. A sharp pain erupted below and Olivia quickly stopped. She pulled away from his lips and rested her head against his muscular shoulder.

"You've no idea how much I've missed you," she whispered lovingly into his ear.

Mitchell pulled her closer to him.

"I just might," he said.

She rested against him another moment, thoughts of the last few days flowing in and out of her memory.

"I have to tell you something," she said finally.

"What is it?"

"I..."

Her body stiffened against him.

"Is everything alright?" he asked.

She sighed.

"Someone just walked in."

Mitchell turned to face the incoming nurse.

"Hello," he said.

"Good evening," she greeted somberly.

"What's going on?" asked Mitchell.

The nurse looked at the floor and then at the two of them.

"I'm sorry to do this," she said. "It's been a long day for the young miss, and we've just entered quiet hours. I have to ask you to leave for the evening."

Mitchell glared.

"You're kidding?!" he stated incredulously.

"But he just got here," protested Olivia.

The nurse shrugged.

"Sorry. I'm just following orders."

Olivia felt the sag in Mitchell's body.

"Could you give us ten more minutes?" she asked.

The nurse gritted her teeth, shifting uncomfortably from side to side.

"I really can't. I..."

"Please..." plead Olivia with her best pouty face.

The nurse glanced over her shoulder nervously.

"Okay," she agreed. "Ten minutes, but that's all."

Olivia smiled at her. The nurse left the room, closing the door softly.

Olivia squirmed out of Mitchell's grasp until she was once again on the floor. She took hold of his hand and made a step toward the bathroom.

"Come on," she said. "If we lock ourselves in there, it should give us a few more minutes."

Mitchell tugged on her arm, pulling her toward him. She gave no resistance.

"Just let me hold you," he said.

Together they lay entwined until the nurse came knocking again. Olivia was certain that it had not been the full ten minutes, but probably would have felt that way even if it had been thirty. She pulled away from Mitchell and slid beneath the sheets, pretending that she had been that way the whole time.

"It's time," said the nurse, poking her head around the corner.

Mitchell nodded, standing from the bed. He leaned over and kissed Olivia tenderly on the forehead, cognizant of the eyes on his back.

"Sweet dreams," he said.

"It's just for tonight," she said reassuringly.

"I'll be by immediately after my morning meeting. I promise."

Olivia nodded.

"I love you," she said.

"I love you, too," he replied, pulling the sheets tightly around her.

The nurse anxiously guided Mitchell into the hallway. He moved at a snail's pace to the elevators, making himself believe that proximity to her room counted as actually being with her. It wasn't until he was at the main entrance of the hospital that he realized that Olivia had never told him whatever it was she wanted to say.

CHAPTER 31

Mitchell's phone rang, the boisterous overture from Robin Hood resounding through the empty apartment. As the exhilarating chords fell away, a narrow hand reached for the device.

"Hello?"

"Yes. Good morning," came a jovial female voice on the other end. "May I speak with Mr. Flynn?"

"..."

"Oh, I see," replied the voice. "My name is Brenda Murray. I'm one of the nurses on the general ward. I'm calling on behalf of Olivia."

There was a pause on the line.

"Uh-huh?"

"I am calling to let you know that she was released from the hospital. She left a little while ago."

"I see..."

"Normally we want someone here to take her home, but after Dr. Moore authorized her release, wild horses couldn't have restrained that girl."

Another pause.

"That's perfectly understandable. Do you know where she went?"

"She said that she was going to meet someone for breakfast, and she would head home right after."

"Ok. Thank you very much."

"No problem," replied Brenda cheerfully. "Have a wonderful day."

The line went silent, and the narrow hand returned the phone to the kitchen island, harder than was originally intended. The owner of the hand gritted her teeth in anger.

"What is she still doing here?!" growled Abigail.

She looked at the newly purchased assortment of groceries spread out across the counter before her. She latched onto an unsuspecting box of cereal and hurled it haphazardly toward the living room. It bounced unsatisfactorily off the side of the couch, making a dull rattle as it fell to the ground.

She put both of her palms down on the island, groaning loudly in exasperation. *That girl is supposed to be in foster care, I saw to it myself. Then why is she still here?*

Abigail suddenly recalled the awkward conversation she had with Harriet and the strange way Mitchell acted on her last visit. *How could I have not seen what was happening?*

Abigail slammed her fist angrily down on the countertop.

That little hussy! she screamed inside her head. *I don't know how she managed to finagle her way back in here, but I'm going to put an end to this once and for all.*

Ignoring the nonperishable groceries, Abigail hurried to the bedroom and flipped on her brother's laptop. When the start screen popped up, she was thankful that he had not bothered to password protect the computer.

Olivia strolled merrily down the sidewalk toward the diner. Though the day was overcast, the temperature was warm enough to not need the coat she was wearing. She was so delighted to be free of the hospital that she wouldn't have cared if there had been rain, sleet or hail.

She thought wistfully of Dr. Libby. Olivia owed her so much, and it was with a heavy heart that they had parted ways that morning. She compulsively patted her rear pocket to ensure the paper was still there. Knowing that she had Dr. Libby's e-mail at her disposal brought a smile to her face.

Olivia turned the corner and saw the diner up ahead. It was conveniently only a few blocks from the hospital. From the sidewalk, it looked like any other hole-in-the-wall place. The awning was worn, but the sign out front was brand new. A man setting out patio furniture greeted her as she moved toward the entryway.

Opening the glass door, she felt a sense of wonder at the extravagant renovations taking place inside. Every bit of linoleum had been ripped up to reveal the wood beneath, several light fixtures were still exposed, a couple ladders were spread around the restaurant, and linens were pushed against the walls, their white color now spotted from dripping paint. A series of intricate oil paintings adorned the floor of the diner, idly resting below their future homes. Olivia took a moment to admire the stunning display of sea port villages and nature trails. A magnificent depiction of a covered bridge caught her eye, drawing her into the image as the ambient music played lightly in the background.

"Olivia," called a voice behind her, extracting her from the reverie.

She turned to see Victor standing beside a booth. He wore black shoes, with black socks, black pants, black coat, and a black tie. She couldn't decide if he looked more like an FBI agent or an undertaker.

"Hello, Victor," she greeted cheerfully.

She approached him, hugging him tightly as she neared. After a moment, he gave her a light pat on the back. When they separated, he gestured for her to have a seat.

The server was quick to notice and approached the table with a cup of coffee. The waiter set the saucer down with a smile and absconded as quickly as he entered. Olivia looked from the mug to Victor with surprise.

"I remembered," he said with shrug of the shoulders.

Olivia nodded appreciatively, fascinated that he could recall how she liked her coffee.

"How are you doing this morning?" he asked.

She lifted the coffee from the table with both hands, blew softly across its surface, watching as steam rose off in a fine mist. She brought the mug to her lips. Bringing the cup down again, she cooed with satisfaction.

"Wonderful," she said with a contented sigh. "There's some very lovely artwork here."

Victor nodded.

"I saw you admiring the one over there."

"Yes," she acknowledged. "It reminded me of a bridge near…near where we used to live when I was a child."

Victor studied her pensively.

"You know…I'm friends with the owner here. I could see if he'd be willing to part with it."

Olivia shook her head.

"Oh, no," she said quickly. "Thank you for offering, but I think it will bring more joy to people here than hanging up in my living room."

Victor shrugged nonchalantly. He took a long swallow from his own mug.

"And how are *you* doing today, Victor?" she asked.

"Honestly…" he began, "I don't think I've ever been quite this happy in all my life."

"Really?" she asked with surprise, taking another sip from her mug.

Victor nodded serenely.

"I have a brand new job, working for the most wonderful boss in the world," he said, toasting her with his mug before downing the rest of its contents.

Olivia blushed.

"Plus, the hours allow me to spend more time with my family, whom I get to continue having, thanks to you."

Olivia looked away, embarrassed at the praise.

"I only did what any decent human being would have done," she said.

Victor nodded.

"I suppose," he replied, "but decent people are hard to come by these days."

The server came by and refilled Victor's mug. He applied additives as he spoke.

"Speaking of which," he began, "we've run into a bit of a snag looking for you-know-who."

Olivia set the mug down gently.

"What kind of 'snag'?" she asked worriedly.

"We located the court records," he said, stirring his coffee. "Apparently, she was emancipated by the courts at the age of fifteen, not surprising considering the transcript of her testimony. After that, the trail goes cold."

Olivia looked disheartened.

"Don't worry," he said, placing a reassuring hand on top of hers. "I've got my best people working on this. They're checking records of her social security number all across the northeast. If she's received a paycheck, opened a bank account or applied for a loan, we'll find her."

Olivia nodded, somehow comforted.

"Just be patient," he advised. "It may take some time to locate her. Especially if she's changed her name."

The two shot each other a knowing glance.

"Ok," she said cheerfully. "What about the other thing?"

Victor beamed at her.

"That," he said with inflated pride, "was a piece of cake."

Victor reached down and lifted a briefcase from the seat. He flipped it around and opened the lid. Olivia's eyes went wide with amazement.

"Wow…" she muttered.

Victor nodded in agreement.

"Just so you know, this is technically more than you're advised to travel with," he warned. "I included a letter in the briefcase with my contact information. It should help explain things if you get stopped for any reason. But honestly, it shouldn't be a problem as long as you don't try to leave the country with it."

"I don't see that happening," she stated. "Not without a passport anyway…"

Victor nodded.

"Yeah…still waiting on those documents as well," he informed her.

The man from outside, who had been setting up the patio, started to walk by their table. He stopped abruptly at the sight of the contents inside the briefcase. Victor glared menacingly at him.

"I think you have someplace to be," he said sternly.

The man looked from the briefcase to Victor and his all black attire. Realizing what the two connected pieces of information might imply, the man quickly glanced at the floor and didn't look up again until he was out of sight. Victor gently closed the lid.

"Probably best not to go flashing that about," he said.

Mitchell exited his morning meeting with Carl walking by his side.

"That was a good meeting," said Carl. "It seems like you always hear exactly what you need to."

"Yep," agreed Mitchell, though his heart was not in the conversation.

Carl reached over, patting him gently on the shoulder.

"Hey…you doing alright today?"

"Yeah," Mitchell said with an unenthusiastic nod. "I'm just a bit tired. It was another late night, and I didn't get much sleep."

It had been a half-truth, not really even a lie, and yet, Mitchell felt guilty anyway. Three full days of talking about moral inventories, defects of character and shortcomings had taken its toll on his conscience. The program had a way of becoming an inexorable lamprey, and it had sunk its teeth into him already.

"Plus," he added, "there's someone waiting for me down at the hospital."

Carl looked at him with concern.

"They still haven't figured out what's wrong?"

Mitchell shook his head.

"The doctors are working on it, but so far they haven't been able to come up with anything."

Carl nodded.

"Would you like a ride there?" he offered.

"Uh…sure," Mitchell said eagerly. "Is it on your way?"

"Close enough," he said, motioning to his car. "Come on."

When they turned the corner to the parking lot, Mitchell was relieved to see an SUV instead of the normal compacts that city-dwellers had grown so accustomed to.

"You know, I figured you might be upset," said Mitchell as they entered the car.

"Upset?" asked Carl, fastening his seat belt.

"You know, about the whole relationship thing."

Carl chuckled.

"It's true that a lot of newcomers focus more on hooking up than on their sobriety and end up going back out, but it's mostly a warning against *any* major changes. 'New' things tend to stress people out: new job, new home, new girlfriend."

He looked over at Mitchell to emphasize that last one.

"Since you were already in the relationship when you came in, I think it's best to stick with it, at least for the time being."

Mitchell smiled to himself.

"But…" said Carl, playfully raising an authoritative finger, "No other exceptions."

Mitchell gave him a salute.

"Aye aye, Captain," responded Mitchell with a playful salute. "Any other orders?"

"Same as before." he said.

Mitchell smiled reflexively, already knowing what he would say without him saying it. *Don't Drink; Go to Meetings; Call Me Every Day.*

Victor parked the car directly in front of the apartment building, completely ignoring the regulation signs. Exiting the vehicle, he moved to the passenger side door.

"Here we are M'lady," he said with a terrible British accent. He held out his hand and aided her to the sidewalk, enjoying his mock role as chauffeur.

"And just so you know," he said in his normal voice, "I'm going to be out of commission for at least a week after the surgery on Thursday. Try not to get into too much trouble before I finish recuperating."

Olivia gave him an affable hug, wrapping her arms around him as though they were old friends.

"Thank you so much, Victor. For everything."

His body tensed.

"I didn't really do much," he stated humbly.

Olivia pulled away.

"Seriously..." she said, looking into his eyes. "I don't know what I ever would have done without you."

Victor averted his eyes from her gaze, trying to keep himself from going red.

"If there's ever anything you need, anything at all, it's yours."

Victor studied her a moment before chuckling with amusement.

"If I live to be twice as old as I am now, I'll never be able to pay you back for what you've given me already," he assured her.

The two embraced one last time before Victor returned to the driver's seat. Olivia waved goodbye as he merged aggressively into traffic.

With her new briefcase in tow, Olivia strolled happily to the elevator. It felt like a lifetime had passed since last she set foot on these familiar floors. All the minutiae, from the sound of her shoes clunking against the old wood to the light of the elevator call button, filled her with reminiscent glee. It was sensational to simply be home.

Her excitement only increased with the ascension of the lift. Her heart skipped a beat as she pictured Mitchell snoozing soundly spread across their bed. Fantasies of varying raunchy detail formed in her mind, her own imagination causing her to blush.

Stepping from the elevator, she moved briskly down the hallway. With key already in hand, she opened the apartment door.

"I'm home," she called out.

The apartment was empty and silent. Olivia sighed with disappointment.

"Oh, well," she muttered, reassuring herself that he would be home soon.

Olivia let the front door close quietly behind her, clicking the lock in place. Setting down the heavy luggage, she slid off her winter coat and hung it neatly on one of the pegs. She was halfway through untying her shoes when a subtle noise sounded from inside the bedroom.

He must still be sleeping, she thought with mischievous delight.

Finishing with her footwear, she slowly crept to the bedroom. With the first steps, she maneuvered out of her socks, kicking them behind her as she walked. Olivia unfastened the button on her jeans, letting them fall behind her as she continued onwards. Never slowing, she pulled the cotton t-shirt overhead, revealing her bare breasts. Tossing the shirt toward the living room, she took hold of the elastic band on her single remaining garment. The elaborate embroidery came to rest a few feet away from the bedroom door.

Olivia surreptitiously advanced, placing her hand quietly against the darkened wood. She eased the doorway open until there was enough of a gap for her to slip through. Taking one last breath to calm her nerves, she proceeded into the bedroom.

"Surprise!" she declared joyfully.

Once inside the bedroom, Olivia stood paralyzed in shock. The room was just as abandoned as the rest of the apartment. On the bed, the sheets were unmade, tossed aside carelessly by its last inhabitant. Even in their unkempt state, it was clear that nobody was lying beneath their protective covering. Olivia narrowed her eyes in confusion.

If it hadn't been Mitchell who'd made the noise...

The bedroom door slammed behind her.

Olivia spun around, gasping in horror at the ominous figure now blocking her only escape route. Advancing toward her, the figure held a pair of scarlet panties dangling from the forefinger. Olivia cowered as its face contorted in hateful accusation, an eerie sneer mocking her as the laced material swung delicately to and fro.

"You know..." snickered Abigail. "I was just thinking the same thing."

Mitchell waved goodbye to Carl as he entered the hospital. His enthusiasm prompted him toward the stairs, but his fatigue led him to an elevator. He soon grew impatient at the slow trundling, wishing he had taken the stairs.

Looking both ways, he stepped into the hallway. Following the numbers on the doors, he located her room and walked inside. A nurse was standing beside her bed removing the linens.

"Excuse me," he called to her.

She turned to face him.

"Can I help you?" she asked pleasantly.

Mitchell gestured toward the bed.

"Do you know where she is?"

The nurse looked at him quizzically.

"You must be Mr. Flynn," she stated. "I left you a message earlier. Did you not get it?"

Mitchell shook his head.

"What message?" he asked with concern.

"Oh, dear," she replied. "I was hoping she would have told you."

"Told me what?" he demanded.

The nurse rolled the dirty sheets into a tight bundle before turning to face him.

"Miss Olivia checked out this morning," explained the nurse. "She wished you were here when it was time to leave, but she couldn't wait any longer."

Mitchell tilted his head to the side, his tired mind unable to comprehend the cryptic speech.

"I don't understand," he said. "Where is she?"

The nurse sighed heavily.

"She's gone home, Mr. Flynn."

The words struck him like a sack of potatoes. It had been the same phrase that his catholic mother used to describe the final journey to the afterlife.

A message sounded through the intercom.

"Excuse me," said the nurse in response. She grabbed the pile of linens and departed the room, leaving him to reflect on his own.

As if in a haze, Mitchell sat down on the edge of the hospital bed. In the last few minutes, his entire world had coming crashing down. He put his head in his hands, though he was still too much in shock for tears to come. *What had she been trying to tell him these last few days? Was it the reason she was no longer here? What if he had been here instead of at the workshop all weekend? Would he have been able to do anything to save her?*

Mitchell continued to berate himself for his behavior until a pair of feet came into view. Lifting his head from his hands, he looked into the face of a woman wearing a white coat. Her black hair was pulled into a ponytail.

"Hello," she greeted pleasantly, extending her hand to his. "I'm Dr. Libby Moore. I was the doctor in charge of Olivia's surgery."

Mitchell unenthusiastically took her hand.

"Mitchell Flynn," he replied. "I'm her…guardian."

Dr. Libby smiled knowingly at him.

"I see…" she said with a playful grin. "And what exactly is it that you're 'guarding', Mr. Flynn?"

He cocked an eyebrow at her.

"What do you mean?" he asked.

She gave him a look of confusion.

"You are her *boyfriend*, aren't you?"

Mitchell's eyes grew wide.

"What?" he said defensively. "Why would you think that?"

She held up her hand.

"It's ok," she said reassuringly. "I know the truth."

Mitchell looked toward the door in preparation for bolting if need be. He turned his gaze back to the doctor, eyeing her up and down nervously. There was something about her that seemed...trustworthy.

"You do?" he asked.

She nodded with a smile.

"It wasn't that hard to figure out," she said humbly. "It's a piece of cake to determine the age of a live patient. You should see the forensics people at work. Now they are the *real* experts."

Mitchell nodded. All things considered, he wasn't really in the mood for idle chitchat. He stood from the bed.

"Wow," exclaimed Dr. Libby. "You're a big one. No wonder you two had problems."

Mitchell gazed at her with concern. *What all had Olivia told this woman?*

"What do you mean *problems*?"

Dr. Libby made a zipping motion in front of her mouth.

"Don't worry, your secret is safe with me," she said. "Besides, now that the surgery is over, you shouldn't be having any more issues, at least not in that department."

Mitchell felt hopelessly lost.

"What surgery?" he asked worriedly.

Dr. Libby tilted her head sideways, clearly troubled by his ignorance.

"I'm sorry," she said sympathetically. "But you really should be hearing all this from *her*."

"I can't," he protested, gesturing toward the empty bed. "She's gone."

Dr. Libby looked at him with the same type of trepidation she might have if his hair had suddenly burst into flames.

"Well, of course, she's gone," said Dr. Libby. "Did you think we were going to hold her here forever?"

Mitchell shook his head with frustration.

"You could have tried to keep her hanging on as long as possible." he stated, his voice beginning to crack. "If someone had only told me I would have been here sooner."

Dr. Libby bowed her head.

"I suppose so," she agreed, returning her gaze to his. "But you know her as well as anybody. Once she had those release forms that was that."

Mitchell narrowed his eyes at her.

"Wait...release forms?"

"Yes." nodded Dr. Libby. "I signed them myself."

Mitchell's face lit up.

"You mean…she's gone home? Like back to my place?"

She looked at him with anxious unease.

"Are you feeling alright, Mr. Flynn? I could…"

Mitchell let out a jovial guffaw, grabbing Dr. Libby in his massive arms and swinging her around like a rag doll. When she made a noise of panic, he abruptly stopped spinning and released her, setting her down delicately on the tiled floor.

Dr. Libby stared at him with alarm.

"I…um…sorry. I got a little carried away."

Her face seemed to relax, even if the rest of her remained tense.

"So, um, she's doing better then?" he asked with embarrassment.

Dr. Libby let out an amused sigh, chuckling softly to herself.

"Go on," she said with a smile. "I'm sure she's waiting for you."

Mitchell nodded once and disappeared into the hallway. He briskly moved through the corridor, down the stairs and breezed out the main entrance. At nearly full gallop, he was able to clear several blocks before fatigue and oxygen deprivation slowed him to an enthusiastic stride.

It was inevitable that sooner or later Abigail would find out about my relationship with her brother. Even our deepest secrets have a way of unearthing themselves, especially in the most inconvenient of circumstances. During my hospital stay, I imagined the ideal situation in which to divulge this information to his temperamental sibling. The scenario I found myself in was not exactly what I had in mind. In fact, I couldn't imagine a worse way for her to learn of our love affair than having been caught with my pants down.

Despite the quick wit and silver tongue, there was no way to talk my way out of this. Abigail continued to brandish the incriminating garment before me, flaunting her advantage. Along with the coolness I felt across my bare bum, it was another shameful reminder of how I'd let lasciviousness lead me to such reckless behavior.

I pushed the thought aside, partly because it didn't help the situation, but mostly because I still tingled thinking about Mitchell's fleshy bits near my own.

With Abigail continuing to bar the doorway, I needed a strategy. With Mitchell due home any minute, all I had to do was hang on until he arrived. Regardless of Abigail's interference, I knew nothing bad could happen to me with him here.

I took a step backward, easing away from her menacing stare. I looked past Abigail to the doorway. If I could lure her away from her post, I could make a mad dash for the living room. I stood a much better chance evading her efforts out there than in this confined space.

"It's not what it looks like," I said, taking another step away.

Abigail didn't budge.

"Funny…" she said. "Because it looks like a slutty little temptress has been trying to seduce my brother with some well-placed parlor tricks."

She jostled the garment in hand to emphasize her point.

Standing there naked with the intimate lingerie prominently displayed before me, it was hard to argue with her. Although the words struck a sensitive nerve, I could completely understand where she was coming from. After all, minus the "slutty" comment, she was right on the money.

"It's not like that at all," I pleaded.

Abigail glared at me with incredulous disapproval.

"Ok. It's very much like that," I admitted. "But it's not like I'm taking advantage of your brother. Mitchell and I are in love."

Abigail sneered at me.

"Love…" she scoffed. "What could a child possibly know about love?"

Facing down her malevolent gaze, I squared my shoulders.

"It's true," I stated with assertive pride. "And I am NOT a child."

Abigail's body suddenly tensed, as though unsure how to deal with my outburst. Animosity quickly replaced consternation, the jaw closed so tightly that a muscle in her neck bulged outwards. Her eyes fixated on me, narrowing into tiny black slits; her slender fingers clenching tightly around the scarlet lace.

"I know it might be hard to believe, but…"

"Hard to believe!?" she shouted.

The scarlet material left her hand and sailed through the air in my direction. It moved with such velocity that even its velvety lace painfully connected with my bare skin. I took another a step back, instinctively holding up an arm to protect myself. Abigail advanced a few feet in my direction.

"You know what's 'hard to believe'?" she snapped. "That you think Mitchell could ever love a girl like you. Just look at you: matted hair, pasty skin…"

Each new insult caused me to flinch inside, but I forced myself to maintain eye contact.

"Not to mention those silly, nonexistent bumps that you probably consider real breasts. At least Evelyn had a buxom physique, not to mention a six-figure salary."

I wasn't sure if it was the mention of my immature body or the comparison to Mitchell's ex-wife, but that last comment hurt more than the previous ones. I turned my eyes to the floor in disgrace. My small act of submission did little to curtail the barrage of humiliation as Abigail continued to berate me on my shortcomings. I listened in silence as she made clear my inferiority in gut-wrenching, pride-demolishing detail.

"So I ask you…" she said, finally reaching the end of her chastisements, "What could you possibly offer my brother?"

At the mention of Mitchell, I suddenly regained my confidence. Looking from the floor, I met her gaze with my own. I inhaled deeply, steeling my nerves against whatever might come *next. Out of my peripherals, I caught a glimpse of myself in the bedroom mirror. Tightening my hands into fists by my side, I smiled defiantly back at her.*

"At least I have a cute butt," I retorted.

Without missing a beat, Abigail took hold of a ceramic knick-knack from atop the chest of drawers. I winced as the trinket sailed past my head, evaporating against the wall behind me.

"You think that's funny?!" demanded Abigail.

I said nothing. Realizing that I had crossed the line, I shrank away from her, withdrawing to the space beside the bed. Having a buffer between me and her felt safer, but I knew it wouldn't last long. I would have to make it to the door.

"Huh?!" shouted Abigail, moving to block my way. "I asked you a question!"

I was trapped now between Abigail and the bed. I would only get one shot at escape. Biding my time, I looked from Abigail to the door.

"I'm talking to you, you insolent little…"

Abigail lunged at me. I leaped into the air above the bed, her bony fingers missing me by mere inches. I bounced once on the bed, landing feet first on the hardwood floor on the other side. Following my momentum, I sprinted for the door. My fingers made contact with the bronze doorknob.

Something large collided with my midsection, knocking me aside. I crashed hard against the side of the computer desk, my body sprawling to the floor. I looked up to see Abigail blocking the exit.

She stormed at me in a fit of rage. Going for the closest thing at my disposal, I pushed the office chair in front of her. It slowed her advance long enough for me to regain my feet. Pushing the chair aside, she raised her left hand and swung wildly in my direction.

Her first attack was easy to prevent by stepping back toward the bed. Sensing another escape, Abigail moved between me and the bed, trapping me close to the computer desk. The next swing I sidestepped, just in time to see her closed fist whoosh by my face. She pulled her right hand far behind her, throwing the following blow with all her might.

Rolling out of the way of the attack, I heard her fist make contact with something solid. Abigail screamed out in pain. Glancing over my shoulder, I could see the cracked laptop screen and Abigail tenderly clutching her hand.

Knowing that it was now or never, I dashed for the door. Taking hold of the handle, I saw a flash of movement from my right side. I ducked low just in time to allow the damaged laptop to fly overhead, crash into the chest of drawers, and shatter into a hundred pieces upon the floor.

I pulled against the knob, opening the door a few inches. Before I could slip through, Abigail raised her leg and kicked powerfully against the solid structure. The bronze handle slipped from my grasp, the door slamming shut with a resounding thud.

Abigail turned to me, a look of sadistic satisfaction showing through. I scurried out of range of attack, standing with my back to the bed. Abigail stepped in front of the door once more. She held her wounded hand pulled back against her torso, blood trickling onto the expensive fabric of her suit.

"Enough!" she growled, panting heavily from the exertion. She pointed her good hand to a stack of papers resting beside where the laptop had once been. "There is a train leaving Pittsburgh today. I've taken the liberty of booking you a first-class ticket to San Francisco. We leave for the station in ten minutes."

Between the hoarse speech and sheer audacity of her request, it took me a moment to process what she said.

"You can't be serious," I replied.

Abigail sniggered ruthlessly at my protests. She awkwardly reached across the front of her body and retrieved her phone.

"Either that or I make a few phone calls and have you deposited in the most abhorrent hellhole that I can find. The gutters you came from will seem like high society compared to where I'll send you."

I took a step away from her, leaning back against the soft blankets of the bed. I stared wide-eyed at her.

"Why?" I asked gravely. "I've never done anything to you."

Abigail closed the gap between us. I winced in alarm as she raised her finger at me, waving it violently mere inches from my face, angrily expressing every point with that bony appendage.

"I have spent the last year trying to nurse my brother out of his depression and away from alcohol. Now that I've finally gotten him sober, I will not have all that effort wasted. It's bad enough that he has been killing himself over a failed marriage without spending a lifetime of imprisonment on top of it on the account of some underage tart."

"Is that what this is about?" I asked, sensing a hope of reconciliation. "You've got it all wrong."

"Save it, hussy," she barked. "You can't talk your way out of this. One way or another, this ends today."

"But you don't understand. If you would just listen…"

Her hand connected solidly, generating a sharp pain in my right cheek. The force sent me reeling to the side, though I managed to catch myself on the edge of the bedpost before completely falling over.

"No!" she screamed. "YOU listen. I want you on that train and the hell out of our lives!"

My face throbbed where she struck me. Water flooded my eyes from the intensity of the impact. Inhaling deeply into my nostrils, I willed the tears back into their ducts. I refused to give her the satisfaction of seeing me cry.

"Ok," I said softly, my back still turned to her. "You win."

Defeated, I faced my tormenter.

"Just let me gather my things."

Abigail smiled with malevolent glee. She watched me like a hawk as I selected a suitcase and filled it with my few worldly possessions. Confident that I had resigned myself to my fate, she exited the bedroom and walked into the bathroom, making sure to leave both doors open just in case.

Moving quietly, I sifted through the stack of papers on the computer desk. Finding a suitable page, I slipped it from the stack. Making a coughing noise to cover the noise, I crumbled the paper into a ball, tossing it on the floor beside the bed.

Putting in the last of my clothes, I zipped the suitcase shut. I exited the bedroom, placing my luggage next to the briefcase Victor had given me.

When Abigail exited the bathroom, her hand was wrapped in gauze. She eyed me intently as I collected the apparel sprawled around the kitchen and living room, sliding them back onto my body.

"Are you ready to go?" she asked when I was dressed.

Taking one last look around the apartment, I gave a solemn nod. I turned my gaze to her, peering into those eerie green eyes. It was not out of hatred or malice, but of genuine remorse that I spoke to her.

"You know," I said tenderly, "for a while there, I was really hoping that we could have been sisters."

Mitchell stepped off the elevator and sprinted down the hall to his apartment. In his zealous excitement, he managed to fumble the keys, dropping them with a jangle on the floor. Mitchell was more successful the second time, pushing the door open with such vigor that it banged against the interior coat rack.

"Olivia, I'm home!" he called out, closing the apartment door behind him.

Not seeing her in the kitchen or living room, he moved to the bedroom. He stopped abruptly in the doorway.

On the floorboards were red droplets that had soaked into the wood. Some furniture had been damaged. On the floor near the chest of drawers, his laptop lay scattered in dozens of fragmented pieces. The only thing he could think was that his bedroom had been the site of a major struggle. *But between whom? And why?*

Looking about the bedroom, there was no sign of Olivia. He moved to the bed and threw the covers off. No Olivia.

Mitchell turned into the bathroom. Not seeing her in the open area, he pulled back the curtain. There was no sign of her. He even looked in the linen closet.

"Olivia?" he called out.

No answer.

He moved back to the living room. Not seeing her on the couch, he pulled off the cushions and checked beneath. He went to the kitchen, throwing open every cabinet and even opening the oven door.

"Olivia?" he called out again, this time with more panic.

He thought about the destruction in the bedroom.

"It's ok if you broke the laptop," he called out. "I don't care. Just come out."

He looked at the coat rack to see that her jacket was not among the lot. *Did that mean that she was not here after all? Where else could she be?*

Mitchell thought about the clothes closet and if she might be hiding in there. He returned to the bedroom, only to find the closet already open. He peered inside. He did not see Olivia. He was just about to close the closet door when he noticed the empty hangers.

All of Olivia's clothes were missing.

Adrenaline coursed through his veins as Mitchell moved to the chest of drawers. He flung open the drawer where Olivia kept her delicates. Her underwear, her sleepshirt and the clothes she kept for cleaning the apartment were all gone.

Mentally fatigued, he took a step back and sat down on the edge of the bed. *What did it all mean? Where was Olivia? Had his absence this past weekend been a turning point in their relationship? Had she left him after all they had been through?*

Mitchell shook his head.

"Calm down," he commanded himself.

Remembering some of the techniques of the program, he recited the serenity prayer until he regained his composure.

"There's nothing to get worked up over," he scolded himself. "There could be a very simple explanation for all of this."

Mitchell focused on what was in front of him. Carl told him that feelings were not facts, so he began to count the facts. Olivia was not home, the laptop was broken, there was blood on the floor, but not a lot of it, and all her clothing was missing.

Mitchell tried to connect the pieces together. *If Olivia had been carrying the laptop across the room, and fell, then that could explain the broken computer. Suppose she cut herself in the fall; that could explain the blood. If she was injured, would she go for help?*

But what about the clothes? Why would her entire wardrobe go missing? It didn't make any sense. Think…Think…Think…

"Laundry!" he yelled to himself. *That explained everything. She was washing her clothes, playing on the computer and then there had been an accident.*

Mitchell rose, intending to go inspect the washing machine. As he stood up though, his foot made contact with something that made a rustling noise. He looked down to spot a wadded up ball of paper. Bending over, he picked up the piece of trash.

He eyed it with confusion. It was not at all like Olivia to leave trash lying around. He took the ball of paper and tossed it lightly into the bedroom trash can.

Moving into the bathroom, he lifted the lid on the washing machine and found nothing inside. He leaned over and opened the door to the dryer. It too was empty. Confusion escalating to fear, Mitchell searched frantically around the laundry machines for any sign of Olivia's attire. Finding none, he wearily took a seat atop the commode, clutching his head in his hands.

None of this made sense. Hadn't the doctor told him Olivia was heading back to the apartment? She had left the hospital before he'd arrived; shouldn't she be back by now? If she hadn't gotten back yet, then why were her clothes missing? If she had gotten back, wouldn't she have waited for him before going anywhere? It was completely unlike her...

Something clicked inside his mind.

It was not at all like Olivia...

Mitchell bolted to the bedroom trash can, retrieving the balled up piece of paper, hastily unraveling its edges. Scanning the page, he deduced that it was someone's trip itinerary, though it seemed that half of the information had gotten cropped off at the bottom. The schedule had whoever it was set to leave Pittsburgh very soon, but without the missing page he had no idea where they were heading.

Mitchell peered into the wastebasket but didn't see any other papers. The printer tray was also devoid of anything helpful. He anxiously paced back and forth trying to make sense of the travel codes. *It couldn't be an airplane; they'd have the listed the airline name beside the flight number. Maybe a bus? What about a boat?*

He stopped dead in his tracks.

The train station.

Clinging tightly to the sheet of paper, Mitchell raced from his apartment. He was halfway down the hallway before he remembered that he forgot to lock the front door.

I have often looked back on the events of that day and wondered if there are any versions of myself in any of the millions of alternative universes that actually managed to board that train. How much different would my life have been if I had arrived at the station only five minutes earlier? What if my interactions at the hospital had been more short-winded? What if I hadn't taken so long in deciphering Olivia's message? What if I hadn't had to double-back to lock the door, and then again to retrieve my phone? What if I'd simply gone left around that group of passengers instead of going right?

If only I hailed a cab after leaving the hospital instead of trying to run back to the apartment, or maybe if I had gone directly home after the meeting that morning, or even skipped the meeting altogether, then who knows, everything could have changed. Since that day, I have come to believe that I was never intended to board that train, that some higher force was at work to stop me. Call it destiny, call it serendipity, but I now believe that everything happens for a reason...

Weaving through traffic at breakneck speed, the cab driver delivered me to the railway's main entrance.

Penn Station has stood as an iconic historical symbol for the city of Pittsburgh for more than 100 years. Towering over the corner of Liberty and Grant, its brick construction serves as a tribute to the architectural prowess of the early designers. Throughout the structure are scores of awe-inspiring masonry, including the famous rotunda, a magnificent circular edifice with a star-like emblem situated high above. Even with the main aspect being converted into apartment housing back in the eighties, it is still among the most majestic sites in the city.

The current Amtrak building is nothing like its predecessor though. The bantam facility stands in the shadow of the once great masterpiece, its gray exterior a gloomy reminder of how even the most elegant beauty is not immune to the sands of time.

When the taxi came to a halt, I reached into my pocket and retrieved a handful of bills. I handed him the wad of money, hoping the extra quantity would constitute a worthwhile sign of gratitude for his efforts.

"Good seeing you again," he called to me as the door shut in my wake.

Overlooking a familiar gray sedan, I raced across the parking lot, barreling past slow-moving travelers. Ignoring their startled looks, I pushed through the automatic doors.

Once inside, I searched for any trace of Olivia. Though the room was vast, covered from end to end in airport style benches, it was wide open. Quickly scanning from one side to the other, I saw no one who matched her unique description. I decided to follow the signs leading toward the train instead.

Almost immediately, I came across a group of idling tourists. With them lingering close to the bench on the left, it seemed logical to go around them on the right. Moving in that direction I accidentally bumped into a brown-haired woman. Catching a glimpse of her face, I recognized her immediately.

"Abigail?!"

If she shared my surprise, it did not show in her face. Instead, she stared at me the way an officer looks at a suspect; the way a hungry cat watches a mouse.

"How did you know we'd be here?" she inquired harshly.

I didn't know how to explain to Abigail that I wasn't looking for her, that I was there for someone else, without tipping my hand and revealing my secret relationship with Olivia. I reached into my pocket and held out the paper I'd found on my bedroom floor.

Abigail took one look at the paper and snatched it from my grasp. She glared angrily at me, as though I had no right to pick up trash from the floor in my own apartment. The last puzzle piece clicked into place.

"What are YOU doing here?!" I demanded.

Abigail pursed her lips tightly together, but said nothing.

"You were waiting for me...making sure that I didn't prevent her from getting on that train."

Her face softened.

"You have to understand," she said. "It's for the best."

I clenched my jaw tightly, shaking my head in disgust. I felt her cling to my arm as I attempted to move passed.

"Mitchell, wait..."

I pulled free of her grip and ran toward the train. I could hear her calling after me, even as she disappeared behind a sea of faces.

I came upon another waiting room. I didn't even bother to look around. The clock was ticking, and I had no time to lose. From somewhere up ahead a whistle sounded, its soul-piercing shrill filling my heart with dread. The world began spinning slower, every detail magnified to terrifying proportions.

Each advancing step seemed to come with great effort, as though I could not gain traction. With the swarm of people in front of me I was forced into evasive actions. I performed a pirouette about an elderly man with a cane, scooted between a couple paying more attention to their phones than their surroundings, and hurdled an annoying child chained to his parents by a leash.

In the distance the train whistle blew again.

I continued to follow the signs, ignoring the outcries and protests of those around me, including some who sounded more authoritative than the others. I could see the platform exit up ahead.

"You can't go in there," stated a stunted man by the door.

Finally free of the crowds, I doubled my efforts, accelerating powerfully toward the doors. The man's eyes grew wide in trepidation at my ferocious approach. Possessing greater wisdom than courage, he surrendered his post as quickly as he'd accepted it. With no further interference, I blasted past the former hindrance.

Out on the boarding platform, I spotted the train far up ahead, gaining considerable speed. Knowing that losing the train meant losing Olivia, I pursued the locomotive quarry with all my effort. I didn't know what I would do once I got close, but I'd seen enough James Bond movies to have an idea.

With every stride, I felt myself pulling closer to the rear car. My legs pumped vehemently up and down; full of fatigue but never slowing. The air in my lungs burned like hot coals as I tried to overcome years of physical degradation. I could hear my heartbeat echoing loudly in my ears.

Only a car length separated me from achieving my goal now. I held out my hand to prepare for that final leap. The scenery before me changed abruptly, acquiring my attention. I tried to reverse inertial tides, throwing on the brakes instead of the gas. I managed to come to a halt just as I ran out of platform.

I looked from the rocky chasm before me to the train departing into the distance, watching until it faded from view. I kept telling myself that it was all a horrible dream, that Olivia would be safely nestled in the bed back at my apartment, that everything would be alright.

I felt a reassuring hand rest on my shoulder. I turned to face brown hair atop a pantsuit.

"I'm sorry, Mitchell," said Abigail kindly. "I had to do it."

I took hold of her, each of my hands clasping the sides of her shoulders. I shook her once.

"Tell me, Abigail. Where is that train headed?"

She looked pleadingly into my eyes.

"Mitchell…it's over. She's gone."

My hands began to tremble.

"Please…" I begged. "You have to tell me."

Abigail gazed somberly up at me, moisture forming behind her fierce malachite eyes. She let her head sag, shaking it once side-to-side. Sensing defeat, I relinquished my grip, letting her arms fall back to their sides. Abigail took a step away, creating a space between us.

"I'll see you back at your place," she said, her voice cracking under the emotional pressure. She began to walk away from me, her shoulders quaking as she moved.

"Abigail..." I called after her.

She stopped, but didn't bother to turn around.

"Take as much time as you need," she said with sorrow in her voice. "But once you get back, I never want to hear about her again."

Abigail moved on in silence, leaving me to stand alone at the edge of the abyss.

Gazing out over the empty tracks, a sense of despair washed over me. Was it true, was Olivia really gone? Over the last few hours I had lost her three times, each bout of hopelessness more heart wrenching than the previous one. After a brief sojourn through paradise, a lifetime without her seemed too heavy a burden to carry.

With heavy heart, I fell back upon my haunches, the cold cement impacting hard against my backside. Wrapping my arms around my knees, I pondered what the future might hold for me now. My thoughts were a pendulum oscillating between futile expedition and aqueous repose. I don't know how long I'd been staring down those pernicious rails when I felt delicate fingers flow through my hair.

I recoiled from the touch.

"Haven't you done enough, Abigail?" I growled.

I felt the fingers again.

I turned to face my assailant, ready to tell her off, when my eyes found those familiar blue sapphires staring back at me.

"I figured you could use some company out here," she said with a sly smile.

My brain felt like mush. I looked down the track, then back at her, then at the track...

"But...you...the train..." I stammered without eloquence.

Olivia glanced down the rails reflectively, as though seeking an answer from the metallic beams.

"That's the eastbound track," she said with a smile.

I shook my head in confusion.

"I don't..."

"Shhh..." she hushed.

She gently rubbed her fingers through my hair again. Cupping my face in her hands, she placed a reassuring kiss upon my forehead. With her face only inches from mine, she spoke in a soothing voice, reminiscent of that first time we lay together.

"Our ride still hasn't arrived," she whispered tenderly.

The way she said 'our' made me relax, somehow she always knew what to say. I eased my head against her chest, letting go of the burden of my emotional roller coaster. As a boy I had been raised to be tough, to man-up, that real men didn't show emotion. It felt wonderful to let go of my instincts and not give a damn about what anybody thought. The teardrops ran down my cheeks in trickling rivulets until they soaked through her cotton top.

All my life, patience has been a virtue just out of reach. From a young age, I fell into the same behaviors as my metropolitan compatriots, always rushing toward the next thing. Waiting, be it for Evelyn to finish getting ready, for the lethargic baristas to retrieve my coffee, or for those Nazis at the DoT to process my paperwork, created more enmity in me on a daily basis than any other source. But for that one day, down by the tracks of old Penn Station, engulfed in the loving embrace of my sweet Olivia, I rejoiced in knowing that, at least in America, the train never runs on time.

CHAPTER 32

I sat by myself in the dining car waiting for Mitchell to finish his phone calls. I took a sip from my coffee mug, enjoying the atmosphere. For all the dilapidated station buildings, the damp platform corridors and unattractive waiting room ambiance, the railroad is still by far my favorite mode of transportation.

Setting my mug aside, I picked up the menu. Though this particular train seemed a bit light on the lunch cuisine, I always enjoyed the food served on passenger trains far more than the box lunches served at 30,000 feet. I wasn't too keen on the inflated prices, but that didn't much matter. Abigail had been generous in purchasing a first-class ticket, which meant a sleeper cabin and free meals in the dining car.

I let out a sigh of regret.

I am not sure what it was she was trying to accomplish with all her antics. Even if I ended up on the other side of the country, then it would have only required a phone call and a plane ticket to be reunited with Mitchell. Nevertheless, I imagined the bridge between Abigail and me had been completely destroyed by our skirmish in the apartment. And yet, when Mitchell asked me about the broken laptop, I couldn't bring myself to throw any more fuel on the fire. I told him that Abigail dropped it from the shock of seeing me.

From across the dining car I could see the server leading a man in my direction. He had little hair on his head, except for the goatee, prominently accentuated by a warm smile. His attire was bland, black shoes, black shirt, black suit jacket, with the only adornment being a white priest's collar about his neck. In his left hand, he carried a tablet device.

Guiding him to my table, she directed this newcomer to the other side of the booth. He complied, setting his device down gently before sliding into the seat across from me. It is common in places with limited space for complete strangers to sit together. I didn't mind *though, I always enjoy meeting new people. After my experiences in foster care, however, I was definitely not looking forward to another debate on religion.*

"Hi," he greeted with a wave of his hand. "I'm Chris."

I noted that he did not introduce himself with a title, which was a good start.

"I'm Olivia," I said, extending my arm toward him.

"Pleased to meet you,," he replied, taking my hand. He eyed me with concern. "Are you traveling by yourself?"

"No," I said quickly. "He's back in our room making some phone calls. He'll be out shortly."

"Your father?" he inquired.

I had spent so much time hiding my identity and my relationship with Mitchell over the last couple weeks that I almost blurted out the lies that had become like second nature. Before I could, something snapped inside me. I don't know if meeting Dr. Libby had given me more confidence in myself, or if my conflict with Abigail had opened up a defiant streak in me, or if I really was just tired of running, but the words that came out terrified and confused even myself.

"No," I said, shaking my head. "He's my boyfriend."

I felt myself give him a challenging stare.

"Oh…" he muttered.

Though he was clearly surprised, he turned away as though he were ashamed.

"I'm sorry," he said remorsefully. "You…um…look much younger than you apparently are."

It was the first time that anybody had ever apologized for treating me like a helpless child. Given the circumstances, I found myself quite inclined to forgive his transgression.

"It's ok," I said, relaxing my menacing look. "I get that a lot."

He nodded, but said nothing, as though he were still fearful of having insulted me. I decided to help fill the void.

"So, Chris," I began, "Where are you headed?"

He raised his head, smiling with relief.

"I'm going to Denver to visit my brother and his wife. I haven't gotten a chance to see them since Christmas."

He reached into his jacket pocket and retrieved a picture from his wallet. On the left stood Chris's brother, Jacob, with his arm around his wife, Megumi. In front of them were three children, only the youngest of which had been born to them. I smiled at the mention of adoption, happy to see those in need of a home find a loving family. I marveled at the diversity, delighted that there were still people in the world who were able to look beyond a book's cover.

"They seem like wonderful people," I said, after he finished telling me more about them.

Chris beamed brightly as he slid the photo back into his jacket.

"Do you have any children of your own?" I asked.

Chris pursed his lips together, as though contemplating some deep philosophical topic.

"No," he said finally.

Chris held out his hand for the soft drink the waitress brought him, thanking her before taking a sip from a diet cola.

"Never found the right woman?" I asked curiously.

Chris chuckled to himself.

"I suppose you could say that," he said with a smile.

"Oh…" I replied, feeling somewhat foolish at my assumption.

"It's ok," he laughed jokingly. "I get that a lot."

I grinned despite my embarrassment.

So much for not judging a book by its cover.

Behind me I heard the sound of the car door open. Turning around, I could see Mitchell duck through the small doorway, remaining stooped as he made his way through the dining area. He was like an overweight dog trying to squeeze through the flap in a pet door. I suddenly wondered how he would fare with the beds in the sleeper car.

It had been a long and weary conversation back in the privacy of our room. I explained all that happened over the past week. I told him about Victor and the money, but left out the part about almost being suckered out of most of it. I told him about Dr. Libby and the surgery, leaving out the part about recuperation time. I also may have forgotten to tell him about the detectives and the leukemia death scare. I also didn't mention how his new job had fallen into his lap suspiciously close to the time I found out about the money.

Mitchell slid in beside me.

"How'd it go?" I asked.

He glanced at the priest and then back at me. I nodded.

"It went well with Kelly. He said he was sad to see me go, but wished me well, even told me to give him a ring if I ever needed anything."

"That's good."

Mitchell nodded, obviously pleased with the outcome. He then glanced away.

"Carl wasn't so pleased."

I raised an eyebrow at him.

"I would have guessed it to have been the other way around," I stated in surprise.

"Me, too," he replied. "Definitely wasn't expecting to get fired right after I quit."

Another eyebrow raise.

"He fired you? Can he do that?"

"Apparently so," Mitchell said with a shrug. "He asked me what part of quitting my job, abandoning my family, giving up my apartment, foregoing my worldly possessions, and running away with a woman I haven't known very long I considered to be 'no major changes'."

I nodded appreciatively. I could see Carl's point on that one.

"So now what?" I asked.

Mitchell shrugged.

"Same plan as before apparently," he said. "Don't drink, go to meetings, and I'm still supposed to call him every day. He said to let him know when I find out where we're staying, and he'll help get me connected with the people there."

Mitchell lowered his head closer to me.

"Do we know where we're going yet?"

I shook my head.

"What about Abigail?" I whispered back.

Mitchell shook his head.

I looked over at Chris, who was trying desperately hard to ignore our conversation.

"By the way," I said, directing Mitchell's attention toward our table companion, "This is Chris. He's on his way to Denver to visit family."

"Mitchell," he said matter-of-factly. "How long are you going to be in Denver?"

"About two weeks."

Mitchell gestured toward the neck adornment.

"Is your flock saved enough to be without you that long?"

I gave Mitchell a harsh nudge in his midsection. He nodded in understanding.

"One can only hope," replied Chris. "Of course, the last time I left the deacon in charge of the copying machine, six states found themselves without power."

Mitchell chuckled, quickly warming to our new companion.

There we were: the atheist, the agnostic, and the priest, conversing as though we were old friends. It turned out that Chris used to be a teacher, so he and Mitchell shared stories about similar problem students. As they chatted, I slid my hand beneath the table, interlacing my fingers with Mitchell's and resting my head gently against his powerful shoulder. When lunch ended, we agreed to meet up with Chris again in the lounge car after a little while.

We headed back to our private room. There was still much left to discuss about our future. At this point, we weren't even certain whether we would stay on the train all the way to the west coast or not.

Before we made it to our sleeper, however, I maneuvered in front of Mitchell, pushing him gently back against the closest wall. Latching onto his shirt with both hands, I pulled him down to my face level, pressing my lips to his. Mitchell wrapped his arms around me, holding tightly to my small frame as we rocked back and forth in the confined space. We had spent so much time apart in the last few days that making out was like reuniting with an old friend. Sadly, after another minute, Mitchell abruptly pulled away.

I opened my eyes and found him frightfully gazing down the corridor. Following his stare, I focused on a young man, presumably the sleeper car's attendant, rubbernecking in our direction.

"Do you mind?" I chastised. "My boyfriend and I are trying to enjoy an intimate moment here."

I felt Mitchell's entire body go rigid all at once. His gaze quickly fell to me, as though seeking an explanation. I was aware that the restaurant incident was never far from his mind, and I didn't want to scare him, but I had to know…

The attendant looked with concern at Mitchell and me. For him, in that moment, there was only an adult kissing on a child. It was up to me to break through that illusion.

"I did not pay good money for our tickets so that I could be gawked at by some voyeuristic little pervert," I stated with impunity. "Now are you going to move on, or am I going to have a word with your supervisor?"

The boy held up his hands defensively.

"I'm sorry," he muttered apologetically. "It won't happen again."

"See that it doesn't."

The attendant quickly disappeared around the corner. I sighed with relief. When I turned back to Mitchell, he was intensely focused on me, a look on his face as though we'd only barely managed to avoid being eaten by a bear.

"What was that about?" he asked.

Staring up into his gorgeous hazel eyes, I ran my fingers across the side of his cheek. Stepping onto tiptoes, I planted a soft kiss on the underside of his jaw.

"I'll tell you later," I whispered.

Resting back on the floor, I wrapped my arms about his midsection. I leaned forward, planting my head against his chest. With my ear placed against him, I could hear the beating of his heart. Mitchell put one hand on my back, holding me against him, as though afraid I might vanish at any moment. With the other hand, he gently stroked my hair. I listened intently as the thumping slowed from its excited state, back to the steady tones of relaxation.

As the train moved ever onward toward its destination, I was once again reminded of how uncertain the future was for the two of us. We had absolutely no idea where we were headed, or when we would get there, or what we would do once we arrived, but as long as we had each other, we could get through anything. My interaction with the attendant had proven that Mitchell and I had hope of finally being accepted. Pushing my face deeper into his chest, I closed my eyes, a contented smile forming on my lips.

In this world, we meet people of all different sizes, shapes, nationalities, religions, lifestyles, skin tones, and gender identities. Regardless of how they are on the outside, we judge them by their appearance, and they in turn derive conclusions about us by ours. There's no getting away from it; it's part of human nature. But no matter how they choose to define us, we are the ones who ultimately establish our identities. In life, we get treated the way we teach people to treat us, and I refuse to be a child any longer.

ACKNOWLEDGEMENTS

Writing this book has possibly been the most rewarding and stressful experience of my life. I know that this project would never have made it this far without the continued help and encouragement that I have received along the way.

First off, thank you to my editor, Joanne, for her critical efforts in dissecting and rebuilding that early manuscript. Thank you to all the staff at Scarlett Rugers for their patience and creativity. A special thank you to Sierra for being so supportive throughout every step of this long process. Thank you to all of my friends and family, especially Corina, Thanh, Tonya, my mother, and my sisters for all of their kind words and assistance. And thank you to my grandmother, Joan, who has always been a source of inspiration and strength, not only for me, but to every single person who knew her.